SETTLING
THE
SCORE

LEN TITOW

SWEETSPIRE LITERATURE
— MANAGEMENT —

*Beloved, never avenge yourselves,
but leave it to the wrath of God, for
it is written, 'Vengeance is mine, I
will repay,' says the Lord.*

—Romans 12:19

1

icki Santana is back in her usual position on the Town Hall steps begging for donations, as she has been for the last year. A woman in her late twenties.

She sits quietly on the steps, with her head bowed with a sign propped up on her knees that reads, 'Help me if you can. I am unemployed and penniless.' She has a black windcheater on, a pair of jeans with frayed knees, and thongs. Her hair looks as if it had not been washed in weeks, and the misery of her life is visibly shown on her face.

It is seven o'clock in the morning, and it is cold.

Vicki slept under a park bench last night with a piece of plastic over her to try to keep the cold from settling on her, but it seems she became uncovered during the night and can feel the aches and pains that the cold has inflicted on her body. The cold forces her constantly to shiver, intensifying as the breeze goes through her.

She has a small open box at her feet for donations. She sits and waits. She has nothing else to do and nowhere to go. This is her life, which many look down upon, and few consider why she has adopted it.

A man approaches her. He is in an expensive suit. He stands for a moment looking at her and the box near her feet, and without warning, he kicks it out of the way, sending the coins scattering down onto the footpath and some rolling down the drain. He kicks the box repeatedly in a rage, sending it down the street. There is no one there to stop him, so he gets away with it.

She recognizes the man as the wealthy businessman Charles Henry, listed as being in the top one hundred most wealthy men in the country. He runs a fashion house and was the instigator of her misery, but he does not recognize her. He walks on, saying, 'They shouldn't be allowed to beg on our streets. There should be a law against it. We should lock them up.'

Vicki quickly chases after the scattered coins and collects what she can from the footpath and gutter and places her box back where it was. She notes some coins had rolled down the drain, but she cannot get them, as the grate is too heavy and the drain too deep. She resumes her position on the Town Hall steps with a somber expression.

The voice inside her tells her that if ever she gets the chance, she should shoot the bastard that keeps kicking her box into the gutter. He deserves it—a low life. She hopes someday he will experience what she is going through. Then she remembers the days when she and her husband went to church, and the minister kept harping on what Jesus said, 'Forgive those that persecute you, your enemies. Don't seek revenge, leave it to God, for He is able to do this, whereas you are not. Seek the Lord's help. Give Him the task of attending to the wrong that's done unto you. Allow Him to deal with retribution, for His judgement will be just, unlike yours.'

Vicki sits and ponders on this and then says under her breath, 'Lord, I will leave it to you to judge this person and administer your judgement on him. Amen.'

Another businessman startles Vicki, youngish in appearance, who stops in front of her. He says, 'My name is Robert. What's yours?' Vicki says nothing while the man stands in front of her. He says, 'I'll give you ten dollars if you tell me your name.' She hesitates and thinks, *Ten dollars? What a bastard. He won't give me ten dollars. He is a liar like the rest of them. None of them can tell the truth.* She stays quiet. The man walks away, not throwing anything into her box. She wonders whether she has done the right thing and ponders on it. She sits there until six o'clock at night and packs up her takings. Twenty-three dollars in coins. It has been a good day.

Vicki makes her way to the park and walks past a couple of benches that may be all right to sleep under tonight. She stops in front of one and throws her bundled-up plastic and rags under one of the benches, reserving the bench for the night, and walks on to see if she can get a cup of soup from one of the charities operating a mobile kitchen.

She approaches one of them in a dark street close to her park bench, and they are happy to provide her with a hot meal and a cup of coffee. She thanks them for their kindness and sits quietly alone and eats her meal. She gives thanks to God for the meal she is about to eat and starts cutting her sausages and baked vegetables. Halfway through the meal, one volunteer approaches her and gives her a cup of coffee. It tasted awful, but beggars can't be choosy, and she must take what is given to her in kindness. It was at least warm. She says to herself; *You have lost the right to object, as you are nothing and no one cares about you. A piece of trash that exists until dumped on the garbage heap.*

She finishes her meal and thanks the volunteers and walks back to her bench and prepares to make herself cozy when a volunteer approaches her from the homeless mission to advise her they can provide her with a room, a bath, and fresh clothes if she desires. She agrees and bundles up her rags and sheets of plastic and steps into their van.

The mission takes Vicki out of town to one of their hostels, and she can shower and spend the night there, warm and safe. They give her a change of clothes, and she feels she is clean and fed, a feeling that she has not had for a long time. She thinks, *Maybe someone cares about me. But I am still a burden on society and still a piece of trash.* She prays to the Lord, 'Father, I thank You for watching over me and giving me food and clean clothing. I ask for Your forgiveness for describing myself as trash, for I am Your creation and in a desperate situation, fearful of what is to become of me. I am in Your hands and have faith in You. Amen.' She gets into her allocated bed, not the softest she has slept in, and falls asleep.

The next morning, Vicki rises early and goes back to her position on the Town Hall steps and sets up her cardboard sign and box for the day.

Vicki waits a while, and several people pass by and give ten or twenty cents, but nothing of any substance. She dozes off for a minute when suddenly, she is startled by a loud noise and wakes up to see the same man who was there the other day kicking her box, sending her money flying. She quickly composes herself and runs after the coins that are scattered on the footpath. She collects the coins and sets herself up again, hoping that he doesn't return.

After about thirty minutes, another person comes by and stops in front of Vicki. 'Hi, I'm Robert. Just checking if you are going to tell me your name. Remember, I will give you ten dollars if you tell me.' Vick keeps quiet and says nothing until Robert leans over her and says, 'Remember me? I am Robert, and I going to give you ten dollars if you tell me your name.'

Robert lifts Vicki up, and she rises to face him. She is scared that he might be like the previous aggressive person who kicked her box down the street. She freezes. She could feel her arms taking the weight of her body. She looks into his eyes and thinks she could trust him. Yet living on the street tells her differently. You can trust no one.

Vicki stares at Robert for a minute and then bursts out, 'Please don't hurt me. I have enough problems to contend with without you adding to them. Please leave me alone. I don't mean to do you any harm. I am a street beggar. Leave me alone. Please.'

Robert releases Vicki and places a ten-dollar note in her cardboard box and leaves. Vicki was surprised and shocked, as she had never received a ten-dollar note from a stranger before and thought he would never give her the money. She sits down and tries to figures out what had just happened.

The day ends, and Vicki goes to the park to find a bench under which she could sleep as night fell. She finds her usual bench unoccupied and places her rags and sheets of plastic under the bench and heads off to see if she can find a charity to get some food. Most of the takeaways are closed, and the charities are some distance away in a different area, and therefore she can't get a free meal from them tonight.

She goes off to where the restaurants are located to see if she can pick up some scraps out of their garbage bins. She goes to Demetriou's Restaurant, as she knew George Demetriou from the days when her husband was alive. She waits outside, and a waiter sees her and tells the boss, who comes out with a lasagna and salad for her.

Vicki bursts into tears when she sees George come out with a meal on a white plate and serviette, as she did not expect this treatment and thought she would be lucky to get leftovers. George calms her down and places a white napkin over her lap, and she eats. When she finishes, she takes out a ten-dollar note and gives it to George, who refuses to take it.

George says, 'Not from my princess. You pay me when you're rich and famous. I will keep a ledger on you.' Both burst out in laughter. It is rare for Vicki to laugh.

Vicki thanks George and gives him a kiss on the check. 'You're a good man. I guarantee to pay you back. I appreciate your support.'

Vicki stares into the restaurant and notices the man who gave her the ten dollars sitting at a table with several other men. Wine is being served, and all seem to be in a jovial mood.

Vicki asks George, 'Do you know the man in the blue suit, George?'

'Yes, he is a regular customer of ours. His name is Robert Somerset, a very wealthy businessman who has just made another takeover of a competitor. They are celebrating the deal, which was completed this afternoon.'

'What does he do?'

'He owns several nursing homes and cares for the elderly.' 'He seems young for such an important job.'

'Yes, but he is very bright and is supported by his parents, who are very wealthy and influential. He came out of the army about a year ago after seeing action in Africa.'

Vicki thanks George and leaves to go back to her park bench to settle in for a chilly night.

The frost comes in early, and it becomes freezing, and Vicki finds herself unable to get warm. She wakes up with a cramp in her leg and must get up to relieve the pain and walks back and forth to get her blood circulating. She cannot get back to sleep, as the temperature is below zero and she is freezing. She stays sitting up and hears some men approaching. One stops in front of her and says, 'At what price, love?'

Vicki recognizes him as the bastard who kept kicking her coin box down the street and knows him to be a violent man with no concern for the welfare of others.

Vicki ignores him, so he and his other two mates come up to her and say, 'What's the price, love?' Vicki could see that they were all drunk, but the one asking the questions was less drunk than the others. She gathers her belongings and is going to move on when suddenly, the man grabs Vicki and forces her to the ground, while the other two look on. Vicki tries to scream, but one man grabs one of her rags and shoves it into her mouth, while the other is holding her down on the ground, trying to unzip his pants. He shoves his hands in her pants, searching for her briefs. He takes a minute to realize she did not have any on and then tries to insert his penis into her vagina while she is thrashing around. Vicki struggles and stretches out her hand to feel if she can grab a rock but grabs a knife, which fell out of her bag when they kicked it under the bench.

She stretches out her hand and, with all her strength, stabs the man trying to rape her on the right side of his torso. She feels the knife penetrating his body and tries to put more effort into the movement to ensure it does as much damage as possible. The rapist immediately gives out a loud yell. 'The bitch! She stabbed me! I'm bleeding!' He grabs his side and tries to get up. His mates grab him and drag him off. Vicki, who is shaken, gets up and runs from the scene, fearing they will be back.

She goes to another part of the park and waits and worries about what will happen next. The fear is playing on her mind. She fears there will be retribution from the rapist, as he will not let this go without some reprisal. She knows these men will be back, so she goes back to where they tried to rape her and makes out as if she has parked herself for the night under the bench by filling the position where she would lie for the night with plastic and covering it over with her rags as if she is sleeping there. She moves away to where the trees are located and waits, sitting on the ground behind one tree.

Sure enough, two men approach where she was. One she recognizes as the rapist, who takes out a gun and fires at the makeshift body under the bench. They move closer and shoot again and again and then run away back to the entrance of the park when they believe they have killed Vicki.

Vicki stays near the tree in the park trembling from both the fear and cold of the night until she can hear the Town Hall clock ringing five o'clock and grabs her rags from under the bench and make her way to the steps of the Town Hall. She notes they aimed one bullet at her head while the others at her body.

Vicki gets to the Town Hall at about five thirty and goes to the toilet to attend to her needs. She washes herself to make sure the rapist's sperm is no longer present on her vagina with paper hand towels and washes her face to get the smell of alcohol off her. She comes out and sets her box up and settles down with her sign near her knees.

A few people pass, but no one drops in any money. Maybe it is too cold for them to take off their gloves and reach into their pockets. Vicki sits there for an hour in the cold, and the sun comes up and warms her shivering body.

At about seven o'clock, Robert comes by and stops at where Vicki was sitting. 'Hi, remember me? I am Robert. Are you going to tell me your name?' At that time, another businessman walks up to Vicki's box and kicks it down the street and walks on. Vicki recognizes him as the same person who has done this to her repeatedly and the one who tried to rape her last night. Robert grabs hold of the man and says, 'What do you think you're doing? Are you a nut or just a bastard?'

The man throws a punch at Robert and hits him on the side of the face. Robert, who is still hanging on, delivers a punch right into the midsection, and the man falls to his knees and bleeds from the wound in his torso. Robert says, 'Who are you, and why did you kick her box?'

The injured man says, 'She shouldn't be here. We don't need beggars on our streets. This is not Calcutta, you know. There should be a law against it.'

Robert asks, 'What's your name?'

The injured man answers, 'Charles Henry. My lawyers will be after you.'

Robert says, 'Well, if that is the way you want to play it, Mr. Henry, let's call the police and the press and see how your lawyers are going to deal with the publicity that will come your way.'

Henry staggers to his feet and, while holding his bleeding side, and no doubt in pain, runs off, leaving the two at the Town Hall steps.

Vicki says, 'Thank you. That was a brave thing to do. That man has done that several times to me and really is just a vicious monster.'

Robert says, 'Well, I don't think he will bother you now, but I recommend you set up somewhere else, possibly opposite a bus or train station, where there are more people bunched together.

'By the way, you still haven't told me your name.'

'My name is Vicki, and thank you for your help.'

'No problem, Vicki, and here is the ten dollars I promised you.'

'No, you already gave me one.'

'Then here is another. You look as if you need a hot cup of coffee.'

Robert walks off, leaving Vicki.

Vicki goes to the hospital to get checked out and gets some of her cuts and bruises attended to and get some painkillers for a headache she constantly has from being thrown to the ground.

2

obert Somerset is the only child of Catherine and Richard Somerset, who, over the years, has become very wealthy from providing aged care facilities to the elderly and acquiring poorly run retirement villages.

They gained old money from their parents and became wealthier as aged care became more in demand. They not only have a reputation for providing high-quality care but also are renowned for their high prices.

There were two children, a daughter and a son. The daughter died from cancer some three years ago, leaving them with their only surviving child, a son named Robert.

They are experiencing great difficulty in accepting the loss of their daughter at such a young age. They always planned on dying before their children, allowing them to benefit from their hard work. But this has not been the case. They continually ask the Lord why He has taken their daughter, but have never received an answer to their prayers. Over the years, they have become bitter towards God as they believe He should have saved their daughter and not just let her die.

Robert is the managing director of Manor Nursing Home and has a few other interests—namely, share portfolios, private investments, and he leases a few commercial premises that he owns.

He went to a private school and was offered a place at Stanford University, where he graduated with degrees in economics and law. He spent time in Europe touring around and working as a financial adviser to one of the larger broking houses.

After five years of being away from home and trying his hand at a few jobs, Robert came back home and was immediately appointed managing director of Manor Nursing Home and has, over the years, built the business up to become the leader in the industry.

The family are Christians and believe in God, but their faith has dwindled since their daughter's death.

Robert is single, and there is no girl that seems to interest him, to the displeasure of his parents, who want him to marry and settle down. He has an apartment close to his office and walks to work every day.

3

*R*obert is working in his office when his secretary comes to the door to say that the minister from the local church would like to have a word with him.

He is about to say that he is too busy, but thinks it might be best to hear what he has to say.

Robert says, 'Ask him in.'

The secretary goes out and escorts the minister to Robert's office.

Robert asks, 'How can I help you?'

Minister replies, 'My name is Allen Sheppard. I am a minister of the local church called St John's. How are you? Thank you for seeing me without an appointment.'

Robert says, 'Normally, I wouldn't, but I was intrigued why you would come here.'

The men shake hands, and Robert directs Allen to a seat.

Robert asks, 'Well, Allen, what can I do for you?'

'Nothing at present. I would just like to introduce myself to you and to say that if you need any spiritual help, I am always available should you need me.'

'Well, that is good to know. At present, I am fine, thank you.' 'Do you go to church on Sunday, Robert?'

'I used to, but since my sister died some three years ago, I haven't attended church.'

'Why is that?'

'My parents, who were good Christians and who went to church every Sunday, stopped going after the death of my sister, and since I didn't have to drive them there every week, I stopped going.'

'Why did your parents stop going to church?'

'I say that they lost faith in God after the death of my sister.'

'Is it possible to get their address? I would like to see them and discuss their rejection of God and try to explain the consequences of their action.'

'Many ministers have tried, but none have succeeded, so I don't think you are going to be any different.'

'I would like to try. I may persuade them.'

Robert gives Allen the address of his parents' house and says, 'Well, you will have to excuse me. I have a lot of work to do,' while trying to shuffle Allen towards the doorway.

Allen says, 'Thank you for your time, but what about you? Do you believe in God?'

'I used to, but over the last ten years haven't had much to do with Him. I guess I am all right the way I am, not needing His help or His miracles, making my own decisions. I came out of the military and saw action in Afghanistan. After being in action and killing people, you often wonder where God is and why He allows this to go on.'

'So, in your mind, you have replaced God, so while things go well, you don't need Him, but when things turn sour, you think you can throw a switch and He will be there?'

'Yes, I guess so, something like that. I haven't needed His services for the last ten years. I guess I won't need them at all.'

'And what services are you referring to, Robert?'

'None, that's my point.'

'I hope you are right, but my experience tells me things are about to change and you may ask for His help. Here is my card. Ring me if you need some help or want to discuss anything.' Robert accepts the card and shows Allen to the door.

Robert walks back into his office and picks up Allen's card and tears it up, saying, 'We won't need this,' and throws the torn pieces into the garbage tin. He picks up the phone and makes several phone calls.

4

icki has picked up a cold from someone and is sneezing and coughing a lot. With no tissues, it is hard to blow her nose. All she can do is wipe it on her sleeve. She sits on the Town Hall steps as the icy wind blows about her, and she can feel the cold going through her body. It sprinkles with rain, and she is worrying about how the day is going to develop if the rain sets in. Her cardboard box is soaking up the water from the steps and soon will not be of any use to her. She collects the coins and puts them in her pocket just in case it pours.

Robert comes past carrying a coffee and stops in front of Vicki and says, 'Hi, Vicki, it is a miserable day.'

Vicki looks up and is happy to see Robert but doesn't get up because she is not steady on her feet and is scared she will either fall over or collapse.

Vicki says, 'Hello, Robert, yes, it is terrible weather and so cold.'

Robert says, 'You look terrible and sound as if you have a cold.'

Vicki replies, 'I do, but I will get over it.'

It drizzles, and Robert can see that Vicki is not well.

Robert says, 'Here, take my coffee. I just bought it and haven't had a sip out of it yet.'

Vicki replies, 'No, you bought it for yourself and you should have it. I will be all right. I will have to move out of the rain. Otherwise, I will get pneumonia.'

'I insist. Most probably you haven't had anything to eat this morning?'

'No, which is not unusual.'

Robert pushes the coffee into Vicki's hands and takes the lid off the cup.

Vicki takes a sip. 'That is good.'

'I have a cheese-and-tomato sandwich in my coat. Here, you need it more than me.' He takes it out of his pocket, still wrapped and in a paper bag. He unwraps it and hands it to Vicki, who takes a bite out of it.

'Thanks. It tastes great. I will be all right now that you have given me breakfast. Next time, leave the pepper out.' Both smile at each other.

'Coffee and a sandwich isn't breakfast. A snack, yes, not breakfast.'

Robert takes out a ten-dollar note from his pocket and hands it to Vicki. She refuses to take it.

'Vicki, stop being silly about taking the money. On a day like today, no one is going to stop by and give you a donation. So take the money and get yourself some lunch later.'

Vicki hesitates and knows Robert is right. She wouldn't get anything today, and it rains.

'Thanks, Robert. You're right. You better be off to work, or the boss will penalize you for being late.'

'I am the boss, so I don't have to worry about that, but I have an early morning meeting, so I will have to be off. Take care of yourself.'

Robert walks off, leaving Vicki.

The rain increases, and Vicki realizes she must get under cover. She tries to stand up but staggers around and falls on her bottom, injuring her hand, which she put out to stop her fall. The rain increases, and she is getting saturated. Her body is shaking from the cold as she gets up. She is dizzy and cannot stand up straight. She tries to take a step forward but does not have the strength to keep upright and falls on her side with a scream.

People are looking at her from under shop awnings, but no one comes out to help her. The rain pelts down, and Vicki lies on the Town Hall steps motionless in the rain, and no one thinks it is their problem.

Allen Sheppard walks out of the Town Hall, puts up his umbrella, and walks down the steps. He sees Vicki lying on the steps. He sees people standing under a shop awning and no one willing to help her. He runs to her side and holds the umbrella over her and rolls her on her back, face up. He can see she is unconscious and needs help. He takes his mobile from his pocket and calls emergency, having difficulty pressing the keys because of the icy wind.

Allen says, 'I need an ambulance. A young woman is lying on the Town Hall steps unconscious and the rain is pouring down on her. She is motionless.'

Ambulance operator replies, 'An ambulance has been dispatched and should be there within five minutes.'

Allen stands over Vicki as the rain intensifies, and both are getting saturated as the wind comes around from all sides. Still, no one comes up to assist or cares about the young woman lying in a pool of water.

The ambulance arrives under siren, and the paramedics jump out and check if Vicki is breathing. One paramedic says, 'She has respiratory problems. Her lungs are not functioning. Her blood pressure is low. We better get her to a hospital, as we will lose her.'

Allen asks, 'What's wrong with her?'

Paramedic replies, 'It looks like pneumonia and her heart can't take the load. We have to get her out of the rain and into hospital or she will die on us.'

The paramedics race back to the ambulance and pull out a bed from the rear of the ambulance. They wheel it up to where Vicki was lying, and both move to pick her up. Vicki is put on the stretcher and quickly taken to the ambulance, where she is placed in the rear, and both paramedics get into the ambulance; one in the driver's seat, the other at the rear with Vicki, checking her blood pressure. The one with Vicki yells out, 'Her blood pressure is low and moving down! We will lose her if we don't get to a hospital!'

The other paramedic grabs the radio and speaks into it. 'Base, we have a female who is unconscious suspected of having severe pneumonia and low blood pressure and irregular heartbeat. Alert emergency. We need help on arrival, which will be five minutes.' He places the radio into his cradle and hits the siren switch.

He looks back at his mate, who says, 'She is on oxygen. All clear. Go.'

The ambulance speeds off, and the rain intensifies further.

The ambulance arrives at the hospital and is immediately confronted by a doctor and several nurses. The doctor quickly checks on Vicki's breathing and says, 'The lungs are not functioning. Too much congestion. We need to put her in a breathing tent to give her support. We need intravenous antibiotics and get her out of these wet clothes.' The nurses take Vicki to the intensive care unit (ICU) and attends to the doctor's orders.

She is linked up to monitors, and her clothes are stripped off her and they placed her in a hospital gown. She is monitored around the clock and is put in a breathing tent to assist her breathing.

Allen comes to the hospital to check on the condition of the young woman taken from the Town Hall. After a few negative responses, he gets to speak to someone that seems to have some information.

Allen says, 'I am a minister of religion and was the person who found a young lady on the Town Hall steps. I would like to know how she is.'

Clerk replies, 'That must be the mystery girl that was brought in with severe pneumonia. She isn't doing too well, but if you go to ICU 3, they will tell you. They are on the third floor, and when you get out of the lift, turn right.'

Allen says, 'Thank you.'

Allen follows the directions and eventually gets to ICU 3. He speaks to the nurse, who says, 'She is in a serious condition and not expected to recover, as her lungs are not responding to the antibiotics. These are early days, and we will know better tomorrow after the antibiotics have time to work. She is comfortable and is under constant observation.'

Allen asks, 'Can I see her to pray over her?'

'Sure, you can. She needs all the help you can give her. By the way, do you know her name?'

'No. I just saw her on the steps and ran to help her. Since she was not responding, I called for an ambulance.'

'Good, that you did. If she was left out there, she would be dead by now. I bet no one went to help her?'

'No one. None of them had the decency to lend a hand. They were all considering themselves. No one wanted to get wet. They would prefer a person die than they get wet in assisting her. What a society we live in.'

The nurse took Allen to where Vicki was lying motionless. The monitor showed her oxygen intake was around 65 and her blood pressure was 45/80. She was in a breathing tent and in a hospital gown with a thermal blanket wrapped around her.

Nurse says, 'Don't stay too long.' Allen replies, 'No, just a few minutes.'

Allen stares at Vicki and wonders what had happened to her. What kind of life has she had to be in a state where she could not get out of the cold and rain and that no one would help her? Has society stooped so low that not one person would lend her a hand? No, they consider her trash and not one of God's creations. It's not their problem, so why should they lend a hand? Allen bows his head and prays for her in a low voice so she may hear if she is able. After a minute, he stops praying and walks away from Vicki's bed and makes his way out of the hospital and home.

The next morning, Robert walks past where Vicki normally sits and notices she is not there. He wonders where she has moved to, but doesn't have the time to find out, as he has a busy day ahead.

Allen goes to the hospital to check on Vicki and goes to ICU 3 and asks how she was. He is told the antibiotics are working, but they still want her in an induced coma to give her lungs time to recover. He leaves the hospital and goes about his duties.

The second morning, Robert walks to work and again notices Vicki was not in her usual position. He gets worried and goes over to one kiosk and asks the man there, 'Do you know what has happened to Vicki? You know, she usually was set up on the stairs of the Town Hall.'

Kiosk operator replies, 'Oh, she's dead. They found her lying in the rain and took her by ambulance to the hospital.'

'Are you sure she is dead?'

'No, but the way the paramedics were working on her, it seems as if she was. Go to the hospital if you want to know.'

'Thanks.'

Robert goes off thinking that would be a waste of time and instead goes off to work. He attends to several matters but could not stop thinking about Vicki until about eleven o'clock, he finally goes to the hospital and see what had happened to her. He hails a cab outside of his office and goes to the hospital. After receiving the usual runaround, he finally gets to ICU 3 and was permitted to stand near Vicki's bed for a minute. He notices she is in an oxygen tent and is fed intravenously, as well as having drips of various kinds leading into her arm. He stays there for a minute and then is approached by a nurse who asked whether he knew the girl. Robert replies, 'Not really. I saw her every morning when I walked to work. She always had a box and was stationed on the Town Hall steps, begging. Her name is Vicki. That's all I know other than two days ago, I saw her and she looked terrible. I gave her a coffee, a sandwich, and ten dollars to get some lunch and then left her.'

Nurse says, 'We wondered where she got the sandwich from that was in her pocket when we took her wet clothes off her.'

'Will she pull through?'

'The doctors don't know. We will get a better idea in the next frorty-eight hours. If she responds to the antibiotics, she should be all right. If she doesn't, then I don't think she will make it. There will be too much pressure on her lungs and heart.'

'Can you keep me informed?'

'Are you a relative?'

'No. Just someone concerned about her welfare. I should have done something two days ago, but didn't.'

'I will put your name down as a point of contact. That way, they will notify you.'

'Thank you. I appreciate your help.' Robert then leaves the hospital and goes back to his office. He attends several meetings but is always thinking about Vicki and blames himself for her condition and hospitalization. He should have acted sooner. It wasn't right to just leave her there.

Allen phones the hospital and finds out that there is no change in Vicki's condition. She is still in ICU3 and listed as critical. He prays for her, asking God to look after her.

Three days later, Vicki responds to the medication and is taken off the coma-inducing drug and is removed from the oxygen tent and placed on oxygen through a facial mask. She breathes normally assisted by oxygen and can talk to the doctors. She tells them her name, and that she lived on the street and what had happened to her. The doctors are happy to see her responding to the medication and advise Vicki that they will release her from the ICU and put her in a bed in the ward in the next few days so she can build up her strength and recover from the pneumonia.

They took Vicki out of the ICU and put in a bed in a public ward to recover.

Day four, Robert arrives and finds that Vicki is no longer in ICU3. He enquires what has happened to her and is advised she was transferred to a public ward and is given directions. He goes down to the ward and approaches Vicki's bed. Vicki recognizes Robert and gives him a warm greeting.

Vicki asks, 'What are you doing here, Robert?'

Robert replies, 'I have come to check on you. You were touch-and-go for a couple of days. What are they intending to do with you?' 'After you left me on that rainy day, I really got bad, and they tell me I nearly died because of the pneumonia. The lungs still feel sore when I take a big breath.'

'What happens when they let you out? Where are you going to stay?'

'Under bench four, I guess. It has more timber across it and should provide me with more cover.'

'You can't go back there. You will end up right back here in no time.'

'I don't have much choice. The park is my home. I don't have a job or a life. I am a burden on society. Even the hospital wants me out sooner than later. They need the bed for a fee-paying person, not a bum like me. They have even taken the ten dollars you gave me.'

'No, you're not going back there. We will think of something over the next few days. Why have they put you in this rotten ward? The paint is peeling off the walls, and it's dirty and understaffed.'

'Because I don't have any money. Stop worrying about it, Robert. I used to concern myself with these things before, but now I thank the Lord, wherever He directs me to be and whatever He gives me.'

'Well, I have to take care of some business now, but I will be back later and see if I can do something about it. You take care, and I will see you later.' Robert leaves Vicki and goes back to work. Towards the end of the day, Allen arrives and was happy to see Vicki sitting up in bed smiling. He goes up to her and introduces himself.

Allen says, 'Hello, Vicki. I am Allen Sheppard, a minister of the church. I saw you on the steps of the Town Hall and called the ambulance.'

Vicki replies, 'Thank you for helping me, but maybe you should have left me there and allowed me to die.'

'That is a terrible thing to say.'

'Is it? I have no job, no money, and live in the park under a park bench with no prospects of getting out of this bind. No one will give me a job so I can earn some money, and no one cares. Not even God by the looks of it. His plans were upset by one of his ministers who refused to ignore the prophecy of the Good Samaritan.'

'Well, I see you know your bible, so you know God would not allow one of His creations to perish without intervening.'

'Swell, I guess not. Thanks for coming to my aid. No one else did. I remember a lot of people were standing some distance away, but none of them came and lent a hand.'

'That's the problem with the world today. Everyone is for themselves, and no one wants to help their neighbor. It is all self.'

'I will call in again in the next few days and see how you are doing and see if we can arrange for you to stay with one of our parishioners.'

'No, thanks. They will look down upon me. I have had that before. Outwardly they're Christians, but really, they care only about themselves and treat you like dirt, worrying about whether you will damage something or steal their cutlery. I have been through that before, and it never works out. Allen, you have got to come to terms with reality in that no one will want to have a bum in their house, Christian beliefs or not. They will help for a day or two, thinking they are doing a good deed for the Lord, but really they want you out of their home. Thanks, but I prefer not to go through that again.' 'I will come back in a few days, and we can talk about it some more.'

Allen shakes Vicki's hand and leaves. Vicki knows Allen has only good intensions for her, but she has been through that before and doesn't want to go through it again.

The next day, the doctors allow Vicki out of bed and allow her to walk down the corridors to get her lungs expanding and breathing naturally without oxygen.

A day later, the doctors agree Vicki could be let out of hospital and allowed to 'go home'. They did not realize home was a park bench in the frosty night, but common sense should have alerted them to this. The circumstances in which they found her were noted clearly on her record, and they could have found this out by reading the report attached to her file. But they didn't care. All they cared about is to get her bed so they would look good statistically for the number of patients treated. It had bearing on the amount of money the hospital received at budget time. That they were sending Vicki out to the extremes that caused her initial collapse didn't matter to them. She was a statistic, and this is how the hospital viewed it.

They released Vicki from hospital with no one caring about her situation or how she came to be in hospital or how she would get home. They gave her antibiotics to take twice a day and an appointment to see a lung specialist at the outpatients in two weeks' time.

Vicki doesn't have anywhere to go other than her park bench, so she walks towards the park and her usual bench. She passes a garbage tin and throws the antibiotics in the bin and walks on.

Two days later, Robert turns up at the hospital to find they had discharged Vicki and no one knew where she was. He intended on going to the hospital and seeing her two days prior, but business matters came up that required him to go intestate and stay there longer than he planned. He kept thinking about Vicki and was annoyed by the fact he could not go to the hospital and see her.

The next morning, Robert goes to the Town Hall steps, but Vicki was not there. He asks a few people if they know where she is, but no one knows but is told, 'Go to the park and you may see her there.' Robert goes to the park and, after looking around for half an hour, finds Vicki cold and shivering under a park bench with a piece of plastic over her to stay warm.

Robert asks, 'Vicki, why are you here?'

Vicki, shivering with the icy wind blowing through her body, says, 'Robert, what are you doing here? This is where I live. They kicked me out of hospital because they needed the bed, and I had no money and nowhere else to go.'

'You are coming with me. Come on, get up. This is no place for you.'
'Robert, leave me. I don't know you and don't intend to go with you.'

'The weather report says icy winds and more rain are coming, and this will settle in by tonight. You will end up dying from pneumonia, so come with me where I can offer you a warm place so you can build up your strength. I will take you to my unit where I live, and you can stay there until we make some other arrangements.'

'No, that is going to be a problem for your wife and family, so, no, thank you.'

'I am not married, don't have any children, no animals, not even a goldfish, and I live alone in a big unit. No, you are not being hired as a mistress. So, come on, and I will settle you in and allow you to rest while I go off to work.'

'Robert, I really would not like to disturb your situation. Please leave me. What God has planned for me will happen, so thanks, but I would prefer not to go. Why would a perfect stranger help a street bum like me? What's the motive?'

'Because I am in love with you.'

'You are mad. You can have any woman you want, and you love me? What is this? Do you think I am Cinderella? No, Robert, this is crazy.'

'How about you come to my place and rest, and we can talk about it this evening when I finish work? If you still feel this way, I will drive you back to the park and you can die under your bench from a second dose of pneumonia. Agreed?'

Vicki, hesitating for a moment and seeing Robert is getting serious, says, 'Agreed, except for the dying of pneumonia bit.'

Both smile, and Robert helps Vicki up, and both walk to Robert's car. He drives her to his unit and directs her to the spare bedroom. He quickly shows her where the coffee and pantry are and lets himself out, as he was running late for work.

The day goes quickly, as Robert has a lot to do. At six in the evening, he drives home to his unit tired and wondering whether Vicki would still be there. He parks his car and goes up to the unit thinking that Vicki has gone back to her park bench. To his surprise, she is there and has cooked a small meal of spaghetti bolognaise for their dinner.

Robert sits down to eat, and after the meal, helps Vicki wash the dishes. Robert asks, 'How do you feel?'

Vicki replies, 'Still weak, and my lungs are sore when I breathe, but other than that, I am all right. Where is the storm you said was coming?'

'They still say it is going to hit. Haven't you switched the TV on and checked?'

'No. In the park, we don't have TV. I am not used to such luxuries.'

'At least you can build up your strength over the next few days. They say it is going to be bad.'

Vicki doesn't believe Robert and thinks that was just something he said to get her to agree to come to his unit. She doesn't know what his motive is, but wonders whether she made the right decision. Robert says, 'Tomorrow I have to leave early for work. I will give you my mobile number so you can ring me if there are any problems. Otherwise, I will see you about this time tomorrow and we can talk. I am going to bed now, so good night.'

Vicki replies, 'OK, I will see you tomorrow.'

Robert goes to bed, and Vicki stays up for another hour reading one of Robert's books and then goes to bed.

Robert gets up in the morning, and it is blowing a gale. He has a light breakfast, has a shower, gets dressed, and leaves for the office. Vicki gets up at about eight and strolls into the lounge room and looks out of the window over the balcony and could see the rain and wind blowing, causing the trees to bend over, and she could see low- level flooding in the street below. She says to herself, *Thank God I am not out there. There is no way I could stay dry in that weather.*

She goes out to the kitchen and gets herself some breakfast and a cup of coffee and settles back in the lounge room and looks around for the controller and switches the TV on. The news is full of the problems the storm has created and the amount of damage done to people's homes. It reported that a tornado had hit a suburb destroying two thousand homes and only thirty were left standing. She again thanks God in a prayer that she is safe indoors and not in the park under her bench.

The wind keeps howling and the rain pelts down against the sliding door leading to the balcony. After an hour, Vicki has a shower and goes to the kitchen and opens the fridge. She spotted a frozen pizza in the fridge, so she decides they will have that with some salad tonight. She takes the milk out and goes and makes herself another cup of coffee and settles back on the lounge and reads her book.

Robert has a busy day of meetings and finishes at about six o'clock. He packs up his papers and puts them into his briefcase, and goes to his car and drives to his unit. He enters and sees Vicki on the lounge watching television.

Robert asks, 'Well, how are we today?'

Vicki gets up and says, 'Getting better. It's a terrible storm. I have been listening to the news, and they predict it will be around for the next few days. Thanks for saving me. I couldn't survive if you hadn't brought me here.'

'At least I don't have to worry if you are safe.

'Tomorrow is Saturday, so I don't have to go to work. We will go to the mall and buy you some clothes that you can change into rather than staying in a bathrobe or my shirt and shorts.'

'No, Robert, I can't allow you to spend money on me, a perfect stranger. I appreciate the food and board, but you can't spend your money on me. Besides, a change of clothes is no use when I go back to the park bench. Other beggars will just steal them from me. No, you have done enough for me. As soon as the weather clears up, I will be gone.'

'Well, at least come and pick out some clothes so I can keep them for you when you next visit me.'

'And what will you tell your family when they ask why you have got women's clothing and underwear in your drawers?'

'I will tell them I wear them when I go out with the boys.' Vicki burst out laughing and says, 'No, I don't think so.'

'We have to go shopping, so we will be there anyhow. If you don't choose something, I will buy what I think will fit you, and you will pay the penalty in wearing oversize garments.'

'All right, but nothing fancy. Just plain things and not expensive.'

Both sit chatting for a while and then put the pizza on and eventually have their dinner. After washing up, they decide to go to bed early so they can get up and do their shopping before the crowd sets in.

The next morning, both get up early, have their breakfast, and set off to the mall.

They first do the grocery shopping and put this in the boot of the car and then go to the shops to buy underwear, a couple of shirts, and jeans for Vicki. This proved a bigger task than first imagined. The underclothing was relatively easy to buy, but the outer garments proved to take the longest in that Vicki refused to pay the prices that were being charged. She would try on a dress and then pants or jeans, and Robert would help her choose which looked best, but when she found out the prices, she refused to have them. Finally, after several hours, Robert got her to agree to accept them, as the alternative would be for her to walk naked, and this didn't appeal to Vicki.

They arrive home and unpack the groceries, and Vicki put her new clothes in the wash to get the starch out of them. Later, she either hangs them up on an inside line or puts them in the drier. Once dry, Vicki has a shower and puts on her new clothes and puts the rest away.

Robert stands looking at her and says, 'What a difference. You know you are a very beautiful girl?'

Vicki replies, 'Stop it, you are making me blush. Besides, I will be the best-dressed girl under the bench. Oops, I shouldn't have said it that way.'

Both burst out laughing and went about their business.

In the evening, they both settle down in the lounge room and talk.

Robert says, 'You know, Vicki, today has told me you are not an illiterate woman who hasn't got her wits about her. You seem an educated person quite capable of handling yourself. Something doesn't add up why a person like that would be out on the streets living under a park bench.'

Vicki replies, 'Well, Robert, it really isn't your business, but you have been good to me, so I guess you deserve an explanation.'

Vicki and Robert sit in the lounge room while Vicki tells her story.

Vicki says, 'I was the only child, and my parents were professional people. One was a doctor, the other a chemist. They lived in a good suburb and had some money, not much, but enough to get them over short-term problems with bills.

'The family was religious, and both parents believed in God.'

'I also learned to believe in God and, through my trials, became stronger in faith and learned to trust God. I believe I would be seven or eight on the POF rating.'

'I graduated from university with degrees in economics and graphics design and went to work as a designer for a fashion house and built up a reputation as a recognized designer. I went out with my boss, who was also a young designer whom I eventually married. Both of us put our souls into developing the business and towards getting a reputation for unique designs.'

'I don't have any children, as there was no time for a family. Every cent we earned went to developing the business, and often we were short of money, as we invested too much of our money in working capital. The rich were demanding in relation to style and fashion but were slow payers.'

'My parents did not agree with my choice of partner, as he wasn't a Christian and didn't seem to be a nice person. He was abrupt and arrogant, a control freak. Money and nothing else meant anything to him. He didn't have time to see my parents, and often I would visit my parents on my own.'

'About a year after I married, my father had a massive heart attack and died while working in his pharmacy. My mother found it hard to be on her own and refused to join some of the senior citizen clubs to make some new friends. She relied on me for companionship, which put a strain on our marriage. My mother died of a stroke about three months after my father died, and I sold the pharmacy and my parents' home to pay off some of our business debts.

'No matter how much I would deposit in the bank, we always found ourselves unable to pay our debts. The more I put in, the less we had in the bank.'

'I noticed the bank account was going down fast and confronted my husband about it. He denied knowledge of any withdrawals, and yet when I investigated these at the bank, they showed they were being withdrawn by him and in sizeable sums. I again confronted my husband, who declared that he was involved in gambling on the horses and dogs and had lost a lot of money, which the bookies were demanding he repaid.

He placed a large bet on what he was told was a sure thing by a friend in the know, and, of course, it came in last. He wouldn't tell me how much was owed other than to say he will pay all his debts off soon.'

'What I didn't know was that he had bought some heroin and pay for it with the money he lost on the races. When the time came to pay for the delivery, there was no money. The dealers were not willing to accept excuses and sent out some hit men to collect the heroin or the money. They came across my husband in the garage trying to re-bag the heroin. They wanted payment, and he didn't have it, so they shot him through the head as a warning to others and took the heroin with them. He died that day shortly after being taken to hospital.'

'I later found out that he owed money to the mob, who demanded payment from me. There were also monies owed to banks on the acquisition of shares on the exchange, which were purchased on a margin scheme, and the stock exchange had fallen substantially over the last few days, making the banks demand that more equity be deposited into the margin account, or they will begin recovery proceedings.'

'Since we held all our bank accounts in joint names, the bank could take all the funds, and they did. I didn't know that I could have taken some of that money out and deposited into an account in my name, but I wasn't thinking straight. The banks took possession of our business and sold it and our family home, which unfortunately was registered in my husband's name only. That was sold, leaving a debt owing to the mob of $1 million. Since there were no assets left, we had to write off our losses.'

'I had no money and nowhere to stay. No one was willing to help me. All of our so-called friends didn't want to know me, as my husband was involved in drugs and was considered a drug taker himself. So I went to the park where I had previously seen people sleeping on the benches.'

'I cried all night the first few weeks and could barely sleep thinking I would be killed by someone who was trying to rob me but later found out that there is an unwritten law amongst those living in the park that you are not to approach anyone else living there or rob them during the night. If you do, all will gang up against you and will inflict injury and ensure you never come back again.'

'I was assaulted twice. Once when I was sleeping under a bench when a man came through the park one night screaming his head off. He sat on my bench talking out loud to himself. He had a large knife, which he was continually sticking into the bench, swearing as he was lifting his knife up and then driving it into the bench. I was scared he would miss the timber rail and stab me. After about five minutes, I ran to a tree, and he came after me and stuck the knife into the tree, hacking at the trunk. The police patrolled that night and saw him and came over to him. He was going to stab one of them when the other officer tasered him, and they took him to the station. One of the police officers said the man was on ice and was under the influence of most probably a combination of drugs. The second time I was assaulted was when three young drunken men tried to rape me. I stabbed one of them and run away. Two of them came back with guns and shot at a makeshift body I made of me under the bench. They ran off after offloading their guns into what they thought was me.'

Robert asks, 'Did you go to the police?'

Vicki replies, 'No, they wouldn't care about us. The mayor wants us out of the city, and if one is shot, that means there is one less to worry about. No one cares about the street people.'

5

llen remembers he must see Robert's parents and decides to see them today. He drives to the address given to him and knocks on the door. Nothing for a moment and then the door is opened by Robert's mother, who says, 'Yes, can I help you?'

Allen stares at her for a moment and says, 'Mrs. Somerset, my name is Allen Sheppard. I am a minister at the local church and an acquaintance of your son, Robert. May I come on in for a minute to discuss a private matter with you?'

Mrs. Somerset replies, 'Our son said you may call us someday, but really, we are not interested in hearing about God and His greatness. It is a lot of rubbish, and while you may decide to fall for the lies, we don't. So, I would say you are wasting your time, and we prefer not to go over old ground again.'

'You believed once, but what I understand, the death of your daughter was the point that turned you from God. Is that right?'

'That was when we decided there was no God and that all of our prayers amounted to nothing.'

'I would like to discuss this with you, if I may. Can I come in just for a moment?'

'I guess you can, since I cannot convince you to leave.'

Mrs. Somerset opens the door and lets Allen in and leads him to the lounge room where her husband is seated. He gets up and introduces himself to Allen, and both sit down.

Allen says, 'My understanding is that you were Christians for many years and, therefore, you had faith in Christ. Over the years, you went through several trials and could get through them with Jesus's help and you believed in Him and were attendees at the local church.'

'Trials are not intended to test your faith but to show you how much faith you have in Jesus. They compound over time and get harder and harder until you reach the point that is the tipping stone that shows you whether you really have rock-solid faith in Jesus or whether your faith is based on sand, which shifts according to circumstances. In your case, the test, by the looks of it, was your daughter, and what I understand, because God took her from you, you decided that there was no God or one that you could not trust, so you went to Satan.'

Mrs. Somerset replies, 'No, we just decided it was useless to trust God, as He just let you down. Time after time, He has let us down. No, He doesn't let you down. You just don't trust Him, nor do you want to give Him the chance of showing you what He is doing and why.'

'You say that God took your daughter. He didn't take anything that was not His. Your daughter was given to you to bring up in a Christian tradition, and you did it. You assumed she was your possession and did not belong to God. We are all destined to die, eventually. God took back your daughter, as she was His to do so, and it was her time. It so happened it was the trial that was used to test your faith in God, and you showed you had lost faith in Him and have not held to his teachings.'

'Mr. Sheppard, we accept what you have said but do not believe in God anymore, and thank you for coming, but I believe you have said your piece and we would ask you to leave.'

'I am sorry you feel this way and that you have gone the way of the world. Unfortunately, you will end up in hell and not have eternal life unless you find it in your heart to ask God's forgiveness and return to the faith.'

'Well, it can't be any worse than what we experience here on earth, so thank you. I will see you out.'

Mrs. Somersby gets up, and so does Allen. They shake hands, and she takes him to the front door and closes it behind him.

Mrs. Somersby returns to her lounge room and says to Mr. Somersby, 'That was a lot of rubbish.'

Mr. Somersby says, 'I am not quite sure. What we are saying is that if we don't have our own way, we say there is no God. We used to spank our kids when they were young, when they thought the same way when we were bringing them up.'

Mrs. Somersby replies, 'Well, you do what you want to do, but I am having nothing more of God and His grace.'

Mrs. Somersby switches the TV on, and they both settle down to watch a movie. Mr. Somersby ponders about what Allen had said and periodically drifts in thought, recalling the points stated by Allen.

6

obert is at the airport waiting for his flight back home. A man sits in the lounge chair near him, and he nods to the man. He then thinks, *Who is this bloke? I recognize him from somewhere.*

He leans over to the man and says, 'Do I know you?'

The man replies, 'You should. I am Steve from high school.'

'Of course. It has been quite a few years, and you used to have hair then.'

'Yes, and life was a lot easier in those days.'

'What do you do for a living?'

'I work for a liquidator as an insolvency consultant. We are trying to sell a fashion house that has gone into liquidation, but there seems to be little interest in this one.'

'Is it a well-known house?'

'Yes. It has contacts overseas and orders on its books. All that it needs is someone who knows fashion and how to operate in the rag trade.'

'What are you asking for it?'

'Whatever we can get. The alternative is to wind it up and get nothing. We must at least cover our costs.'

'Give me your card, and I will see if any of my contacts are interested.'

Steve gives Robert a card and then hears his flight being called and makes a dash for the departure lounge.

Robert sits thinking about what Steve had said and wonders whether it would help get Vicki a job. He had some money put aside in investments, which he could call upon if necessary, so capital would not be an issue unless Steve's idea of a cheap price differed from what Robert was thinking.

Robert hears his flight being called and makes his way to the departure lounge and boards the plane for home. He keeps thinking about what Steve had said to him and decides to discuss it with Vicki and, if she was interested, call Steve and see what assets are being offered with the deal and the asking price.

Robert finally gets home tired and keen to get into bed.

Vicki has already gone to bed, as it was eleven o'clock, and all the lights are off.

Robert gets up early the next morning and was surprised to see Vicki up and sitting at the kitchen bench having some coffee.

Vicki says, 'Good morning. You certainly got home late. Did you have a good business meeting?'

Robert replies, 'Yes, it went well. We agreed to acquire the chain of retirement villages they control and set a date ninety days from yesterday for settlement. The owners of the retirement village are going to retire, and we will be in total control.'

'Why, don't they have children who can take over the running of the business?'

'Yes, but they are not interested in running a retirement village. Both the kids are professional people. One is a doctor, the other is an engineer. I met them, but they do not seem to have business skills and therefore would find it hard to make a profit.'

'That's a shame. What you were telling me was that it is a well- known retirement village with an excellent reputation?'

'That's right. That's why I went and checked their books and did a due diligence on the company. After that, I made them an offer, which they initially rejected, but after we discussed the issues, they agreed that our price was fair and reasonable and had their lawyer checked the contract for sale before signing.'

'On another matter, what have you got planned for today?'

Vicki replies, 'Nothing much. I thought I'd take a walk in the park.'

'And sit on a bench, or under one?'

'Something like that. I have been here for the last few days, and let's face it, you don't want to have a reputation for having a mistress in your apartment, do you?'

'A fellow has to do something to uphold his profile.'

'I have a job interview with the department store here in town. They are looking for a shop assistant, and I thought of applying to earn some money. I don't intend to tell them about my qualifications. Otherwise, they will say I am overqualified for the job.'

'I may have something better for you. Last night, while I was waiting for my flight, I bumped into an old schoolmate of mine who is a liquidator. He is trying to sell a fashion house who has gone broke. He is trying to find a buyer for the business. Would you be interested in running it for me if I acquired it?'

'I think I know who they are. I believe it's Marque International, or MI as they are known. I heard they went into liquidation, and they appointed a liquidator to sell them or their assets. I think you will be talk big money to acquire them?'

'Not if no one is willing to step up and have a look at them. Are you interested?'

'Robert, I have been out of the industry for a few years, and things have moved on. I have probably forgotten what it takes to run that type of business. Besides, everyone in the industry knows what happened to me, and it would be embarrassing to trust me now.'

'Rubbish, most people will remember your husband's death and that he was involved in drugs, but take you as you were, an honest, decent person who got caught up in his scheme and paid the price. You don't have to tell them you were living in the park or anything about where you ended up. Just say you kept a low profile to try to get over his death. They will understand that and allow you to re- establish yourself.'

'I think this shop assistant's job is more to what I should aim at present to build up my confidence.'

'Why don't I make the phone call and see what we are looking at? You are going to be bored going up to people asking, "Can I help you?" when none of them want to buy. All they want to do is try on a new dress or pants and see how they look in them. Most won't have the money to buy a new dress or whatever and are only wasting your time, and you will earn fifteen dollars an hour, which won't be enough to pay for your rent.'

'What do you think is the cost of a park bench?'

'You can't go back to a park bench with all the good clothes I bought you.'

'Well, you threw out my other clothes that the hospital gave me, so if you take this back, then I will have to be a streaker under the park bench. Do you want to see me naked?'

'Yep, I have the time.'

'I'm sure you have. So, it is either go along with your plan or undress. Is that the case?'

'No, let's not make it that difficult. Just undress.'

Robert gets up, and so does Vicki. He takes her in his arms and gives her a big kiss on the lips.

'You shouldn't have done that.'

'I told you I am in love with you, and that just proves it. Don't worry, I will not demand that you sleep with me before the wedding. I know you are a Christian and will stick to your beliefs. So don't get drunk on our wedding night?'

'Robert, stop saying things like that. Your parents will not allow you to marry a girl like me, who has no money or reputation, someone who lived in the park under a bench.'

'We won't tell them that. If we buy the fashion house and I appointed you manager, it will give you all the credibility necessary for you to meet my parents and get back your self-esteem.'

'I don't know. Spend all that money just for me. It seems a lot for you to do just for me, and the risk of losing your money on the acquisition is high. It might be easier for you to start up a business on your own, but you may not have the reputation that MI have gained over the years.'

'Well, the first thing to do is to phone Steve and find out what they are actually selling of MI's and at what price.'

'No, I am scared that I may mess things up for you and you will lose your money.'

'Or make a lot of money. If we go ahead with it, I will tell my parents that I have diversified and that I have hired a designer/ manager to run the business. I will pay you a wage and share the profits with you on a percentage basis.'

'Well, they may accept me on that basis. We can only wait and see, I guess, but I can't stay here indefinitely. What will your parents say?'

'I have the answer. I will take you to the park and you can stay there.'

'The park? But I thought you said you didn't want me to go back to the park.'

'Get your things while I make a phone call to Steve, and then we will be off.'

Vicki realized she was in love with Robert and found it hard to accept his comment that he was taking her back to the park. She went to her room and gathered her clothing and put them in a plastic shopping bag, while Robert made his phone call. She came out of her room tearful just as he finished his call.

Robert says, 'Steve is in his office, so I will see him and find out what he wants for the business. I'll leave you at the park so you can soak up the atmosphere.'

By this time, Vicki was close to tears but doesn't want to upset Robert. She picks up her plastic bags and makes her way to the door. Robert follows her, and they go down to the basement, and Robert puts her clothes in the boot of his car. They both get in, and Robert drives off.

Vicki is upset, and she takes about fifteen minutes to get over the shock that she is being taken back to the park. She looks up and wonders, *Why are we driving north when the park is south of Robert's unit?* Another minute and they pull up outside a unit block called Park Royal Apartments. Vicki bursts into tears upon seeing the name of the block of apartments. Robert tries to calm her down but couldn't, and she weeps until he opens her car door and looks at her and says, 'Why are you crying?'

Vicki replies, 'I thought you were taking me back to the park bench, not Park Royal.'

'I never thought about that. I have always referred to these apartments as the Park. Sorry to upset you. But why didn't you ask me instead of bottling it up?'

'It was such a shock I couldn't understand what was happening.'

'I own an apartment in this block that no one knows about. I bought it a few years ago during the property slump and have kept it, thinking I will get around to renting it out someday. Since you are worried what my parents would think about me having a mistress around, well, I thought of having you stay here until we can get some clarity about what we are going to do. I will l leave you here and speak to Steve and then come back for you. You can decide whether you want to stay here or stay with me. Leave your things in the car, and I will bring them up when I come and tell you what transpired with Steve. You can stay in the unit and get a feel for it.'

'What should I say if someone knocks on the door?'

'Tell them to mind their own business. If you like the unit, tell them you are the new tenant. If you don't like it, tell them you are the new cleaner or, better still, the French maid. They will believe that in this place.'

Vicki and Robert go to the eighth floor and get out of the lift. They walk to apartment 8002, and Robert takes out a key and opens the door.

Vicki says, 'Wow, it's beautiful.'

Vicki walks around and checks the bedrooms and lounge room. She stands in the kitchen and can see right over the balcony. She checks the linen cupboard and sees it has towels and sheets in it.

Robert says, 'I will leave you here. You can make a cup of coffee for yourself. I will be back in a couple of hours.'

Vicki lets Robert out and locks the door. She goes into the kitchen and opens the cupboards and checks where the coffee is located. She presses the jug to heat the water and, when it boils, makes herself a cup of coffee. She opens the door to the fridge, but there is no milk. She sits on one of the kitchen chairs and looks over the balcony and sips her coffee, wondering how Robert is getting on. After a couple of hours, she hears a knock at the front door and gets up and opens the door. Robert is on the other side and says, 'Can I interest you in some insurance?' Vicki lets him in, and both sit down in the lounge room opposite one another.

Robert says, 'He wants $5 million for the lot, building's artwork, designs—the lot. He wants to deal on a walk-in, walk-out basis.'

Vicki replies, 'It sounds a lot of money. What did you say?'

'Goodbye, not interested.'

'Good. Well, that finishes that off. Thank God you didn't go ahead with it.'

'They value the property at about $3.5 million, leaving a valuation of $1.5 million on the business.'

'It is far too expensive. I don't think anyone will pay that type of money.'

'What do you think of this unit?'

'It is great, but I can't let you allow me to stay here at the Park. There is only one bench, and that's a kitchen bench, and it is too small to sleep under.'

'What do you want to do? Do you want to stay here or come back to my apartment?'

'It seems that you will not be proceeding with Steve's deal, so I think I should go to the interview that I had arranged for this afternoon for the retail job and then try my luck at the YWCA or see if I can get a bed at one of the charities. I have imposed on you enough, and you should get on with your life and business. Otherwise, your parents will be suspicious of where you are.'

'No, I will take you back to my apartment, and you can stay for a few more days. No one will know or find out I am keeping a maid in the cupboard.'

'I have to get a job, Robert. I can't rely on you all the time.'

'And why not? We are going to be married, aren't we?'

'Oh, Robert, be serious. You haven't even proposed, let alone taken the time to know me. If you did, you would find out that I am really a witch and I turn people into frogs, so be careful.'

'Us frogs will do anything to get a kiss.'

Robert and Vicki hold each other in a passionate hug and kiss just as Robert's mobile rings.

Robert says, 'Just when I was enjoying it. Hello. Yes, Steve. Just a quick look at the figures but thought your estimate of the sales price for the building and business on the surface looks high. What would I be prepared to pay for the business? That's a good question. I would say no more than $3 million. Yes, I am prepared to talk to you. Say ten tomorrow at your office. OK, I will see you then. Goodbye.'

'That was Steve. He is prepared to discuss $3 million. I will see him tomorrow to discuss it further with him. I want you there so you can start looking over their designs and graphics to get an idea of what they have and what they should have.'

Vicki replies, 'I can't go. I only have jeans and tops. You need someone with a dress that looks like they mean business. That's going to leave them with an impression.'

'Then we come back to your suggestion of being naked. That will impress them?'

'Yes, I am sure it would. No, you will have to go by yourself.'

'Look, a decent dress or business suit won't cost that much. Let's go down to the shopping centre, and I will buy you one.'

'I can't let you do that. You have spent enough on me as it is.'

'And what did you intend to wear to the interview today?'

'I never thought of that. I will need something. Otherwise, they won't even see me, let alone interview me for the job. All right, let's see what we can get, but nothing expensive and nothing other than what's in Kmart or Target.'

'Or the Reject Shop?'

'Funny.'

Vicki and Robert go to the shopping centre and start window shopping. They go into one of the large department stores and find a dress and a suit that may be suitable. Vicki goes in and tries on the dress and comes out to see what Robert thinks.

Vicki says, 'It looks all right, but not sure if it's classy enough for the design business?'

Robert replies, 'Well, don't you look great in that? It will create an impression. If not on them, then definitely on me.'

'Yes, it is a good fit. I will try on the business suit.'

Vicki goes back into the booth, changes, and comes out with the business suit on and stands in front of Robert, who currently has his mouth open staring at her.

Vicki says, 'Well, Robert, how does this look?'

Robert replies, 'Great, we will take both of them.'

'Robert, be reasonable. They both cost over a hundred dollars each. Which one is suitable for tomorrow's meeting?'

'We will take both because we will have to meet with them frequently before the deal is clinched, and you need different clothes for each meeting.'

'I never thought of that.'

Robert goes over and takes another dress off the rack and says, 'We will also take this one just in case we have to see them three times.'

Vicki says, 'Let's get out of here before you buy up the shop.' As they walk out of the shopping centre, Vicki says, 'Aw, no, I can't go because I have no shoes to wear with these dresses.'

Robert replies, 'Then let's go back and get you a pair of eleven-inch heels.'

'I wouldn't be able to walk in them. No, a standard heel in black will do me.'

They go to a shoe shop, and Vicki tries on a few pairs of shoes and picks out a five-inch heel, which she can get used to. They then make their way back to the car and get in.

Vicki says, 'I just thought of something. I can't go to the meeting without make-up.'

Robert replies, 'Don't worry about that. I will give you some of my aftershave.'

'Gee, I must really look awful. I thought I only needed a lipstick and a blush, but now, come to think of it, I really need a foundation, eyebrow pencil, lipstick, and stockings. We better go quickly as we have a lot to buy. Thanks for telling me.'

'I should keep my big mouth closed. All it does is open my wallet.'

They head off to the make-up counter, and Vicki approaches one of the make-up girls, who advises her what she needs. Two hours later, she comes out and says to Robert, 'Gee, that's cheap, only $350.' Robert is not too happy that he has spent close to $1,000, and they didn't get to Target.

Again, they walk to the car, and Robert opens Vicki's door and says, 'Quickly you better get in.' Vicki gets into the car, and Robert gets into the driver's side.

Vicki asks, 'Why did we have to get in quickly?' Robert replies, 'Because it might cost me more money.'

Vicki laughs, and Robert calms down after thinking about the meeting tomorrow.

Vicki says, 'Look at the time. My appointment for the interview has passed. What will I do?'

Robert replies, 'Just tell them you were there and got caught up in the marketing pitch and lost track of the time.'

'It's too late to ring them now. I will have to ring them straight after I get back from the meeting tomorrow. Robert, you didn't keep me going so I would forget the meeting, did you?'

'Heaven forbid such a thought. I couldn't devise such a plan. You have to be a woman to think that way.'

'Sorry, I thought you intentionally tied me up with all the things I needed so I would forget the appointment.'

'Never mind. We will see how we go tomorrow.'

Robert pulls into McDonald's on the way home and gets some Big Macs and drives home. They eat their hamburgers, and Vicki goes off to watch some TV, while Robert answers some emails.

The next morning, they both get up early and have breakfast, and both have their showers.

Robert comes out dressed in a navy-colored suit and sits on the lounge. It is eight o'clock. At eight thirty, he gets worried and yells out to Vicki, 'Is everything all right?'

Vicki replies, 'Yes, just putting on my make-up.'

'How long will you be?'

'Soon.'

Robert waits, and it's nine o'clock and gets worried. He says to himself, *Two hours to get ready. You have got to be joking.* He yells out to Vicki, 'Come on, we are going to be late!'

Vicki replies, 'Coming.'

Vicki steps out, and Robert's mouth drops open.

Robert says, 'Gee, you look fantastic. They will not be able to take their eyes off you.'

Vicki asks, 'Was the wait worth it?'

'Yes. Forget about the meeting. We are going to the Town Hall now to get married.'

'Let's see what they have to say, lover boy.'

'Lover boy. I'm making progress.'

They go down in the elevator and get into Robert's car and drive off to Steve's office.

7

Steve is waiting to introduce Robert to his principal partner and is surprised to see Vicki. Robert introduces Vicki to the two gentlemen.

Steve asks, 'Vicki, what is your role in today's meeting?'

Vicki replies, 'I would like to see the designs and graphics you are selling with the business, as I am aware what styles were designed by MI. Possibly you could show me where you keep the records so I can have a quick examination of them.'

Steve says, 'By all means, you can use the office next door, and I will bring in the registers.'

Steve directs Vicki to the office next door and goes out and brings in two large thick arch folders.

Steve says, 'These are the main ones. I'll leave you for a while so we can start negotiating with Robert.'

Vicki replies, 'Thank you.'

Vicki looks through the records and, after two hours, has come up with a list of irregularities. She makes several telephones calls and takes careful notes on what they said to her. She gets up and walks to the front of the office where Robert is sitting and shows she wants to talk to him.

Robert comes out and says, 'You don't look too happy.'

Vicki replies, 'No. What I believe they have done was to sell the designs to garment manufacturers instead of licensing them to manufacture the garments while still keeping the rights to and control of the design.'

'Was this hidden?'

'Yes. I had to make several telephone calls to some manufacturers I know, and they told me that most of the designs were sold by Steve, and the only ones kept by MI are the ones no one wants to take a risk with. This means that the deal comprises the name, which is worthless, as most people know the fashion house has gone broke, and the building, which, it seems, no one has made an offer for. If you don't buy it, the building will have to go to auction, and who knows what they will get for it?'

'We argue that the business name is worthless, as it has been tarnished, but can you use it to re-establish the business, as what I understand, it has been around for years and is a recognized brand for design and innovation.'

'Yes, it could be used and resurrected, but this will take time and money.'

'How much would you say?'

'Two million at least.'

'That's what I thought. Let's go in but say nothing and let me do the talking. It may get heated, so sit quietly and keep smiling at them. It may calm them down.'

Robert and Vicki go into Steve's office and sit down.

Steve says, 'Nothing wrong, I hope, Vicki? Do you need anything explained?'

Robert replies, 'Yes, she does, Steve. First, why did you think we were fools, and, second, why didn't you tell us you had sold the copyrights to the designs instead of licensing the manufacturers, as is the custom?'

Steve turns red, knowing that his credibility is at stake now. 'All the other parties that were interested in the business didn't pick up the things you have mentioned, so we thought you would miss this, and afterwards, once I sold the business, well, it's your problem and not ours. You know it is up to you to do your due diligence, not for us to do it for you.'

Robert replies, 'Due diligence, yes, that's our responsibility, but misrepresenting what you're selling is a fraudulent act, which says a lot about your honesty, Steve.'

Steve says, 'It has nothing to do with honesty. You agreed to look at the proposition with a view of making an offer. Are you still interested in the business, or are you walking away from it?'

'I am not interested in dealing with a crook, Steve, as at the end of the day, I will end up with nothing but problems.'

'Make an offer if you are still interested.'

'One million for the lot.'

'You have to be joking. The building alone is worth $3 million.'

'Is that before or after Town Hall resumes it?'

'That's only hearsay and not definite.'

'According to Town Hall, it is definite, and you know it, Steve. You're peddling lies just to get your money and don't care about the consequences. Therefore, all the buyers have been scared off, and we are the only ones interested in the business or were interested in it.'

'What, you are pulling out, are you?'

'Yes, I can't see any value in the proposition and don't want to waste my time with a rotten deal that's going to cost me more money or blow up in my face.'

Steve, looking at his manager, says, 'We will accept $1 million if you are prepared to settle within sixty days.'

Robert replies, 'I want to know exactly what we are buying, and none of your fraudulent dealings.'

Steve says, 'Give me a couple of days, and I will put a package together for you that will contain all the information you will need to make the right decision.'

Vicki adds, 'You better include any outstanding orders for design the fashion house had committed itself to and any contractual obligations that exist as regards fashion shows.'

Steve replies, 'Yes, it will take me a while to get those together, particularly the contractual obligations entered into by the company, which could impact upon you later.'

Robert says, 'I will not be buying the company. You can liquidate that. All I want to buy is the assets and the business name.'

Steve replies, 'That might be difficult if there are outstanding contractual commitments, and we might not get out of them.'

Robert gets up and makes a move towards the door. Vicki gets caught off guard, stands up, and follows Robert to the door. Steve follows them out and sees them to the lift. Robert and Vicki go down in the elevator to the car park and sit in the car. Robert starts the car and prepares to drive out.

Robert says, 'It was good that you picked up the fact that he sold off the designs.'

Vicki replies, 'I didn't, that's why I made the telephone calls. I guessed there must be something wrong with the deal, and after speaking to some of my old friends in the industry, they told me what Steve was doing. How did you know about the building being compulsorily acquired by Town Hall?'

Robert answers, 'I didn't. I heard that Town Hall wanted a new place for its library, and this is the only building that would meet its requirement as to size and position. It is the only one that would not interfere with anyone and be an easy compulsory acquisition.'

Robert drives home and decides to let Vicki rest. So he lets her out and goes off to the office to see what was happening.

Vicki makes a phone call to the department store to see if the job was still available. They tell her that if she is interested, she should get there quickly, as they had several applicants for the position. She agrees to be there by two thirty in the afternoon for an interview. She goes through her things and finds twenty dollars in her jeans, which she forgot to give back to Robert when they went shopping. She quickly grabs her purse and goes down to the street and walks about a block and realizes that there were no cabs around. She walks another block and turns towards the main expressway. As she approaches it, she notices a bus is standing at the bus stop and waves her hands showing the driver that she wants to board the bus. The driver waits for her, and she gets on the bus and pays the fare to Town Hall.

As they approach the city, she notices a major shopping centre and indicates to the driver she wants to get off. He pulls up at the bus stop, and Vicki goes off. She walks to the shopping centre and then looks for the department store and finds it on the second floor. She goes to enquiries and asks for the manager. They directed Vicki to where the office is and she walks there and asks for Mrs. Jones. After a few minutes, Mrs. Jones, the store manager, comes out.

Mrs. Jones asks, 'Hello, Vicki, how are you? Didn't you have an appointment yesterday?'

Vicki replies, 'Yes, I did, but, unfortunately, I took ill and had to go home. I didn't want to take the risk of passing it on.'

'That was very thoughtful of you. It is quite common for that to happen in a place like this where there are always a lot of people. Thank you for being so considerate.'

Mrs. Jones asks, 'You look like a very attractive woman. Why would you want to take up a position as a sales assistant?'

Vicki replies, 'I am interested in fashion and like to dress people.'

'That's a very nice dress you're wearing. What is the name of the manufacturer?'

'Roberts designed it and it was manufactured in China under license by your store.'

'Well, that tells you how much I know. I should have bought one myself. I might look as good as you do. We have a problem at one of our counters, so you will have to excuse me for a minute so I can lend a hand?'

'May I come along? I may be able to help.'

'Yes, by all means.'

Both ladies go down to the section Ladies Apparel and could see there is a problem in that two of the staff have been taken ill and there are only two members of staff to handle all the enquiries and man the register.

Vicki asks, 'Can you handle the register while I attend to the enquiries?'

Mrs. Jones replies, 'Yes, that is a good idea.'

Vick suddenly realizes she knew nothing about their product range, so she had to use her wits and overcome any problems. She approaches a lady that seems furious and says, 'Can I help you?'

Lady replies, 'Yes, I have been waiting for fifteen minutes for help. Don't you people want to make a sale?'

'Sorry, madam, two of our girls took ill and we are short-handed. Now, what is that you were looking for?'

'Something like this in a size 16.'

'You know, that style would not flatter you at all. May I suggest this style, which will make you look taller and give you a shape?'

Vicki gives the lady two different dresses of that style and directs her into the fitting booth and goes to the next customer and does likewise. Within half an hour, she has all the ladies trying on dresses and out of the way.

A lady comes out of the fitting booth, and suddenly, there is a wolf whistle, and her husband appears.

Husband says, 'Fantastic. Don't you look like a spring chicken with style?'

Lady replies, 'Yes, and I chose it by myself.'

Vicki looks at the lady and smiles and looks at her husband, who couldn't take his eyes off her.

Vicki asks, 'Madam, which one do you intend to take?'

Husband says, 'How many do you have that look that good?'

Lady replies, 'Three, and I can't decide which one to buy.'

Husband says, 'Take the three.'

Lady asks, 'Do you think so? That is going to be expensive.'

Husband replies, 'If you look like that, it's worth it.'

Lady goes up to Vicki.

Lady whispers, 'Thanks. Sorry, I was rude before.'

Vicki replies, 'No worries, madam. We are here to help,' and directs her to the register.

At four thirty, the crowd seems to have thinned out as people were going home. Mrs. Jones comes over to Vicki.

Mrs. Jones says, 'It's no use interviewing you. You have proven to be an experienced assistant. You certainly gave our clients the right advice. All of them commented on your suggestions and how well they looked in what you selected for them. You certainly must have been in this business a long time.'

Vicki replies, 'No, for the last few years, I have been in the park sleeping under a bench.'

'Good one. You're hired, and I will see you tomorrow at nine. Don't be late.'

'I will be here.'

Vicki gets her things and walks out of the department store wondering what had happened. She got a job without an interview. She stops for a minute and says a prayer to the Lord, thanking Him for his help and giving her the job without the need for lying.

Vicki walks to the expressway and sees people lined up for a bus. She stands there waiting with the others, but right at the back of the line.

Robert finishes work and drives out onto the expressway to go home. He is stopped by a red light and just glances at the people trying to get on the bus outside the shopping centre. He glances at the line and thinks, *I hate to be waiting for a bus at this time of the evening, especially now that it has started drizzling.* He glances at the last person in the line and suddenly recognizes that it is Vicki. He says to himself, *It can't be. She's back at the apartment.* He looks at her again and realizes it was Vicki. The light turns green, and he turns onto the freeway and stops behind the bus. He opens his window and yells out, 'Vicki!'

Vicki turns around and sees it was Robert and runs towards his car and gets in.

Robert asks, 'What on God's earth are you doing waiting for a bus?'

Vicki replies, 'I went for the shop assistant's job, so I went for the interview. But two girls took ill and was asked to assist and stayed a couple of hours serving customers. They were very happy with me and gave me the job. I start tomorrow.'

'You got the job?'

'Isn't that great?'

Robert could see she was very pleased with herself and didn't want to throw cold water on her achievement.

Robert says, 'We will have to drop off at the takeaway to get some dinner. So, what do you feel like eating?'

Vicki replies, 'Anything as long as it isn't too heavy.'

'Let's get some Chinese?'

'Yes, that will be fine.'

They pull up outside one of the Chinese takeaways and order some assorted dishes and rice and drove onto their apartment to have dinner. After Robert goes and checks on his emails and notes, there is a message from Steve. He phones him.

Steve says, 'We will have all the documents you requested by tomorrow. So, can we arrange a meeting and conclude the deal?'

Robert replies, 'Not that quick after what we have been through today. We would want time to look at the records and make any relevant enquiries, so we know what we are buying.'

'So, what do you suggest?'

'Deliver the records to my office and give us a few days to go over them, and I will get back to you as soon as we can.'

'All right. I will drop them off tomorrow at about ten.'

'That will be fine.'

Robert hangs up and goes into the lounge room where Vicki is sitting, staring out the lounge room window.

Robert says, 'He is keen. I got him to drop off the documents at my office tomorrow.'

Vicki replies, 'That's great. I can work tomorrow and Saturday at the department store and look at the documents on Sunday and chase up any leads on Monday, as I have Monday off for working Saturday.'

'I guess so, or do we just dump the idea?'

'Let's see what he has before we can it.'

'How are you going to get to work tomorrow?'

'With the change I kept from the shopping the other day, which I owe you.'

'I forgot about that.'

'Good idea. Thanks,' and she bursts out laughing.

'It is good to see you happy again.'

'Thanks to the Good Lord and you. Isn't it strange how things take different turns? You think you are on top of the world and the carpet gets pulled out from under you, or you think you are heading into a storm and suddenly the sun comes out and things improve. You never know what's around the corner.'

'You put that down to God, do you?'

'Believe in Him and you will come out all right. That's what I was taught, and life has proven it to me. Have faith in Him. Take a look at where you found me. He used you to bring me out of that environment.'

'So I am just a servant doing the work of the Lord, am I?'

'No, to me you are the master, for without you, I would still be in the park. That's why I love you.'

'Now you are talking. When do we get married?'

'Are you a Christian?'

'Not dedicated, but I believe in Jesus Christ.'

'Good, then there is hope for our relationship.'

Vicki gives Robert a big kiss, which sends him swooning, and he blushes.

Robert asks, 'How are you going to get to work tomorrow?'

Vicki replies, 'I will come with you, and you can drop me off at the shopping centre and pick me up at night at the same place.'

'Yes, I can do that. But you will have to get up at five o'clock in the morning.'

'Why five o'clock?'

'It will take you three hours to put on your make-up.'

'Men. You don't appreciate the effort us women go to make ourselves pretty for you.'

'I will take you with or without make-up. You'd better get to bed. It will be a long day for you tomorrow.'

'I guess you're right. Goodnight.'

They kiss, and Vicki goes off to her bedroom.

The next morning, Robert has to go into Vicki's bedroom and wake her up.

Vicki asks, 'Robert, what are you doing in my room?'

Robert replies, 'Trying to make love to you before you go to work.'

'I forgot I have a job to go to. Put the kettle on so I can have some coffee.'

Robert goes out and switches the kettle on and goes and has a shower.

He comes out after dressing and makes some toast for himself.

The toast pops up just as Vicki comes out of her bedroom with make-up on dressed to kill.

Robert looks at her and is momentarily speechless and then says, 'You certainly look beautiful.'

Vicki replies, 'I think so too, and thanks for the toast.'

Both have a bit of a laugh, and Robert puts more toast in the toaster.

After breakfast, they wash up and grab their things and go down to the car and drive off.

They get to the shopping centre, and Vicki gives Robert a kiss and was ready to get out, but Robert hangs on to her.

Robert asks, 'What are you going to have for lunch?'

Vicki replies, 'I haven't thought about that. I know I will get a cardboard box and place it discreetly in a corner, asking for donations and use that if I get enough or if security doesn't find it.'

'You can't take the park out of the girl, can you? Even when you take the girl out of the park?'

Robert adds, 'Here is fifty dollars for lunch or whatever you need. I will pick you up tonight at the same spot.'

Vicki replies, 'Fifty dollars is too much. I will be all right. I will just take ten out of the till.'

'I thought you were a Christian?'

'Oops. I guess you're right. I will give you the change tonight.'

Vicki kisses Robert again and gets out of the car and goes inside the shopping centre.

Robert drives to work and starts dictating some letters on his recorder.

At ten, Steve arrives with his assistant, and they drop off four binders containing all the information. He gives Robert an engineering report on the building and gets him to sign a confidentiality agreement and leaves.

Robert looks through the first folder, which contains profit-and-loss details and information about the novation of leases and other contracts.

He reads the documents and makes some calculations, getting a feel for what the business could generate. The other folders contained details about contracts that were entered for design work and estimates that these could amount into the millions of dollars if the parties were agreeing to continue with the contracts. He spends most of the day going through the binders, getting a feel for what the business is worth and believes the figure of $1 million is fair and could go as high as $2 million if necessary.

Vicki was introduced formally to the staff with whom she will work with, even though she introduced herself to them yesterday while she was filling in. She filled out her record sheet, and the HR department entered her up on the computer as an employee. She was rostered to work Saturday but was told that they have enough girls this week to cover the weekend, so she can have Saturday off and begin the new week on Monday.

She unfortunately had one problem in that her wages were to be banked every week in her nominated bank account, but she did not have one.

To get a bank account, she would need to have one hundred points identification, which would consist of a driver's license, passport, and/or birth certificate. She had none of these. She rang Robert from a pay phone and got his bank account details so they would bank the money into his account. She gave HR the BSB and account number, and they were satisfied.

Vick goes on the floor after the formalities and assists customers in selecting appropriate garment for their needs or occasion. She gets a lot of compliments from satisfied customers who advise they will come back, as the service has improved, and the advice was spot on.

She works till lunchtime and goes and gets a wrap for lunch and a Coke. After a half an hour, she goes back to work, and before she realizes it, the day has gone, and it is time to go home. She signs herself off in the computer and goes and waits at the entrance of the shopping centre, watching out for Robert.

After about fifteen minutes, Robert pulls up, and she gets into the car. She gives him a kiss, and Robert drives off onto the expressway and home.

Robert says, 'I just love the drop-offs and pickups.'

Vicki replies, 'Thanks for helping me out with the bank account.'

'That's no worry. I will be a rich man by the end of the month.'

'Yeah, on eighteen dollars an hour?'

'Are you working tomorrow?'

'No. They rostered enough people on for Saturday, and I don't get rostered until the new timetable. So, I have Saturday and Sunday off.'

'That's good because we can concentrate on the acquisition and see if we are going through with it. I brought the folders home Steve dropped off so you can have a look at them tomorrow, while I pop over to see my parents and tell them the good news that I am going to get married.'

'You can't tell your parents that. They will reject me, thinking I am going to marry you for your money.'

'What a girl will do to keep fifty bucks?'

'That reminds me, I have to give you back the change, I bought a wrap for lunch. I hope you don't mind, but I was hungry and only had half an hour for lunch.'

'Keep it just in case one day I don't turn up to pick you up. You can at least catch a bus home.'

'I will look through the documents while you see your parents on Saturday, and then we can talk after you come back in the afternoon.'

'I only plan on staying an hour or two.'

'What do you normally do when you see them?'

'Stay the whole day.'

'Then you will have to spend the whole day there. Otherwise, they will get suspicious and start asking questions.'

'No. I will spend half a day with them and make some excuse about why I have to leave.'

'Don't upset them. They haven't seen you for a few weeks, so be careful what you say to them. They deserve to spend some time with you.'

'If they ask, I just say I met a girl on a park bench and fell in love with her. No one will believe that.'

'I can see you are going to blow it.'

'What are we going to have for dinner?'

'Let's go home and I will make us something. We bought enough things when we went shopping last week. I should be able to put something together.'

They drive home and go up to their apartment and get out of their work clothes into something more relaxing. Vicki goes to the kitchen and starts making dinner, sausages, and salad.

Robert goes to the cupboard and takes out a Cabernet Sauvignon and uncorks it, and goes to the kitchen and gets two glasses out of the cupboard. He fills the glasses and hands one to Vicki. They touch glasses and say cheers, and each has a big drink.

Vicki says, 'It has been a long time since I have had wine. This tastes good.'

Robert replies, 'Yes, we need it after a full day's work.'

Robert empties his glass and refills his and then tops up Vicki's glass. She pulls it away and says, 'Not for me. I'm not used to alcohol. Unlike some of the bench dwellers, I couldn't afford plonk and therefore left it alone.'

Robert says, 'Don't worry. If you get drunk, I will put you to bed. I will even leave your clothes on, promise.'

Vicki replies, 'Thanks. What a gentleman.'

Vicki finishes cooking dinner and prepares the salad and puts everything on the kitchen table, and both sit down to eat. Robert fills his glass, and Vicki points to hers and he tops it up.

They have their dinner, and both wash up and sit on the lounge to finish the wine.

Vicki says, 'This is a nice red.'

Robert replies, 'I only drink it for medicinal reasons.'

'Yes, I am sure. What, to make you go numb?'

'To relax. Tomorrow we will go to the shopping centre and buy what we need for the week, and then I will go to see my parents while you have a quick look at the records Steve has given us. I will stay a couple of hours and then come back and take you to dinner.'

'No, it is too expensive, especially when you go to Demetrious.'

'How do you know which restaurant I go to?'

'I was hungry one evening and went there to see if I could get some leftovers from George and saw you there. He told me who you were, and that you had just signed up a new acquisition and was celebrating your success.'

'Isn't he going to get a surprise when we walk in?'

'No, we can't be seen together yet. What will people think of if they see us?'

'Vicki, you are not a murderer, and you are going to have to come to terms with the fact that some people know of your circumstances and, if they are your friends, will say nothing but wish you the best. If they ask me, I will say I forced you to come and live with me and kept you from escaping.'

'You would say that?'

'Do you think it will make any difference what I say?'

'No, I guess it wouldn't. But I would prefer to be employed for a while and stand on my own feet before people think I have caught onto you as a sugar daddy—me being so young and you, so much older.'

'They can think what they want, but they will see us anyhow, going shopping or going to work.'

'I never thought of that. Looks like I will have to go places with a paper bag over my head.'

'You are allowing this to become too complicated, and that is when people have to make excuses. I met you after you got a job and took you in as a renter. We share the expense of the apartment, and each lives their own lives. What could be simpler than that?'

'You're right, but roommates don't take each other to Demetrious for dinner. They go to McDonald's where they pay for their own meal.'

'All right, it will be McDonald's for a while, but I am not keeping you under a bushel for too long.'

'Let's see what comes out of the acquisition, and then I can become more confident of what people will think about me and the fact that you will be robbing the cradle.'

'Robbing the cradle? You're not a teenager, you know. I am having another glass. Do you want another glass of red?'

'Yes, thanks.'

They finish another bottle of red and then went off to bed, to a relaxing sleep.

The next morning, they get up and have breakfast and go off to the shopping centre and do their grocery shopping.

Vicki says, 'I will have to buy a dress or a pair of slacks to cover two more days of work. I only have three days of clothes, and I will have to work five days next week.'

Robert replies, 'Well, let's see what is available.'

Vicki walks into one clothing shop and immediately walks out.

Robert asks, 'Too cheap for you, are they?'

Vicki replies, 'Too dear for poor quality stuff.'

Vicki goes into another shop followed by Robert and spots a dress that looks good. She goes and tries it on in the fitting booth and comes out to let Robert see how it looks. He nods his acceptance, and she goes back into the booth and changes back into her street clothes. She comes out with the dress and then spots another one hanging on a different rack and then a third one. She hands the one she had just tried on to Robert and tries the other two on. After about ten minutes, she comes out with the two dresses and was just walking to the counter when she spotted a pair of slacks and a blouse. She hands the two dresses to Robert and goes into the booth to try on the slacks.

Robert is standing there with three dresses over his arm when the store manageress walks past him and says, 'Can I help you?'

Robert replies, 'Not really. I have to decide which one I will take.'

Manageress asks, 'They are for you, are they, sir?'

Robert says, 'I guess you can say that, since I will pay for them.'

Vicki comes out of the fitting booths and says, 'Don't worry about my partner. He just likes to stir people up. I bring him along as a coat hanger to hold the stuff I have tried on, and he has agreed to pay for them.'

Manageress says, 'Of course, madam, I thought he was buying something for you and wanted some advice. That's all.'

Manageress scans the five garments and says, 'That will be $660, sir. Will that be card or cash, sir?'

Robert replies, 'Have you any dishes you want washed so I can pay it off?'

Robert hands over his credit card, and the manageress folds the garments and places them in a carry bag and hands it to Robert and says, 'I hope you enjoy wearing them, sir,' and smiles and goes to the next customer.

Vicki and Robert go out of the shopping centre and head off to their apartment. They carry all their groceries and purchases up to their apartment and start putting things away. When they finish, Vicki takes one folder and puts it down on the kitchen table and says to Robert, 'Thanks for buying those things for me. Take it out of my wages that are being deposited into your bank account.'

Robert replies, 'No, that's your money. While I might gripe about spending the money, I am glad to make you happy and to see you come from where you were too now. It is an investment in my future wife, if you will have me?'

Vicki says, 'Robert, don't be silly. You know I really love you. It's just that I think you might be better off with someone else that doesn't come with the baggage I come with and someone that will do you justice rather than embarrass you. You deserve better.'

Robert gives Vicki a kiss and says, 'I agree. But I want you, and you are the only one I have loved. So, for good or bad or indifferent, we must make it work. I think God has a plan for you—I seem to be part of it. You must acknowledge it and see where it leads us.'

Vicki says, 'You better see your parents and allow me to get to work, as I cannot review the folders tomorrow.'

'Why not? You're off.'

'It is a day of rest, and, besides, I want to go to church on Sunday. I noticed there was one about five or six blocks from here. I will drop in and see what it is like.'

'I will come with you. It is about time I thanked the Lord for allowing me to find you.'

They kiss, and Robert gets his things and heads off to his parents, leaving Vicki to review the folders.

8

Robert pulls into his parents' driveway and gets out of his car. His father comes out of the house and greets him and tells him that his mother is not feeling well. Both go into the house, and Robert goes to the bedroom and sees his mother lying in bed.

Robert asks, 'What's the problem, Mum?'

Catherine replies, 'Just didn't feel well, and decided to rest. I'm all right. I will get up and have coffee with you.'

Catherine Somerset gets up and walks to the kitchen, followed by Robert and his father, Richard.

Catherine asks, 'What have you been up to since we last saw you?' Robert replies, 'I took over the Wilson's retirement village complex, and it took longer for me to bed it down than I thought.'

Catherine asks, 'Any problems with the acquisition?'

Robert replies, 'Yes, but I expected the problems. I had to dismiss the entire management structure, as they had a different business culture than we have. They only cared for the profits and not the quality of service they provided.'

Richard says, 'We learned years ago that will not work and it comes back to bite you.'

Robert says, 'That's why I had to get rid of them and put in our own management team in there to ensure they ran it our way. The feedback I get from the elderly there and their family is that it is definitely working, and both the staff and patients are happy about the changes we have made.'

Richard asks, 'What did you pay for it?'

Robert replies, 'Six million, which means we get a payback in eleven months.'

Catherine says, 'That's great, or you have overestimated the returns.'

Robert replies, 'Underestimated the returns, you mean. Currently, we have 100 percent occupancy and could place another one hundred beds if we had the room. We are going through an appraisal to see what it would cost to double our capacity to cater for demand.'

Richard says, 'That sounds like a great acquisition.'

Robert adds, 'So far, it shows that we have done our homework and, if anything, have underestimated the potential of our investment.' Richard says, 'Well done. What about your private life? Any changes? Have you found a girl to marry? We would like to see you settle down before we die, you know.'

Robert replies, 'Well, to be honest, I found a girl on a park bench and asked her to marry me, and she said yes.'

Richard says, 'Great. You should bring her home so we can get to know her, but leave the bench in the park.'

Richard adds, 'It is hard to find time to socialize when you are running a large organization like you have been, but you have to put aside some time for yourself and go to places where you get to mix with young people.'

Robert says, 'Not hard, but near impossible, as things always crop up. Like today, I will have to cut short my visit to get back and finish some work.'

Richard asks, 'You are not going back to the park bench, are you? If you are, I will come with you and meet your girlfriend.'

Robert replies, 'No, I am not going to the park.'

Richard says, 'What a pity.'

Robert stays with his parents for about three hours and then goes home. He tries to get his mother to see a doctor, but she refuses, saying it is something she ate that disagreed with her.

Robert leaves his parents and drives to his apartment, where Vicki has finished looking over the papers and has prepared a baked dinner for them. They sit down and have their meal and do the washing up and then sit at the kitchen table to discuss what Vicki had found.

Vicki says, 'It seems the business went broke because their designs were copied from other fashion houses who took legal action against them for breach of copyright. They lost their money because they had to pay all the profits back to the designers and couldn't afford to pay their everyday running cost. At the end, they had no new designs of their own but had contracted to provide designs for shows throughout the year. If you acquire the company, you will have to fulfill these commitments, but if you only buy the trading name and not the company, you will not have to honor these contracts.'

Robert asks, 'What is your estimate of the profit we would make if we completed the fashion shows?'

Vicki replies, 'When I did this before, we used to make a profit of $5 million to $10 million a show if all went well, but we don't have the team to design for a show. I have lost contact with my people after we went broke, and besides, they may not want to come and work for me again.'

'How much money would we have to have to carry us along until the first fashion show?'

'About $2 million with a staff of about ten to fifteen. But we haven't designed anything yet, and it will take about two months to get a team together. We won't have time.'

'Then we will have to buy the name only and not take on the contracts.'

'Or forget about it altogether.'

'Is that what you want?'

'I don't know. I used to enjoy designing things before we went broke, and I have a few designs in my head that I would like to try out, but things have progressed, and are they going to be good enough today?'

'We will offer him $1.5 million for the business name and building. If he accepts, we will try to establish a team around you. If he doesn't accept, then he will get nothing, as there are no other bidders.'

'There is nothing else left in the business, as they have sold all of their designs to the manufacturers instead of licensing them.'

'I will wait for him to call me on Monday rather than ringing him. That way, it won't seem that I am too eager to buy the business.'

Vicki and Robert decide to go for a walk around the block to get some fresh air. They walk a couple of blocks and bump into Allen, who was coming back from seeing one of his parishioners.

Allen says, 'Vicki, it's good to see you so well. The last time I went to check on you, they told me you had checked yourself out of hospital and they couldn't give me a contact number.'

Vicki replies, 'Allen, this is Robert, who has been looking after me and who came to my rescue when the hospital wanted to discharge me back into the park. He has allowed me to stay with him to recuperate.'

Allen says, 'Yes, I know Robert. I came to his office some months ago, and he was glad to get rid of me. No, I shouldn't say it like that.'

Robert replies, 'Yes, I remember you. You came to my office just to see if you could help to connect me with God.'

Allen says, 'I also went to see your parents. It is a shame they have turned from God, especially in their later years. If they die, they will not have eternal life. It is a pity they have hardened their hearts against God.'

Robert replies, 'Well, you keep at them, Allen, and tell me if I can help.'

Allen asks, 'Will I be seeing you in church tomorrow?'

Vicki says, 'We were thinking of going to the one over the next block.'

Allen replies, 'That's good. That is the one I run. I will see you tomorrow. No loitering outside, Robert.'

Robert, surprised, says, 'Yes, we will be there, or Vicki will.' Allen says, 'I will see both of you tomorrow.'

Allen walks down the street, and Vicki and Robert stroll back to their apartment and settle down to watch some television. They hear about the royal wedding in England and the interest it is gathering and after a while decide to go to bed.

9

On Sunday, Vicki and Robert have breakfast and get themselves ready for church. They walk the few blocks rather than having to take their car out. They arrive a little before ten and go into church and sit in a pew.

Several of his work friends and colleagues approach Robert and he shakes their hands and starts talking to them for a few minutes until the service begins. They all look at Vicki and smile at her. You could read their minds, and no doubt the question that will be asked of Robert is 'Who's that girl? We have never seen her before.'

The service begins, and everyone takes part in the singing, and then Allen moves into the pulpit.

Today, we will consider why has sin taken a hold on us and our society in such a dramatic way? A big and important question. Before we can answer this question, we must get an understanding of the two major players in the spiritual world, and why is there an emphasis on mankind instead of just an outright battle occurring in the spiritual world?

We have already covered the chief characteristics of God and have previously described him as *omniscient,* all knowing; *omnipresent,* present everywhere; and *omnipotent,* all powerful; and we know the Father always appeared in the world through the person of His Son Jesus Christ. While we cannot initially see the Father, we can see the Son, and the Father, through the Son, has rendered us holy. It is our sinfulness that keeps us from the Father, yet the work of the Son has reconciled us to the father through the cross. I am sure you have a good understanding of God, and therefore I we will not go over what we have dealt with previously.

So today we are going to concentrate on Lucifer, whom you also known as Satan or the Devil. We will use these names throughout this sermon.

The Bible tells us that the angelic rebellion led by Satan precedes the creation of man, which explains much about the Father's plan of working through the One who will ultimately replace Satan as ruler of this world—namely, His Son Jesus Christ. In recognition of His victory on the cross, the Father has appointed Him the Lord anointed to rule the world and not Satan, as some would lead us to believe.

It is important to understand what happened to Satan and why he rebelled against God. It also gives us an understanding of why God created Satan, why He allows him to sin against God to this day and why hasn't God brought Satin's existence to an abrupt end but allows him to linger on.

Lucifer was the highest-ranking angelic creature in heaven and had considerable influence and authority over other angels. None would have rebelled against the Lord on Lucifer's say so, but he envisaged that with proper planning and opportunity, he might persuade some of them to follow him. Satan's plan was not to overthrow God by force but to affect a takeover by way of authority. By winning over the allegiance of the angels, Satan thought to present God with a fait accompli, which He would be powerless to reverse. For if the angels were to choose Satan over God, then he felt God would not seek divine retribution against him and the fallen angels, but cave into their demands.

These same tactics are used on earth by Satin today. He makes sure that all on this earth bow before him and gives allegiance to him. The purpose again is that if all bowed before Lucifer, then this would protect him from divine retribution, as God the Creator would not destroy all His creations along with Satan. There would be nothing left of earth if that was to happen.

Lucifer was able to entice one-third of all the heavenly angels to join him. This is a staggering number of angels that he convinced. Before any would follow him, the fallen angels would have to be convinced of success because if they failed, there would be a swift retribution from the Lord Almighty. Yet he would have to convince them that there must be more than just a political change of leadership. Lucifer could not have persuaded fallen angels to join him by offering them existence in Paradise, as their existing place of abode would not have been terrible or slum like, to force a rebellion against God. There had to be something more that he offered, something that the angels did not have, something that would be worth risking God's retribution if they failed.

Many academics have considered this point and agree that the risk those angels took would have been very high and unlawful by God's decree. The elements do not affect angels, as we humans are, not plagued by disease or the ravages of time, not in any need whatsoever that might incite the lust for acquisition that so inflames mankind. Yet it is precisely the fact that liberates the angels from all the cares and concerns we humans feel so intensely that Satan found his chief selling point, the prime inducement to his fellow spirit- creatures to gamble their eternal futures and bind their fate to him forevermore—namely, their lack of a corporeal body.

While we humans possess both a spiritual and a physical body, angels are primarily spiritual creatures only. The absence of true corporeality (body) such as we humans possess is in many respects a blessing, for it spares the angels the pain, suffering, and tears, which are the common heritage of mankind since the fall. But this lack of corporeality seems to have left many of the angels wondering what might have been, as they observed the animal life of the original earth prior to its cataclysmic destruction following Satan's rebellion. It seems that God had showed his intention to create mankind with a body who would take control of the earth, and some angels, no doubt, considered they should have a physical body rather than God making a new creation and placing them in control of the earth in preference to the fallen angels.

From everything we know about the angels from scripture, it is contrary to the will and law of God for angels to possess bodies as humans do or enter such bodies. They wanted to experience what humans could experience, which was denied to them. They considered the only way to get what they wanted was to fall in behind a new leader and take what they had been denied in defiance of God. Satan found the angels curious about the experience of material existence, and he inflamed this curiosity into outright lust, and rebellion took shape so that they became obsessed with the possession of material bodies.

When the devil and his angels had confirmed their evil and rebellious intentions, God Almighty executed an awful judgement upon the prehistoric earth where they existed. In a terrifying judgement, all life on earth was annihilated, and the universe plunged into utter darkness, an event that must have been incredibly traumatic for all the angels, as they were creatures of light.

The ruination and destruction of the earth under Satan's prehistoric rule is aptly described by the phrase 'ruined and despoiled'. The state of the earth in Genesis 1:2, described as in 'darkness' is only understandable when a judgement of this sort is assumed to be the source and cause of the darkness. For God is a God of light and everything He creates is perfect, while darkness is synonymous with evil, like the fallen angels. God's retribution left the earth scorched and in ruin.

A re-creation of the earth was essential to make the universe habitable once more for creatures with physical bodies. The account of the seven days is a description of this renewal of the heavens and the earth, and everything God accomplishes within the period of re-creation is specifically designed to make life supportable for mankind.

The Bible tells us the creation of man was the culmination of God's work. The process begins with the divine conference of the Trinity announcing God's decision, 'Let Us make man in Our image.' Man is then created in the image of God, blessed and given rule over all other creatures on earth. He is provided with food, as are other creatures, along with an environment to support mankind. Only after the earth has been restored to viable conditions, man created upon it and placed in charge of it, does God conclude all He has made is *very good.*

Besides being a sign to the devil and his followers of their fate, the Lord's cataclysmic judgement upon the earth, also showed the faithfulness of the angels who had rejected Satan's appeal. These amounted to two-thirds of all the angels in heaven. They trusted instead in God that He would somehow not allow His universe to remain cloaked in darkness and devastation, and they were not disappointed. For truly, the Lord's solution was an eventuality that Satan and his followers did not expect in their wildest imaginings, the complete *re*-creation of the heavens and the earth in seven literal days, accompanied by the creation of something completely new—*man,* a creature who would be God's means of exposing all of Satan's slanderous lies, a creature who, while possessing obvious limitations, had what Satan and his demons coveted most, a physical body to house his spirit.

While there is indeed a conflict of the deadliest kind being played out between God on the one hand and Lucifer on the other, the latter nevertheless continues to abide by certain mandatory restrictions and commands on account of the awesome might and irresistible power of God. Satan is therefore 'free' to act on earth but only within very distinct parameters laid down by God and well-known to the devil and his angels.

These 'rules of engagement' allow the devil and his minions to tempt mankind in a variety of ways, but generally do not allow an overt attack upon human beings without specific consent from God.

Satan's reign over the earth was not taken from God or awarded to the devil by God but was rather relinquished by Adam, and by default, the devil has temporarily usurped the authority over planet earth. To put the matter in legal terms, Satan's rulership of the earth is based only on a *de facto* control—his reign has never been and will never be one of legitimate right to earth.

Over time, the devil has tried to frustrate God regarding His plan for the earth in manipulating or controlling mankind to ensure God's intentions regarding retribution towards Lucifer are either delayed or prevented.

Lucifer's first attack on mankind was against Eve when he persuaded her to reject the word of God and put herself above God by eating from the forbidden fruit. Lucifer contemplated God would destroy His creation, allowing him to take control of earth without opposition. Mankind was expelled from the Garden of Eden and lost its authority and control of the earth, giving de facto control to Lucifer.

The devil's second counterattack on the plan of God after Adam and Eve were banished from the Garden of Eden, had the potential of being just as effective as the outright elimination of humanity — namely, it was intended to pollute mankind to where he no longer would be truly human at all as God had created him.

Unable to prevent the inevitable replacement of himself and his followers that was taking place by human beings, the devil cunningly surmised that if he could introduce a measure of impurity into the human line, and once that impurity had affected the entire human race, there would be no more *true humanity*, no pool of legitimate replacements, and most importantly, no way of bringing his ultimate nemesis, the Seed of the woman, into the world—namely, Jesus Christ. The means whereby the devil sought to accomplish this was to promote the cohabitation of his fallen angels with human women.

The fallen angels took human wives for themselves in contravention of God's order, and consequently, the population growth increased rapidly. The female progenies were singled out, as they became the objects of the attentions of these 'Sons of God'. They were the main point of interest for the devil's minions because it is the female who carries the essential seed of our humanity.

Should Satan have succeeded, he would have prevented God from carrying out the judgement He had already proclaimed against Satan, because it would have made the birth of the Jesus Christ, the woman's *pure* human seed, an impossibility.

Rapid expansion of humans brought with it an increased carelessness about acknowledging, let alone following, God and His natural law. This increase in depravity of human behavior, seen here on earth for the first time, formed the basis for a divine displeasure, so extreme that the great flood became the only acceptable remedy.

These conditions provided Satan with his first major strategic opportunity since his success in corrupting Adam and Eve. Apparently prohibited from direct outright destruction of human beings and stymied in his abortive attempt to have human beings slaughter each other to the point of extinction (by God's prohibition of murder in the wake of Cain's killing of Abel), he now found himself confronted with the intriguing prospect of introducing a fatal disease, so to speak, amongst the growing ranks of the spiritually weak.

Offering the possibility of cohabitation with some of his followers would be an attractive proposition that would soon infect the entire population on earth. The insidious nature of the plan was that this seed, once planted, would quickly spread. Although the majority might refuse to take part in the first place, there would be some who would accept or even seek such alliances given the 'talented' offspring that would be produced. Once the angelic seed was introduced into the human gene pool, eventually, every human family would become infected and spread that infection (always by choice), until at last there would be no possibility of a pure line for the Messiah.

God decided as punishment for breaking his laws that all life on earth was to be exterminated except Noah and his family and brought on a flood over the entire surface of the earth, which lasted forty days and forty nights. Those that cohabitated with human beings were punished with the most severe penalty possible this side of consignment in the lake of fire. The penalty for 'not keeping to their own realm' was to be plunged into the lightless abyss, a terrifying prospect for these creatures of light, even in their fallen state. This awful prospect motivated the 'legion' of demons who had possessed the demoniac at Gadara to beg Christ frantically not to have them confined to that terrible place and instead to be allowed to enter the bodies of swine that were nearby.

Lucifer's third attempt was the construction of the tower at Babel. This massive and impressive construction project could not help but be the universal subject of conversation in the cultural, lingual world that existed. Like the ark, it was unique and completely unprecedented. Unlike the ark, however, which had been commissioned by God as a sign of impending judgement (as well as a vehicle of deliverance from that judgement), the tower of Babel was not only not *of* God but was instead decidedly *anti*-God.

The primary aim here was to build a tower to reach into the heavens, so contact could be made with the gods. The method of doing this was to unite all mankind in the construction of this structure, ensuring that the devil had control over all of mankind and their tower. Once the precedent had been set and enough time had passed in such a unified, all-out effort, the roots of a monolithic world would have been firmly set. It would then be possible to assume complete political control of mankind.

The worship of demons in place of the true God was undoubtedly a major hidden purpose in the tower's construction, for the symbolism of a tower reaching into the heavens was clearly an attempt to contact the gods and not God. After it had cemented political unification, the tower would be used for pagan religious activity. This pagan devil worship would (as in later times in Babylonia) be a mandatory part of life in the new society, and, as this would be the only society on earth, all true spirituality would forever be fatally compromised. God knew what Lucifer was up to and caused mankind to speak different languages, preventing communication and the completion of the project.

The fourth satanic strategy was to eradicate all Jews from planet earth. Before Christ, the Jewish people were a special target of the devil because the Messiah would come from Israel. If he could not eliminate, corrupt, or subject humans to his complete control, destroying the line of the Promised One would bring the plan of God to an abrupt end. Complete annihilation of the Jewish state and the Jewish people was the only sure way to accomplish this objective, and so it was that Satan devoted considerable resources to attacking Israel, both internally and externally. Internally, Israel became the target of every corrupting influence the devil could bring to bear. One needs only to read the prophets, especially Jeremiah, to get a sense of the idolatries into which she was led, while, externally, Satan worked tirelessly to array the nations of the world against her for the purpose of her destruction.

The Messiah was the object of Satan's destructive intentions throughout His earthly life. From Herod's attempt to destroy Him (death of the firstborn), to the devil's personal, intensive temptation of Christ in the desert and attempts to oppose Christ, to his active role in the betrayal of Christ (Judas), Satan spared no effort in undertaking to frustrate the Father's plan for Him.

Since the time of Christ, Israel has continued to be a prime focus for the devil's destructive attentions, though for a different reason. Although Satan failed to prevent the coming of the Messiah by extirpating the people from His heritage, he still has hopes of rendering His Second Coming pointless by eradicating the people to whom He is destined to return. For without Israel's continuation as a people, there would be no way of fulfilling the many specific promises made to them by God, the majority of which will only be brought to complete fulfillment under the millennial reign of Christ. Without an Israel for the prince of Israel to rule, the devil would effectively have frustrated God's plan and thereby prevent his own demise. Israel is today still under threat from militants in the region determined to destroy the Jewish state.

The fifth attempt by Lucifer was to attack the body of Christ— the persecution of the church. Since the resurrection, ascension, and session of Jesus Christ, the devil's primary focus has been Christ's body on earth, His church. Having been defeated in all four of the campaigns, the devil is faced now with the sure and certain prospect of being replaced along with his followers by the church as it continues to grow. Satan has therefore been reduced to fighting a futile rearguard action in the vain hope of somehow staving off the inevitable. Despite this, the devil is forcing upon true believers worldwide, an attack which is more furious than before, as he attempts to prevent the growth and completion of the church. This means opposing believers and attempting to prevent our spiritual growth, but it also means taking all measures to prevent unsaved humanity from coming to the light of Jesus Christ. The church in modern days faces problems associated with the move to not follow the true word of the Bible but rather a reconstruction of the Bible to make it suit the occasion. These days, the church is under attack from the State, who, most times, operate a policy in opposition to the church's doctrine. Politicians who proclaim themselves to be true Christians vote in opposition to the teachings of the Bible and criticize those who follow the teachings in accordance with God's word. The purpose of these challenges is to have the State control religion and, over a period, have the Bible changed to suit the trends of society.

The sixth attempt by Lucifer is to infiltrate the church and have some of God's ministers do despicable things to children and alike, causing mankind to revolt and reject religion and the church and lose faith in the establishment. Those with faith will find it impossible to fight against the onslaught, forcing the State to take control and dictate what the church can and cannot do. This is happening now, along with the churches in many countries being destroyed by opposing militant activists in the name of Allah and stirred up by Lucifer.

The primary target during this era, however, is true Christian orthodoxy. Wherever believers are seriously attempting to pursue a close and genuine relationship with their Lord, we can expect to find active opposition. There is a point of view that suggests that major persecutions of the church are largely a thing of the past, but such opinions are not informed by events of today taking place in countries such as China, India, the Philippines, Malaysia, Indonesia, Ethiopia, Sudan, Egypt, and Iran, where to be and to walk like a true Christian is still to take one's life in one's hands. Even in places where no such direct threat of persecution exists now (such as Australia, England, and the United States), more subtle forms of attack are being employed. One thing is certain, if the Church-Age continues, the devil will continue to make a priority of targeting Christians who are advancing spiritually to dissuade others from following suit. The sphere within which the devil now operates on earth is much larger than was the case in the Garden of Eden. Instead of a single tree to test the hearts of mankind, we now face an entire world filled with multifarious temptations. And instead of the limited lying influence of the devil, satanic lies and influences are everywhere in this world we inhabit, ranging from the patently obvious to the almost invisibly subtle. The limited avenue of opportunity in the Garden of Eden proved to be enough for Satan to instigate humanity's fall in Adam, and the world gives Lucifer a greater opportunity to secure his position.

The devil has an extraordinary advantage in his quest to lead humanity astray. The sin nature now lives in the flesh of all of Adam and Eve's descendants. Indeed, it is not too much to say that the devil has kept our sinful tendencies in mind in constructing his worldwide system of temptation, deception, and control. It should come as no surprise why the world is the terrible place that it is, given the evil resident in the heart of man and Satan's ability and opportunity to exploit that evil. Bearing this in mind, it may be of benefit to point out that when something goes wrong, it is God that gets the blame and not the devil, and it's God's creation, man, that blames God.

Satan's control over earth is restricted by the will of God, as the devil can only do what God allows him to do. Much as he clearly would have liked to, Satan was not permitted to lay a finger upon Job until God expressly gave His consent, and despite his unique sufferings, Job never was destroyed because God would not allow it. Satan's request to 'sift Peter like wheat' was denied in response to a prayer on his behalf by our Lord, and there are at least two New Testament cases of rebellious believers being 'handed over to Satan', plainly showing that the withdrawal of God's protection had to be sought by apostolic intercession before the devil could have free rein with them.

A primary purpose for mankind's creation was and continues to be God's replacement of unwilling fallen angels with willing, faithful human beings. Much to his surprise, Satan's successful seduction of our first parents did not head off this inevitable eventuality—it merely changed the circumstances and timing of the numbers required of willing worshipers from the ranks of human. It goes without saying that if humanity could be eliminated from the earth or be subjected to manipulation so severe that the exercise of a free will, choice for God would be impossible, God's plan would have been in jeopardy. Therefore, while God allows the devil to operate within a wide range of latitude in this world, which Satan claims as his own, his sphere of operations is not absolute and is unquestionably more restricted with those of us who have become followers of God than it is with those who have given allegiance to Lucifer.

God has incorporated into mankind's make-up certain safeguards to help him resist the influence of Lucifer. The first of these being a conscience. After eating of the tree of the knowledge of good and evil, Adam and Eve gained an internal, mental, and emotional sensitivity that could distinguish between right and wrong, between good and evil. God graciously constructed the necessary test of their obedience in such a way that disobedience would provide them with this essential internal compass, a mechanism without which moral navigation through a satanic world would be impossible, especially for persons in a sinful state. Once the protection of the perfect environment of Eden had been removed, an 'internal guidance system' became a necessary element for humanity. For while in the garden there was only one straightforward test about which the Lord God had given specific instruction, the devil's world would be full of many tests and temptations, ranging from the completely obvious to the quite subtle. Without some way of judging the rightness and wrongness of our actions, we humans would be completely at the devil's mercy, master of deception that he is. Eating of the tree of the knowledge of good and evil resulted in our first parents gaining just such an ability, the *conscience,* and they have since physically passed this capability down to all their offspring.

In addition to the internal check that conscience provides on the devil's manipulation of mankind, God also limits Satan's control of human affairs by *law,* by *nationalism,* and by *direct divine intervention.* Since God's destruction of the tower of Babel, law and nationalism have been and continue to be the two major visible barriers that keep Satan from complete world domination.

Law is an outgrowth of conscience, a society-wide codification of our collective impulses to protect what is right and restrain what is wrong, built on tradition, experience, and experimentation, but always for the general purpose of good. Imperfect human beings produce imperfect systems of governance, but the fact of orderly, generally good-oriented legal authority is from God.

Lucifer's attempt to rule the world can be seen in the world 'getting smaller' and communication and use of the internet becoming well entrenched throughout the world. What he had tried to do at Babel, Lucifer was trying to reproduce the concept of the 'tower' in the internet. He now has a worldwide structure without borders used by all of mankind that has a single language, allowing him to rule without obstruction worldwide rather than in each country. Globalization is giving Lucifer much of what he is seeking, and the internet is replicating the philosophy of Babel. Internet allows cybercrime, bullying, pornography without checks or control, gambling, and the passing of information without detection.

Nationalism acts as a serious check on the devil's earthly operations. A universal society with an identical culture and language is much easier for the devil to control and manipulate, as for a single biological entity. As soon as any virus invades it, the disease quickly spreads and infects the entire organism. A one-world state thus offers no more resistance to gross forms of evil, once initially penetrated. A multinational world, however, is more resistant to Satan's influences, precisely because of its diversity.

Communism or Nazism or sexual libertinism or what have you must be introduced and promoted in every country individually, giving time and space resistance to whatever new strain of evil the devil is currently promulgating. Satan is pushing for globalization to eliminate borders and obstructions, such as seen in Europe with the EU.

Christ's 'head-on' or mortal attack on Satan and his kingdom began at the cross and will be effectively completed at the second coming when the Son of God returns to regain complete, direct control of the earth for mankind on behalf of God as the God-Man. Even until that time, Christ is the authority over all the earth, even though Satan says otherwise.

God's plan for the defeat and replacement of the devil through Jesus Christ has been rolling on irrepressibly forward ever since Adam and Eve departed from the Garden of Eden. Since the Kingdom of God became imminent with the arrival of our Lord Jesus Christ in human form, the devil has stepped up his operation, and these will find their most intense expression during the Great Tribulation when he is finally excluded from the heavens once and for all.

The primary aim of the devil's system is to reverse the concentration on serving God and focus completely and firmly instead on this earthly life. For Lucifer, every human being who looks away from God and towards this world is a triumph; just as for God, every person who turns his gaze away from the devil's dark world unto Jesus Christ is a victory.

As he proved in his cunning seduction of so many of his fellow angels, Satan has a tremendous grasp of how best to prey upon his fellow creatures. He understands his subjects (angelic and human alike) and does not shrink from boldly exploiting all weaknesses. A common theme in his approach is his focus upon whatever one of his intended victims lacks; the angels lacked physical bodies, so he promised these to them. The fact that engineered, possessed bodies would never have amounted to the real thing doesn't concern the devil, only that the lie he is selling be believed. Adam and Eve lacked the knowledge of good and evil, so he tempted them to acquire it—no matter that it meant their ultimate physical death. Following the fall, human beings are in many respects, much easier targets for Satan.

The devil's main tactical aim is to increase his influence and control over humanity, and he mercilessly exploits any opportunity, any weakness to do so. The essence of his approach, the premier weapon aimed at the battleground of the human heart, is *the lie*. Satan is the deceiver of the entire world and the father of lies. These titles suggest his central tactical aim, to obscure *the truth* in any and every way. Satan's world system, however, is no mere disinformation campaign. The devil is out to win the 'hearts and minds' of all human beings. He is very aware that we can be influenced, pressured, and tempted physically and emotionally as well. Much of his system is directed towards the body with the purpose of affecting the heart thereby. The satanic world system is, for that reason, a network of interconnected lies, emotional appeals, and physical pressures, which, at their most effective, are difficult to disentangle and, in the minds of the weak, are plausible.

Satan's world system, the lie, extends like a spider's web into every corner of the globe, into every area of human activity, and thus making its way into every human heart, blocking, denying, opposing God's truth however, wherever, and whenever it can. It is important to note at the outset that the satanic world system encompasses not only behaviors that anyone and almost everyone would view as satanic, and areas that are acknowledged as sinful, but also very many areas that are normally deemed 'good'. In his choice of tactics, the devil has no scruples. He will encourage all behavior—what men may see as good or what they may see as bad— to block God's truth and thus increase his own influence in the world. Adam and Eve knew they needed God, recognized immediately their own inability to atone for what they had done, and accepted the promise of Him who would die in their place rather than attempting to solve the problem by their own actions.

Most of humanity has in fact lived their lives as if the *opposite* of each of the basic principles listed above were true. A large part of the reason for this is the system constructed by Satan to turn these essential truths of human existence on their head, and to replace them instead with a system of lies to blind mankind to the truth, a *world system* designed to capture and ensnare as much of humankind as possible. Satan's world is thus based on a complex system of propaganda, which he and his demons foster throughout the world, a clever and elaborate network of lies that at their root are simple refutations of the basic truths of which the following are the main ones:

1. **'You don't need God':** By all rights, the reality of death should bring every human being to the realization that without God, there is no hope. But in human history, the devil has been very effective at using the fear of death to enslave humanity. This is because in our post-Eden world, life is lived very close to the edge. Without work and effort by the sweat of our brow, there is no bread, and without bread, there is nothing to sustain life. Fear is therefore a major element in our collective psychology outside of the garden, because we are all aware that without material means, life will not, cannot, be sustained. Satan concentrates on intensifying this worry, hoping to turn people away from the issue of ultimate mortality towards the everyday problems of survival instead. It is a very common and a very human reaction to ignore the big problem, impending death with no solution and to focus instead on the immediate smaller ones on how to provide food and clothing today so I can survive. But as our Lord has told us, this is turning things inside out. We should first seek the kingdom, God's solution to death in eternal life through Jesus

Christ, and then everything else we need to survive in this short life will be added to it. But when the devil's teachings are accepted instead, unsaved humanity strives instead for material success, so that whether out of failure and panic, 'God isn't helping me; I need money, not God'; or out of success and self-confidence, 'I have helped myself; I have money; I don't need God', the true need for God to deliver us eternally is blindly overlooked or bypassed in the quest for temporary substitutes that can provide only temporal benefits. This first satanic lie always seeks to undermine the authority of God by undermining His truth. We know from His Word, we all know from the way He has constructed the universe and from the obvious inevitability of death that we need God more than anything else, but the devil tells us that there is no hope of eternal life and so no point in seeking God, so that we may take our eyes off the truth and focus them on life's material needs and accumulate as much of these as possible, and in time they displace God.

2. **'I am like God':** Once we reject the truth that our lives are completely and dependent upon God and that He is the only hope for eternal life, once we take matters into our own hands and worship the work of our own hands, our creation, once we come to believe that success in providing for ourselves in this material world can somehow compensate for our complete helplessness in the face of impending death, it is a small step to believing that the will we are exerting, is equal to God's will. For after we reject God's will to learn the lesson of this world's futility and of our hopelessness without Him in the face of our mortality, we become reliant on our own will in place of His. After God's authority was destroyed in Eve's eyes, the temptation to 'be like God' was great, and just as she ate of the forbidden fruit in anticipation of becoming divine but only became alienated from

Him who is divine, so also we, by substituting our will for God's will in this life come to think in our heart of hearts that we are the true 'masters of our fate' on an equal par with God. Just as the devil used fear instilling in us desperation about our material needs to cause us to focus upon this temporary world instead of the eternity, which should be our primary concern, so in this second lie, the devil appeals to our subjective pride. In ignoring our eternal needs, we ignore God. In this second lie, by taking unjustified pride in our own abilities, accomplishments, and will, we reduce God in our thinking to our own level. With the first lie, we think we have no need of God, who is greater than we are. With the second lie, we become so self-secure that we now see ourselves on an equal footing with God. Though we have been given free will by God to respond to Him in this life, we now use our will as if we were God, responding to the. devil's lie and our own pride instead.

Putting ourselves in the place of worship instead of God (for that is what arrogance and pride amount to) results in seeking our own glory instead of God's, glorying in our own accomplishments, instead of realizing that they have come from God, and attributing the gifts, abilities, and successes we have to ourselves instead of God. We, in fact, do not recognize God at all.

Satan's second lie in this progression encourages us to love self instead of God, and to do so requires not only that we ignore God as in lie one above but also, that we take this to the next step and belittle Him, for that is what comparing ourselves to Him amounts to. In responding to lie number one, we ignored our own mortality and our need for God's help to overcome it to think we had no need of God at all but material things instead, which take the place of God. In responding to lie number two, we ignore our own sinfulness and our need of God's help to overcome it and don't recognize our sins and end up craving praise on ourselves instead. A large part of this lie and indeed an essential component of it is Satan's preaching of relativism. For only by denying the absolute nature of good and evil could we ever deceive ourselves into thinking that we are good, and only by being good could we possibly be 'like God'. As the devil convinces us to worry about the material concerns of the day instead of the 'distant' day of death, we begin to believe that instead of being concerned for the eventual judgement upon our sins that we have true worth that ought to be praised. In falsely building up our righteousness in our own eyes, we dispute God's truth. By substituting our own flawed character as worthy of praise and in blinding ourselves to our inherent sinfulness, we dispute God's perfect character.

3. **'God needs me':** The third satanic lie seeks to blot out the issue of the incurably evil nature of the world and instead to suggest the possibility of establishing a new man-made Eden on earth .. . by *helping* God! By the time we have bought into this third lie, we have moved from worshiping things and worshiping self to worship what we esteem, what we do, what we make. We create an idol (a personal good or goal) and glory in its accomplishment. That good or goal is not God's good or goal, but we assume in doing so that our intentions trump God's desires. We assume God needs us to accomplish this good or goal, and that without us, it wouldn't be, couldn't be done. We assume we are helping God, but we are only helping the devil. But by the time we have bought into this third lie, we have jumped from confidence in self instead of God and esteem for self instead of God to looking to self for ultimate truth instead of to God.

In reality, of course, we end up relying on, esteeming, and looking to the devil in self, but that, of course, is the purpose of this integrated system of deception and fraud. As outrageous as it is to assume that we pitifully limited human beings could ever rise above the sin and evil that is in us and create our own personal paradise on earth (individual or collective), it is really a small step from assuming that we have no need of God and that we are in fact equal to Him to assuming that our view of the world and of our lives is 'better' than what He proclaims in His Word, to assuming that we are superior to God. For when we try to 'help Him' apart from His will, when we determine it is for us to decide what is good to do for the world and for ourselves, how are we not establishing ourselves and our standards as superior to Him? While this may seem not only an outrageous but also an unlikely mindset, it is in fact the principle upon which most of the world's population is currently operating. For whether in the social, political, or religious realms, most mankind is of the opinion that what they are doing is 'good', even though it is patently obvious to any Christian that most of what is happening in the world is far from good in the divine definition of that word. But most people and most groups are adept at justifying their actions—not because of divine standards of truth (for the truth of God reproves and corrects us and moves us back to the truth when we respond and repent) but because of their own self- constructed standards, standards that are flexible enough to bend to whatever they desire at any time, standards that are really diabolical at their base. But it is important to understand that it is what God says is good that is good and that, conversely, just because we may say something is good does not make it good.

This third satanic lie is based upon denying the truth that God's will is the issue, not our will; that God's righteousness is the perfect standard, nor our own pathetic self-righteousness. It is, of course, right and proper for every Christian to want to please His Lord—*but only according to His will*. When Paul went to Damascus with every intent to have the leaders of the Christian community there, arrested and brought back to

Jerusalem for trial and what amounted to judicial murder, on some level, at any rate, he felt he was 'doing good' and 'helping God' by working to eradicate this blasphemous sect. In reality, of course, he was persecuting Jesus Christ and His church, the cause to which he would later devote his life and for which he would ultimately lose it. Jesus Christ is the only *true good*—the center and focus of all God's solutions, the number-one thing that the devil would like to replace and substitute. 'Doing good' apart from Jesus—worse yet, 'doing good' while denying Jesus subverts the entire purpose of the plan of God for history and for the lives of every individual. Claiming to do good apart from God, to improve a world that God has long ago marked for complete destruction to burn the evil out of it entirely, is, to deny the need for a Savior, to deny the need for God's help, to proclaim arrogantly instead that we can somehow 'help God' by these paltry activities. As an example, the movement to help the planet, climate change, discrimination when it really prevents freedom of religion are some modern-day examples of this.

The lie is the basis for Satan's world system. He gained a following through on the lie that seduced many of his fellow angels. He regained control of the earth through the lie that corrupted Adam and Eve. He exercises control over his cosmos through the lie that seeks to ensnare all of mankind. Our common human responses to the devil's propaganda— namely, greed, pride, and self-righteousness— culminate in an integrated system of organized sin and evil that is better known as the chaos called 'human history'. Human history (as opposed to the plan of salvation, which God is carrying out in the course of history) is not progressive at all from the divine point of view but actually and inherently regressive. Without organization and help from the evil one, this would not have been the case. Given active divine restraint of gross evil (the flood being one prime example) and given the internal mechanism for evaluating right and wrong contracted at the fall from the tree of the knowledge of good and evil (i.e., the conscience), the sensible efforts of good and just men may well have moved humanity 'forward', or at least have retarded its decline. As it is, however, humankind and human civilization are accelerating on the downward spiral that has been our track since being expelled from the Garden of Eden. The widespread fallacious assumption that we are now somehow better off than mankind of ages past certainly does not proceed from a divine or even a humanistic, moral point of view.

Plunging headlong into the myth that scientific, technological, social, cultural human progress is the ultimate value is merely helping the devil to build the new tower of Babel. Faith in technology (instead of faith in God), hope in political solutions (instead of God's solutions), and love for human cultural accomplishments (instead of for God and the sacrifice of His Son) are common variations on the devil's theme of working to make heaven on earth. But cutting God out of the equation is not only impossible but also foolhardy. For only God can satisfy the genuine needs of humanity: forgiveness, spiritual peace, and eternal life. Satan's offer of a re-won paradise here on earth is insanely laughable for sinful, mortal creatures. Or it would be, if so, many had not bought into this myth. It is the height of absurdity to openly flaunt a disbelief in God while proclaiming unreserved faith in sinful mankind's 'progress'. The pseudo-trees of life offered by the devil merely hold out false hopes. In worshiping progress and the new innovations, we are merely establishing a new system of idolatry here on earth, behind which has a new god— namely, the devil—and our children are being taught to follow suit. Satan's integrated world system has inserted its tentacles into the entire amber human life. For our purposes, however, it will be helpful to concentrate on three well-recognized categories of human experience where the devil's influence bleeds through most clearly in the modern world.

Religion and the occult: This area is perhaps the most obvious of Satan's infiltrations of influence into the world of mankind, since it is in the field of religion and the occult, where the devil opposes the truth of God most directly.

The devil is anxious to find something for everyone, anything to intrigue the spiritual side of man, anything but the truth of Jesus Christ. All religious activities that do not put Christ in the undiluted centre of things put Satan there by default. For by helping to still the innate desire to seek their Creator, such activities merely perpetuate separation from Him.

Organization is one of the keys to satanic false religion. The devil knows well that people will do things in a group that they would never do on their own. Corollary to this and equally important is the principle that if enough people are doing something in a highly organized manner, then an air of legitimacy will be lent to the enterprise, a false patina of orthodoxy; in effect, that will help to blind initiates new and old to the fact that God and Christ may in reality be entirely absent and the organization subtly evil in every way. Once enough people become involved in such religious organizations, a momentum and critical mass is achieved that allows pseudo-groups to present to the world a false picture of spirituality (even though in truth, God is not in their midst at all). Many of today's churches fall into this category where it is considered lawful to ignore some of the Bible's teachings and to substitute or intentionally misinterpret other passages or sections to accommodate minority interest.

There are several common factors, present in varying combinations, that connect paganism, cults, the occult, and organized pseudo-religions. Foremost is the fact that by denying the power of the gospel of Jesus Christ, they are fellow participants with the devil in the process of 'blinding the minds' of potential believers, 'stealing the seed' of the gospel out of hearts that are seeking God before they can turn to God in Christ and thus be saved.

False teaching within the flock of true believers in Christ is a deceitful satanic attack that requires special individual treatment. As the body of Christ, the church universal (those who genuinely follow Jesus Christ) understandably comes under more severe pressure and more insidious attack than any other segment of humanity. Often unable to persecute and destroy the godly outright, Satan reverts to false teachers and false doctrines, hoping to turn believers in Christ from the true path.

For believers, economics and technology are, of all the areas of modern human activity, arguably the most difficult from which to maintain a healthy degree of separation. These all-pervasive forces are inseparably interwoven with the need for us to earn our daily bread from the sweat of our brow. And, in turn, these two powerful forces interweave with culture, politics, and society, thus making Satan's integrated system that is virtually impossible to stay completely clear of.

Modern rationalistic materialism has, in fact, reached such a pitch that any belief in the spiritual, non-material dimension is considered 'ignorant'. Mass communication, technological advance, and economic globalization are moving ever more rapidly towards the diabolic dream of one integrated world—a world where there are no firewalls to resist the implementation of the devil's will, a horrible prospect destined to come to full fruition in the Great Tribulation. Faith does not oppose development in these areas, but it is a fact that increased reliance upon *and faith in* techno-economic progress cannot help but undermine faith in God—it is impossible to serve two masters. Possibly the best example of this is the phenomenon of modern medicine. As believers, we understand that God's will is paramount and that His plan has taken all the various circumstances of our lives into account. It is all too easy for the public to see medicine as the new religion, hospitals as the new temples, and doctors as the new priests, even gods. For it is in the sphere of and the fear of death where our mortality is most acutely felt, and it is exactly this fear of death that is one of the devil's major weapons for the enslavement of humanity. Just as excessive worry about the economical means of life (food, clothing, shelter) is used by the devil to induce fear and turn us away from trusting in God, so also Satan makes use of excessive worry about threats to our health to persuade us to rely on medicine more than on God as the solution to our problems. But these two worries are similar and have similar consequences when allowed to triumph over faith. A further example is the move to voluntary euthanasia by some countries instead of relying on God.

God's plan of salvation in the promised person of Jesus Christ caught Satan completely by surprise. With the commencement of human history outside of Eden under the promise and potential of salvation, God's plan for the final disposition of Satan and his followers began its inescapable forward march. Left unopposed, it would only be a matter of time before fallen angels would respond to the gracious offer of a Savior and return to a merciful God. Faced with this inevitable progression, Satan's only possible alternative, his only recourse in the face of God's plan for redeeming willing humanity through the person and work of Jesus Christ, was to oppose the plan of salvation in every possible way and with every available means at his disposal. As redemption through Jesus Christ summarizes the plan of God for human history, so opposition to faith in Christ is not only at the heart of the devil's world system but also the guiding principle in his reactions to the grand movements of the plan of God as they become manifest.

After Eden, the devil, as we have seen, was left without a strategy. Being a mere creature and having no actual use for mankind, any strategic operations on his part are of necessity merely reactions to God's actions. The devil really has no grand plan of his own—except to try to stop God's plan. Having been thwarted in his attempt to halt the progress of the plan of God through his seduction of Adam and Eve (failing to anticipate God's promise of redemption through the woman's Seed), the devil has now been left with little choice but to oppose the ultimately unopposable plan of God for human history.

Despite the essential futility of their actions, the devil and his forces are and always have been extremely active in their attempts to turn mankind away from God. Every human being—and believing human beings in particular—has always been an important 'target of opportunity'. But besides this general policy of using all means to deceive and to destroy humanity at large, Satan has also concentrated significant resources throughout human history on more specific 'prime targets' to prevent God's plan from coming to fruition and delay inevitably the retribution God plans for Satan and his fallen angels.

In the course of daily activity, most people don't consider God and go about their business relying on their own judgement and not on God. They are, in fact, doing what Satan requires of them and has them set their minds on material things, occupational matters, or pleasures to ensure their thoughts are not reverted to God. They act in their best interest for self and not for the Creator. While the majority think and act this way, the minority cast their thoughts to God in varying degree and form the bulk of the pool of faithful worshipers. However, a good portion of these lack faith in Jesus but still consider themselves as Christians. Satan ensures this group is continually confronted with trials who never seem to get out of the pits of misery. The only way to overcome these attacks is to pray to God and seek His strength and assistance, and He will lead you away from Satan's influence. The persecution of Christians will continue until they unite and gain a voice to combat the lies and injustices that continually confront them and challenge the State on social issues while preventing the State from encroaching into biblical doctrine as has been the case in same-sex marriage legislation and other such issues. What we have covered is only the tip of the iceberg of Satan and what he has been doing and is doing on this earth and with our faith, but it gives you at least some idea of what you have to look out for so you don't make the same mistake made by Adam and Eve.

Let us pray………..

1 0

Vicki and Robert get up early and have their showers and dress for the day. They have a quick light breakfast and are soon on their way to their respective places of work.

They dropped Vick off at the shopping centre, and Robert goes to his office. He goes and gets a coffee and walks past where Vicki used to sit. He goes back to work and at about ten receives a telephone call from Steve.

Steve asks, 'How did you go in looking through the folders?'

Robert replies, 'We covered everything we wanted to look at and have concluded you don't have much to sell. First, we cannot consider taking over the holding company, as it has contracts we could not fulfill and the penalties on default will bankrupt us. Second, it would take time and a lot of capital for us to build up a team to handle the fashion shows.'

'Make us an offer, and we will consider it.'

'One million dollars, and that really is the best I can do.'

'You have to be kidding me. The building alone is worth more than that.'

'No, not if Town Hall is going to reclaim it for a library.'

'That's only hearsay with no truth in the rumor.'

'Come on, Steve, you know it and so do I that it is on the cards, and most probably you have got enough swing with Town Hall to make sure they kept it under wraps until your sale goes through, and then surprise.

No thanks. My offer is $1 million, take it or leave it. The offer stays for forty-eight hours. After that, I withdraw my offer.'

'I will pass it on to my boss for consideration. I don't think he is going to be happy about the offer.'

'Give me a ring when you decide. Thanks.' Robert hangs up and goes about his tasks that he has set for the day.

Vicki is busy helping women make their selections and is overwhelmed by the number of women that came in on Saturday and Sunday that came back on their flex day to get her advice. The word has gotten around that the department store has a person on staff that knows their garments and who helps select the right garment for your shape and size. Sales are brisk while Vicki is working, and everyone can see the difference.

In the afternoon, Vicki is called into Mrs. Jones's office and is complimented on her approach to providing a service to the customers. They also asked her to cast her eye on the new designs and asked to comment on which one she believes would be winners next season. Vicki notes that the designs she is reviewing were from the Henry Fashion House and still remembers the scumbag Charles Henry, who would kick her change box down the steps of the Town Hall.

Vicki gives her opinion but makes it clear she is not keen on any of the designs, as they seem to be the same other designers have put forward with minor changes. She points out that the store could be in trouble if they showed they stole the designs from other designers, a point that management was concerned with. She leaves the meeting and goes back to work. Before too long, the day has ended and Vicki was out at the front of the centre waiting for Robert.

Robert pulls up, and Vicki gets into his car and they drive off home.

Vicki asks, 'Did Steve ring?'

Robert replies, 'Yes. After discussing what he did not have to sell, I offered him $1 million for the lot. He was not too happy, as he thought he would get a minimum of $3 million, as he still believes the building was worth at least that. I told him I believe he has made a deal with Town Hall regarding announcing the compulsory acquisition until he finds a buyer and gets them to sign a contract.'

Vicki says, ' I am happy you didn't offer any more. Even $1 million would be too much for the business.'

They drive into their apartment complex and park their car and go up to their apartment. They get changed, and Vicki prepares a meal for them comprising chicken and rice.

Robert says, 'You know you are spoiling me with your great cooking. Before you came here, I was lucky to get takeaways.'

Vicki replies, 'When I was in the park, a dinner was what someone threw out in the garbage tin, and I had found by scrounging around. I do not want to go back there, not while I am working. I enjoy cooking a quick meal for us. It's how I relax.'

Robert says, 'You're a champ, do you know that?' Vicki smiles, and they get on with eating their meal.

They watch a bit of television and then go to their rooms and to bed.

The next morning, the same grind, and Robert is at work casting his eyes over some figures when Steve rings.

Steve says, 'Good morning, Robert. We have considered what you have said and the reason for such a low figure. We understand your reservation in taking over the company with the tight contract dates and the penalties if you default. We have been in contact with the fashion organizers, who advise that they will not hold a fashion expo this year owing to the likelihood of a terrorist attack, which they knew was being planned when the fashion expo was first announced to the world. They are prepared to renegotiate all contracts, so they hold the fashion expo eighteen months from now and not this year. This will guarantee an entry into the fashion expo and allow you to exhibit your designs to the world. Both fashion parades that MI have will be extended, which means whoever buys the business will exhibit their designs in two major fashion shows, getting maximum exposure. It also means that we cannot sell the name and building separately, as the IFS will hold us to the contracts entered.'

Robert replies, 'That changes things to some extent, but you have to understand, Steve, I don't have a design team behind me and therefore will need to hire the personnel to fulfill the contracts. This would be a proposition for someone already in the business, but, of course, none of them want to buy the business, as they would prefer it went broke and out of existence. It would mean one less competitor. Let me think about it and I will call you tomorrow with my answer.'

'Can you ring me today?'

'Sorry, too many meetings and commitments today. It will have to be tomorrow first thing.'

'All right, tomorrow. We must tell the International Fashion Show, the IFS, what is happening with the contracts MI has made with them.'

Robert goes about his business, but still thinking about the potential to make good money if the deal goes through.

Vicki is at work and approaches a lady with her back to her, looking at some dresses on a rack. 'Can I help you, madam?' The woman swings around and stares at Vicki. Vicki stares at the woman, and both hug each other.

Vicki says, 'Alex! What are you doing here? No, I don't mean that. How are you?'

Alex replies, 'Vicki, it has been a few years. I heard they took everything away from you and you ended up on a park bench?'

'Alex, it is true, and I nearly ended my life, but the Good Lord had something planned for me, and here I am. What are you doing these days?'

'Doing casual work wherever I can. After the business went bust, my husband met another woman and left me. We divorced, and I am on my own with two kids, no money, and trying to keep myself from sinking.'

'But you were the best in the business. I would have thought that the other fashion houses would snap you up.'

'You would think so, but no one wanted any of us. I try to keep in touch with the old team, and none of them are doing well or what they used to do before. All found it difficult to find work, and some have given up trying.'

'I am sorry for causing you and the team all this hardship.' Vicki cries.

'Stop it. It was that bum of a husband of yours that did it, not you. The price you paid was higher than ours. Here is my mobile. Ring me when you get a free moment, and we will chat. I have to get back to work.'

'What about the dresses you were looking at?'

'You're joking, aren't you? They are poorly designed and made. No thanks. I can sew up something for myself far better than this trash. Who designed this stuff?'

'Charles Henry.'

'He must make a packet of this garbage. Sorry, love, I must run. Please ring me.'

Vicki fixes herself up and works through the day and again is whisked away home by Robert that evening.

Robert says, 'Steve rang, and the fashion organizers will cancel the fashion expo scheduled for this year and put it on in eighteen months' time. They want to know whether we are interested. I told him it would make little difference to us, as we do not have a team ready to go into action and prepare for the expo. I said I will give him a ring first thing tomorrow.'

Vicki replies, 'I came across my former seamstress, who tells me that after I went broke, all the staff had found it hard to get a job with other fashion houses. They do not want people that competed with them. If we go ahead, I bet I could get my old team back and we could be in production within weeks.'

'What should we agree to pay him?'

'If we do the two fashion expos, we could make anything from $5 million to $10 million if we win. If we get other orders in the meantime, we will make more profit and be able to cover our overheads. We would have to get to a stage where we can support ourselves quickly. I would stick to what you said before. Go to $2 million and no more. Tell Steve it is an enormous risk from your point of view and you don't know if you could pull a team together quickly.'

'Yes, I am comfortable with that.'

They arrive at their apartment and go in.

The next day, the routine repeats itself, and both Robert and Vicki are both at their respective workplaces.

At nine o'clock, Robert takes a telephone call from Steve.

Steve says, 'Robert, have you reconsidered what we spoke about yesterday?'

Robert replies, 'Yes, I have, Steve, and we have been able to get our bid up to $2 million.'

'Two million? I would have thought the potential would have allowed you to go to at least $3 million.'

'We considered it, Steve, but we are starting off from scratch and have to create a team that could attend to all the design and production work. That will not be easy and will require us to invest at least $1 million in costs for the first year with no income. I am not made of money, you know, and it would be stupid of me to think I could employ designers without paying them regularly. That's why we are $1 million short of your figure.'

'I will have to discuss your offer with my manager and see what he has to say.'

'That's all right. Come back to me when you have decided.'

Robert hangs up the phone and works through to one o'clock and is just in the process of walking out of his office to get a sandwich when Steve rings again.

Robert asks, 'Steve, what's the news?'

Steve replies, 'I have spoken with Mike, and we both agree your offer is too low for us to consider.'

'Well, I am sorry to hear that, Steve. It is a pity we have put in all that hard work, and it has come to nothing. Well, give me a ring if you change your mind.'

'Yeah will do. Bye'

Robert did not believe Steve and did nothing about the offer and went about his business. He told his secretary that if Steve rings, say he is tied up with clients and cannot be interrupted. Sure enough, at about four o'clock, Steve rings again, and Robert's secretary advised him that Robert was tied up with clients and he most probably will not be able to get back to him until late tomorrow.

Steve says, 'It is urgent that I speak to him now. Can you please get him to come out of his meeting and take my telephone call? I will be brief.'

Secretary replies, 'I am sorry. He left instructions not to disturb him, so I can't interrupt.'

'This is an urgent matter, and I insist you interrupt his meeting. I will take the blame for it.'

'One moment. I will see what I can do.'

Robert's secretary goes into his office and advises him that Steve is on the phone and insists on interrupting his meeting, as he has an urgent matter to discuss with him.

Robert picks up the phone. 'Steve, what is the problem?'

Steve says, 'Robert, are you able to go to $2.5 million? If you can, we can call a creditors' meeting and ensure the deal is done.'

Robert replies, 'Steve, you can do it at $2 million. All you are doing is putting the best deal before the creditors. They must decide whether they want to accept some money being returned to them or not.'

'We have already put two million to them when we were in discussions with Charles Henry from a competing fashion house. He also refused to go any higher, and the creditors refused his offer because they hated his guts and were not prepared to sell the company to him. Believe it or not, they preferred to get nothing than to see him own this business.'

'Steve, you know that under those circumstances, you can go to the court and they would overrule the creditors' decision and order you to accept the $2 million offer.'

'I know, but it would be a lot of messing around just for $500,000.'

'Steve, I will have to call you back in the morning. My money tree died a year ago, so I cannot just pluck the money from it. I will have to see if I can borrow the extra $500,000 or walk away from the deal. I will call you tomorrow. Bye.'

Robert looks at his watch and realizes he has taken longer than he intended to, as he has to pick up Vicki from the shopping centre.

He drives into the front of the shopping centre and notices Vicki is there looking out for him. She comes to the car and gets in and gives Robert a kiss.

Robert says, 'Can you go out and come in again?'

Vicki smiles and shakes her head.

Vicki asks, 'Any problems that you were so late?'

Robert replies, 'Yes. Steve. I told him I was not willing to go over $2 million, and he rejected the offer.'

Robert drives onto the freeway and home.

Vicki says, 'Well, that might be the best thing. It is a lot of money, and I would hate for you to lose it.'

Robert replies, 'But, wait, I haven't finished telling you the full story. He rang back at four o'clock and basically said we can have the lot at $2.5 million. He said he cannot accept a $2 million offer, as Charles Henry already made this and the creditors rejected him and his offer. They would prefer to get nothing than to sell to him.' 'I don't blame them. That creep, you had to stop him from kicking my money down the Town Hall steps. The same creep that tried to rape me and then came back and tried to kill me because I stabbed him.'

'You never told me about that.'

'No, because I reckon you would start a fight with the creep. I have left it to God to handle and have put it behind me. He will handle the retribution.'

'The best way of fixing that bastard is to take the business away from him and let him go broke. That's the way you can get at him.'

'No, Robert, he is too rich and powerful for us to take on. Besides, as I have said, I am leaving up to God to handle. He has brought down a lot of highflyers and kings over the years that think they are invincible or gods.'

'Yes, I guess you're right. Putting my fist into his face won't achieve anything other than give me the satisfaction of knowing that creep has got some of the pain he inflicted on you.'

'He got just that, that night. I stabbed him on the right side, and he left bleeding and holding his side. I bet he didn't report it to the police.'

Robert drives into the car park of his apartment block, and both get out of the car and go up to their apartment.

Vicki prepares the dinner, and both eat in silence thinking about the deal. They finish their meal and wash up and sit in the lounge room and discuss the offer.

Vicki asks, 'You agree we should let it go, don't you, Robert?'

Robert replies, 'Not really, considering I was willing at one state to pay $3 million for the business. The eighteen months' period changes the dynamics and gives us breathing space to get on with pulling a team together and put on a fashion parade. Are you sure you're not scared of failure rather than lacking in confidence, design wise?'

'I am scared what others will think of me resurrected and taking on an iconic name like MI. The only thing that is positive about the deal is that there are two guaranteed fashion shows in eighteen months' time on a world stage, which does not present itself often. If we were starting off fresh, we wouldn't get a consideration. It is only that they invite the best and there was no out clause in the contract ending it, should the business go broke.'

'Vicki, have you ever ridden a horse?'

'No, I haven't. I went to a farm once, and the farmer's son got on a horse but was bucked off. I decided there are easier ways of getting transported around than to get on one of them. Why do you ask?'

'I just wonder what you would do if you got bucked off a horse. Would you get back on it or walk away?'

'If I was a country girl, I most probably say, "Bugger you, horse, you will not get away with this," belt him, and get back on the horse and ride him to prove it and not feed him for two weeks.'

'That's my point.'

'What is your point? I don't get it.'

'You think about it? I am going to bed.'

Robert leaves Vick in the lounge room thinking about what he had said. Vick decides she is not good at riddles and therefore could not be bothered working it out. She gets up, switches the lights off and goes to bed.

At about one in the morning, Vicki wakes up and realizes the answer to Robert's riddle. She gets up out of bed in her shortie pajamas and switches her light on and storms into Robert's bedroom, waking him up.

Vicki says, 'You expect me to get back to where I left off in the fashion industry, don't you? This acquisition is your horse, isn't it? You expect me to get back in the industry and make a name for myself, don't you?'

Robert, half asleep, replies, 'Why don't you get into bed with me, and we can discuss it?'

Vicki makes a move to do just what Robert said and then realizes he was trying her on.

Vicki asks, 'Get into bed with you?'

Robert replies, 'Who else? Just me and my teddy bear are here.' 'You promise no sex?'

'It never crossed my mind. Never.'

'I bet it didn't. No, I will go to my bed and talk to you in the morning. Not that I am going to get much sleep thinking about this for the rest of the night.'

'Just get into bed with me?'

'Men—they can only think about one thing.'

Vicki storms off into her own room and closes the door, leaving Robert to himself and his teddy bear.

The next morning, Robert gets up, showers, and gets dressed for the day ahead. He puts the coffee on and makes toast. Vicki comes out of her room with her eyes just about falling out of her head.

Robert says, 'You had a rough night. I see you have been riding horses all night.'

Vicki replies, 'You and your bloody horses. I couldn't sleep because of your riddle, and then instead of discussing things with me, you want to have sex?'

'What do you think a hot-blooded male would think of if a girl in shortie PJs comes storming into his bedroom at one in the morning? He would ask, "Have you fallen off a horse?" Would he?'

Vicki takes a cup of coffee from Robert and a plate containing two slices of toasted bread. She puts it on the kitchen table and goes to the fridge and gets some butter and jam and opens both up and spreads it on her toast. Robert does the same.

Robert asks, 'Well, are you going to get back on the horse or not?'

Vicki replies, 'I don't know. I am terrified I will lose your money and have a repeat performance of my past.'

'If it was your money, would you risk it considering what we know about the proposition and the company and why it went broke?'

'No, if that is all I had.'

'If you had enough to carry you over a downturn, would you take up the offer?'

'Not without you. You're the only one I trust.'

'How about you get back into those shortie pajamas of yours and we take the day off?'

'You know we are going to have to get married soon or live apart.'

'I agree, my poor teddy bear can't take much more of it.'

Both burst into laughter and clean up and head off to work.

Robert, while driving in the car on the way to work, asks, 'What am I going to say to Steve this morning?'

Vicki replies, 'I can't think clearly with all that sex you were having last night. What do you think?'

Robert says, 'I think this is the best deal we are going to get out of Steve and therefore we should go for it. I think you know fashion, and this is God's way of giving you an opportunity to get back the ground that has been lost over the past few years. If I am right, we will get our investment back in two years, plus a handsome profit, and will re-establish you as an iconic designer. If I am wrong, I at least will have a very expense pair of shortie PJs and something better than a teddy bear to cuddle.'

Vicki bursts into tears as they drive into the shopping centre car park. She takes out a tissue and blows her nose and dabs her eyes and gives Robert a big kiss, and leaves.

Robert drives to work and thinks about what he is going to do. At nine o'clock, Steve phones.

Steve asks, 'Robert, we have a creditors' meeting scheduled for today at ten. What's your decision?'

Robert replies, 'Steve, the amount of turns you have taken in the negotiations doesn't leave me with much confidence in you and your proposal. Two and a half million is a lot of money, especially when you do not have it and need to borrow it. I would like to attend the creditors' meeting and present an offer to them, and if we get the majority vote, we will take up the offer. If not, we will let it slide.'

'We will agree to that. I will email you the address and alert security that you are coming to the meeting.'

'I will be there.'

11

Robert arrives at the address Steve emailed him and goes up to the twenty-third floor, where there are about eight to ten men standing around. They all look at Robert, who is looking for Steve.

Steve comes from the front of the room and shakes hands with Robert. Robert takes a seat at the front, and Steve calls the meeting to order.

Steve says, 'We have called a meeting of creditors to discuss an acquisition proposal put forward by Mr. Robert Somerset and to vote on the proposal after answering questions that you may have. I may mention that we as liquidators have been active in trying to find a buyer for the company and to date have had no success. We have tried to market the company on the world stage, but most of the fashion houses refuse to take it over as each believes they have a different culture and do not see any benefit in trying to incorporate the two together. Also, I must again point out that the creditors' meeting agreed that we could sell the designs of the company rather than license them, and therefore the company has no credible designs to sell in an acquisition. I will now pass you over to Mr. Somerset to outline his proposal. Robert, it is all yours.'

Robert says, 'Good morning, ladies and gentlemen. I have looked at the company's books, and it has only one asset—namely, the building that it is in and that I am told is going to be compulsorily acquired by Town Hall, possibly at the next month's meeting.

'I have been told that it also has two contracts that allow the buyer to present their designs on the world stage in eighteen months' time. None of the major fashion houses consider this to be an asset, as they are already invited, and the minor fashion houses would not accept the invitation, as the demand would be too great on them and they wouldn't have the resources to fund a fashion parade on that scale.

'The IFS have already clarified that they will begin legal proceedings against the company for breach of contract if the company does not fulfill its obligation under the contract. It is therefore a liability to any purchaser rather than an asset, and I have treated it as such in my appraisal.

'My understanding is that they sold the designs, and the proceeds were used to pay the liquidator's fees and half of what the creditors were owed, leaving a debt of $2 million still owing.'

'My proposition is that I acquire the company for $1 million, which will mean that the creditors receive 85 percent of what is owed to them.'

Steve replies, 'The liquidator supports the proposal, but it will mean that after we deduct costs, the distribution to the creditors will cause each creditor writing off 20 percent of the debt owed to them. Has anyone a question or an opinion that they wish to raise?'

Steve says, 'Yes, sir.'

Creditor asks, 'Why would you buy the company with the risk of being sued for non-performance of the contract? It doesn't make sense.'

Robert replies, 'Because the liquidator refuses to sell the trading name without selling the company. I was only interested in the trading name, not its building and the problem of Town Hall's compulsory acquisition of the building. There are no designs we can acquire, as you had agreed to sell these outright, leaving very little left.'

'You're no fool. You have interests in several areas. So it doesn't make sense for you to buy this company, knowing you have to put a fashion parade together and stage it in eighteen months' time. Otherwise, you will be sued.'

'I am gambling on being able to bring together a team quickly and meet the timetable. If I do, I can make some money out of the venture. If I cannot, I will go down making an enormous loss.'

'Do you have a designer lined up?'

'I have found a designer who, over the last few years, has had a very rough go of it, and she will come and work for me to get these two fashion parades on the world stage.'

'Who on earth could that be? Most of the fashion houses keep their designers under contract, and therefore most would not allow them to go over to you. Who is the person you think can do this miracle for you? We want you to be honest with us, as most of us would prefer to sell the building and take a loss and move on without worrying about reputations or otherwise. However, if you are conning us, then I do not believe we would agree with your offer. We will sell the building to Town Hall and distribute the proceeds, which should give us the million you are offering.'

'That is assuming Town Hall will pay you $1 million. I am guaranteeing $1 million, which makes it a certainty and not just a possibility.'

'Yes, but you still haven't answered the question who is going to do the design work for you. We don't want you to go broke.'

'I appreciate your concern, but the person has not agreed to come on board until I acquire the company. I am prepared to divulge her name on the understanding that there is no mention of her until I have time to complete the acquisition and her employment.'

'You can trust us not to say a word.'

'Then can I say we have a deal or don't we have a deal?'

'No, we do not have a deal until we know who the designer is.'

'Her name is Vicki Santana. She has been out of the industry for the last few years, and I believe I can get her back to the work she loved doing, before the tragedy of her previous marriage.'

'I remember her. She was a talented designer but had a husband dealing in drugs and gambling and was taken out by the Mob who put a bullet in him. She lost everything because of him. She, I understand, had a breakdown and went off somewhere. No one has heard of her in years.'

'I really don't know the full story, but will try to get her on board and back to her trade.'

'You are undertaking an enormous risk. If she has lost her touch, you will go broke.'

'Well, do we have an agreement or not?'

Steve asks, 'Shall we put it to the vote?'

Creditor says, 'Don't rush it. I won't to know more about your plan before I vote on it.'

Robert replies, 'My plan is my business and not for general publication. Your concern is whether you are prepared to take the offer as full satisfaction of the money owed to you, not what I intend to do.'

'Well, I won't vote for it.'

'Good, then lose the money owed to you. If you want to be a fool, you can, but the liquidator has to present the proposition to the court, and it is up to the court to decide if you are unwilling.'

'We will tell the court that we will get the same deal if we reject your deal, as Town Hall will buy the building and pay $1 million, the same as you will pay.'

'The difference is my amount is guaranteed, whereas with Town Hall, you may only get half a million. The amount is uncertain.'

'Yes, but I still feel we should reject the offer.'

'What do the other creditors say? Will you accept the offer or not?'

The creditors talk it over amongst themselves, and 50 percent are for the deal with an equivalent number against it, leaving Robert 25 percent short of the numbers he requires.

Robert says, 'I sense that there is an indecision amongst you, so why don't I try to sweeten the deal for you? Not only will I agree to pay $1 million now, but should we present a fashion parade in eighteen months' time, I will then pay you a further $1 million, which will mean you recover all the money owed to each of you.'

Creditor replies, 'Yes, that is paid only if you can present a fashion parade. If you do not, we don't get any more money?'

Robert says, 'You can take some of the risk or take all the risk by rejecting my offer.'

Creditor replies, 'No, I will reject it.'

Steve says, 'We have an offer put to the meeting by Mr. Robert Somerset to acquire the company outright on the basis that he pays $1 million now for the acquisition and $1 million in eighteen months' time, when he attends the IFS. If, however, he does not attend these two contractual parades, he will not be obliged to pay the second $1 million as proposed.

'For this proposal to succeed, there must be 75 percent of creditors in number attending this meeting to voting for the proposal and 75 percent in value voting for the proposal. Otherwise, the proposal fails.'

'All those in favor of the proposal, please raise your hands. I see nine hands. All those against the proposal. I see one hand. The proposal is carried and will be presented to the court for ratification next week. Thank you, gentlemen. I now close the meeting.'

Steve goes to Robert and says, 'Congratulations, you got the company at a very good price.'

Robert replies, 'I hope so. I have a lot of hurdles to jump over. I hope I don't go broke in the process.'

Both men shake hands and move towards the lift. Two men who ask to see him interrupt Robert. He sits down with the men.

Robert asks, 'What can I do for you?'

Creditor replies, 'We were interested in what you said about Vicki and would like to help her achieve her goal.'

'Well, if I am not mistaken, no one was willing to help her before, and that's why she had no alternative but to do the best she could.'

'We supported her and helped her when she was getting a reputation in design. We tried to help her, but that bum of a husband always prevented us. Could you give her our cards and ask her to call us so we can see her and assist her where possible?'

'I will pass the cards on to her, but it will be up to her to contact you. Agreed?'

They shake hands, and all go their way.

Robert gets in his car and notices it was one o'clock and went to the shopping centre and give Vicki the news. He drives to the shopping centre and walks to the department store. Vicki was sitting outside having a sandwich. He walks up to her and gives her a kiss.

Vicki says, 'Oh my god, that means you bought it, doesn't it? How much?'

Robert replies, 'One million now and one million if we win the fashion parades.'

Vicki asks, 'How did you pull that off? You were going to pay $3 million for it?'

Robert replies, 'Well, I tried to get away with paying $1 million, but there was a creditor that refused to accept just $1 million. In fact, he still rejected the $2 million offer. However, the vote was carried by a majority, so it now goes to the court in a week's time to be ratified.

'I met several people that were interested in you being appointed as designer to the company. They gave me their cards and asked me to pass them on to you. They seem very interested in what you are doing and what had happened to you. Here are their cards. I will have to go back to work. We can talk about it tonight at the apartment.' Robert gives Vicki a kiss and walks away from her. Vicki looks at the cards and bursts into tears and becomes upset and weeps uncontrollably.

Robert asks, 'What's the matter?'

Vicki replies, 'This man is my uncle, and the other is a close friend. They were very close to my parents and tried to look after me when my parents died. I left without telling them where I was going, as it scared me that the thugs that went after my husband would turn on them. So, I didn't want them to get hurt, so I didn't tell them of my plans. What am I going to do about them?'

'Well, pull yourself together and get back to work. How else are you going to pay me back for all the money I spent on you?'

'You mean to tell me that all you are interested in is the money I owe you?'

'No, but it was the only thing I could think of at the moment to snap you out of your misery and get you back to work.'

'Thanks, but I think I will go home. I am not in the mood to see customers.'

'That's not good enough. Back to work, and we will talk about the problems tonight.'

'I guess you are right. We have a lot to talk about, and we do need privacy.'

Vicki and Robert kiss, and Vicki goes back to the department store. As she walks in, she passes Mrs. Jones, who was in tears.

Vicki asks, 'Mrs. Jones, what is the matter?'

Mrs. Jones replies, 'Nothing you can help me with, Vicki. But if you must know, I have just been retrenched and my job given to a younger person. This is all part of the store's cost-cutting exercise. I have been here for twenty years and worked my way up from a junior and thought I was contributing to the profitability and doing a good job, but management wants to bring in a new culture that they believe will entice younger buyers to come in. What they have not considered, they are not the ones with the money—it is the more mature persons that are spending these days, not the younger ones. They are going to go broke, these idiots.'

'Mrs. Jones, what are you going to do? Have you got any contacts that will help you get a job?'

'No, and at my age, it will be difficult.'

'Mrs. Jones, can I ask you to do me a favor that may seem odd?'

'What is it?'

'Accept my resignation and backdate it to one hour before you got retrenched.'

'I couldn't do that. You need the work, and you are so natural with design and people. No, no, you stay on until they tap you on the shoulder.'

'Please, I insist, and I will ring you in a couple of days to explain what I am doing and when you can start at your new job.'

'What new job? I haven't been to an interview yet.'

'How about both of us walk out right now and meet tomorrow to discuss the matter?'

'Where do we meet?'

Vicki gives Mrs. Jones Robert's work address and says she would meet her there at eleven o'clock. She calls Robert and tells him she has resigned from the department store and she is waiting for him, but if he is tied up, she would catch a bus. Robert was more than happy to pick Vicki up earlier than usual.

Mrs. Jones goes back into the office and processes Vicki's resignation papers and then leaves the department store for the last time.

After fifteen minutes, Robert pulls up and Vicki gets into the car. Vicki tells Robert what has happened, and he is glad she has resigned from the department store.

Vicki says, 'Mrs. Jones is an excellent operator and knows the rag trade better than most people I know. I asked her to come to your office so I could talk to her and maybe offer her a job with us.'

Robert asks, 'Doing what?'

'Running the operation from design coordination to getting people on the stage. She knows how to handle staff, and I really will need a person of her experience to handle the day-to-day problems, while I concentrate on the design work.'

'Well, talk to her, and if she doesn't want the earth, give her a job starting in one week's time. I have spare space up on the floor above us I could set you up so you can start work immediately getting your crew together and start working on what you are going to do and what you need as to staff.'

Robert pulls into his apartment's car park, and both get out and go up to his apartment. Vicki prepares dinner, and both sit and eat in silence. They wash up and sit in the lounge room talking about the deal and what will happen.

Vicki says, 'You know I am going to have to tell my uncle everything what had happened to me.'

Robert replies, 'I guess so. They sounded concerned what happened to you and why you didn't seek their help.'

'Robert, I want you to come with me when I meet them and tell them what has happened.'

'Why? You can explain what happened. I am not married to you yet. They will wonder, "Why is he here?"'

'I can't explain it to them without your support. You are the only one I can trust to help me when I get into difficult moments. Their wives were always with me and worked with me in the design and production of the garments. When I lost everything, they lost their jobs, and no one would give them work because of their ages and their loyalty to me. We will need their help and expertise.'

'It is going to look odd if I am there. They will say to me, "Why did you come to a family gathering?" and I will say, "Because I am her employer."

'No, you say we are going to be married, or we are married and you're my husband.'

'No, we can't start telling lies.'

'No, I guess you are right. All we can say is that we are engaged and will be married shortly.'

'No, just say I came along for support, and don't mention anything about marriage or that we are engaged or any of that.'

'Why? Don't you want to marry me?'

'It seems you have no option. Either you marry me or you're back under a park bench. That is not the way I want it to be. I want you to have a proper choice, not as it is now.'

'I still will love you and marry you, anyway. You are the only one who has looked after me and loves me.'

They kiss and head off to their respective bedrooms.

12

Vicki gets up and starts making breakfast for Robert and herself. She puts everything on, the kettle and toaster, and goes and has a shower.

Robert can hear the kettle boiling and gets up and has his shower, and then goes off to the kitchen for some breakfast.

Vicki comes out all dressed ready for work. They both have breakfast and prepare to head to Robert's office. They descend to the car park and get into Robert's car and drive off to his office.

Robert says, 'I will get you settled in upstairs and then let you plan what we need to meet the deadlines for the international fashion shows. That will basically tell us what staff we need to meet the deadlines.'

Vicki replies, 'That will be great, but I need you to phone these two and make a time when I can call in and talk to them. I don't think I could do that now, and I think it would be best I see them sooner than later.'

'All right, I will give them a ring and tie up a date and time.'

They arrive at the office, and Robert and Vicki go direct to Robert's office.

Robert says, 'I will take you up to the office upstairs and let you settle in. Once you have done that, come down and we will have to discuss what we are going to do.'

Vicki replies, 'Sounds good to me. Let's go.'

Vicki and Robert go up in the lift to the floor above and get out. Vicki is impressed because it is fully furnished and ready to be used. She looks around and finds the largest office and places her bag and things there and says to Robert, 'This will do me.'

Robert says, 'I will leave you to get familiar with the layout, and when you are ready, come down and we will set down a plan.'

Robert leaves Vicki and walks down the stairwell and goes to his office. He looks at his diary and notes the appointments that have been made for him.

After about twenty minutes, Vicki comes down and goes into Robert's office. As soon as she walks in, the telephone rings, and Robert picks it up.

Robert says, 'Hello, Robert speaking.'

Steve replies, 'Robert, this is Steve. I have the contracts ready and would like to call in to get them signed.'

Robert asks, 'Can you be here within the hour?'

Steve replies, 'Yes, I am just at our lawyer's office. We can be at your office within a half an hour. We will see you soon.'

Robert says, 'They want me to sign the contract and pay them the $1 million. After that, it is ours.'

Vicki says, 'I have called the organizers, and they will email you the design themes and criteria we have to meet to fulfill our part of the contract. That should be done within the next hour.'

Robert replies, 'I will make the call to your relative creditors to see when we can come over and talk.'

Robert picks up the telephone and rings the number on the card given to him.

Robert says, 'Hello, I am after Tim O'Brien.'

Tim replies, 'Tim speaking.'

Robert says, 'Tim, you asked Vicki to ring you to organize a time for you two to get together. Unfortunately, she is tied up and asked me to ring on her behalf. When would be a good time for you?'

Tim replies, 'I am busy all next week, but if she can come to my house at two o'clock tomorrow, we can spend some time chatting. Tomorrow being Saturday will make it less stressful.'

Vicki is nodding to Robert that she agrees.

Robert asks, 'Where does she go? What is your address?'

Tim replies, 'Vicki knows it. She has been to my house many times.'

Robert says, 'OK. She will be there at two tomorrow.'

Robert hangs up the telephone just as Steve walks in with his lawyer.

Steve says, 'Robert, this is John Malcolm, our lawyer.'

Robert shakes hands with John and introduces Vicki to the two men.

Steve asks, 'Robert, do you want me to go through the contracts with you and you sign afterwards, or do you want me to leave them with you and you ring us when your lawyer has had time to read through them?'

Robert replies, 'I am concerned that it will take a week before we check the contracts and, if necessary, get amendments made to them. In the meantime, I want to bring a team on board to prepare for the task ahead of us. What I propose is that we sign heads of agreements, which you can draft up fairly quickly, and I pay you, say, $100,000 today so neither of us can withdraw if the contract reflects accurately what we agreed to.'

'That sounds fair. We will leave the contract with you and John's business card, and your lawyers can ring John whenever they are ready for you to sign and pay the balance of the money owed. We will have the heads of agreement drafted and be back at two for you to sign.'

'That seems reasonable. We will see you at two.'

Steve and John go out, and Robert phones his lawyers and asks them to attend a meeting with him in one hour's time. They agree as they have had a cancellation.

Vicki was sitting there seeing Robert doing all these things and is amazed.

Robert picks the phone up and makes a call.

Robert says, 'Roger. Robert. I wonder if I could see you at my office this morning. I know it is on short notice, but I need to speak to you urgently. Good. Then I will see you within the hour.'

Vicki asks, 'Who is Roger?'

Robert replies, 'He in advertising and public relations.'

'Why do we need them?'

'Once I sign the agreement, I want Town Hall to drop any moves it intends to make on the building. So, I have to begin a campaign against them so we can establish the company MI.'

'I never thought of that. Robert, I am out of my depth.'

'Don't worry. You may be, but I'm not.'

As Robert hangs up, Roger Norton walks in.

Robert says, 'Roger, thanks for coming in on such short notice.'

Roger was not looking at Robert, but at Vicki.

Roger says, 'Vicki, is it you, really you, after all these years? Come here and let me give you a hug.'

With that, Roger goes over to Vicki and gives her a gentle hug, while Vicki bursts into tears looking over Roger's shoulder.

Roger asks, 'Vicki, where have you been all these years? I tried to find you. Where did you go?'

Robert says, 'Roger, it looks like you know each other.'

Roger replies, 'We were the PR firm handling Vicki's account. That bastard of a husband of hers would not pay his debts, and I nearly lost my job because of it. Vicki paid us all the money owing, and he took it out on her. She saved my hide, and I owe her a lot for it.'

Vicki says, 'Yes, he did a lot of bad things. Roger is the best in our industry, and if he is on board, we are in excellent hands.'

Roger replies, 'Thanks, Vicki.'

Robert says, 'Roger, we have a problem that we need you to handle for us and do the PR for our new acquisition.'

Robert explains to Roger what has happened with the acquisition and that they need Town Hall to vote against the acquisition because most libraries are now going digital and it would be a waste of taxpayers' money to acquire a building that will not be used after a few years. Second, Roger was to promote the credentials of the newly acquired business and that Vicki was to be named as the chief designer of MI.

Roger says, 'Let me draft up an advertising and promotion campaign, and we can then discuss or refine it. It will take a week to come up with some concepts, and I will call you as soon as we have something.'

Robert replies, 'That will be good, as it will take us a week to get things moving.'

Vicki says, 'Thanks for taking us on, Roger. I know how busy you must be. Do you have any other designers on your books?'

Roger replies, 'No, they prefer to use the overseas agencies rather than us. They think they are getting better and more creative work from them, but all they are getting is a bigger bill with little to show for it. I will be in touch.'

Robert shows Roger out and comes back to his office.

Robert asks, 'Vicki, have you worked out the theme of the fashion parade?'

Vicki replies, 'They were going to email you the information. Can you check if they have sent it?'

Robert checks his emails, and, sure enough, it is there. He prints it off and gives it to Vicki, who says she is going back to her office upstairs.

Robert receives a telephone call from Steve that they have drafted the heads of agreement and that he wants to come to his office to have them signed. Robert agrees to see them at three in the afternoon.

Steve arrives at three and hands the heads of agreement to Robert for his consideration. Robert reads them and agrees to sign. He signs the HOA and gives Steve a cheque for $100,000 made out to Steve's company. Both men shake hands, and Steve takes the document back with him for his boss to sign.

At four o'clock, Steve faxes back a copy of the signed HOA and confirms that they expect the contract to be signed within a week and the balance of the monies paid then.

Vicki has spent the last couple of hours reading through the papers to get a precise idea of what is required by IFS. The theme is 'Modern America' for the first parade, which could be anything. One designer's approach would differ from another, as each would interpret the requirement and design differently.

The theme for the second parade is 'Youth of Today', which again is an open requirement, as it could mean anything, and both are very challenging, as a world audience would appraise the designs.

Vicki checks the credentials of the other fashion houses that are invited to present at the parade. Most she knows, but there are a couple of new international ones she has never heard of. She then notices that they also invited Charles Henry to attend, and her blood boils. She is determined to beat him and make a better presentation and designs than what he could come up with.

Vicki makes a list of what staff she would need to employ to undertake the task ahead. She remembers Alex and Mrs. Jones and rings them.

Vicki says, 'Mrs. Jones, this is Vicki. How are you?'

Mrs. Jones replies, 'Resting but still upset with the way the department store retrenched me. I looked at the newspapers to see if there were any jobs going that I might apply for, but there are none listed, unfortunately.'

'Could I see you on Monday at nine to discuss a proposition?'

'I will take it. When do I start?'

'Well, let's discuss it and see if you will be interested in the job, and we can then discuss a commencement date on Monday?'

Vicki gives Mrs. Jones the address where to go.

Mrs. Jones says, 'That sounds great to me. I will see you on Monday.'

Vicki then rings Alex and speaks to her.

Vicki says, 'Hi, Alex. Hope you are well.'

Alex replies, 'Yes, as good as can be expected without a job.'

'That's what I want to speak to you about. Can I see you on Monday, say, about ten, so we can discuss what I am doing and if you are interested in joining me?'

'Sure, but I will see you on Saturday, so we can discuss it then.'

'No, Alex, on Monday. So, I will see you then. Here is the address where to go, and I will see you then.'

Vicki sits back and wonders why Alex said, 'I will see you Saturday,' but is interrupted by a call from Robert.

Robert asks, 'Have you done everything you wanted to do? Can we go home?'

Vicki replies, 'I am coming down now. I will be in your office as soon as I switch the lights off.'

Vicki goes down to Robert's office, and both go down to the car park and drive home. They call into a pizza place and buy a pizza and salad for dinner.

While eating their pizza, Vicki remarks, 'I phoned Alex to get her to come into the office on Monday so we could talk about a job, and she said, "I will see you on Saturday." Strange. Never mind, maybe she misunderstood me.'

Robert replies, 'Possibly. It has been a busy day with the acquisition and Steve trying to rush things. Well, it is over until next week. We have a couple of days to unwind.'

'Well, tomorrow is going to be hectic with shopping in the morning and then off to speak to Tim, which shouldn't be a long session. It is at his home, so his wife will be there.'

'Do you know her well?'

'Yes, she was one of my concept designers until everything went pear-shaped. I hope I can get her to join me, as she is one of the best in the industry.'

'If she is that good, why hasn't she found a new job?'

'Fashion houses don't want to take on designers from other places, as they may steal some of their concepts or designs and then leave them and go elsewhere.'

'No one trusts anyone in that industry.'

'Yes, that is right. The thing I noticed from the papers you got from the International Body was that Charles Henry was also invited to take part in the parade.'

'That crook. You better be careful once you design that he doesn't get an idea of your designs. Otherwise, he will steal them and say they are his.'

'Yes, I agree. Anyhow, let's wash the dishes and go to bed. It's going to be a busy day, and I am tired.'

They clean up and shortly afterwards give each other a hug and kiss and walk off to their respective bedrooms.

13

oth Vicki and Robert get up early, shower, and have breakfast. They head off to the shopping centre to do their usual Saturday shopping for groceries and meats. They come home and put everything away, and Vicki divides the meat up into portions and then places them in the freezer. Once completed, they sit down and have a cup of coffee with a cake they bought. By the time everything is done, it is one o'clock, and Vick says to Robert, 'We better go and see what Tim has to say. We don't want to be late.'

Robert says, 'No, let's go. He said you know the directions.'

Vicki replies, 'Yes, I think I remember. It is about an hour away.'

They go down in the lift and get into Robert's car and they drive off with Vicki giving directions.

Robert says, 'Now, don't forget, we don't want them to know we are going to get married or that we live together. If they ask, tell them you live at the Park and our relationship is purely a business relationship.'

Vicki asks, 'The Park?'

'Yes, the Park Royal. Remember, I took you there.'

'Oh, yes. I remember. I hope I can remember all the things I have to remember and things I am not about to say.'

They drive on with Vicki giving instructions like 'Turn left—no, I mean right. No, this is not where you turn', which leads to a few heated words between them. Eventually, they arrive at Tim's house. They park the car and get out. They walk up to the house, and Robert rings the doorbell.

After a minute, Tim comes out and shakes Robert's hand, and Tim stars at Vicki and then says, 'Life hasn't been good to you, love. You have aged but still look beautiful.'

Vicki says, 'Tim, I am sorry for the trouble I have caused you.'

Vicki cries, and Tim says, 'No, no Vicki, that is now in the past. We have to look to the future.' All three go in the house. Tim says, 'Why don't we go out back to where my wife, Pat, is? She wants to see how Vicki looks.'

All three walk to the rear of the house and enter a large entertainment area. As they walk towards Tim's wife who was seated by herself, there was a roar of 'Surprise!' and people come out of everywhere giving Vicki hugs and kisses. Vicki immediately grabs Robert's hand, which was noticed by everyone.

Robert knows that Vicki's reaction in grabbing his hand had given their game away and that he could not say that it was purely a business arrangement. Vicki bursts into tears and tries to bury her head in Robert's chest, crying uncontrollably, and trembles.

Everyone notices Vicki got a shock from the welcome and could see her shaking as she sobs.

Robert takes Vicki into the house and seats her on the lounge. He tries to move away, but Vicki would not let his hand go. He takes a tissue out of his pocket and gives it to Vicki, who then releases Robert and blows her nose. She is given a glass of water by Pat O'Brien, Tim's wife, and she sips a little. She finds it hard to concentrate on what to say and would like to get up and go home, but knew she could not; she would have to face the music.

Pat says, 'I told you it was a silly idea to have all of those who knew her come over at the one time. What did you think of? It is not a birthday party.'

Tim replies, 'Vicki, I am sorry. I have done the wrong thing and scared you with what I thought was a coming-home surprise. I will tell everyone to go home, and we can talk amongst ourselves.'

Vicki says, 'No, Tim. Now that they are here, they want an explanation of what happened and where did I end up.'

Robert asks, 'Are you up to it, Vicki?'

Vicki replies, 'No, and most probably will end up in tears more than once, but I have to do it now. I want you with me.'

Vicki walks out of the house into the entertainment room and pauses looking at the gathering that was there. She remembers most of them, as they are very close to her. She steps forward and lets go of Robert's hand and pauses, and everyone stops talking.

Vicki says, 'I am sorry. I burst out in tears. I was not expecting all of you to turn up, and it came as a shock to me to see you suddenly. Sorry. I am very sorry.

'I guess most of you are looking for an answer to what happened to me after I lost everything.'

From the crowd, 'And how you made your millions.'

Vicki says, 'Shortly after my husband was killed by the mob, they came after me and, since I had nothing, told me they were going to come after every person who was related to me and our business to get the money, they had lost in dealing with my husband. This meant that they would come after all of you—everyone I loved. I couldn't let that happen to you and your families. They would stop at nothing to get their money.

'It wasn't any use to go to the police, as the mob have paid the police to pass on the information. So, they are hand in glove with the police, and they would come after you as soon as the police gave them your names.

'To protect you and your family, I had to get away. I had no money and could not approach you, as they would know who you were and where you lived. I knew I was being followed day and night. So, I left the suburb and ended under a park bench in the city park. I would sleep there at night covered in plastic to keep out of the cold. I would find food in garbage tins and get a hot meal once a week from the charities. I tried to get some money for food by begging on the Town Hall steps in the heat and better cold in winter. I did not have a spare shirt or enough money for a pair of underpants. I did this for about four years until I got pneumonia and was rushed to hospital, near death and not expected to live.'

By this time, some people were in tears themselves, for they thought Vicki had a glamorous life, not the life she was describing. They understood from the conversation that she sacrificed herself for them.

Vicki says, 'sometimes in the park when I had to fight off men who came to rape me, and on one occasion, one of them came back and fired three bullets into my pile of rags that I filed up. So, they thought it was me under the bench. They ran off. One of them was Charles Henry, and you all know what he is like.'

'When I was in hospital, they wanted my bed, and because I was a no one with no money or reputation, they forced me out with nowhere to go but back to the city park. Robert, who used to walk past me when I was sitting begging on the Town Hall steps, recognized me and took me to his apartment just before a big storm and cold snap hit the state last month. I have stayed there since trying to build up my strength.

'Robert has made a bid to take over Marque International, or MI as most of us know it. They are an icon in the industry before it went broke. As part of the contract, the company must present two fashion parades based on the themes "America Today" and "Youth of Today". Robert hired me to do the design, and I am now trying to put a team together to get the designs and production work done. At present, I am the only one employed, and they will sign the contracts next week to complete the acquisition. I hope this answer all your questions.'

Vicki, who by now is in tears, moves away but is stopped by those present, intending to apologize for scaring her. Robert stands close by, and Vicki keeps glancing at him to make sure he does not leave her there alone.

Pat says, 'If you are looking for staff, we are here, or do you consider us of no use now or too old and decrepit?'

Vicki replies, 'I have put you all to enough trouble already, and the next eighteen months will be hard with the competition and what Charles Henry will get up to when he knows he has a competitor. You know the mob that supports him, and they play rough.'

Pat says, 'Well, we can handle Mr. Henry, and as for him using a gun, we will wrap it around his bloody neck if he uses any of his thugs on us.'

Pat adds, 'Look, Vicki, we all tried to get jobs after the breakup, but no one would give us a job, not even take us on as cleaners. We were the best in the industry, and they did not want us. Now they can get stuffed. If they come and ask us to jump ship, we will say, "Is your company up for sale?"

'Vicki, you were the driving force before, and we were the most creative fashion house around. We were the best in the industry. Now we are nothing. We just want to be recognized for our talent. We want to finish the job we started before. We want to be recognized as the best. You really cannot deny us the opportunity to finish what we started. You owe nothing to us other than the opportunity we are seeking. All of us are here. We are a family. Yes, we thought you were doing well, living the life of luxury and therefore didn't want to know us, but now we know what they did to you, and we want to get back at them and make it harder for the scumbags that treated you and us like dirt. You need our support both morally and physically to ensure they don't get at you again.'

Vicki says, 'I'm not the boss, so I will have to discuss it with Robert.'

Pat replies, 'Good. Now that is settled. If there is any difficulty with Robert, just tell him if we are not all employed, you will not marry him.'

The group bursts out laughing and moves towards Vicki, asking questions about the project.

Vicki says, 'Listen, everyone, the theme I have already told you about. The designs have not even started, let alone reach the conception stage, and I really have not thought of what we are going to do for the parade. Remember, there are two fashion parades, which makes it harder to achieve. Robert will sign the contracts next week. It is best if he tells you what he has planned.'

Robert replies, 'Nothing is in concrete, but I have already commissioned Roger Norton to attend to our PR and advertising requirements. As soon as we sign the contracts and pay the money, all the staff will be at the MI building and we will do all the work out of there.

'We want the world to know what is happening and that we are open for business, so they can get used to the idea that we are in business to provide the best design works available and are out to get any design contracts we can to generate a cash flow.'

Pat says, 'I will call my overseas contacts and see if they can give us some work.'

Robert replies, 'I prefer you didn't. We do not want to seem to beg for work. I would prefer they came to us. We will spend money both locally and overseas to build up a reputation and to tell people we are back and open for business.'

Pat says, 'Good. I see where you are coming from. We will meet at your office on Monday and plan what we need to do and who is to do what.'

Vicki says, 'Thanks, everyone, for your support and trusting me again.'

The crowd stays talking to Vick, and then slowly they leave and go their way, leaving Robert and Vicki to say goodbye to Tim and Pat.

Vicki and Robert say their goodbyes and drive off home.

There is very little said while driving home, with Vicki going over in her mind what has happened and Robert realizing she needs time to confront what her family has told her and to recognize their loyalty and support for her.

They arrive at their apartment, and both get out of the car and go up to their apartment. Vicki sits in her chair, and Robert switches the television on and gets a beer and sits down. Robert was surfing the channels when suddenly Vicki yells out, 'Stop! Leave it on that channel for a minute.' Something has caught her eye. It is a documentary on the fashion industry covering the International Fashion Shows. Vicki quickly grabs the controller from Robert's hand and starts taping the show while sitting there watching it. Robert goes to his computer and brings up the show and records it. Vicki sits for the full one hour and finally, when it ended, asks if they could screen the show on Monday.

Robert replies, 'Yes, we either take the TV box with us or the laptop and we can replay it so everyone could see it. Is it important?' Vicki says, 'Thank God we were here to see it. I think it has given me an idea of what is going to be required, design wise, to make an impression on a world audience.'

'I'll be blown if I could see anything coming out of the show other than some good and some hilarious outfits and some undernourished, tall women.'

'Men. I guess that is why you need us women around you to ensure you dress well in sweatshirts, shorts, and thongs.'

Robert smiles and sits down and watches the rest of the show while drinking his beer.

Sunday, they go to church, and Allen is there to welcome them. After the hymns and reading from the Bible, Allen moves into the pulpit.

Robert thinks, *Not another long sermon like last week's.*

Allen says, 'The sermon today is in the recognition of Christ. Believe in Him and have faith in Him.

'The unfortunate aspects of life are that most good ideas or projects come from the inspiration of the Holy Spirit, but because of man's intervention, the thing never gets done or are completed in a mess or there is a disastrous outcome in the future, and God generally is left with the blame, not man.'

'When I refer to man, of course, I am using the generic term, which also includes women, so please do not think that I am being sexist.'

'Ideas or inspirations from God should be recognized. You hadn't thought of what has popped into your head before, nor had you considered the matter, but suddenly, the seed grows in your mind as to what should be done and, in time, how it is to be done.

'God advised Adam as to what was required in the Garden of Eden. Noah was told how to build the ark. He told David a few things and conversed with the likes of Abraham, Solomon, Moses, Jesus, and others. He told them, or as they say in modern terms, "He gave them the good Word."

'The good ideas come from God, but, unfortunately, man does not give God the credit, thanks, recognition of the concept, or thought, or opportunity to complete the task.'

'What invariably happens is man gets the concept and says, "That's a good idea. I am glad I thought of it," without recognizing that the inspiration came from God and thanking Him for it.'

'The other problem is that you get an idea, but do not wait for God to advise you on its detail or implementation. God will never give you half a concept or idea. He will give you everything you need to do the job. The only difference is that He will give this to you in His own time and not when you demand it. He wants you to have the best idea and best outcome, but He also wants you to give Him recognition that it came from Him and that you have faith in Him to help you complete the task.'

'God is giving you a means by which you can judge your faith in Christ and to see the outcome of such faith.'

'Shallow faith evaporates quickly, and the person goes back to using their own idea to complete the task.'

'Compounding faith is faith in God, knowing that He has performed in the past and believing He will do it again for you in the future. Trust in Him. He may not do it your way or as quick as you would want it to happen, but the outcome will be far better than you had planned, and it will fit into His overall plan He has for you. 'Some people think that their daily lives comprise just a routine of getting up in the morning, having lunch, dinner, and then going to bed. There is no recognition of ideas popping into their heads or things happening around them because they are like robots and do not bother thinking, "Why am I in my current position? What does God want of me?" In fact, most have forgotten about God and don't bother communicating or praying to Him. It is their life, and they will decide what is going to happen, not God.'

'You are, in fact, a small ball on the road or footpath, waiting until you acknowledge God and show you are prepared to be pushed or kicked along in the direction He has planned for you. You can stay there all your life and get nowhere, or have faith in Him, move along, and serve the Lord.'

Sometimes you may question the Lord's intention or why things are happening to you and only to you and not to others. Everyone else seems to enjoy life, but not you. Why? It is because the Lord believes you have to experience what you are going through to get His job done but also to allow you to gain increasing faith in Him so you know He is there with you, for you, and will get you through what is happening to you, even if it seems impossible. 'He opened the Red Sea to let his people through and closed it on his enemies.'

'The message today is to believe in God, have faith in Him. Recognize what He is saying to you and let Him do the job and finish it His way through you, for it is you who serves the Lord and not, as some believe, the other way around.'

'Let us pray . . .'

The service ends, and the congregation moves outside.

Vicki and Robert wait to say hello to Allen, who, after shaking hands with other parishioners, finally catch up with Vicki and Robert.

Vicki says, 'Allen, you must have been listening to us all week, for your sermon was spot on what we are doing.'

Allen replies, 'No, but He has been. What is happening with you two?'

Robert says, 'We have concluded the acquisition of a fashion house that has gone broke, and we are now moving to put on two fashion parades that will be screened worldwide, which we never thought possible some weeks ago.'

Allen says, 'I am sure that God has a plan and a reason for you two being brought together and the opportunity presenting itself.'

Vicki replies, 'That is the problem, Allen. I ended up under a park bench and now have been given the opportunity to present a fashion parade on a world stage. It is surely not for my benefit, and yet I cannot understand what we do that will be for the Lord's benefit.'

'If we do not consider His requirements, we will go our own merry way, doing what we believe is what we want to do and not delivering His message. That is it. It is His message that He wants us to deliver to the world. But what is that message?'

Allen replies, 'Possibly. But you will have to pray and ask Him to give you wisdom to understand what He wants you to do. He will tell you in His own good time.'

Robert says, 'I think we are taking this too far and reading too much into the matter and your sermon.'

Allen replies, 'Well, I am sure time will tell you otherwise, as it is not normal for someone to be placed in Vicki's position without a reason. It is also the same when the disciples asked Jesus, "What sin did the blind man do that made him blind?" Jesus said, "He has not sinned but was placed on earth so I can prove to the non-believers that I can do miracles in the name of the Father, and he can bear witness to these miracles." The same with you, Vicki. You are part of God's grand plan, even though Robert may not think so.'

Vicki says, 'I agree. It is too coincidental for all these things to happen on their own. There is a spirit driving us towards a goal, but we cannot see what that is.'

Allen replies, 'In time, the Lord will reveal it to you. You just have to have faith in Him and ask His guidance about what you are doing.'

Robert says, 'Thank you, Allen.'

Vicki adds, 'We will say a prayer for guidance, Allen.'

Both Vicki and Robert go off and walk back to their apartment. They have lunch, and Robert goes off to do some work, while Vicki makes notes for tomorrow's meeting.

14

The next morning, everyone is gathered at Robert's office, ready to get started.

Vicki says, 'Good morning, everyone. First, I want you to meet Mrs. Jones, who will oversee administration. Please fill in the forms she gives you, so we know who we have working for us. Once that has been completed, I want you to see a one-hour documentary on the international fashion parade, and then we hope to have a presentation from our advertising people as to what they are intending to present worldwide regarding our acquisition. Any questions?'

Robert gets a call from his solicitor saying contracts have been reviewed and are good to sign. Robert telephones Steve and arranges for him to come around in an hour's time to sign the contracts. He prepares to move funds into his trading account so he can pay the remaining $900,000 owing to acquire the business.

Roger arrives and goes straight to Robert's office. He has his presentations on a CD and asks Robert for access to the large TV. He inserts the CD, and both sit down and watch the presentation, which goes for thirty seconds. There are three presentations that will be broadcasted in each country in Europe, Asia, and throughout America. The first video clip declares we have placed the fashion house under new management, and the chief designer is Vicki Santana. This is to run for one week and basically will tell everyone that MI is open for business.

The second video clip outlines the designs the company is involved in and again advises of the unique designs and world-class fashions they were renowned for and intend to continue and that they are open for business.

The third video advises that the fashion house will enter the international fashion parade in Paris in eighteen months' time.

Robert says, 'Roger, they are great, and I cannot falter them. We have all our staff upstairs, and I would like them to see the videos and get their feedback.'

Roger replies, 'That would be a great idea. When do you want to go upstairs?'

Robert says, 'Let's go up now.'

Both men go upstairs, and all the staff are looking at the end of the documentary. They take a seat.

The documentary ends, and Vicki steps up to the front.

Vicki asks, 'What do you think of that?'

Pat replies, 'They are giving everyone a message as to what type of designs they believe will fit into their concept and what is to be exhibited.'

Vicki says, 'That is what I thought was the case. What we will need to do is to run it again so we can all get an idea of the designs we should concentrate on.'

Robert steps to the front of the meeting.

Robert says, 'Before you get down to talking shop, can I introduce you to Roger, who has some videos that he is recommending we screen worldwide so we can get some recognition and penetration of our brand? Roger?'

Roger says, 'It is good to see so many old faces. We need your critical appraisal of these because if they don't impress you, they won't impress an international audience and we will get no work placed with the company.'

Rodger puts the first video on and then the other two. Afterwards, he asks for comments.

Vicki says, 'Video one basically says I am the key person in the company and all designs are mine when in fact we all help in the design.'

Roger replies, 'Yes, but the final decision is yours, and you can say yes or no.'

Vicki asks, 'Can we say who the support staff are and maybe have shots of us all rather than me? That way, it will show a team of people and not just an individual.'

Pat says, 'Vicki is right. We want to say, "You didn't want us before. Now you will regret it."'

Vicki adds, 'We were the best before, and we will be the best again in a short period.'

Roger asks, 'Any comments on the second and third video?'

Pat says, 'Can't you expand it to show that we are not only entering the international fashion parade but also intending to design for other main events?'

Roger asks, 'Like what?'

Pat replies, 'The royal wedding, Ascot, Kentucky Derby, Melbourne Cup, just to name a few.'

Roger asks, 'Have you got orders for these events?'

Pat replies, 'No, but if asked to design a garment, then we will do it. We are not saying we will do it, but we will design for special events, and these are some events that come to mind.'

Roger says, 'Yes, I see your point. I will get the team on to recasting the videos and will come back to you in a few days' time.'

Vicki says, 'Thanks, Roger. Girls, we have to get back to our designs, so we have to see the documentary again to make sure we haven't missed anything.'

Robert says, 'Our contract has been finalized by our lawyers and will sign it within an hour. We will pay the balance of monies owing and from then on, we own the company, and are locked in. As of tomorrow, the fashion house will be in its own building, and I have already appointed a security company to control who goes in and out of the building. CCTV is already being installed and operational and will be manned twenty-four hours a day, seven days a week. We will complete all design work on designated computers. I will give you your temporary ID cards this afternoon, and you will have to have your picture taken tomorrow so the computer can check facial recognition for unauthorized entry.' Robert escorts Roger to his office, and after some discussion, Roger leaves to attend to the revamping the videos.

Vicki and her team watch through the documentary again and note what they believe is being discreetly said and note the direction the organizers want the participants to take and the main points that will be judged on.

After the documentary finishes, Vicki advises the group of what she believes the message is and the type of garments the organizers are intending to be designed.

Pat disagrees, and they hold a discussion as to what the group thinks. This goes on until twelve, when they break for lunch.

Steve meets Robert at his office at eleven o'clock and turns up on time and is shown to the boardroom.

Robert turns up, and both shake hands.

Robert says, 'I have the amended copy of the contracts that you have agreed to. So, do you want to have a quick look through it?'

Steve replies, 'Yes, thanks, to make sure it incorporates the latest amendments.'

Steve looks through the contracts and, after twenty minutes, agrees it reflects the final agreement.

Robert asks, 'So it is all right to sign it?'

Steve replies, 'Yes.'

Robert signs the contract first, and then Steve signs. A second copy is also executed, and both men take one executed copy as their copy.

Steve asks, 'The money, Robert?'

Robert gives Steve a bank cheque made out to Steve's company for $900,000.

Steve signs the documents transferring the title of the MI building to Robert's company, and both men shake hands, and Steve leaves to bank the cheque.

Lunchtime over, Vicki and the girls meet at the upstairs office and again are debating the style and designs that will be made for the fashion parade. They continue their discussions until it was time to go home when they break, and Vicki again reminds them that tomorrow they must meet at the MI building and not at Robert's office.

Vicki heads down to Robert's office, and the rest make their way home.

Vicki asks, 'How did it go?'

Robert says, 'Yes, it went well, and I now own the company and the building. Did you finalize the design schedule?'

Vicki replies, 'No, that will take another week before we all agree what we have to design and balance it against the time that we have on the catwalk.'

Vicki asks, 'Are you turning up at the MI building tomorrow?' Robert replies, 'Yes. We will go straight there from the apartment, and 'I will spend an hour there and come back here and leave you to keep me informed with what is happening.'

Vicki asks, 'When is Roger going to start his broadcast?'

Robert replies, 'I hope by the end of the week. I do not want the world to just find out about us. I want to tell them who we are to make sure there are no lies told about the company or what it stands for.'

Vicki and Robert close the office and drive back to their apartment.

After dinner, they are sitting in their lounge room discussing the day's events.

Robert says, 'You will have to decide when or if you are going to move into the Park Royal and get some independence back into your life.'

Vicki asks, 'Don't you want me around anymore?'

'That's not the issue. You are a single girl and need some independence to run your life the way you want to.'

'But I have that here. We are going to get married, so I can't see the point of moving away just to move back.'

'Vicki, I don't want you to marry me out of gratitude. You may find someone better, someone that will make your head swirl and sweep you off your feet, someone in the industry who wears modern clothes and calls everyone darling.'

'Except for the modern clothes you have described yourself. You always call me darling.'

'I still think you should move into the Park and see if you prefer to be independent and, overtime, save some money and not be so reliant on me to support you.'

'I think you are trying to get rid of me.'

'Rubbish. I love you and will always love you, but I think circumstances have put you in a position, and I think your love for me is more gratitude than love.'

'How would I get to work, buy groceries, and do all the things I am doing now?'

'I will buy you a small car so you can drive yourself around and have your independence. You are being paid a wage, so we will apply for your identification documents to be reissued to you and get your license reissued as well. Once you have these, I will arrange for you to open a bank account in your name, and your wages will be deposited directly into that account. You will then be independent and not rely on me. I will meet you once a week at the office, and we can go over what you are doing and whether we are on target.'

'I don't like it. But if it helps you come to terms with our love, then I have no choice. Do you want me to move there tonight?'

'I don't want you to move anywhere. I just think you would think differently about our relationship if you had some independence.'

'When do you want me to move out?'

'Tomorrow, you have to settle in at the old building and get everyone motivated and working. We will have a look for a car for you, say, on Wednesday and lodge your request for copies of your identification documents, which they can hand over to you right away over the counter. So let us make it the day after tomorrow.'

Vicki bursts into tears and runs to her bedroom and doesn't come out that night.

The next morning, Vicki comes out looking as if she had not slept that night.

Robert looks at Vicki and says, 'You look as if you have been crying all night.'

Vicki replies, 'I have.'

'Why? I thought you would be happy to get some independence.'

'Thanks.'

They have breakfast, and both go down the elevator and get into Robert's car. They drive off to MI building and enter it and have a look around.

Vicki finds the manager's office and puts her things there. Robert looks around and notes there seems to be a lot of space and rooms within the building. Eventually, everyone comes in, and the group gathers in one of the large meeting rooms.

Everyone notices Vicki looks upset and not her bright self, but does not want to comment, thinking she may have disagreed with Robert or an argument.

Vicki and Robert greet everyone.

Vicki says, 'Mrs. Jones will advise you where you can seat yourself or which office has been allocated. Most of our meetings will be held here. Everyone, you have half an hour to look around and find where your workstations are. After that, we will meet and try to complete our design schedules.'

Mr. Jones says, 'Girls, please follow me and I will give you all the grand tour.'

After everyone has left, Robert advises Vicki of his intention to go back to his office to attend to his work. He tries to give Vicki a kiss, but she walks away, leaving him somewhat bewildered why she did what she has just done.

Robert drives to his office and starts his day's work, still thinking about what has happened. He works all day and does not realize that it is six o'clock and he has to pick Vicki up at five. He drives to MI building and notes it is shut and locked. He phones Tim and asks to speak to his wife, Pat.

Robert asks, 'Pat, do you know where Vicki went to after work?' Pat replies, 'No, she didn't seem herself all day, but all of us were on edge trying to complete the design schedule, which we unfortunately couldn't complete. No, I am sorry, I don't know where she could be.' Robert drives to the apartment thinking Vicki may have misunderstood the plan, but no sign of Vicki. He drives to the Park Royal, thinking she would be there, still no sign of Vicki. He goes back to his apartment thinking she is tied up with a design problem and would be late home, but thinks it is strange she has not rung to say she would be late.

Robert sits in his apartment waiting for Vicki, watching some television, and then goes to bed.

The next morning, he gets up and checks Vicki's room. He could see she had not slept there last night. He gets worried, so he makes some breakfast and showers and drives to the MI building and waits for Vicki.

All the staff arrive but not Vicki.

He goes back to his own office to see if she is upstairs but finds the doors locked and again, no Vicki. He does not know what has happened to her. He could not go to the police and report a missing person, as she is not related to him and is just a person occupying a room in his apartment. He doesn't know what to do.

Robert works all day getting through his schedule but not functioning as he would like to have, as he always is thinking about Vicki. She is always on his mind. He finishes his day and drives to his apartment. Still, there is no Vicki. He worried, but could not think of what he should do. He has something to eat and watches some television and, after a few hours, goes to bed.

The next morning, he gets up, and the weather has turned cold, and it is raining. The forecast is for three days of blizzard conditions. He showers and goes to work, realizing that Vicki has walked out on him without a word. Something has happened between them that turned Vicki away from him.

He goes to MI's office and tries to get to understand what designs are being planned for the show, but finds it hard to understand the points raised by the staff. Mrs. Jones is more in tune with what is happening, and he basically leaves it to her for the moment. He makes sure that the staff has enough work to go on with and then leaves for his office to attend to his work. The staff were also getting worried as to what had happened to Vicki, and they ask questions as to what they should do.

A week has passed and no sign of Vicki or any word from her. The weather worsens. A bitter cold snap grip the state. It is back to jumpers and coats to keep warm.

Towards the end of the second week, Robert receives a telephone call from Allen.

Robert says, 'Allen, no doubt you're ringing to find out why we haven't been in church?'

Allen replies, 'Well, now that you mention it, why haven't you?'

'Unfortunately, Vicki and I had a disagreement, and it appears she has walked out on me, and I don't know where she is.'

'But what about the relationship you have with God? It appears you have walked out on that too.'

'Yes, I must agree I have. I have only been going to church to give Vicki some support.'

'That is no reason to attend church and have people think you are a Christian when you really have no belief or faith in God.'

'I agree, but that is the type of upbringing I have had and really haven't had much use for involving God in my life. I cannot see the point. I am well off and can do the things that most people cannot do. He can't give me anything that I haven't already got.'

'I am sorry to hear you say those things and would still welcome you at our church should you change your mind.'

'Thanks, but I can't think of any reason for me to attend.'

'The invitation is always there. By the way, I walked past the Town Hall steps yesterday and sighted Vicki sitting on the steps in her usual position—'

Robert interrupts, 'What? You must be mistaken. That wouldn't be Vicki.'

Allen says, 'If you say so, Robert.'

'It must have been someone that looked like her. It could not be her. She has a good apartment to come to, and me.'

'It looks like you wanted her to leave, and since she had no home of her own, she went back to the only place she knew, her park bench.'

'No, you must be mistaken. She could always stay with me.'

'No, you made it clear she was to have independence, and she took that as you wanted her to go back to where she came from.'

'Where is she? I will bring her back immediately. It is freezing out there. She cannot stay in the cold. She will get pneumonia again.'

'That's why I am ringing. She collapsed with pneumonia and was taken to the local hospital. Unfortunately, she is not expected to make it, and they asked me to give her last rites, as the hospital does not expect her to last the night. It is a pity you're not a religious man, as I would ask you to pray for her.'

'Why didn't you tell me this before?'

'You led the conversation, Robert. I just thought you would like to know her whereabouts.'

'Thanks, Allen. I will go to the hospital straightaway.'

'You can save yourself the journey. The roads are blocked with traffic and accidents caused by the icy weather, and for another, they will not let you in to see her, as you are not her family.'

'What can I do?'

'Pray. But you say you are not a believer. I guess nothing. I do not want to be rude, but all your money and influence seem to mean nothing when it comes to the crunch. I can only recommend you try to find God and ask for His help.'

'Fat chance of that.'

'I will leave you to ponder over your options, Robert.'

'Thanks for calling, Allen.'

Robert hangs up his phone and sits and wonders what he could do. The news on the television warns people not to go out that night, as the conditions are extreme and there are a lot of accidents. He knows he would never make it to the hospital and sits for a while and decides he could do nothing that night and thinks about how he would go about replacing Vicki as head designer for the company.

He sits there for about an hour and then goes to bed.

Robert keeps waking up during the night with bad dreams. He could not get Vicki out of his mind. Again and again, he would wake up with her calling him, and he knew he could not just leave her to die and replace her with another. He knows all his money could not give her life back to her, so he gets out of bed and prays to God for help and to guide him as to what he must do to be a Christian. He goes back to bed and sleeps for about two hours, and then it is time to get up. He gets out of bed and switches on the news and hears that the storm has passed over and they forecast reasonable conditions for the rest of the day.

He showers and gets into his car and drives to the hospital and once there asks at Administration which ward, he would have to go to see Vicki.

Clerk says, 'Sir, I will just check. I think they have taken her to the morgue.'

Robert asks, 'The morgue? You mean she died?'

Clerk replies, 'Yes, sir, let me check our records.'

Robert is beside himself, thinking he is too late and a lot of good his praying has done. *Have faith, they say. What rot.*

Clerk says, 'Sir, our records are incomplete. Go to the ICU on the seventh floor and ask the nurses there.'

Robert asks, 'What is ICU?'

'Intensive care unit, sir.'

'Thank you.'

Robert makes his way up to the seventh floor and asks to see Vicki.

Nurse says, 'Sorry, sir, she is in a terrible condition and not expected to recover.'

Robert says, 'I am her fiancé. Can I see her?'

Nurse replies, 'Fiancé? You must be joking. She is a street girl that got pneumonia from having to stay out on the street with nowhere to go when the storm hit. No, sorry, she didn't have a fiancé, not even a close friend. We tried to call the person who took her out the last time, a Mr. Robert Somerset, but he did not bother returning our calls.'

'That's me, but I didn't receive any calls.'

'Is this your telephone number?'

'Yes, except for the last digit. My number ends with a seven, not a one.'

'That must be the reason we couldn't get hold of you. I will let you see her, but only for a minute, and I really mean a minute.'

'Thank you.'

They placed Robert in a gown, and he must wear a facial mask. He was taken to Vicki's bed and allowed to stay for a minute. He is seated near her. Vicki is white without color and breathing through a machine. She is monitored, and the nurse at the end of the bed keeps an eye on the monitor to ensure they give her the best chance to pull through.

Robert says to the nurse at the end of the bed, 'Will she pull through?'

Nurse shakes her head without saying a word.

Robert takes Vicki's hand and can feel the cold that her body had to endure. He cannot see why she did it and decides that God is the only one that can help. He prays to God to help her pull through and asks that He does not take her from him.

Nurse says, 'Sorry, sir, your one minute is up. You will have to leave. We will call you if there is any change in her condition.'

Robert replies, 'Thank you. Please do.'

Robert holds Vicki's hand momentarily and stares into her face and then lets go and walks away when suddenly the nurse at the end of Vicki's bed hits the red alert button, and the siren goes off, and over the loudspeaker, 'CPR, CPR' is broadcasted.

Nurses and doctors quickly run to Vicki's bed, and they rushed in a defibrillator, and the doctor yells, 'All clear!' He places the two pads on Vicki's chest and presses the button. Vicki's body raises itself upwards as the shock goes through her. The doctor looks at the monitor showing her blood pressure and yells out, 'No effect. One more time.' Everyone moves back. The doctor again places the pads on Vicki and sends a charge through her body.

Robert is about ten yards away from the activity and realizes Vicki is in a life-and-death situation and looks at the monitors and sees that Vicki has given up and cannot make it back to him. He stands there not able to do a thing knowing this is it; he has lost Vicki. He sits in a chair and prays to God, asking for His help and intervention.

Doctor says, 'No change. Third and last charge.'

The doctor once again sends a third charge through Vicki, but there is no heartbeat.

Doctor says, 'We can't bring her back. Her heart is not responding. Time of death is 1500 hours after three attempts to restart her heart.' Robert stands there in disbelief, staring at a motionless Vicki and hears, 'She's dead.' He looks as everyone disburses, and only a few people left around Vicki, her body open and lifeless on the bed. A nurse approaches Robert and says, 'Sir, you will have to leave.

There is nothing more we can do for her. We must prepare her for transportation to the morgue, and this will take some time before all of us finish what we have to do and take care of the paperwork.' Robert looks at the nurse in bewilderment and then moves to where Vicki was lying. He leans over her with tears running down his face and takes her hand and kisses her on the lips. The nurse says, 'Please, sir, leave.'

The nurse tugs Robert away and moves with him towards the door.

Robert lets go of Vicki's hand, kisses her again, and wipes his tears from her lifeless face and turns and leaves the ICU ward. He goes down in the lift and sits in the hospital's foyer, trying to fathom out what has happened and bursts into tears and cries uncontrollably. After ten minutes, he controls himself and walks to the car park and drives back to his apartment. As he enters, the telephone rings. He finds out it is Allen on the other end.

Allen says, 'Robert, just checking to see how Vicki is.'

Robert replies, 'She died about a half an hour ago, Allen.'

'I am sorry to hear that. Unfortunately, so will we all.'

'I did everything you instructed me to do. I prayed to God, but a lot of good that did Vicki.'

'Can I come over so we can discuss this face to face?'

'Not now, Allen. I am not in the mood to hear all about the great things regarding God when He won't help Vicki when she needed Him.'

'I think it's better I come over and we can have a cup of coffee and just talk about what is going through your mind now.'

'Not now, Allen. I am too upset to even think straight, let alone hear about Almighty God.'

'I will be over in about twenty minutes.'

Robert sits down in the lounge room and wonders what he is going to do. He rings Tim and Pat and tells them so there is no misinformation going around.

Robert says, 'Hello, Pat, Robert here. Yes, I have located her. Unfortunately, she contracted pneumonia and has died in the local hospital.'

As soon as Robert said died, Pat faints and drops the phone. Tim, who is close by, runs up to her and gets her into a chair. He then picks up the phone and says, 'Who is this?'

Robert replies, 'Robert, Tim.'

Tim asks, 'What has happened? Pat just fainted, and she dropped the phone.'

'I told Pat that Vicki has died of pneumonia.'

'Oh, Robert, I am sorry to hear that. No wonder Pat fainted. That is bad news.'

'Will you phone the others and tell them? I just cannot do it and don't know their telephone numbers.'

'Yes, leave it to me. I will ensure everyone gets the news.'

Shortly afterwards, there is a buzz from the phone, and it's Allen downstairs wanting entry to the building. Robert lets him in, and Allen makes his way up to Robert's apartment. He rings the bell, and Roberts let him in.

Allen says, 'I am sorry about Vicki and believe we should have a discussion about her death.'

Robert replies, 'Really, Allen, there is very little to discuss. I prayed to God to help and allow Vicki to pull through, but He either didn't want her to make it or didn't care since I was not a committed Christian.'

'God has a plan, and what has happened is part of that plan.'

'If He has a plan, then what is it? Can you enlighten me as to what it is?'

'No, because none of us are privileged to know this.'

'So, it is a load of bullshit, isn't it?'

'Just because we don't know doesn't mean it isn't real.'

'Well, Allen, all I know is you said, "Pray to God and He will help you." Yet when I prayed, He did not answer my prayer. He took Vicki from me. That, in my book, is one of two things—He either doesn't exist or doesn't care.'

'He does care, and all I can say to you is He has a plan and have faith in him, and it will turn out better than what you imagined. At present, you are upset over Vicki's death and the position this has left you in with the new acquisition. But I am sure, given time, things will unravel themselves.'

'Thanks for coming around, Allen. I think we have to leave it where we disagree when it comes to God.'

Robert and Allen shake hands, and Allen leaves.

Robert goes to the lounge room and ponders on what he should do.

He has a fashion company without a designer and a contract that must be honored. If he does not comply with the contract, he stands to lose basically all the money he has, which will force him to move into the park and live under a bench himself.

Roberts sits there till nightfall and then goes to bed. At about two in the morning, he has a dream.

Vicki comes to him and says, 'Robert, I am all right now. The Lord has allowed me to return home to heaven, so do not worry about my spirit. It is with the Lord. You must find some young designers and complete the contractual obligation you committed yourself to. Do not blame yourself for my death, as it is part of the Lord's plan and not something He did not intend. It was my time to go, and you must carry on ensuring our contractual commitment is fulfilled. I will be with you always. Do not blame yourself for my death, as it is part of the Lord's plan. I always loved you.'

Robert wakes up abruptly, thinking Vicki is in his room, but realizes it is only a dream. He is in a cold sweat and goes to the bathroom to wipe his forehead. He sits in the lounge room for a minute thinking about what he had dreamt. He could brush it aside and put it down to his active imagination or Vicki truly saying her last words to him. He decides it was the latter and goes back to bed. In the morning, he wakes up and goes off to the MI building and goes through Vicki's notes. She had sketched out her designs for the first fashion show. As he is reading the notes, the staff arrives for work. They all go to their desk until all have arrived. Then Pat approaches Robert.

Pat says, 'We are deeply sorry about what had happened to Vicki, and the only way we believe we can ensure she is not forgotten is to finish what she started.'

Robert replies, 'That is my intention, but it seems she hasn't completed her sketches of all the garments. I will have to bring in some designers to finish the designs, but if I do this, it will not be Vicki's designs but theirs.'

'Vicki had made sketches of the garments we should concentrate on in the first parade and rough sketches of the second one, which we can transcribe into full production sketches.'

'We will still have to have a designer on board to design the various off-the-cuff projects we may get from time to time.'

'Yes, but that would not be urgent, and it will be Vicki's ideas that will make the fashion show.'

Robert asks, 'Mrs. Jones, what do you think? Vicki trusted you and said you knew fashion more than anyone.'

Mrs. Jones replies, 'Look, the name is Emma. I agree with Pat. Vicki gave us enough sketches for the first parade, and we can fill in what was required for the second, as we know her ideas and what she was trying to achieve. If we end up with extra work, then we will need a designer quickly to undertake that task. Hold off advertising for at least a week to enable us to cremate Vicki and attend to the mourning process.'

Robert says, 'All right, I will agree to your suggestions as long as you agree to come to me anytime you think I am off the track.'

Pat says, 'Agreed.'

They all go back to work.

Robert go back to his office.

Robert works for an hour and then receives a telephone call from Roger.

Roger says, 'Robert, I heard about Vicki's death from Pat. I think we should meet to see what changes you want to make to the advertising.'

Robert replies, 'I agree. Are you able to come at two this afternoon?'

Roger says, 'I will be at your office at two.'

Robert thinks about what changes he should make but cannot decide, as it was still early days and they have not decided on who the new designer will be. He thinks of advertising internationally and sees what comes from his enquiries, but keeps it low key for a while until he is ready to give it some thought.

At two, Roger turns up at Robert's office, and Robert greets him with a handshake.

Robert asks, 'What do you think we will have to change, Roger?'

Roger replies, 'Nothing in the first video or second video if you are still soliciting for work and your doors are going to open to the rich and famous. The third video will have to change because, no doubt, the designs will not be Vicki's but someone else's, whoever the new designer is.'

'The team thinks that Vicki had left enough sketches and notes for us to put on a fashion show as she wanted. We will need the new designer to take on any additional work that may come in through our advertising. So what do you recommend?'

'We should run the first two advertisements as planned, but hold off on the third until you can get a designer on board.'

'I agree, but don't commence the ads for two weeks.' If anyone asks, we will tell them we are just bedding down the acquisition.'

'That will be all right, as we will need to examine which countries we are advertising in and which will be the best time to place the advertisements to gain maximum impact.'

'That will suit me and give me enough time to get my head around all the issues and what is happening with Town Hall and the MI building.'

'Town Hall intends to vote on the acquisition of the building at their next meeting, which is in two days' time. We have done a lot of work on trying to convince the mayor and alderman that it would not be in their interest to throw ratepayers' money away on a building when the move is towards digital, and the community already has a library that is functional. They seem to buy the idea, but it still must go to a meeting to decide what they intend to do. I have been given the right to make a presentation to the council before the vote and have got community support not to buy this building for a library.'

'Telephone the details to my secretary as to where and when the meeting is taking place, and I will attend with you to answer any question that may crop up.'

'I will ring through the details tomorrow.'

Robert shakes hands with Roger and escorts him out of his office.

He comes back into his office and sits down at his desk to review some papers when his secretary advises him that the hospital is on the telephone.

Robert says, 'Hello, can I help you? Robert Somerset speaking.'

Hospital replies, 'Mr. Somerset, we're not sure whether you are the best person to speak to regarding Vicki Santana.'

'What about her?'

'Well, the coroner has released her body for burial, and we were going to arrange for a pauper's funeral for her. We noticed they listed you as her fiancé and thought to call you before proceeding to complete the arrangement.'

'Thank you for calling, but I will handle the funeral arrangements myself. Where do I direct the funeral parlor to go to collect Vicki's body? I will take care of everything.'

The hospital gives Robert the details, and he writes them down carefully, repeating the address to make sure he has it right.

Robert looks up on the internet and speaks to a few funeral parlors before deciding on one that he thinks would handle the matter with dignity. He gives them the details, and they say they would collect the body the next day and that they could attend to the service and cremation next Monday. Robert agrees and makes an appointment to see the funeral director at his chapel the next day at eleven o'clock.

The next day, Robert goes to work and then drives to the funeral parlor and meets with the funeral director.

Robert says, 'I need to book a chapel for Monday that can hold about twenty to thirty people. I also need to locate a cemetery that will intern the ashes with a plaque with Vicki's name on it and inscribed "Vicki Santana, Always in Our Hearts".'

Funeral director replies, 'I am sure we can meet your requirements, sir. Will you follow me so you can select a coffin and flower arrangements?'

The funeral director leads Robert to a room that contained about fifteen different coffins and large pictures of flower arrangements.

Funeral director says, 'As you can see, we have several coffins. Some are plain and economical, and some are very expensive. Now, this one is quite comfortable and may suit the occasion.'

Robert asks, 'How do you know they are comfortable? Have you tried them out, or has one of your clients returned and gave you a rundown?'

'Very good, sir. No, we say comfortable referring to softness and size.'

'Does it matter if the person is dead? They will not feel it, will they?'

'No sir, but if the size is right, it adds to the dignity of the funeral.'

'I guess you're right. What about this coffin?'

'This is one of our mid-range coffins suitable for cremations and is the most popular coffin. It looks good and is ideal for an open service.'

'We will have a closed service but a viewing the day before for those who want to attend.'

'Yes, we can arrange for that. Leave all the arrangements to us. If there are any problems, we will get back to you.' Both men walk back to the funeral director's office.

Funeral director says, 'My recommendation regarding the interning of the ashes is to have this to the local cemetery, which is not too far from here.'

He shows Robert some pictures, and Robert agrees.

Robert says, 'Let me check with the minister whether he will be available on Monday.'

Robert telephones Allen and says, 'Allen, Robert here. Sorry to interrupt you, but I am with the funeral director completing plans for

Vicki's funeral and would like you to hold the service if you are available on Monday?'

Allen replies, 'I would be glad to do it, Robert, and, yes, I am available at eleven o'clock on Monday. Will that fit in with your plans?'

Funeral director says, 'Yes, that will be fine.'

Robert replies, 'Yes, Allen, that will be fine.'

Allen says, 'I will have to meet with you on Saturday to discuss the type of service you want. Are you available at around two in the afternoon?'

Robert replies, 'I am not sure what we have to discuss, but sure, come on over at two.'

Robert hangs up and says to the funeral director, 'Will that be all, or are there other formalities that need to be attended to?'

Funeral director replies, 'Well, there is. As I understand, the person we are cremating is a pauper and died with no money. Who is going to pay for the cremation and plaque?'

Robert replies, 'I see, a matter of money. Well, our company, which runs several nursing homes, has over time sent you quite a lot of business, and you have the hide to confront me with who is going to pay the bill.'

'Sir, don't misunderstand me. I am not trying to get you to pay this minute, just wanting to note on our records who will pay the bill so we can send you an invoice.'

'Send it to my office. I will take care of it immediately. Is that it? Thank you for your help.'

Robert gets up and walks out of the funeral director's office and drives to the MI building.

The staff are all busy at work finishing what they wanted to do for the day.

Robert approaches them and says, 'The coroner has released Vicki's body for cremation, which will be held on Monday at eleven o'clock. We will close the office on that day. All are welcome to attend the service at the North Side Chapel. Rev. Allen Sheppard will handle the service. We will have a small gathering after the service where finger food will be served and drinks.'

Robert waits around answering questions and then moves to go home.

15

Mayor says, 'This is the last item on the agenda for today. It is to vote on the proposal to acquire the Marque International building on a forced sale basis, offering the existing owners $1 million for the property. The floor is open to discussions on this matter.'

Alderman, representing ward 1, says, 'Mr. Mayor, I move that the acquisition proceeds without delay.'

Mayor replies, 'We cannot proceed with your recommendation without allowing the parties who oppose the acquisition to state their case. We have Mr. Roger Norton, who is a resident of this ward and represents the new owners of the building. Mr. Norton?'

Roger says, 'Thank you, Mayor. I know it has been a long meeting for everyone, so I will make my representation short. Town Hall has within the district, several community libraries and all but for the one in town center has been operating on a reduced patronage. In fact, compared to five years ago, there has been a 50 percent reduction in the number of people using the services of the library. In comparison, the digital library has over the same period increased its operation by 50 percent. With the reduction of patronage in the libraries, council has reduced its staff in those centers by 50 percent, which has been a substantial saving for our community. The increase in the digital volume has not necessitated an increase in staff, as the books are described as electronic books and are sourced and controlled electronically by the registered member. Council, I understand, will consider in the next few months as to what it intends to do with all the libraries and come up with a plan to phase them out and possibly sell the premises. I believe council will make an expensive acquisition to house a library when, in fact, the move is to a digital base and not a physical hard copy base. Council will, under the circumstances, be wasting community money, which could be better used for upgrading current facilities and roads for the community, rather than wasting money.'

Mayor says, 'Thank you, Mr. Norton. Are there questions? No. Then I present our next speaker, Mr. Robert Somerset, the current owner of the MI building. Mr. Somerset?'

Robert replies, 'Thank you, Mayor. I support Roger in what he has said to you all and would like to add that this building currently houses an internationally recognized company. Yes, its' brand has been tarnished recently in that it went into receivership because of poor management and not because of inferior designs. We have a chance to again resurrect this iconic brand and bring and establish it here, attracting overseas interest and trade to our city. To forcefully acquire the building will remove the name from a building, as the move to alternative offices will not give naming rights to the building and loss of recognition. It will also mean that within a short period, council will have to close the building as you intend to do with some of your other libraries owing to the move to digital books and sell the premises, which could result in a loss. Council is currently receiving an income from the building in the form of rates and other fees levied on commercial businesses, which it would not receive if it acquired the building. I can only urge you to reconsider your intention of acquiring the building. I would request, considering the substantial risk that council faces, that the names of the aldermen who voted for the proposal be published so that when the time comes to sell the building, the community knows which aldermen were at the center of causing the loss, even though the risk had been clearly presented to them.'

Mayor says, 'This being a public meeting, the names of the aldermen that will vote for the proposals are recorded and can be printed in the local papers. That is a matter for the paper's editor and not for council. I take it that there are no other speakers on this matter. No. We will therefore call for the vote. Those in favor of council acquiring the MI building, please raise your hands. None are raised. Those against, please raise your hands. Twelve hands are recorded. The motion to acquire the MI building is unanimously rejected. There being no other matters before council, I close the meeting.'

Robert and Roger go up to the mayor and are congratulated. They stay a while talking to other members of council and eventually leave and go their own way home.

16

Claudia Simpson is a young designer trying to make it on her own. She could not afford commercial premises and runs her business from her apartment. When she has to see clients, she would meet them at their homes or their office or at a cafe to discuss their requirements. She had won the right to design for a fashion parade in Paris, beating several larger fashion houses, including Charles Henry, who did not take it lightly and began proceedings against her for theft of copyright saying she stole his designs.

They brought proceedings before the court, and she does not have enough money to hire a lawyer to defend herself in the action brought against her.

She not only has little money but also does not know what to do or what the procedure is for defending the action brought against her. She contacts all the fashion houses to see if they have any work available so she could earn some money for rent and food. All that she called are not interested in dealing with her, as they do not want to start a legal war with Charles Henry or get him offside, as he has a reputation of being a ruthless businessman who would do anything in getting his way, including resorting to extortion and lying.

She remembers Pat O'Brien and, as a last resort, telephones her and asks if she could come and speak to her. Pat agrees, and that day, she goes and sees Pat at the MI building.

Pat says, 'Claudia, it has been a while since we have spoken. You must be in a desperate state for you to now telephone me.'

Claudia replies, 'Pat, I don't know whether you have kept up with what has happened in the industry, but I have recently won the right to present a fashion parade in Paris.'

'Yes, I know about it, and congratulations. It is good to see an up-and-coming designer make it. So, what is the problem? You don't seem too enthusiastic about it.'

'I don't know what to do.'

'About what? About the design, the venue? I don't understand.'

Claudia tells Pat the complete story of how Charles Henry is trying to ruin her and claim her designs.

Pat says, 'I really can't help you other than mention it to the boss. He is looking for a new designer, but you are self-employed, which would make it difficult to hire you. Look, I will mention it to him after Vicki's funeral and see what he says. Are the designs yours, or did you take some ideas from Charles Henry's company?'

Claudia replies, 'I never knew he was bidding for the right to put the parade on, nor did I know what he was designing. I kept to my own designs and won the right to the fashion parade purely on merit. Now I am finding myself being sued and do not know what to do or how to defend myself. They are going to keep the legal action going until I am ruined.'

'I will mention it to Robert on Tuesday. He has enough to attend to with Vicki's funeral and running this business and his own.'

'I will attend Vicki's funeral. I was her best friend. We were very close. I will see you there.'

Claudia and Pat stand up, and Pat escorts Claudia to the front door and says goodbye.

Pat comes back into her office and sits down at her desk and thinks, *I wish someday that bastard would get it in the neck for what he has done to so many people. He shouldn't be allowed to get away with it.*

Pat packs up and goes on home.

17

On Saturday, at two in the afternoon, Allen comes up to Robert's apartment and is let in.

Allen says, 'I have to discuss the type of service we are going to have for Vicki. Who are going to be the speakers, and what prayers are going to be said?'

Robert replies, 'Well, let's keep the service to a minimum, and all those who want to say a word about Vicki can get up and speak about her.'

'What prayers are to be said for her, Robert?'

'Allen, I am going to leave all of that in your hands, as I really don't know much about praying, and as I already have spoken to you, I don't think the Lord cares too much about those who pray to Him.'

'Don't prejudge the Lord, as He has a plan, which you will get to know about in His good time. I am sure.'

'I will leave it to you to conduct the best service you can under the circumstances, as you know the problems that were associated with Vicki both past and present.'

'Have you got any photos of Vicki so we can place a picture of her on the coffin?'

'No, not one except the photo taken for her employment ID card.'

'That will have to do if that is the only one you have. I will get it enlarged and placed on her coffin for Monday.'

Robert goes and gets Vicki's ID card and gives it to Allen.

They chat a while, and Allen leaves and to see if he can arrange for the photo to be enlarged. Robert escorts Allen to the front door of the apartment, and Allen leaves.

Robert goes and see his parents, as he did not want to be on his own. He gets his keys and wallet and goes down to the basement car park and drives off to his parents.

An hour later, he pulls up outside his parents' home and goes on inside.

His parents, Catherine, and Richard Somerset are in the lounge room watching television. They get up as soon as Robert walks in and switches the television off.

Catherine says, 'Well, it has been a while since we have seen you, Robert.'

Richard asks, 'What have you been up to? How is that romance going with your friend in the park?'

Robert replies, 'Unfortunately, she died of pneumonia with the cold whether we have had.'

Richard says, 'I am sorry to hear that. I thought you might bring her home for us to meet her.'

Robert replies, 'So did I, but God had different thoughts and took her from me.'

Catherine says, 'Same as your sister. She was taken from us unexpectedly. It took us a long time to get over it, which we never have. We have accepted it but still think about her.'

Robert says, 'I now can understand what you two went through when that happened.'

Richard asks, 'When is the funeral?'

Robert replies, 'Monday at eleven.'

Catherine and Richard could see that their son was deeply hurt over the loss of Vicki and therefore does not mention her again. They change the conversation to work and tell Robert what they have done since the last time he visited.

They have dinner with him, and Robert advises them about what has happened with the acquisition of the new nursing home group and how it has been incorporated into the parent company.

Robert's visit ends at about eight, and he leaves to return to his apartment.

18

Sunday is a relaxing day. Robert tries to rest and not think too much about Monday's service but keeps thinking of the good times with Vicki. He goes to church as Vicki would have insisted if she had been alive, and Allen would also like to see Robert. He changes his clothes and walks to the church. After a twenty-minute walk, he arrives at the church, and Allen meets Robert at the front door, welcoming him and the other parishioners as they enter. Robert has some words with Allen, who moves in and sits down in one pew and waits for the service to begin. While sitting there, two ladies come to his pew to sit alongside of him. He doesn't know them and therefore doesn't start a conversation with them. He moves left to allow them to sit down without having to crawl over him.

After ten minutes, Allen begins the service, and all stand up for the first hymn, which is then followed by reading from the Bible.

Allen then comes to the pulpit for the sermon.

Allen says, 'several you have approached me and have been honest enough to tell me you are having difficulty in spiritually finding God, communicating with Him, reaching Him, and even feeling His presence. You feel as if God does not want to have a relationship with you, and you end up back on your own, not knowing what to do. Most of you say you have been with God for many years and do not understand why suddenly this is happening. Others are saying they are relatively new Christians and do not seem to find or relate to God's presence.

'I can for most advise you that God wants to have a relationship with you on His terms and not on yours. Many come to God on a bargaining basis. "If You give me this, I will do that for you." This never works, and you can save your time and energy if this is your approach. However, I believe this is not the case here.

To come to Jesus, you must declare Him the Creator of the world, the one who died for your sins on the cross and who has been resurrected from the dead by God and the ruler of this world. You must accept He is the Almighty and does control heaven and earth. You come to Him on your knees (in your heart) having faith in Him and genuinely asking for forgiveness of your sins.

'At times of trouble and during trials, the belief and faith part becomes the hardest thing to accept, as most times you have told me, it seems as if God has stepped back and has left you to the ravaging of the world. He does not come close to you as if He has gone on a holiday, leaving you to your faith or your own ingenuity.

You ask what you should do when this happens, as you still want a relationship with God, but it seems He does not want to know you. 'As I have previously advised you in other sermons, God steps back and gives you the freedom to explore the degree of faith you have in Him. He wants you to know whether your faith is built on sand or on solid rock. The longer the trials go on, the harder it is to maintain faith in Jesus, as He seems not to be there or caring enough to make His presence felt. He does not need to do this, as He already knows what's in your heart. But He wants you to find this out for yourself. Possibly to make sure when the time comes, and He challenges you on this, that there can be no misunderstandings or conflicts of opinion.

Many lose faith if there is no immediate resolution to their problem or turn on God when some disaster strikes them, such as a loved one is struck down, dies, or sustains an injury. The degree of faith you have in Him is showed to you through these unexpected events or sudden disasters in your life.

'When Jesus walked the earth, He had many times referred to Himself as the "Light" and/or the "Truth", and these two concepts are synonymous with God. So, when you speak of God, you speak of the truth and light and not darkness, which represents Satan. 'When something happens in your life that causes you to question God's actual intentions, go back in your mind as to what has transpired and not to fabricate the facts or try to blame God. You hear from people all the time declaring, "If there was a God, this would not have happened, which proves there is no God." They either don't know what they are saying or refuse to accept that God gives mankind the freedom to do what they please, and sometimes, this leads to terrible things happening to those on earth, like your young daughter is raped or killed at the hands of a stranger, or your neighbor or you lose all of your finances in a stupid financial deal or gamble it away on a horse race. Your entire world is turned upside down in a split second, and you find yourself alone in a crisis. 'In these instances, many Christians pray to God for His help, guidance, and are encouraged by His presence and the help He provides them while answering their prayers. But as we have stated at the beginning of the sermon, this seems to come to a halt quickly, leaving you in no man's land, not knowing what to do. The obvious is still to maintain your faith in the Lord, but this, most times, is easier said than done.

'This has happened to many prominent men, as stated in the Bible. Look at what happened when Abraham was told by God to leave his father and enter Canaan. On his journey, he found himself alone, and none of his prays were answered by God. His family was dying from thirst, and something had to be done. God would not speak to Abraham or come close to him. Abraham decided he had no choice but to go into Egypt and risk the wrath of the Pharaoh. He entered Egypt telling Pharaoh that his wife was his sister, and they fed Pharaoh this lie until he took ill and forced Abraham out of Egypt.

"I am the Truth," said the Lord, and it is the truth that you must maintain. You know what has transpired. You know what God has stated to you in the Bible. You know who He is, and that He is with you, and it is your faith in Him that will carry you through these crises. The truth is what you should concentrate on and believing in Him, for this tells you that God will lead you eventually out of the wilderness to better times.

'We have been told that Christians were fed to the lions in the Colosseum. You may say, "Where was the truth there?" Men directed this to happen and not God. That His people were treated in this manner and forced to adhere to so great a suffering would have horrified the Lord, but He did not intervene because He gave mankind a free will. The lions attacked the bodies of those Christians. Their belief in Christ is not held in the body of mankind but in their soul, and they believed in the resurrected Christ, for that was the truth. The lions may have devoured the body but not the soul, which maintained the truth and faith in Christ. So, you, too, must maintain your faith in the truth.

'When you come to a problem, you know the truth and must therefore maintain your perspective of the truth, for in doing this, you will maintain your faith in Christ. If you feel Jesus has abandoned you, then concentrate on the facts of your trial and seek the truth regarding the aspects of it and what God would do in this situation. Maintain the truth as the Bible tells you and your faith in God and you will find the Lord has not abandoned you, but He is there watching over you. You will not be allowed to make the wrong move or decision, as He will guide and nurture you through it.'

'The truth will carry you through, for you know it is right. God may step back and give you room and time to think and allow you to question your belief, but if you concentrate on the truth that is before you and not the lies, then no one can persuade you otherwise or no snake can tell you otherwise unless you are seeking something other than the truth. Remember, God knew Satan would test Adam and Eve as He knows you will be tested.'

'God will never leave you. This is His promise. This is the truth as stated in the Bible and by Jesus, no matter what your circumstances are.'

'Now, we have many parishioners who are not Christians but still come to church every Sunday, and they are their own man for the next six and a half days of the week. They mostly find it hard to rely on God, for most times, they are their own god and not followers of Jesus Christ. Here, the truth is according to what they want to hear and not what the Bible says. Matters of divorce or marriage are followed, not what the Bible declares but what society dictates, yet they declare themselves to be good Christians. When it suits them, they vote to pass their rights on to the State to act rather than stand up for their Christian religion and values, and yet they declare themselves to be good Christians even when they follow their interpretation of the Bible, which is contrary to and oppose the teachings of Jesus.'

'The argument stated is "I believe in God and have always been a good Christian. On this occasion, I will vote . . .", which is contrary to what the Bible teaches, yet they declare themselves to be a "good Christians." So, they follow an interpretation of the Bible, which is populous and worldly, rather than the teaching of Jesus Christ, no doubt a worldly interpretation to suit the occasion. As time goes on, they continue along this path with the inevitable result that they have rewritten the Bible to a degree that it totally follows the world's interpretation and not Christ's teachings.

'By concentrating on the truth, it will lead you along the correct path and not one that is falsely declared to you by Satan's snake. Remember, Satan does not want you to have a relationship with Jesus at all. He is there to throw you off your path to faith in Christ, and he is an expert in doing this. He most probably is the one that caused the situation you are experiencing and will declare to you that this would never have happened if there was a true God. You must see the truth and, through it, understand what is happening and have faith in God that He will make sure the outcome is as He had planned and not according to Satan's manipulation.

'Remember, Peter refused to accept the truth when he openly declared he did not know Jesus and denied he was a Christian. He denied the truth and wept when he realized what he had done.

'In these times, take a moment and pray to God. See what He does and evaluate what transpires from your prayers. If you cannot see why this has happened, then pray to God and ask for His wisdom and comfort and declare your continuous faith in Him. He will not leave you or let you down.

'You always remember that Satan's purpose is to get you to a stage where you decide his alternative is the better one, or you lose faith in God and turn to the dark side. He wants you to give up your claim to eternal life and bend your knee before him, declaring him to be king and not Jesus.

'God wants you to have faith in Jesus and through your faith, have eternal life. The truth is what you must seek at all times even if the trouble at hand, is insurmountable and unclear and seek the path the Lord will direct you on to, bearing in mind that those around you will immediately turn on God and try to tell you things that are contrary to your belief and have you do the work of Satan.

'The disciples all fled God when the soldiers came for Him, as will be the case when you are in trouble. Your friends will not want to hear about what God has to say on the matter, but will be critical of Him and not of Satan. If you seek support, you will find a few avenues and, on most occasions, you will get negative responses from friends and relatives, for they do not believe in Christ.

'The truth will always lead you back to God, and if in times of doubt or the happening of a heart-wrenching event in your life, then by concentrating on the truth of God during unclear or indecisive times, will always see you through these problems, for He has given you this promise, which is the only one you can rely on.

'The other matters raised regarding the truth is when you as a Christian are confronted by untruths or statements by a non- believer who has made either accusations against the Christian faith or inflammatory comments about Christ. We all have been in this situation with the dirty joke about Jesus being the most common remark. The question is, as a Christian, what do you do about it?

This is not a simple question to answer, as it depends on your relationship to the person and the environment you are in. Most people in these situations walk away without making a comment. I personally cannot do this and say, "Not another religious joke. I would have thought after the last half a dozen, you would give them up," and then walk away. In times like this, it is not worth starting a fight or an argument, but showing your displeasure and ending the conversation there.

'The other times when this occurs are when you are at a meeting, and they formulated a plan to benefit from handling lies or dishonest transactions. At times like these, you should make your thoughts known and the fact that you object to the intention to tell lies to clients or falsely represent fact and declare that you thought the people about you had more credibility and honesty about them rather than having to resort to these tactics. Your position may put you in conflict with others, but you should hold your Christian beliefs and not have a foot in both camps.

'Remember, Satan will challenge your belief of the truth, and if you refuse to give this up, then he will see that others do his work for him. You will find yourself in compromising situations, which could force you to resign your job or be dismissed on cropped up lies. To hold on to the

Truth will never be easy, but is always rewarding and always have God's blessing.

'Another matter that I should alert you to is the feeling that God has placed you in a compromising situation and has walked away, leaving you with a problem or to be blamed for something. For example, you may have lost your job for refusing to alter your belief, or you may know you are heading for a financial problem and pray to the Lord for help. Your situation may be genuine, desperate, and through no cause of your own, you pray for the Lord's intervention and help. Without this, you will find yourself in an embarrassing situation, and this could discredit you as an individual and reflect poorly on you as a Christian.

'I am told that the situation becomes more desperate and the prayers unanswered with the person not knowing what to do and eventually, through no fault of their own over time, realize that God has abandoned them to their own resources, which are limited. You should never believe that God would leave you in such a situation like that after being told, "I will never leave you," yet here you are on your own looking down the barrel of a disaster. What should you do when you consider that you have been told a lie by Jesus?

'Most people in this situation would abandon God and make their own decisions, as was the case of Abraham, who made the journey to Egypt during the great famine after his prayers were not answered and many of his household were dying from starvation on route.

'Will you tell God He is a fraud and a liar and that you have made a mistake in following His teachings only to find out that He doesn't support His followers in time of need but ignores them when they need Him? Are you going to change direction and move to Satan's camp and imbue yourselves with assets and consumables to fill the void of Christ?

'You, too, will have to confront this situation as many have told me they have had to, and many have decided after a long period of isolation and separation from the Lord that it is not worth having faith in a God that does this to His people and who is a Charlotte. They still believe in Him but will not have faith in Him, as He does not assist them, answer any of their prayers, doesn't make His presence felt or known to them, or in fact is non-existent. It is a situation that is described to me that is contrary to the teachings in the Bible—remember "I will never leave you," and yet He does and leaves the person in a situation of disbelief that Jesus would do such a thing. Yet many have described this to me, and some of you are sitting in the pews now agreeing with what I have said and are witnesses to this. You believe you have become an Israelite forced to walk the desert for forty years until you die and understand how they must have felt.'

'Why? Why has God done this to you after promising He will never leave you? Is He now deciding to join Satan and become an outright liar, telling you one thing and doing something else? I do not think so. After evicting Satan from heaven, there must be another purpose, motive, or reason.

'We, of course, are not told as to why God does this. We can only try to assume, and when our time comes to be in His presence in heaven, ask Him personally as to why He abandoned you, or did He?

'I believe the answer lies in two areas. Jesus while on the cross was left on His own bearing our sins with the Father turning His face away from Him. "My God, my God, why have You so forsaken Me?" This must have been an awful situation for Him to confront and never had Jesus experienced this before. I believe when you find yourself alone, without God's presence, you are experiencing some of what Jesus went through while He was hanging on the cross. You, too, must come to your final stage of being tested, as was Jesus. The difference with you is that Jesus promised not to leave you, and He hasn't but does not make His presence felt or known to you as He promised, and you are expected to accept His promise and rely on it. A test of the truth and, in turn, faith. As Jesus's faith was tested on the cross, so now yours is being tested.

'The second point here is that Jesus did not have the Holy Spirit with Him. God turned from Him, whereas you have the Holy Spirit within you to guide you through these tough times, to strengthen and guide you. He did not have this. So, what should you do?

'It comes back to the truth we have been seeking. The truth is Jesus. The light. If you find yourself not able to relate to or find Jesus spiritually, then you must relate back to the truth, the teachings of the Bible. If Jesus is not there, then do not pursue Him, as He will reveal Himself to you when He is ready. Concentrate on the truth, His teachings, the facts of the situation, and what the Bible tells you. Make your mind up as to what you are going to do based on the teachings of the Bible and adhere to this plan, as you know it to be in line with your faith in Jesus Christ. If you stay strong on this path without deviation, and this may be hard to do as one cannot contemplate the number of logs that are going to be thrown across your path to ensure you slip up. The road on which you are traveling will be dangerous. However, while it may seem a lonely road, it will not be. Jesus will be there with you, and this is where the faith aspect comes in. You must have faith that so long as you are abiding by His teachings and following the truth that He will ensure you are protected, guided, and directed to a good outcome showing the Lord and yourself that you can hold on to your faith in extreme circumstances, and abide by His teachings. You of all can be trusted to do this.

'In my belief, you have reached a point in your life where your faith is being tested and tested under extreme circumstances, and in most cases, if you adhere to your faith, then this will be your final major test. If you don't, you may abandon your faith and never come back to this point again and never hold faith in Jesus again, only believe in Him and not have faith that He will support you in times like these. The test is real and has been described by many to me with a lot not able to endure it. Some end up being Christians for an hour on Sundays and thereafter, their own masters. Others endure the test and base their faith in solid rock and will never leave the faith.

'If confronted with such a situation, be strong and know you are special to be selected for such a trial and hold on to your faith in Jesus, whatever happens and whatever confronts you. Pray constantly for guidance, wisdom, and the Lord's support. Seek the truth.'

'Let us pray...'

19

On Monday, Vicki's friends gather at the chapel to remember her. The coffin is already in the chapel when Robert arrives, and the flower arrangements are on top of the coffin, and they look stunning. On top of the coffin is a picture of Vicki, which has been provided by Allen.

Everyone takes their seats, and Allen begins the service.

He describes Vicki's life and what went on with the business and her husband and his involvement with drugs and gambling and her life in the park.

Many that are there are crying and find it hard to accept her tragic life and that she was so young when she died.

He then asks if anyone wants to come up and say a few words about Vicki.

No one stands up, not even Robert, who still blames himself for Vicki's death. She would still be alive if only he had not told her to move out to the Park Royal. But he could not bring himself to get up and tell her friends the truth, that it was his fault and how much he loved her and that they were going to get married.

Allen says, 'Vicki was a religious girl who believed in God and had faith in Jesus Christ even when she was under the park bench trying to remain warm and out of the rain. She knew she was in God's hands and doing his work.'

'Each of us must die someday, but in Vicki's case, we consider it was too early, as she had much to live for and achieve and could have become a recognized designer on the world stage. But this was not meant to be, and God decided it was her time to go back home to Him, to heaven. She had completed all the tasks that were designated to her on this earth, and so her life was ended.

'Most of us think we are here on the earth to do as we want to do. Free spirits, as they say, and not consider or care about the real purpose as to why we are here.'

'We are here to serve God in whatever capacity He chooses and to have faith in Him to see us through life until He calls us back home. 'Vicki knew this and did the Lord's work. It was not easy for her.'

'She was threatened by men who could have killed her, along with her husband. She was deprived of a roof over her head and sought refuge under the stars. She had no money to buy food yet found all that she needed in garbage tins and, sometimes, from charities and some good folks who were kind enough to give her their leftovers and scraps from their table.'

'Vicki believed. Her faith in God was stronger and more important than Satan's offerings and refused to sell herself to any man for a quick profit or do as the world does in these circumstances by lying and cheating to get personal gain at the expense of others.'

'She found a friend in Robert, who was a Good Samaritan, who took her in and tried to get her back on her feet. She went back to the trade she knew and was ready to tackle the world stage in design when she was struck down again with pneumonia and died from a heart attack because of her deteriorating health.'

'No doubt all of us who knew Vicki find this very hard to accept, and she leaves a deep hole in our hearts, which we cannot find comfort for, other than through the powers of our Lord Jesus Christ.'

"Some of you here today are not Christians and do not have the belief or faith that Vicki had. While Christ gave you a free will to decide your own destiny, I can only warn you of the dire situation you are in. Should it be your time to pass on, then you will not have eternal life but will end up with the other cheats and robbers in camp.

You will not be given the chance of even having a glimpse of heaven, but will go to hell for a thousand years. These, unfortunately, are the grim facts of life.

'So I ask those in this situation to accept Christ and ask Him to help you in becoming a true believer like Vicki. If you need personal help, I am more than happy to meet with you and discuss your situation . . .'

'Let us pray . . .'

The service ends with the curtain being drawn in front of the coffin and everyone standing looking on and no doubt considering Allen's comments about Vicki.

Everyone moves next door to the chapel, into a private room, where hand food and refreshments were served.

Allen goes to where Robert is standing.

Allen asks, 'Was the service appropriate?'

Robert replies, 'Yes, it was very good. I am, unfortunately, going to come and see you about the last part of your sermon.'

'Take your time. No doubt it is private and difficult to talk about.'

'You're right there, but I don't know where to go to find some peace or relief. I feel guilty as I cause Vicki's death.'

'When do you want to meet? In a week or two?'

'In about one hour in your office.'

'Sorry, I have another matter to attend to shortly and won't be free until three or four o'clock today. Why don't I come to your apartment when I have finished, and we can talk?'

'That would suit me fine. I will see you there. Thank you for taking care of the service.'

Robert goes off to see the funeral director to pay him and stays to talk to other people there and, as the crowd thins out, leaves the function room and makes his way home.

Robert sits and watches a bit of television and dozes off on the lounge when the security buzzer rings. Allen is waiting downstairs, requiring entry to the building. Robert presses the button to release the door, and Allen is in Robert's apartment within a few minutes.

Robert says, 'Thank you for coming.'

Allen replies, 'A pleasure. What's on your mind?'

Robert says, 'In your service this morning, you gave a good outline of Vicki's life, but there was an obvious gap between when she was with me and when she got pneumonia and died.'

'I am to blame for her death.'

Allen says, 'Aren't you being dramatic?'

Robert replies, 'No. I was concerned about marrying Vicki, and afterwards when she got a reputation as a designer, she might meet someone in the fashion industry that she might like better, and then we have to go through a divorce. I recommended she go to my other apartment and live there for a while, on her own, and see if she still feels the same way about me afterwards. But it appears she misunderstood me and went back to where she came from—namely, the park. If she had not, she would be alive now.'

'So, what you are telling me, you also controlled the weather and arranged for a blizzard to come in unexpectedly, which went for four days.'

'No, I can't control the weather.'

'Then don't you think that was an act of God? You may have had an indifference, but that did not give Vicki her pneumonia. It was the icy winds and rain that did that. If you knew where she was, you would have gone and tried to convince her to go to your apartment. But since you could not find her, you couldn't do anything. Robert, you must recognize this is God's world, and you have been placed here to serve Him. He has a plan for you, and your life will flow according to His plan.'

'I sure miss her and wished it never happened.'

'Why? Because you now find a lot of time on your hands to sit and ponder the course the world has taken or is heading?'

'No, not really. Work keeps me busy enough, but I sit and think about what happened and what I could have done to make it turn out differently.'

'Of course, we all think that, but the Lord guides us to where

He wants us to be. That is why I am trying to get you to believe in God and have faith in Him and have a relationship with Him—that you know it is His will and not yours that is governing what is happening.'

'I guess you are right. I will give it some thought and catch up with you soon. I appreciate you taking the time to talk to me. It hasn't eased the ache in my heart but has made things a lot clearer in my head.'

'Good, and I will see you on Sunday in church?'

'Vicki and I will be there. I will light a candle for her.'

'I will see you at least there.'

Both men get up and walk to the front door. They shake hands, and Robert opens the front door and lets Allen out.

20

Robert goes to the MI building to see if there are any outstanding issues to be attended to and to make sure all the staff are occupied. Emma Jones and Pat approach him, who ask if they can see him for a minute.

Emma says, 'We have made some enquiries as to the number of models that are going to be available in Paris with the view of booking some for our fashion parade in Paris. We know it is still some time away, but these things have to be booked in advance.'

'What we have found out is that the word has already gotten around that you have acquired the fashion business and that you are determined to honor the contract and put on your two shows.'

'What the other fashion houses have done is sign up all the known models for their catwalks, which will leave us with no models to show off our designs.'

Robert says, 'That is easy to resolve. We will get you, Emma, Pat, and two more to show off our wares.'

Emma replies, 'Yes, I would do it if I was twenty years younger and twenty kilos lighter.'

Pat says, 'Tim will never let me go to Paris on my own and especially get back on the catwalk.'

Robert asks, 'You mean you were a model some years back?'

Pat replies, 'Yes, I started my career as a model and then progressed to other segments of the industry, including design and manufacture.'

Robert asks, 'What about our local models? Will they be available?'

Pat replies, 'Any model that is experienced here and overseas will be booked, no doubt, by Charles Henry, so we cannot source anyone from here.'

Robert sits for a moment and then says, 'Hang on, we are looking at this the wrong way. We are an old traditional company who has given many opportunities to models throughout the world. Why should we stop now? We can set down the criteria we believe are necessary for a person, male or female, to be a successful model. We will interview young people and select the number we want and train them to be models. We will guarantee payment for the next two years, and we will get them work outside, so come Paris, they will be trained and ready to become internationally recognized models.'

Pat says, 'What a great idea.'

Emma adds, 'I agree, and I am sure we can get some of the world-renowned models to drop in and give the young ones some tips when they are in the country.'

Pat says, 'Well, that means we have to sacrifice our careers as models for the new generation. Thank God you came up with a solution. This one had me beat.'

Robert says, 'All right, set up a plan as to what we need to train a model. There will have to be an emphasis on the practical side, as this is one of those jobs where you are trained on-site doing what is required. Set up a training schedule, and we will review it in the next couple of days.'

Pat adds, 'There is another matter we would like to talk to you about.'

Robert asks, 'Can it wait? I am late for a meeting.'

Pat replies, 'Not really. I said I would get back to this person today.'

Robert asks, 'What's the problem?'

Pat replies, 'There is a young designer—her name is Claudia Simpson—that has had some success on the world stage of design.

'She has won a minor competition in Paris recently. Unfortunately, she was competing against Charles Henry's group, who now has begun proceedings against her for breach of copyright.'

Robert asks, 'Well, did she steal the designs?'

Pat replies, 'Knowing the girl as I do, I would say no. She is an honest girl and an up-and-coming designer just making a reputation for herself, but as usual, she does not have the money to fight Henry and his dirty tactics.'

Robert asks, 'What is it with this bloke that he does this to people?'

Pat replies, 'He has used these tactics a few times with people who get in his way and doesn't care about them or what it will do to their reputation. Don't be too surprised if he tries this with us just when we are going to the fashion show.'

Robert says, 'Yes, that is a thought. What do you want me to do about it? We are after a designer, but not one that is going to be discredited.'

Pat asks, 'Can you have a word with her? She is scared and doesn't know which way to go or what to do.'

Robert replies, 'Surely she can get a lawyer with the prize she got from the fashion show she just won?'

Pat says, 'Yes, but Henry has already advised her she better have ten times that amount, as he intends to put her under and ensure her reputation is thrashed.'

Robert says, 'A real nice block, isn't he?'

Pat says, 'At least have a word with her.'

Robert replies, 'All right. Get her in at three, and I will come back this afternoon and see her. Make sure you are both here with me just in case we can get something from her about the International Fashion Show and what we should look out for.'

Both ladies agree, and Robert stands up and makes his way out of the building and into his car.

He drives to work and attends to his meetings and, at three, heads off back to the MI building.

Pat and Emma are waiting with Claudia.

Robert walks into the room and introduces himself to Claudia and says, 'I remember you. You came to church last Sunday and sat near me. The lady you were with kept saying to you, "Introduce yourself to him."'

Claudia replies, 'That's right. How embarrassing. That was my mother, who was determined to have me married on Sunday.'

Robert says, 'Well, Claudia, the girls tell me that Mr. Henry is giving you a hard time?'

Claudia, with tears in her eyes, replies, 'A terrible time. He served me with these papers today, and I do not understand what they mean or what I should do. I am a designer, not a cheat like him.'

Robert asks, 'Tell me what actually happened?'

Claudia outlines the competition she entered into and that she borrowed the funds from her mother to fly over to Paris to put the exhibition on. She won the competition by coming up with new and enervating ideas in design. Henry presented garbage, and everyone there can confirm that. 'I won the competition fairly. Now he is saying that the ideas were his and I must pay him all the profits earned, or he will sue me for breach of copyright and take everything I have.'

Robert says, 'I am sure he will do it. He is that type of person. I saw him once kick the box of a beggar off the Town Hall steps and walk off in spite.'

Claudia adds, 'I don't know what to do.' Robert replies, 'Get a bloody good lawyer.'

Pat says, 'Come on, Robert, you know how to handle this type of person, but Claudia doesn't.'

Robert sits for a minute and stairs at the seated girls, considering what Claudia has just told him? He then smiles a cunning grin, and everyone looks at him, wondering what he is thinking.

Robert says, 'Claudia, I don't think you will agree with my proposal, as it is radical and will switch the emphasis from you to my company.'

Pat asks, 'What do you have in mind?'

Robert replies, 'Claudia comes and works for us on a two-year basis. Her designs are owned by MI, as she was doing them for our company, which means Henry is suing the wrong person. He will waste a few thousand dollars before he figures that one out, and in the meantime, we can prepare for our catwalk event.'

Claudia smiles and says, 'Agreed. That's a great idea.'

Robert says, 'Go home and think about it, and we will meet here tomorrow morning to discuss it further.'

Everyone agrees. Robert leaves to go to his apartment, while the three girls stay to chat.

21

obert is in his office at MI building attending to some correspondence when the staff turn up for work. Pat goes into Robert's office.

Pat asks, 'Has Claudia arrived yet?'

Robert replies, 'No, not yet, unless she went straight to her room.' Pat says, 'I will check.'

Pat walks out and walks to Claudia's office and finds Claudia sitting at her desk staring at the door in a gaze.

Pat says, 'We were wondering where you were.'

Claudia replies, 'I came in early and found this office and assumed it was Vicki's old office and looked at her designs for the fashion show. They are excellent designs.'

'Yes, we are working off them and should be able to fill in any missing pieces by adapting her method.'

'No, some designs need more than that whoever takes over will have to attend to that.'

'What do you mean, whoever takes over? Aren't you taking up Robert's offer?'

'No.'

'We better speak to Robert.'

Both ladies head off to Robert's office. On the way, they are met by Emma Jones and Alex Moss, who had just turned up for work.

Pat says, 'Girls, put your bags in your rooms and come immediately to Robert's office. It is urgent that we all hear what is being said.'

Pat and Claudia go directly to Robert's office and sit down. A moment later, they are joined by Emma and Alex and then by all the other staff who had been unofficially informed of what had been happening with Claudia.

Robert says, 'Well, I didn't expect everyone to join us this morning, but it may be helpful for you all to hear it for yourselves rather than through the grapevine.'

Robert asks, 'Well, Claudia, are you going to join us?'

Claudia replies, 'I thought about it all night but decided not to accept your offer.'

Robert says, 'I am surprised.'

Pat says, 'Claudia, you can't take on Henry by yourself. He will ruin your reputation and bankrupt you to make sure you don't come back again.'

Claudia replies, 'Yes, I know, but I will not put you all in danger. Some of you I have known for many years, others from childhood, and you have helped me and my mother through tough times. I will not endanger you just for my sake.'

Robert says, 'Hang on, Claudia, what are you not telling us? Something happened between our meeting yesterday and this morning. Why don't you tell us why you have changed your mind?'

Claudia replies, 'I would prefer not to and would ask you to respect my decision, which I can say was not made easily.'

Robert says, 'Sorry, Claudia, I am not accepting what you have said, as I feel you have made the wrong decision and are not telling us what has happened. If Henry is after you now and crushes you, we are going to be next in line. If you say you know some people here and do not want them hurt, then that is garbage, as they work here and will be subjected to the same treatment you are going through. You better tell us what has happened to you to make that decision.'

Claudia is near to tears and shaking, and everyone can see she is under a lot of pressure.

Alex says, 'Claudia, I have known your family from the time you were born. I was at your father's funeral when you were ten and have helped you and your mother over the years. So, I deserve to know what is happening and why you have changed your mind. We will shortly start our advertising campaign worldwide. Henry will see us as a threat and come after us, so whatever has happened! You must tell us!!'

Claudia ponders for a moment and is torn between protecting those she loves and putting them and others in danger.

Claudia says, 'All right. I believe you deserve to know. When I left here yesterday, I was ready to take up Robert's offer. I thought it was the right thing to do. I drove to my apartment and went in and locked the door and had something to eat and sat down to watch some television. There was a knock on my door, and I looked through the spyhole in the door and saw two men standing there. The one who was knocking lifted his hand up, and I saw a gun. I went to the phone and called the police. They arrived while the two men were trying to break down the door and arrested them. One of them said they will be out within the hour. The police asked if I wanted to press charges, and I said no, so they ended up releasing them. I slept the night at my mum's place, as I couldn't go back to my apartment.'

Robert says, 'You should have gotten the police to charge them to prove to Henry he could not intimidate you.'

Claudia replies, 'I was scared and couldn't think straight. They are doing the same thing to me what they did to Vicki.'

Robert says, 'Did you know Vicki?'

Claudia replies, 'Yes, we would talk on the phone and discuss different designs and sometimes meet up for coffee before they forced her to run for her life. They are doing the same thing to me as what they did to Vicki.

'We kept close even when she was living in the park. I tried to help her as best as I could with money when I was in the country, but most of my time was spent overseas, designing and attending to fashion parades.'

Robert asks, 'What do you mean the same thing to Vicki?'

Claudia asks back, 'Don't you know?'

Robert says, 'Claudia, you better tell us what you know about Vicki.'

Claudia replies, 'The day you dropped Vicki off at this building and went to your office, she received a phone call early in the afternoon from Charles Henry telling her he knows where she lives and works, and he was sending some of his men over to speak to her about leaving the industry. Otherwise, he will arrange for her and those around her to get some special treatment.

'Henry is tied in with the drug bosses who protect him and give him the muscle, so there is no competition, and he helps them to lauder their money through property investments and on the stock exchange. They are tied up with bookmakers and the gambling industry. That is how he became wealthy through the mob's money and contacts.'

'Vicki's husband lost a lot of money and could not pay his gambling debts to the bookmakers who were controlled by the mob. He tried to get involved in selling drugs to get the cash he needed to pay off his debts. He did not realize that he was treading on the toes of the crooks that were protecting Henry.'

'They killed him because he was competing against them. Vicki only found out after his death. She did not know about her husband's gambling or drug business until they killed him, and creditors came knocking on her door to collect their debts. The gangsters also came after her, and they took everything. Vicki had to get away. Otherwise, they would have hurt or killed her friends, you, her family. They were determined to know about her family so they could collect any shortfall from them.'

'I met her shortly after you took her in. She went for an interview at the shopping center for a job, and I bumped into her by accident that evening. We had coffee the next morning, and she told me all about what had happened to her, her husband, and her business. She also told me about you, Robert—that you cared for her, and she hoped the nightmare was over and she could start a new life with you, but that was not meant to be.'

'After receiving the phone call from Henry, she decided it was too dangerous to go back to her apartment, so she went back to the life she had before on the streets and the park so they could not find her.

'What I understand happened was that a cold snap occurred that week, and she got pneumonia and died shortly afterward.'

'Now, these same people are coming after me, and I must go away. Otherwise, they will hurt my mother and me and possibly you all to find out where I am.'

Robert says, 'Those bastards. I blamed myself for Vicki's death when that skunk was the one who drove her back to the park. Like hell you are going to run away.'

Claudia replies, 'I must. They will come after every one of you to get to me.'

The girls talk between themselves and finally stop.

Alex says, 'Claudia, we all find it offensive that, first, Vicki and now you won't allow us to help you. Yes, most of us are family to you and all were family to Vicki, and thugs will not intimidate us, and we want to finish the show for Vicki and to ensure Henry finds out he can't treat people this way. You owe us the opportunity to help you. We all cannot run away. Someone must make a stand against these men. Yes, they are powerful and have muscle, but we must stand up to them. If we don't take a stand now, they will pick us off, one at a time.'

Claudia replies, 'I can't let you take my fight on.'

Robert says, 'Fight, or did you mean flight?'

Claudia smiles at the joke.

Claudia replies, 'Both.'

Robert says, 'Well, that's settled. We all agree to be involved and help one another and Claudia. I will arrange for my solicitor to draw up the papers today for you to sign, and we will backdate them to a year before you won the show in Paris, so they can't say you were not working for me. I will arrange for my lawyers to file a defense today in court, advising you own no designs, which will stop them coming after you. They will have to wait to the court case until they can find out I own the designs, or MI does.'

Claudia says, 'It is too dangerous for you. They will hurt all of you because of me. I cannot put you through it. Please let me go away and they will hurt no one.'

Robert replies, 'No, we have a fashion parade to attend to. They will try to stop us, but we will have to be one step ahead of them. Does everyone agree?'

The group outside Robert's office yells out, 'Yes!'

Claudia bursts into tears and cannot stop crying. Eventually, she stops, and someone brings her a glass of water and she takes a sip.

Robert says, 'I will arrange for the building to be watched twenty-four hours a day. I will also arrange for armed guards to be stationed at the front door to make sure none of Henry's thugs get inside the building.'

Claudia says, 'I can't go back to my apartment. They will wait for me there.'

Robert replies, 'You will have to come and live with me for a while until we can think of something else. They will not try to get at your mother after we file the defense that the designs are not yours and you were acting on instructions of an employer. We will arrange for them to be filed today.'

Robert adds, 'Claudia, go over Vicki's designs and see if they need to be amended. Start working on the designs for the second show as Vicki was concentrating her time on the first show.'

Robert asks, 'questions, anyone?'

Everyone outside pours into the office to consoles Claudia and welcome her on board. Robert leaves and walks to his car and drives to his office. He phones his solicitor and explains what has happened and gets him on to drafting the relevant papers.

Robert phones Roger and advises him what has happened and tells him that Claudia would join his fashion house and for him to complete the videos and still show that the first fashion show would be Vicki's design and the second one would be of Claudia's design.

Robert then phones a Joe Arnold, a friend of his who owns a security firm, and explains what has happened.

Robert says, 'Joe, I need twenty-four-hour surveillance of the MI building and protection for the staff during office hours. I also would like you to get me two guns—one I will keep at the office, the other on me. This could turn nasty if they come after me.'

Joe replies, 'I will have one of my men accompany you wherever you go until this matter is over.'

'Do you know whom we are dealing with?'

'Yes, and they don't play by the rules.'

'Well, neither should we.'

'I will arrange for everything right away. Whom will the men speak to at the MI building?'

'Get them to ask for Emma Jones. She is the manager there.'

'I will arrange for one of my girls to accompany Claudia from her apartment to the office in the morning and back home after work. She will stay with her at night.'

'I was going to get her to stay at my place to give her some protection.'

'Not a good idea. They don't know you are involved yet, so let us not tell them until the matter goes to court.'

'I believe it will be best she stays in her own apartment even though they know where she lives.'

'Yes, that would be the best plan. When they come and knock on the door, we will wait for them and give them a bit of a surprise.'

'I will tell her this evening when I see her.'

'All right, I will put everything into action.'

'Just one thing. How come you know of Charles Henry and his connection?'

'What they are doing to Claudia, they did to my sister. They drove her to commit suicide. She was just finding a notch in the fashion industry, designing clothing and jewelry, when they came at her threatening the family when I was overseas in the army. I have to settle a score with them.'

'I will leave it up to you. When can I expect the guns?'

'I will deliver them to you this afternoon at the MI building. Your name will be used to register them, and they will be brand new. I know you have used guns before and can shoot straight, so I have no worry about you handling a gun.'

'I will see you this afternoon.'

Robert settles down to attend to some work, and about two hours later, his solicitor arrives with the papers for him and Claudia to sign. He drives to the MI building and walks into his office. Pat sees him going in and follows him.

Pat says, 'The security guards are here and have briefed all of us, and we each have a tag to wear to prove who we are.'

Robert replies, 'That's good.'

Pat says, 'They want to see you after you have signed the papers.'

Claudia walks into the office and was introduced to Robert's solicitor.

Robert says, 'Right, John, why don't you show Claudia where to sign?'

John says, 'She can't sign without reading the documents.'

Claudia replies, 'John, I am a dead person already. Do you think you are going to make it any harder for me? I am amongst the only people that care about me. I do not think they are going to rip me off. Where do I sign, John?'

Claudia signs, and then Robert signs on behalf of his company. They date the documents eight months prior to the date on the entry form for the registration to go into the fashion show.

John Armstrong then rushes out so he could lodge the defense for Claudia.

Everyone gathers to see the event and applauds Claudia for signing.

Robert says, 'Well, everyone, it is time to go home. Just be careful who approaches you, and if possible, stay together. Claudia, I see your escort has arrived.'

A young, well-dressed lady comes up to Claudia.

Security says, 'Hello, I am Sharon, your escort.'

Robert says, 'Claudia, the security firm considered for the time being, until the court case, that it would be best to have Sharon with you, as she can take care of any problems that may arise from unsolicited men calling you. She will stay with you overnight and escort you to the office. She will then come and collect you after work and take you back to your unit.'

Claudia asks, 'But what happens when I go shopping on Saturday or see Mum?'

Sharon replies, 'I am your best friend. I will be with you at all times unless you go to the toilet. At all other times, socials and weekends, I stay with you until the court case. Just one thing— if there is trouble, you do not help me. You are to step back behind me and give me the room to smash heads or move completely away.'

Claudia says, 'Great. I will leave all that to you. I can see you get your kicks out of that.'

Sharon says, 'Robert, here are your guns.'

Everyone stares at the guns given to Robert.

Pat asks, 'Do you know how to use them, Robert?'

Robert replies, 'I think so, since they licensed me in the army. Special Services.'

Robert stays for a while and then goes down to his car and drives off and goes to his unit, taking the guns with him.

Claudia and Sharon drive off in Sharon's car and go to her apartment. On her door is a message reading, 'We will call back tonight to discuss your health.'

Sharon calls her boss, and they organize several additional guards to be stationed inside her unit as a welcoming committee.

Claudia cooks a meal for everyone, and they sit down to have their meal.

There is a knock at her door. Sharon gets up and looks through the spyhole. She signals it is them, and both men stand near the doorway, while Sharon answers the knock.

Sharon says, 'Yes, can I help you?'

Gangster replies, 'We would like to speak to Claudia. Is she available?'

Sharon says, 'No, she's not.'

Gangster replies, 'Well, we will just go in and wait for her.'

The two men try to push Sharon aside, but she gives one a kick in the groin and knees the other.

Sharon says, 'I said you are not welcomed, so please leave.'

The gangster tries to grab hold of Sharon. She gives one a kick in the head, sending him crashing to the wall. The other tries to throw a punch, and she ducks and knees his midsection. She grabs him and knees him again, and he falls to the floor. She walks inside and closes the door. She calls the police, who arrive to take the men away.

Sharon says, 'You better grab your things. We have to get out of here. They will be back with reinforcements. Pack a bag with all your belongings and another with your clothing. I will take you to my place, which will be safer.'

Claudia packs all her things and heads off with Sharon.

The police release the men, and they come back to Claudia's apartment. They break the front door down and enter her apartment but couldn't find anything to assist them as to where she had gone. Neighbors phone the police, who are waiting for the men as they come out and arrest them for unauthorized entry, destruction of property, and intending to assault a person.

It is Saturday, and Claudia and Sharon go shopping to buy what they need for the week. They go to Sharon's place and unpack their shopping, and Sharon chills out the rest of the day, while Claudia works on her designs for the second fashion show.

22

Robert is in his apartment when Allen buzzes to come up. Robert lets him in, and Allen knocks on the door and is let in. Allen says, 'I thought I would check in on you to see if you were coping with Vicki's death.'

Robert replies, 'Well, you wouldn't believe it, but you were right about God having a plan and we don't know what it is. We came across one of Vicki's friends who was a fellow designer and who also had been harassed by Charles Henry.'

Robert tells Allen what he learned from Claudia and the criminal history of Charles Henry and his fashion house and association with gangsters and money laundering.

Robert says, 'I would like to put a bullet into that bloke for the misery he has caused and what he did to Vicki.'

Allen replies, 'If you really want to punish him and get it off your mind, leave it to God to settle the score His way. What you have told me clearly shows he is very wealthy and is protected by men who would not think twice about putting a bullet in you. You don't have the resources, strength, or ability to knock this bloke out of the ring, but God can. You can only kill him, but leave the matter of retribution to God. He will punish the person and do a better job of it than you.'

'Allen, I know you have faith in God, but, unfortunately, God and me, well, I don't believe He would punish these people the way I would like them punished.'

'And how would you like justice administered?'

'A bullet between the eyes.'

'Well, that would mean a quick and easy death. I am sure God can do far better, and His justice will be equal to the crime. It will be divine retribution. Robert, you must recognize you don't have the means to fight them, but God has. All that it takes is for you to have faith in Him and say a prayer, asking for His help and leaving the matter in His hands. From then on, He will attend to it in His own way in His own time, and it will be everlasting.'

'I don't think it is going to be that easy. These people have guns and are paid thugs. Do you think God can stand up to them? If you do, you are in fairyland. They are too powerful. They are not in heaven but on earth.'

'Yes, God knows, but He moves mountains, which they cannot. He controls tornados, which they cannot. He decides who lives and dies, not them.'

'I will think about it. Thanks for coming around. I would just like to even the score on Vicki's behalf.'

'Leave it to God. He will do a far better job of it than you can.'

'How about I buy you some dinner?'

'That sounds great.'

Both men go down to the basement and notice someone standing near Robert's car as if they were going to let a tire down. They see Robert approaching and runoff out of the car park.

Allen sees what has happened and says, 'It could be pranksters.'

Robert replies, 'Not likely. Thank God we came down in time.' Both men get into Robert's car and drive off for some dinner.

The next morning, Robert goes to church, it being Sunday, and he knows it would disappoint Allen if he did not turn up.

Robert has breakfast and walks to church. On his way there, he pauses outside the church to get his breath and is surprised to see Claudia, her mother, and Sharon.

Claudia says, 'Mum, this is my boss. Robert, this is my mum.'

Mrs. Simpson replies, 'Nice to meet you, Robert. Yes, you have my permission to marry my daughter.'

Robert says, 'Thank you. I wasn't aware I had proposed.'

Mrs. Simpson replies, 'Well, get a move on it, will you? She is aging by the minute. Something is troubling her, and when women are so uptight, it's men.'

Claudia says, 'Mum, stop that. Sorry, Robert. Mum is always trying to marry me off, and on one occasion to a married man.'

Mrs. Simpson replies, 'Only on one occasion? I thought it was more.'

Robert says, 'That's all right. She has given her permission, so all I have to do is propose.'

Sharon asks, 'Do you want me to twist his arm, or are you going to just smile at him?'

Claudia says, 'What is going on here? Leave me alone.'

All go into the church and sit upfront where Allen can see them as he conducts the service.

Allen performs the service, but Robert was not interested in what was being said. He is concentrating on a stained-glass window that is installed in the church depicting an angel of the Lord with a sword in his hand and God directing above what must be done.

Allen enters the pulpit and looks over the congregation for a few seconds and then says, 'A concerning matter has come to my attention this week that was never flagged by the government of the day, nor was it part of their election platform for obvious reasons. The matter I refer to is abortion, which is still prohibited in this state and which, this week, the government has declared it will move to decriminalize. The government declared it was completing the legislation to affect this and that, within a week, it intended to allow a conscious vote in parliament to ensure the legislation passed without delay. News reports on television, radio and in the papers, of course, declared this "to be about time" and that our State was behind the rest of the country, and we should accept this as being a women's right. The rent-a-crowd was brought in to stage their usual protest with prepared placards. You see them constantly in similar protests and who are repeatedly pointed out to be on Centrelink's Newstart allowance or doing a further university degree, unemployed of course.'

'Our church leaders did their usual protest comprising a paragraph on abortion in the newspapers with nothing new said or any headline declarations being made, and of course, no television interviews or insistence on appearance on ABC 7:30 program. On that day, I rang and spoke to the radio presenter of the number-one rating morning drive time show in the country and, in the course of the conversation, declared that this matter should be protested by our church leaders, and he should invite them on to his program to put their view forward against the legislation. I also was able to register my protest against abortion and that society would benefit if these unborn children could be adopted.

'Two days later, the Archbishop from the Catholic Church came on the program and was given approximately three minutes of airtime to put his case. Thirty seconds was taken up with the objection of terminating life by an abortion, and the presenter took the rest of the time up wanting to know why the church did not know this legislation was being presented in parliament for debate.'

'This is not good enough in that the church is not showing leadership in this matter but deciding to be reactive and not proactive and take a position of protest, which it is declaring it must do to defend the principles of the Bible. Here, the church is trying to portray itself as doing something when it is doing nothing other than mouthing a few words in protest.'

'My view is that a lot more should be done. I tried to telephone Members of Parliament and left messages on their phones to call me back, but as usual, I ever received no return calls.

'My view on this matter may coordinate with yours. If it doesn't, don't let me persuade you from having a view, but allow me to express mine.'

'First, to abort a pregnancy is the same as killing a life. Just because the child is unborn is irrelevant. It is still a life, and to end pregnancy is to kill or stop a life, and this is contrary to the teachings of the Bible. If you do not believe me, then ask to see an ultrasound of the fetus, and you will see the heartbeat is there verifying it is alive. It lives and is not just a piece of garbage imbedded in a women's body that is removed or aborted and left to die on an operating table.'

'When Caine killed Abel,

> 9   The Lord said to Cain, "Where is Abel your brother?" He said, "I do not know; am I my brother's keeper?"
>
> 10   And the Lord said, "What have you done? The voice of your brother's blood is crying to me from the ground."
>
> 11   "And now you are cursed from the ground, which has opened its mouth to receive your brother's blood from your hand."
>
> 12   "When you work the ground, it shall no longer yield to you its strength. You shall be a fugitive and a wanderer on the earth."
>
> 13   Cain said to the Lord, "My punishment is greater than I can bear."

14   "Behold, you have driven me today away from the ground, and from your face I shall be hidden. I shall be a fugitive and a wanderer on the earth, and whoever finds me will kill me."

15   Then the Lord said to him, "Not so! If anyone kills Cain, I shall take vengeance on him sevenfold." And the Lord put a mark on Cain, lest any who found him should attack him.

'Is killing an unborn child any different from Cain killing Abel? God has made it clear how He views this intentional termination of life and the consequences of such action. Are you the keeper of your unborn child? Yes, no one else has this responsibility but the mother. The mother will therefore receive the same treatment Cain received if she pursues with the abortion being a willful termination of a life. She is the one who makes the choice, so we are told.'

'Many say it is lawful to end a pregnancy because the State allows this. Yes, the State, in an effort to make religion irrelevant, has legislated to allow this to happen and agrees not to take any action against those who act in this regard. But the Bible does not support the State in this legislation and, in fact, says this action is contrary to the will of God, and God will not hesitate to act as he did when Cain murdered Abel.

'Many who end pregnancies will not care what the Bible says on the matter. All that they want is to expedite a termination and get on with their lives, which may entail falling pregnant again and repeating the procedure. They are of this world and do not believe in God. Believe it or not, belief is not the question. The Bible makes it clear that God protects the child, and His judgement will be upon you if you intentionally abort your pregnancy, and in this instance, it is irrelevant whether you believe in God. You will suffer the consequence of your decision, for here you are your baby's keeper. God, the Creator, has created a unique life within you, and you have been given the choice to either take care of this life or give it to someone who will. God has not given you the choice of deciding whether the unborn child lives or dies. This is up to Him to decide, not up to you.'

'The problem these days is the persons who are given a free will think they can do what they want to do, and, unfortunately, this is not the case. Yes, God has given you a free will to act responsibly and not selfishly knowing that the wrong decision made specifically against the laws of God by you will invoke retribution according to the teachings of the Bible. God specifically brought this to the attention of the Israelites in the Old Testament. Accept it or not, the Bible declares God created us in His image, and certain of His aspects have been incorporated in our make-up. Murdering unborn children is not one of them.'

'Cain recognized God as the Creator and accepted his judgement when he killed Abel. If you reject God at the time of making your decision to end your pregnancy, there will come a time when you confront this decision and agree that He is the Creator and you, too, have killed a life and must pay for your sin. His retribution will not be any less than that imposed on Cain. You will be forced to confront what you have done, and you as a murderer will be banished from God's protection, losing the presence of the Holy Spirit if it lives in you. You cannot have the Holy Spirit if you intentionally murder an unborn child knowing you are going against the teachings of the Bible and God's laws or continually repeat this owing to your adulteress lifestyle. You will be left to your own devices, and Satan will be the only one available to claim you by default. There is no doubt you can ask for forgiveness for your sins, and the cross is the place where this happens, but most people who go down this path rarely fall on their knees and seek God's forgiveness and mercy.'

'You see on the news, women demonstrating that this is their decision, as it is their bodies that are being decided upon. Stupidity reigns supreme here, as they are demonstrating on a point that is not even being argued about. God gave women the right to decide what they are to do with their bodies, and no one is arguing this point. They have free control over what they do, as God Himself has granted them a free will. Therefore, their decision regarding the fetus is so important because this is the argument, not what they are doing with their bodies. They either accept that by terminating their pregnancy, they are killing God's distinctive living creation within them, a life that only He could give them, or they declare they do not care and will take the consequences.

'We are not told the statistics experienced in other States where this has been legislated as to how many women end up seeking services from psychiatrists or other mental professionals once their action dawns upon them. I believe this decision will lead to a problem down the track, which is not being declared in this debate with the politicians trying to change the emphasis from a debate as to right to life to one arguing a women's right to do what she wants to do with her body. The unbelievable aspect here is that most women have fallen behind this argument without understanding that God has given them this right of choice and that this is not the argument at hand but rather the argument is the right to life, or are they smart enough to realize this but refuse to confront the truth, as they are willing parties to the shame of being portrayed in our news and on live television?'

'Our church leaders do not in reality want to fight this battle but will prefer to stand on their religious pulpits and mouth a few words in protest and allow the matter to take its course, which, no doubt, will end with the legislation being voted upon in the affirmative.'

'We are told the legislation contains several safeguards requiring a doctor to sign off on the abortion. It does not require a psychiatrist to check to see if the woman is mentally capable of knowing the ramification of her decision and the likelihood this will have on her mental state now or in the future. Nor is there a requirement that a religious minister sign off declaring they have brought the religious arguments to the person's attention. All that is to happen is a medical GP to sign off, and the operation is performed, and society then picks up the bill for psychiatric services later on when the person realizes what they have done—namely, killed their unborn child— and get depressed over this.'

'I, for one, will try to stop the legislation or at least try to get amendments made to it where a minister of religion must first counsel the person as to what they are doing in terminating their pregnancy before the operation can proceed. The minister must make it clear that the Bible states the termination of the pregnancy is viewed as terminating life, and in biblical terms, this is not a lawful termination in the eyes of God. Second, the minister must make it clear that there are alternatives to an abortion. Today, there are a lot of couples unable to have children. If the person was genuine in not wanting the child, they can at birth give it up for adoption, giving a couple the right to start a family. The religious minister appropriately trained should interview the person before they gave an authority for the abortion to proceed.'

'The argument where there is a life-or-death situation of the mother does not enter this debate, and in these instances, we must do all to save the life of the mother. While they throw this up as a norm, it is rare and should not be used as a red herring during this sensitive debate.'

'I will say that this will not be an easy debate to have, as my current experience is that calls to the news outlets result in no one willing to return calls to arrange for a discussion of the issues. Calls to ministers of religions also lead to no return phone calls, as they to do not want to involve themselves in the debate. One could think that we have decided, and all they expected us to do is go through the motions to ensure it passes.'

'I phoned the office of archbishop to be told that he does not take calls from members of the public and rarely returns their calls. I asked, could one of his ministers or deputies return my call, to be told it is doubtful that this will happen. They thanked me for ringing. What a kind gesture from his office.'

'When the phone was hung up by the archbishop's office, I contrasted this with God. The archbishop and his team must put themselves on a level well above God, as Lucifer did. I can pray to God at any time and do not need to make an appointment, and God personally will answer my prayers. The Archbishop and his team, who declare themselves servants of God, make it clear no one will talk to you or call you back irrespective of why you rang. It is above them to do so. Why should someone with status, self-esteem, pride, and dignity of office want to discuss an issue with a Christian, especially a commoner? My thought immediately went to thinking about the Pharisees and how they distorted religion to suit their lifestyle and wonder, is this part of our present problem with the church? Is this why we are having no debate on the abortion issue? I wonder what our religious leaders are saying when, at Easter time, their backs are to the cameras, and they wash the feet of the twelve selected men. A humbling sight, no doubt.'

'Calls to Member of Parliament again got no action, as the respective parliamentarian does not return your call, as he, too, only wants to get the legislation passed and not to be forced to debate it or have their conscience pricked. Our premier, who declares herself a Christian, has openly declared she will support the legislation on abortion. Again, another one saying she believes in God, but not what the Bible says.

'I would ask all of you to join in this debate and register your protest with your local Member of Parliament and have the legislation postponed, allowing appropriate debate to take place and amendments made to ensure the best outcome. The amendments should contain not only what has been discussed but also provision for counseling services by a religious minister if required, possibly an add on Lifeline.'

'I would also ask the church to establish a policy on this matter so society can clearly see and know where the church stands on this issue and the reason for them taking such a position. I would ask that the church's position be recognized in legislation so discrimination does not raise its ugly head, as the State will use its powers to ensure religion does not have a say in this and similar matters.'

'The last point, of course, is that if after all these safeguards are incorporated into the legislation, we should be able to receive reliable reports as to the number of abortions that are being performed, say, quarterly and the geographic areas where these are done. This will give us an indication of where resources need to be deployed to address this social issue.'

'May God give our religious leaders the strength and wisdom to bring this battle on and to establish a panel to address social issues confronting the community, and in particular, the poor and needy.

'Let us pray . . .'

The service ends, and everyone goes outside and chats for a while and eventually makes their way home.

Robert sits in his apartment and wonders what the Lord could do. He googles some searches and reads for an hour on what he could find on the internet and interpretations of the Bible from some free commentaries.

He decides that there may be something in what Allen has said to him and kneels down and prays to God to accept him and to help him in his journey to belief and faith and to take from him the hurt that these men and Charles Henry have inflicted on him and to leave the retribution to God to carry out. He asked God to bless the soul of Vicki and hopes she is with Him in heaven.

Robert finishes his prayer and gets up off his knees and makes himself something to eat. He does some paperwork till about nine o'clock and decides to have an early night.

At about one o'clock, he dreams Vicki is standing in his bedroom and talking to him.

Vicki says, 'I am glad you have found the Lord, Robert, as I had hoped you would. These men you spoke about are murderers, and it is good you have handed the matter of retribution over to God to handle. I know you still love me, Robert, but I am in heaven, and you must seek a life without me on earth. Find happiness for yourself and trust in the Lord.'

Robert wakes up, saying, 'Vicki, I can't. Where are you?'

Robert then realizes he was having a dream. He goes to the kitchen and gets himself a drink out of the fridge and sits pondering on the dream. He then goes back to bed.

The next morning, Robert gets up and, after breakfast and a shower, goes straight to his office to settle the advertising campaign with Roger, which he wanted to come out after the court case.

23

Robert's father is sitting on his front veranda with a cup of coffee in his hand, enjoying the mid-morning sun. His wife, Catherine, is in the kitchen making him a sandwich when two men pull up in a car and walk up to his house.

Stranger asks, 'Are you Richard Somerset?'

Richard replies, 'Yes. What can I do for you?'

'Nothing other than give your son some advice.'

'He doesn't take advice from anyone.'

'Tell him to get out of the fashion industry before he winds up dead.'

Richard, getting up on his feet, says, 'Why don't you tell him yourself? You know where he works, so tell him yourself.'

Stranger replies, 'We have tried, but he won't listen. This is his last warning. We hope you may get him to see reason.'

Richard says, 'He won't listen to what I say to him.'

Catherine comes to the front door and sees the men standing talking to Richard. She goes back into the house and telephones Robert.

Catherine says, 'Robert, there are some men at our house threatening your father. They have guns under their coats. I am afraid they are going to do something bad to him. Please help us.'

Robert replies, 'Mum, I am calling the police and am on my way.'

Catherine goes back to the front door and sees the men move closer to Richard.

Richard says, 'I will pass your message on to him. I will ask you to leave.'

Stanger moves closer to Richard and says, 'Just to make sure he gets the message.'

Stranger hits Richard in the face with a fist and, as Richard keels over, hits him in the midsection and then a blow to the back of his head as he falls to the ground. The men then walk away, leaving Richard motionless.

Catherine witnesses what has happened to Richard, immediately calls emergency, and comes out and kneels in front of Richard, who tries to extend his hand to touch her and, in his dying breath, looks at her and says, 'I love you.'

Catherine bursts into tears and screams out, 'Richard! Richard!' But Richard is motionless.

The police arrive just as the ambulance turns up. The paramedics quickly run to Richard's side and try to listen to his heartbeat, but there was none. They declare him dead and radio base that they arrived too late.

Catherine is in hysterics, and the paramedics must sedate her to calm her down. They decide to take her to the hospital. At that time, Robert arrives and goes up to his mother, who is being sedated by the paramedics, and sees his father lying on the veranda motionless. He goes up to his father and kneels over him, saying, 'Dad, Dad.'

Paramedic says, 'He won't respond. We believe the hit to the head or midsection caused a heart attack. There was no heartbeat when we arrived. He died from the blow.'

Robert bursts into tears and sobs over his father's body and says, 'Why, Lord? Why do the innocent have to pay?'

The police approach Robert and ask him questions as to what had happened or what he knows.

Robert tells them about acquiring Marque International and the commitments the company has with putting on a fashion show in Paris in about a year's time. He tells the police of what he knows of Charles Henry and his thugs. They advise him they know of Mr. Henry and his association with the gangs, but, of course, do not tell him they are taking money from them to turn a blind eye to their activities.

Catherine is taken to hospital and sedated for observation and care.

They took Richard to the morgue for an autopsy to find out the cause of death.

Robert stays at his parents' home, not knowing what to do and trying to cope with what has happened.

Two deaths and both in tragic circumstances make Robert want to kill Charles Henry for what he has done. He doesn't think about leaving it to God, but wants immediate retribution, whether they considered it legal.

Reporters arrive, and the death of Richard Somerset makes headlines in the news with the police declaring they have no leads.

Claudia and Sharon are in their apartment watching the day's news when they hear the grim story about Richard Somerset.

News reporter says, 'two men who beat an elderly man to death on the front veranda of his home this morning. His name was Richard Somerset, aged eighty-four. Police are investigating the incident. The attack was witnessed by the man's elderly wife, who has been sedated and remains in hospital. Police will try to get a description of the men when Mrs. Somerset can be interviewed.'

Claudia says, 'Oh my god. No, not Robert's father.' She takes her mobile and rings Robert. No answer. She tries again, still no answer.

Claudia adds, 'I have to go to see if he is all right.'

Sharon says, 'He is dead. That's what the news said.'

'Not Richard. I mean Robert.'

'We don't know where he is.'

'Your organization would have his address. Telephone them and get his address. I am getting my coat.'

'I don't think this is a good idea. Robert is all right.'

'Is he? His father was just beaten to death by gangsters and his mother has been hospitalized, and you tell me he is all right? I knew I should have disappeared. Now people are being killed because of me.' Claudia waits while Sharon gets the address from her office, and both go down to the basement and get in Sharon's car and drive off. Robert sits and ponders as to what has happened and decides that the police will do nothing, as they are being paid by the mob. He decides to take things into his own hands and to pay Charles Henry a visit at his office. He switches everything off and locks up his parents' house and gets into his car. He reaches out to the glove box and takes a gun from its cradle and slips it into the belt of his trousers and drives off to Charles Henry's office.

After an hour of driving, he parks his car about a block away and walks to Charles Henry's office. Several men are standing around the front of the building. He goes around the back and tries a few windows and doors and forces one of them open and gets inside the premises. He makes his way upstairs in the stairwell, checking to see if there is any activity on the upper levels. He can hear people speaking on the upper floor. He walks up the stairwell until he reaches the top floor and opens the fire door and listens for noises. Charles Henry is one of the people he can hear speaking. He opens the fire door and steps onto the top floor and walks in the shadows until he reaches the office next to where people are speaking. He opens the door and goes in, leaving the door partly opened so he can hear what was being said. There are three people waiting in the room. After about half an hour, he could hear some men walking away from the office next door and steps out into the hallway and approaches the office where they came from. He looks inside and notices Charles Henry sitting at the desk and no one else in the office. He draws his gun and sneaks into Charles Henry's office, crouching behind a large chair. If they catch him, he knows he will be in trouble, possibly ending up like his father. He stays behind the chair to make sure he can surprise Charles Henry.

In the meantime, Claudia and Sharon arrive at Robert's father's place. Claudia runs to the front door ringing the doorbell. She knocks and still no answer. A neighbor comes around to see who is making the noise.

Claudia says, 'We are friend of the family. Can you tell us where Robert is?'

Neighbor replies, 'I don't know. He was here until the police left, and then I saw him drive off. I don't know where he has gone.'

Claudia says, 'He may have gone back to his unit. We will go there to make sure.'

Sharon asks, 'Make sure of what?'

Claudia replies, 'Make sure he doesn't try to kill Charles Henry?'

Sharon says, 'Yes, I guess if I was in his shoes, that will be what I would do.'

Claudia asks, 'Can I give you my mobile number, and could you ring me if he comes back here?'

Claudia gives the neighbor her number, and both girls get into their car and drive off to Robert's unit.

Sharon says, 'You must be in love with Robert to go to this amount of trouble.'

Claudia replies, 'I just don't want him to get killed for my sake. I knew I should have done what Vicki did and just hid out in the park.'

Sharon says, 'But it was his father that got killed, not you.'

Claudia remained quiet, hoping she could get to Robert before he does something foolish and gets himself hurt.

Robert stays behind the chair and notices Charles Henry get up and move to the window and look out. Robert moves behind Charles Henry with his gun drawn. Charles Henry sees Robert behind him as a reflection in the window and yells out. Robert hits him on the back of his head with the butt of his gun, and Charles Henry falls to the floor. Robert says to himself, *now what? Do I put a bullet into the bastard?* He hesitates as Allen's words come to haunt him: 'Leave the retribution to God. Have faith in God. He will handle it and do a far better job of it than what you can do.'

Robert aims the gun at Charles Henry's head and is ready to pull the trigger when he hears someone coming and moves to the doorway behind the chair. Two men come in and immediately see Charles Henry lying on the floor bleeding from a head wound.

As the men come in, Robert slips out and down the hallway to the fire stairs and makes his way down to the ground floor. He notices no one has closed the window, so he slips out of the building and walks to his car in the shadows.

Robert sits in his car for a minute, contemplating why he didn't put a bullet into Charles Henry. He was not sure why he hesitated. Possibly he did not want the retribution to be instant but prolonged and anything but merciful.

He starts the car and drives off to his apartment. Midway, he makes a detour and checks on his mother, so he heads towards the hospital. Half an hour later, he drives into the hospital car park. He takes out his gun and puts it back into its cradle in the glove box and walks to administration. He asks where his mother is and is told her ward and bed number and walks to her bedside.

Robert looks at his mother, who is still under sedation. She is still on oxygen and looking very frail. He wonders how she is going to cope without his father, who was her reason for living. He stays there until a doctor comes over to him and advises him she will be sedated for at least twenty-four hours, and they would then decide to bring her out of it slowly. Robert stays there for a while and goes home. He walks to his car and drives off.

In the meantime, Sharon receives an official news blitz from her office. They have taken Charles Henry to hospital with a concussion. He was admitted unconscious, bleeding from the head.

Sharon says, 'Someone got to Charles Henry and knocked him out. He has been admitted to hospital with a head injury. Do you want to visit him?'

Claudia replies, 'Very funny.'

While the girls are chatting, Robert pulls up into his underground car park and goes up the lift to his apartment.

He enters his floor and is surprised to see Claudia, who runs up to him and gives him a big hug, saying, 'Thank God you're all right. I thought you may do something silly and get yourself in trouble or hurt.'

Robert opens the door and lets the girls into his apartment. They all sit down and stare at each other.

Sharon says, 'Thank God we found you. She was driving me crazy looking for you. She thought you were going to do something silly.'

Robert asks, 'Like what?'

Claudia replies, 'Kill Charles Henry.'

Robert says, 'Not so silly. I got close, but hesitated. Some of his men came in, and I had to get out.'

Claudia says, 'My god, don't tell me it was you who got to Charles Henry.'

Robert replies, 'Yes, but I hesitated, which I shouldn't have done. I kept hearing Allen's voice telling me to leave it to God.'

Claudia asks, 'What would you have achieved in killing him? The mob would only replace him with another Charles Henry, and nothing would have changed. We would be back where we started with more killings.'

Robert replies, 'I guess you're right, but it would have given me satisfaction to know the mongrel didn't get away with killing my father.'

Claudia says, 'God will take care of it. Leave it alone, Robert. Promise me you won't make another attempt.'

Sharon says, 'We better get back home now that we know you are all right. Does Charles Henry know it was you?'

Robert replies, 'I don't know, but I don't think he had a good look at me, as it was only a split-second reflection in a window before I hit him, and he went down. I would say he doesn't know who did it.'

Sharon says, 'We will get you a driver who will also act as a bodyguard. If Henry knows it was you, they will come after you. Claudia, I will wait outside in the car park for you. Don't take too long.'

Sharon walks out of the apartment and closes the door behind her, leaving Claudia inside.

Claudia gives Robert a big kiss and hug.

Claudia says, 'Don't do anything silly or both of us will be dead.'

Robert replies, 'No, I won't, but there is going to be more to this as time goes by.'

Claudia fixes herself up and leaves, making her way to the car park, she gets into the car and closes the door.

Sharon asks, 'Is everything all right?'

Claudia replies, 'Yes, we just had some words.'

'Yes, I can see that.'

'What do you mean?'

'Well, have a look at your face.'

Claudia pulls the sun visor down to investigate the mirror and sees her lipstick had smeared across her face and down her cheek. Both girls stare at each other and burst into laughter.

Claudia says, 'I guess I better fix my face up.' She takes out a handkerchief and starts taking the lipstick off her face. Sharon starts the car, and they drive off.

Charles Henry is released from hospital a day later and declares he does not know who the person hit him. He stays home for a week and then resumes work.

24

Catherine Somerset is kept in the hospital for a week. She knows things would not be the same without Richard and finds it hard to accept that he has been taken from her. She has witnessed what had happened and does not blame God, as she knows men had done this, but doesn't know why her Richard was treated so brutally by them. Richard's funeral is arranged by Robert, and Allen is the minister presiding. It is a tense affair with all those who are in the nursing home industry attending to pay their respects. Richard was one of the pioneers in the industry and was well respected.

Those in MI who know Richard are given the day off, and they attend the service.

The casket had already been delivered and had been placed at the front of the church with flowers on top, and a picture of Richard stood in the middle of the coffin.

Robert goes and collects Catherine, and on arriving at the church, both walk to the front pew and sit down. Catherine stares at the casket and Richard's picture and sobs. Allen puts his hands over her shoulder and gives her a hug.

Claudia comes to the church with her mother and Sharon, and all stand outside for a while hoping to see Robert. Allen approaches her and says, 'Claudia, nice to see you.'

Sharon asks, 'Have you seen Robert?'

Allen replies, 'Yes, he just got here and took his mother up to the front. I think you better give them a few minutes with Richard.'

After about five minutes, Claudia goes in and walks up to where Robert and his mother are seated.

Robert says, 'Mum, this is Claudia, the designer from our firm.'

Catherine replies, 'Nice to meet you. Thank you for coming.'

Claudia sits near Robert, and both hold hands for a moment. After a few minutes, they are joined by Claudia's mother, who is introduced to Robert and Catherine, and afterwards, they are joined by Sharon, who sits down next to Claudia's mother.

The service begins with Allen making a brief speech that Richard was taken from them under tragic and unexpected circumstances and this is how the world has become, with no thought about our fellow man.

Many rise to speak about Richard and that he was a good family man and a leader in the industry, with some mentioning the death of his daughter and the impact this had on him and Catherine.

After all had spoken, Allen moves to the pulpit.

'I had reason to visit Richard and his wife, Catherine, on a number of occasions to see if I could be of help to them, so they got to understand the death of their daughter, and why it was not possible to blame God for this. I must say that I failed, as, too often, people do not want to listen to a point of view after they have consolidated their thoughts and need to blame someone, and in these cases, it is God.

'The Creator is the one that is usually blamed in these circumstances, with little ever said regarding Satan and his cause of the death of their daughter. This thinking repeats itself monotonously whenever a sudden death occurs, as most people never take the time to understand what is happening and why God allows this to happen. 'Richard understood what I was saying and came to church several times to find God. Whether he did, I really cannot say, but I know he was trying, and I had prayed several times with him. So I cannot say whether he believed in Jesus and resumed his faith or whether he had joined those who rejected Christ. I cannot say he found internal life through Jesus Christ. I can only hope he had.

'Life is an unexpected period when we really do not know what is going to happen next or in the future. It is out of our control. Many plan on things happening, and if they eventuate, they believe things will go according to their plan. The other day, one of my parishioners who was a Sunday Christian finally decided to follow the Lord and not have a foot in each camp because he noted he was being led to a pinnacle but could never complete a deal as something always went wrong at the eleventh hour. He was meant to pay for shares he acquired on a delayed contract (two days after purchase) and was going to sell them the same day he paid for them, giving him a quick, neat profit. Unfortunately, when he went to transfer the money into his trading account, the bank system was down, preventing him from doing so. The share transaction was dishonored, and the shares sold at the best price, leaving him with a loss and not a profit.'

'Life is unpredictable and does not go according to plan. You don't know how much time you have left on this earth. You get up in the morning to go to work but never make it back home.'

'If those present have not considered this, then I would urge you to consider this point that it is only through Jesus Christ you will find internal life. If you have not sought Him out, then you will be destined to a life with Satan.'

'You are on this earth to decide whether you will follow Jesus Christ and have eternal life, or Satan and live in hell.

'I believe Richard made the choice to follow Jesus and will be in heaven with the Lord. I hope you to have thought about your life and make the right decision.'

'Let's bow our heads and pray . . .'

The service ends, and all stand up while the curtain automatically is drawn. Once closed, Robert and Catherine walk down the aisle and out of the church and stand with Allen at the entrance. Claudia stands near Robert, while Claudia's mother and Sharon stand about twenty meters away.

Robert has arranged for light refreshments and sandwiches to be available, and everyone partakes in some refreshments and, after about an hour, makes their way either back to work or home.

Robert takes his mother back home and stays with her that week to make sure she could cope. Catherine finds life is lonely without Richard. Everywhere she looks reminds her of him, and she often talks to him and realizing it is a mirage and that in reality, he is not there. Robert could see she was not coping and stays the month to give her some company and time to adjust.

Catherine tries to make new friends but could not without Richard. Robert decides to partly move back home to keep Catherine company and stays one or two days during the week and on weekends.

25

Charles Henry is at his desk waiting for the people to turn up from Lehman Brothers. At about ten, three men appear and introduce themselves to him.

Charles says, 'Gentleman, you said you had a good investment proposal that would make me quite a bit of money.'

Frank Dwyer replies, 'Lehman Brothers has bundled together mortgages, which are thirty-year mortgages based on real estate in United States. These mortgages are secured on bricks and mortar and, therefore, can be described as secured investments. Most are on a 3 to 5 percent per annum rate, which avoids market fluctuations. 'We are prepared to sell these mortgages to you at a discount.'

'The rate of discount will depend upon the amount you buy. We are currently selling these in every country throughout the world, and they are in demand, especially where earnings are important. Compared to the current 1 to 2 percent offered by the banks, they are an attractive investment. A lot of the sovereign superannuation funds and church groups have bought our bond and mortgages and are currently reaping the rewards compared to the cash rate being offered by banks.'

Charles says, 'I will have to make some enquiries before agreeing to invest in the scheme, but it sounds a good secure investment if what you are saying is true. Can we meet after lunch and talk further about the securities?'

Frank replies, 'Sure, we will come back at two this afternoon.'

Charles sees the men out and sits at his desk thinking about the deal. Lehman Brothers has been around for many years and has had an excellent reputation in the security industry. America's real estate is appreciating, and money is easy to get after the government has forced banks to lend to people who want to buy a home for themselves.

He makes a phone call to his contact in the mob to see if they are interested.

Charles says, 'Jimmy, I had several people from Lehman Brothers come to see me to sell me some securities. They say that they are selling these worldwide and specifically to organizations that want a secure investment. They are based on bricks and mortar properties located in USA. The investments are paying an interest rate of 4 to 5 percent, but that could be higher if we buy a sizeable chunk of them.'

Jimmy replies, 'Yes, I have heard of them, and we have seen some of our contacts buy into the scheme. We would not be interested in buying in, but what are you proposing?'

'It is a secure way of laundering money.'

'Yes, I agree, as you end up with thirty-year mortgages secured on appreciating property. Well, we will be prepared to lend the money to you at bank interest rates of 1 percent, but it will be a loan only, and you will have to pay it back to us. How much were you thinking?'

'Two hundred and fifty million. At 5 percent, that should bring in a good steady income. Will you be able to fund that amount?'

'Not all at once but can do it over a week.'

'Then let us get it going. How much can you give me now?'

'One hundred million.'

'Get the paperwork done so I can sign what is required and have the first hundred transferred into my personal account straightaway.'

'The boys will be there this afternoon with the papers you have to sign, and as soon as you have signed them, we will transfer $100 million to your account.'

'Great. I will wait for them.'

At two, Jimmy's lawyers turn up, and Charles signs the agreement, giving Jimmy the right to take all of Charles's assets if he does not pay the interest on a monthly basis. They point out the risk he is taking, but Charles Henry is not interested in what they say and signs the documents willingly. They made arrangements to transfer the money into Charles's account.

Frank turns up at two but is kept waiting. After the contracts have been signed by Charles and Jimmy's lawyers left, Charles ushers Frank into his office.

Frank asks, 'Have you considered our offer, Charles?'

Charles replies, 'Yes, and I am prepared to invest $200 million into your securitization scheme.'

'We thought you might go as high as half a billion dollars.'

'Not at the moment. I want to see how I go with the first lot and if there are any problems with this form of investments.'

'We will arrange for the papers to be drawn up, and the mortgages transferred to your account. When did you want to pay the money for the investments?'

'At the end of the week. Here are the details of my lawyers. They can check the contracts, and they will ring me when they're satisfied with the paperwork. As soon as they are, I will arrange for the money to be transferred to your account.'

'All right, we will plan on finalizing everything on Thursday.'

'No, make it Friday so I can pool all the money together.'

Both men shake hands, and Frank leaves to attend to the securitization contracts.

Frank arranges for the contracts to be sent to Charles's lawyers, who check them and advise Charles they are in order. Charles signs the contracts and pays over $200 million to Lehman Brothers.

Lehman Brothers arranges for the notification letters to be sent to all the people affected, advising them to deposit their monthly repayments into Charles's nominated account.

Charles is not satisfied with this investment. He is told to never put all your eggs in one basket. He remembers that one of his contacts said he knew nothing about securitization and mortgages, but knew about equities and the way the stock exchange operated. He has made a lot of money by acquiring shares on margin call, which required only 10 percent of the acquisition price.

Charles telephones his bank, who agrees to set up an account for him and explains that he could trade or invest in any share he wishes, but should the share reduce in value by 10 percent of the purchase price, he would have to make good the loss in equity within seven days of being advised. This will enable him to buy more shares on a rising market and maximize capital gains and dividends earned, but should the market turn down or collapse, then he would be required to put in more equity to make up for the loss in value of the portfolio being held.

Charles agrees to the terms and employs several people to monitor his investments for him. He opens his account with $10 million, which would enable him to acquire $100 million of shares on the stock exchange.

One of the persons he employs is a share broker who knows about equities and begins trading shares and making good profits through trading.

Charles is very pleased with what he established and believes within a year or two, he would be a very wealthy man.

As for Claudia, he issues instructions to bring the matter to court and take whatever action is necessary to discredit her. He will spend whatever it takes to send a message to other fashion houses he would not accept being second in a contest and that if they are trying to outdo him, they better have a lot of money, as he is going to use all avenues available to him to ensure he succeeds and no one tries to beat him or tries to win a fashion show that he is competing in.

26

Pat and Emma have established a program to train models. They believe they have the right approach and are ready to place their advertisement in the newspaper advertising for young people interested in a modeling career.

They placed the advertisements in the papers, and both Pat and Emma estimate they might get about twenty enquiries.

After about three days, the applications come in. Within a week, they have over three hundred applications, and all look as if they could do the job. They sent letters out to all the applicants, inviting them to telephone and make an appointment for an interview.

They eventually compiled a short list of one hundred applicants after several weeks of interviewing all applicants.

All the finalists are put through their paces, and after about a month of trials, they cut this back to fifty applicants.

Most of the applicants are pencil-shaped figures, but they also taken a few fuller figures along with two applicants that are amputees. The intent is to reflect society by not making out that we all have perfect figures.

This approach is not the norm, and everyone knows it may backfire on them, as all the other fashion houses have models that are well figured, anorexic, and well trained.

Emma and Pat decide those selected would be more reflective of the community. They know they would have to select at least ten slim-figured models that would be groomed specifically for the International Fashion Show, but they also decide to select several applicants with fuller figures and a number of ladies that best could be described as plus sizes. By the time the modeling school starts, they have thirty-five on their books to be trained.

They would teach the applicants the art of grace, poise, how to walk along the catwalk in a straight line without tripping or veering left or right, and how to speak to the press on what to say and not to say.

They established the school on the fourth floor of the MI building and it began after they have constructed the catwalk.

Two trained teachers were specifically employed to prepare the curriculum and to put the students through their practical work. Each student was progressively examined, and any problems rectified immediately they are noticed.

Pat and Emma make continual trips to the fourth floor to see how things are going and are the examiners on the catwalk.

The training is rigorous and is enhanced by professional models attending class and giving further tuition to the students. It is not long before the school gains a reputation for excellence, and those who completed the course are very much in demand as models.

The course also covers not only poise but also design and how to show off a garment from swimsuits to fur coats. It also gives the students' insight into what to do when a mishap occurs, like you tread on your dress going down the catwalk and it tears off, leaving you exposed. A reality in the trade and one that needs poise to overcome the embarrassments.

Local businesses prefer the models from the school, as they are cheaper and want to get on with showing off their client's garments, whereas those of fame are more interested in their reputation and not so much of providing a service to the client.

They established an agency that would take the students that have graduated and find work for them, which is easy to do owing to the demand.

The school proves very popular, and within a short period, there is a waiting period of six months before someone could begin the course, but this does not deter them from putting in their application.

27

All stand, please.'

Claudia stands with her lawyer, John Armstrong, at the bench table as the judge walks in and bows to those present and sits down. Everyone in the courtroom sits down.

Robert is sitting at the back of the courtroom and notes that Charles Henry is sitting to the left of Claudia with his lawyer, Ron Stevens.

Charles Henry looks aggressive and is giving last instructions to his lawyer, no doubt intending to crush Claudia.

Claudia looks nervous and out of her depth. She keeps looking at her mother, who is sitting behind Charles Henry to Claudia's left.

The judge looks through the papers and says, 'Mr. Stephens, you may begin since you are acting for the plaintiff.'

Mr. Stephens says, 'Your Honor, the proceedings have begun with an initial application and supported by an affidavit by Mr. Charles Henry, who is the managing director of the litigating company.

'Our application shows that Ms. Claudia Simpson took our client's designs and portrays them as her own at the recent fashion competition held in Paris. We claim damages of one million dollars and all profits she received from the show, which we estimated to be a further one million dollars.'

Judge says, 'Mr. Armstrong?'

Mr. Armstrong replies, 'Your Honor, I believe our case has been appropriately defended in our defense, and the affidavit of Ms. Claudia Simpson has been filed. We contend the defendant does not own the designs and was merely employed to design the garments for a large fashion house and that Mr. Henry's application is not possible of success. This we have pointed out in our defense, and as Mr. Henry has pursued his claim against an innocent party. We claim costs of $50,000. We also contend, Your Honor, that Mr. Henry's application is faulty and should be rejected by the court, as at no time does he provide evidence as to which design he is disputing ownership over, nor does he provide proof that he had designed the garments.'

Judge asks, 'Mr. Stephens, what do you say about these claims?'

Mr. Stephens replies, 'This is the first I have heard about these allegations, Your Honor.'

Mr. Armstrong says, 'Your Honor, they are clearly stated in our defense, which had been served on Mr. Stephens well before the scheduled date. We will not accept ignorance of these facts as an excuse. We, of course, would like to see the evidence that Mr. Stephens will present today as to how he can lay claim to ownership of these designs.'

Judge says, 'Mr. Stephens, I would like you to address the matter raised whether you agree you are pursuing the wrong person, and if not, why do you say Ms. Simpson owns the designs?'

Mr. Stephens replies, 'Your Honor, we would ask for an adjournment of these proceedings for one week so I may get instructions from my client and clarify the issues you have raised.'

Mr. Armstrong says, 'We object to any adjournment of these proceeds at this preliminary stage. Your Honor has experienced these tactics before by the plaintiff. The real purpose here is to use up the defendant's funds, so they must discontinue their defense and therefore, by default, lose their ability to gain justice. In short, Your Honor, the idea is to continue the proceedings on a piecemeal basis until the defendant goes broke. The plaintiff then does not have to prove their case and leaves as the winner. We ask Your Honor to reject Mr. Stephens's request and direct his client to produce the evidence that he owns the designs and that Ms. Simpson has claimed to be the owner of the designs.'

Judge replies, 'I agree with Mr. Armstrong. This is a simple matter and is one that goes to the heart of this case. I do not believe an adjournment is warranted now and instruct you, Mr. Stephens, to begin your case proving that Ms. Simpson has put herself out as the owner of the designs. If you cannot prove this, then your case falls apart, as you are proceeding against an innocent party.'

Mr. Stephens asks, 'Your Honor, may I have a moment with my client?'

Charles Henry goes out with Mr. Stephens and is gone for about ten minutes.

Mr. Stephens comes back to the courtroom alone.

Mr. Stephens says, 'Your Honor, I am instructed by my client that he does not wish to seem a monster pursing an innocent party and therefore wishes to discontinue action against Ms. Simpson.'

Mr. Armstrong stands and says, 'Your Honor, my client has always maintained her innocence, and therefore we claim costs in this matter.'

Judge says, 'Mr. Stephens, I believe your client has begun proceedings against an innocent party and advice that you have presented no evidence to prove ownership of the said designs. I dismiss the plaintiff's case and awards cost of $50,000 payable within twenty-eight days to the defendant. Case dismissed. This court is now adjourned.'

The attendant yells out, 'All rise!' and everyone gets to their feet.

The judge stands and walks out of the courtroom.

Claudia thanks her lawyer and goes and hugs her mother. Claudia says, 'Thanks for coming, Mum, and lending me support.'

Mum replies, 'Good that I was here to see what that bastard looks like. Now you have $50,000. You can buy me a cup of coffee.'

Claudia says, 'Love to Mum, but I better thank Robert.'

Claudia turns to see where Robert was but could not spot him. All she could see was Sharon, her escort, standing at the rear near the door.

The three ladies go off to get a cup of coffee.

There is a coffee shop near to the courthouse, and they go there and order and sit down. Their order is delivered, and they each have a sip out of their cups.

Sharon says, 'Well, Claudia, you don't look too happy for a girl that just won her case and $50,000.'

Claudia replies, 'I am thrilled, but I thought I could thank Robert for his help, but he didn't think enough of the case to stay around.'

Sharon says, 'That not right at all. When we saw that Charles Henry could not prove his case and his lawyer asked for five minutes to speak to his client, we knew you had the case won. We did not want Charles Henry to spot Robert in the courtroom and link him back to you. Remember, we do not know if he spotted Robert before Robert hit him over the head. So, we immediately grabbed hold of Robert and whisked him away in one of our cars back to the MI building. This way, Charles Henry will still try to find out who was the person who really owned your designs and maneuvered $50,000 out of him. Why are you worried about whether Robert was there? You're not falling in love with him, are you?'

Claudia replies, 'Oh, no. I just wanted to thank him.'

Mum says, 'You can do that when you get married.'

All three burst out laughing and finish their coffee and walk to Sharon's car.

Claudia's mum asks, 'What is this about Robert knocking Charles Henry out?'

Claudia replies, 'Don't worry about it, Mum. Robert got into Charles Henry's office and was going to kill him but didn't and only knocked him unconscious.'

Claudia's mum says, 'What a pity. He should have finished the job. That bastard deserves it, what I hear. The misery he has caused people, someone should finish him off.'

Claudia replies, 'Yes, Mum, someone will—God.'

Sharon drives off and drops Claudia's mum off at her apartment and drives off to the MI building, and both go in.

As Sharon walks into the building, everyone she meets congratulates her on her fantastic win. Finally, she gets to Robert's office and sees both Pat and Emma there sitting, having a meeting with Robert.

Robert spots her outside his door and waves her to come on in.

Robert says, 'Congratulations on your win.'

Pat and Emma get up and congratulate Claudia, and all sit down.

Claudia says, 'Thank you all for your support and help. I really could not have gone through this without your support. I was very scared in that courtroom.'

While they are talking, all the other staff are mingling outside to congratulate Claudia. Robert signals for them to come on in, and they do, and each congratulates Claudia to where she is in tears.

Claudia says, 'Thank you all for your support. I really could not have gone through with it without you all supporting me. Thank you.'

Robert says, 'Now let us get down to business. As we progress through to the International Fashion Show, the IFS, Henry, is going to get more desperate and try to cripple us. He may try the same trick he pulled on Claudia or a different version of it.'

Pat asks, 'What do you mean, a different version of it?'

Robert says, 'Just think about it. What is the best way to stop us from showing our designs at the IFS?'

Emma replies, 'Do exactly what he did to Claudia.'

Robert says, 'No, he will not pull that again. He knows we have money, so he will not attack our bank accounts. No, if I wanted to stop someone from showing their designs, I would steal them just before the IFS is scheduled. Without your garments and designs, you would be out of the competition. No one would believe you if you claimed he stole your designs, even though he has a reputation that would have people thinking of this.'

Claudia asks, 'Well, thinking the way you are, what are we to do about it?'

Robert replies, 'I want you to design a program for the IFS that would not be the type of designs that would win. They must seem to fit the bill, but not quite there. They must incorporate ideas from other designers, so the industry will immediately recognize plagiarism even though they may not say it, they should be able to recognize it. In my opinion, he will steal these designs and our garments, and this will happen in Paris, not here, possibly en route to the show.'

Pat says, 'That bastard taking what we designed and showing it off as his. Does anyone know who Henry's designers are?'

Claudia replies, 'Yes, I know three of them, and they are very good. They were the ones who tipped me off as to what he was going to do. They are honest designers being paid a lot of money to keep Henry at the top of the industry, but there are some who hate Henry and will try to prevent him from getting the reputation for being the best in the industry.'

Robert says, 'Well, I would reason he will have little faith in his designers and will steal our designs. So let us work on that basis. You will have to design four lots of designs, two of which we know will be claimed by Henry.'

Pat says, 'We don't have the designers to do all that work. Claudia can't handle all that on her own.'

Robert replies, 'hire two junior designers and put them to work.'

Claudia says, 'I know two young designers that were working under me at the Paris show. I had to put them off to make sure Charles Henry did not hurt them. I know for a fact that both are unemployed and, like me, were finding it hard to find a job or get back into design.'

Robert replies, 'Get them in and let us have a word with them. Now, on another note, all finished garments and designs are to be kept on the sixth floor of my office except for the phantom shows. No one is to know, and we will transfer the designs and finished garments to my office under security and in crates, so no one knows what they are or where they are located. We will store all designs done on tablets and touch screens in the cloud. Questions? None. Good. Then let us get on with it?'

Robert then slips away and makes his way to his apartment.

Claudia, who did not see Robert go, looks for him to thank him but can't find him.

Sharon senses Claudia is down in the dumps and says, 'I will drop you off at our apartment and then go off to Robert's apartment to discuss a few things with him, if that is all right.'

Claudia says, 'Like hell you will. Let us go.'

Sharon drives into Robert's apartment and parks her car near his. Claudia gets out and starts heading towards the lift when she suddenly realizes Sharon is not with her. She walks back to the car and says, 'Aren't you coming?'

Sharon stares at her and shakes her head and says, 'You have five minutes.'

Claudia realizes what is happening and walks to the lift. She goes up to Robert's floor, but when she gets out of the lift, she can see two men kneeling at Robert's door and stops some ten yards away from them. One man sees her and says, 'That's the bird Henry was suing.' Both get to their feet and rush towards Claudia, grabbing her. Claudia gives out a high shriek as one man grabs her and puts his hand over her mouth. Claudia tries to kick him as she struggles.

Robert hears a noise outside his door and opens the door with a gun in his hand. He sees Claudia being held by one man and shoots, hitting the man in the leg, forcing him to the ground. As he falls, he releases Claudia, who runs towards Robert's apartment. The other man takes out his revolver and aims it at Claudia when, suddenly, a shot rings out, and the man falls to the floor, face down. Sharon stands at the lift door with her gun raised. Robert raises his gun at the man he previously shot and says, 'Get down and don't make a move.'

Sharon runs into Robert's apartment and calls the police and her office, informing them of what has happened. Claudia goes into Robert's apartment shaking and crying. The police arrive within minutes and recognize the men as part of the mob and Henry's protection team. No doubt they were instructed to pay Robert a visit and possibly try to get the $50,000 back out of him.

The police take statements from everyone concerned and try to get the man shot in the leg to talk, but he refuses, and they take him to the hospital to get his wound attended to. They rushed the man Sharon shot to the hospital, but he died en route.

Claudia says, 'They were going to kill us.'

Sharon replies, 'Yes, thank God Robert opened his door when he did. I should not have let Claudia go up here by herself. Shortly after you got into the lift, I realized there may be trouble and came up intending to stand at Robert's door.'

Robert says, 'I'm glad you did. They were not here for the fun of it.'

Claudia asks, 'What are we going to do? They know where you live, Robert.'

Robert replies, 'I will go to Park Royal and stay the night. I cannot go to Mum's, as they will call there. It is best I leave her out of it. Tomorrow

I will stay with Mum, and you better arrange for some of your people to stay with her around the clock to protect her.'

Sharon says, 'I will make the arrangements now.'

Claudia and Robert hug and kiss as Sharon makes her telephone calls and arranges for protection for Catherine, Robert's mum.'

Sharon says, 'We better get going, and you better go off to Park Royal. In the future, we will go there instead of here, as they will be back soon.'

Robert and Claudia kiss, and Robert says, 'She is still shaking.

She is not coping with this well.'

Sharon replies, 'She will be all right. I have a sedative I can give her when we get home. She will be all right after a good night's sleep.'

Robert grabs a suitcase and packs a bag and locks his apartment as Sharon and Claudia wait outside. They all go down the lift to their cars and drive off, each heading in a different direction.

The shooting made headline news the next morning, with Robert being named as the person who was marked by the mob and Charles Henry.

The next morning, Claudia telephones her two young designers and finds out that they are both living with their parents, and both have found it hard to find design work or employment. One works retail part time, the other at a cafe serving and cleaning tables. Both are keen to speak to Claudia and are happy to come on over to discuss anything that Claudia may have in the way of design work. Both want to speak to Claudia that evening and are thrilled that she won her court case against Charles Henry, which they heard on the news.

Both designers turn up at Sharon's apartment, and Sharon opens the door.

Sharon asks, 'Can I help you?'

Beth says, 'Yes, I am Beth, and this is Anna. We have come to see Claudia about some design work.'

Sharon replies, 'Please come in. Claudia is expecting you. Can I ask you to raise your hands above your heads so I can quickly search you?'

Anna asks, 'What trouble is Claudia in?'

Sharon replies, 'None, but I am sure with you two, this will change soon.'

Sharon gives the girls a once-over to make sure they do not have any concealed weapons and then directs them into the lounge room where Claudia was waiting.

Claudia stands and gives both girls a great big hug. Anna asks, 'Claudia, why the frisk? Are you in trouble?'

Claudia explains to the girls what has happened at the trial and at Robert's apartment the day of the trial and the plan Robert devised to outsmart Charles Henry.

Beth asks, 'Where does that leave us?'

Claudia replies, 'We require two junior designers to assist me in finishing Vicki Santana's designs for IFS first show. I must design the second, and we have two other comprehensive works that will need designs. It will require both of you to sign a two-year contract of employment and confidentiality agreement and will require both of you to assist at our modeling college.'

Beth says, 'I am in. When do I start?'

Anna asks, 'Claudia, is this going to be like the other job where we were fired without notice?'

Claudia replies, 'Girls, I had to do that to protect you. Otherwise, that weasel Henry would have hurt you. If you are asking, could it happen again? Then the answer is yes. However, at that time, I was on my own with no help. Now we have a reputable international-recognized designing house behind us with a lot more staff, and we have Robert, who is very smart and seems to have money behind him. If you want a regular job with security, then I suggest you stay serving at the cafe. I cannot guarantee that type of job. The only thing I can say is that we have a boss that is taking most of the heat off us and putting on himself. Girls, go home and think about the proposition, and if you are interested, I want to see both of you at MI at nine. If you do not turn up, then I will understand.'

Claudia asks Sharon to take the girls to their cars to ensure no one gives them a hard time, which Sharon was happy to do. Sharon then comes back and locks the door.

Sharon says, 'They're scared.'

Claudia replies, 'Yes, I know. Henry threatened they would kill their parents and rape the girls if they ever worked for me again.' Sharon says, 'A real nice bastard. A pity Robert didn't shoot him.'

Both girls watch a bit of television and then decide to call it a night and go to bed.

The next morning, both are ready early and decide to get to the office for an early start. They arrive at eight thirty, and both Beth and Anna are waiting for them.

Claudia says, 'Girls, we said nine. How long have you been waiting?'

Anna replies, 'Thirty minutes. Neither of us could sleep. We have talked it over with our parents, who think we would be mad to give up this opportunity. Also, they are fed up with our attitude after we left the industry and would support any idea to get us back into design.'

Claudia says, 'I can well imagine how hard it would be for your parents with you two. Well, girls, what is the decision? I assume you're in since you beat me to work.'

Anna replies, 'I am most definitely in.'

Beth says, 'I am in as long as you stop protecting us. We can handle the bad whatever form it comes in.'

Claudia replies, 'Agreed. Let me show you around.'

Claudia shows the girls the facilities, the design rooms, and takes the girls to the model college and lets the girls sit in on one of the classes.

Anna immediately notices an international model giving a lecture to the girls and is impressed.

Claudia introduces the girls to Pat and the other girls, who welcome them aboard, and then she takes the girls up to see Robert.

Robert is on the telephone with Roger and waves them in. Pat, Emma, and Alex soon joined them, who all sit down and are listening to Robert's conversation.

Robert says, 'Roger, I want the videos to hit the airways worldwide. Start with Europe tonight and the rest of the world tomorrow. In relation to our designer, I still want Vicki's name mentioned, as we will show her designs at the IFS first show. I also want our new designer mentioned, Claudia Simpson, who recently won the Paris exhibition. Lay it on for two weeks that everyone knows we are here and then broadcast the last video declaring we are open for business.'

Robert says, 'Pat, tell the other girls that the videos are being broadcasted tonight in Europe and tomorrow the rest of the world.

'Now, you two girls, I understand, are very talented designers.'

Anna says, 'That would be Claudia telling you that.'

Robert replies, 'No, it was your parents.'

Everyone bursts into laughter.'

Claudia says, 'Robert, this is Beth and Anna. They were the two designers who helped me when I won the Paris competition. They know of Charles Henry, who threatened their families and them. He said he would rape them if they worked for me.'

Robert asks, 'Girls, do you really want to work for us knowing that there could be trouble? You are both very young and, no doubt, talented, but things could get rough, and we don't want any of you hurt.'

Claudia says, 'I promised to tell the girls if there is trouble, and they want to see it through this time.'

Robert asks, 'Sharon, what do you think?'

Sharon replies, 'I don't like the present situation. With Claudia, we can look after her 24/7, but I believe we will have to come to some arrangements with the girls, possibly take them to and from work and put an emergency button on their phones at their homes with GPS on their phones so we can track them until IFS is over.'

Robert asks, 'Girls, are you prepared to allow us to limit your freedom, as Sharon outlined?'

Beth replies, 'I am OK with that.'

Anna says, 'Me too.'

Robert asks, 'Well, when can you start?'

Beth replies, 'Immediately.'

Anna says, 'Tomorrow. I am doing casual work, so I must turn up for work today and then I can resign. They will not pay me any entitlements because I am casual.'

Robert says, 'Well, I don't want you girls to resign your jobs yet until you have heard the rest of what we want you to do. You may not agree with it.'

Robert explains they expected the girls to design a phantom wardrobe and intentionally take ideas from other designers and incorporate them into the garments they were designing to ensure it would outrage those designers over theft of their ideas.

Robert also explains that we would expect the girls to accompany Claudia to the IFS and assist her in all her design work, including any extra work that may come in over the next eighteen months.

Robert asks, 'Well, girls, do you want to think about the proposition?'

Anna replies, 'No, I love it. That bastard deserves what he gets, and the plan is great.'

Beth says, 'I'm definitely in. What restrictions or limitations are going to be imposed on us in our designs?'

Robert replies, 'You will be directly under Claudia's control. We will incorporate any ideas you have into our main IFS show, and the designs you want introduced will depend on Claudia as to how they fit in with the general theme. As for the phantom show, we don't want it better than our own with the likelihood that it will be stolen.'

Beth asks, 'What if it is not stolen?'

Robert replies, 'Then our designs will compete with Henry's on an honest, contested basis and we have lost nothing, but I will take a lot of convincing that it will happen that way.'

Emma says, 'Girls, come with me, and I will sign you up and get all of your paperwork completed.'

The girls go out with Emma, and everyone moves out to begin their day. Claudia stays back to speak to Robert.

Claudia says, 'I wanted to thank you for your help, but you left the courthouse early.'

Robert replies, 'Yes, on security's advice that Henry didn't link us two together and knows whom he is dealing with.'

'But he has found where you live and will find out as soon as the advertising starts.'

'No, not for three weeks. Your name is mentioned only in part in the last advertisement. Until then, he still cannot link us together with the IFS. After the ads start, he will assume I hired you because you were proved innocent in the court case and will not go after you.'

'No, but he will come after you.'

'I can handle myself. Besides, I have a bodyguard with me, or should I say, driver.'

'Robert, take care. Do not take any unnecessary risks.'

'Don't worry, I will be all right.'

Claudia stops for a moment and looks into Robert's eyes and gives him a hug and goes off to put Beth to work and see Anna off.

28

Roger arranges for the advertisements to be rolled out progressively. In the first week, most competitors do not worry about MI, but after the third week, they recognize that a major player has re-established themselves within the industry.

By the third week, the rich and famous who want to be aligned with a fashion house seek out Claudia, and they made appointments to discuss their design requirements.

Unique designs are presented, and these are transformed into finished garments and are shown on red carpet events receiving accolades for the use of different materials, color, and shapes, so much so that MI's prices have to be increased to slow down the demand that is flowing into them.

The fashion house receives a reputation for honesty and innovative design and, because of the volume of work coming in, has to hire additional designers to accommodate the demand.

Only the inner group knows of Robert's plan, with the new staff being brought in to handle the new orders and to address short-term fashion parade requirements and special orders in design.

The modeling college also progresses and becomes the source of providing models to MI and other designers and agencies. The models who graduated from the college are in high demand because of their skill, professionalism, and dedication.

One evening, Claudia receives a telephone call from the president of a small sovereign nation whom she has known for many years and has kept in contact with, over the years. They are like family to her, as she used to visit them when she was a child, with her mother particularly on school holidays. The country is small, and the economy well run, but they do not have the resources like some of the European countries have. Claudia meets with them at their hotel at the end of the month to discuss their need.

The fashion house continues to get a reputation for its design work so much so that Robert can recoup his initial investment within nine months of opening MI's doors, and the business becomes profitable from the fifteenth months from commencing business.

The fashion house receives a reputation for being a place to work in who looks after its employees both remuneration wise and training.

Claudia makes her way to where the president is staying and, after passing through security, finally meets the president and his wife.

They discuss old times and talk about the family and the fact the president's daughters have grown up and are independent and are trying to establish an identity of their own. During the conversation, the president opens up to Claudia and advises her they have been invited to the royal wedding but intends to decline as the cost of costumes would be prohibitive for all his family to bear. The royal couple is insisting they attend, as the president and his family are close to the royal couple, but they do not want to stand out in the international press as paupers and disgrace their country.

Claudia thinks about the problem and finds out that there would be a party of five, comprising the president and his wife, his two daughters, and their son. Claudia telephones Robert and discusses the situation with him. Robert is prepared to attend to the designs and prepare the outfits conditional on payment of $100,000 and that the fashion house keeps ownership of the garments and copyright to the designs. The president agrees, and Claudia would design the garments for the prestige event.

Claudia wants to handle the designs personally and knows that if they are spectacular, the fashion house would benefit, as the wedding is to be televised worldwide. She knows you could not get better exposure than this throughout the world.

Claudia takes the measurements from all present and thanks the president and his wife and tells them not to worry and to accept the wedding invitation. She would ensure that they will look like heads of state should, and that the whole family would present well and be a credit to their country.

Claudia goes back to her office and designs the garments she feels are appropriate for the occasion. Anna comes in and looks at her designs and makes comments about them.

Anna says, 'These are old-fashioned designs, and we have used most of the styles on other dresses to clothe heads of state. You need something new and vibrant. Clean lines without ruffle.'

Beth walks in and sees the designs and says, 'This is wrong. You need the curves to go away from the back. Here, let me show you.' Both girls sketch what they thought was appropriate for a royal wedding, with long lines and curves for the ladies and straight lines for the men. After an hour, Claudia could see that the girls made sense and their designs are more superior to hers. They then move off to selecting materials and, after a couple of hours, know exactly what they want and how the president and his family would appear. They send the measurement and sketches to their wardrobe department, who make up the garments, and after two weeks, all have been completed.

Claudia gives each garment a thorough check to ensure they are well sewn and look spectacular. She telephones the president's wife and arranges for all the parties to attend her office for a fitting.

One week before the wedding, all arrive, hoping they will look elegant and not be criticized when the wedding is televised. All know that the world would watch them, as they are personal friends of the queen and that they would be the talking point if they were not clothed appropriately to the standard of such an occasion.

The five arrive at the MI building and are welcomed by Claudia, who is accompanied by several dressmakers and Anna and Beth. They take everyone to a room that had a lot of mirrors on the walls. Each is shown to a fitting room, and their garments are brought out for them to try on, with the designers moving from room to room. Eventually, everyone comes out wearing their garments, and they look very modern, elegant, and confident.

President says, 'Girls, you look stunning. I look twenty years younger and very striking.' The president then looks to his wife, who is wearing a simple-style dress that looked very modern and befitted her position. They all look at each other and could see that everyone was well dressed and in outfits that would impress even the most hardened critic.

President says, 'Claudia, you have done wonders for our country and us. We will be always in your debt.'

Claudia replies, 'You should thank the designers, Anna and Beth, as these were their designs. Remember, you are part of the inner circle who will be seen worldwide, and make sure they see you as we hope the designs will stand out and be noticed by the viewers and critics worldwide.'

I took the president and his family back into their fitting rooms to take off their garments and get back into their street clothes. They packed their suits and dresses into special suitcases, along with their designed shoes, handbags, and jewelry, and given to men who were brought along to carry the heavy suitcases.

The president and his wife thank Claudia and her team and leave to go home and then to England for the royal wedding.

The president flies back to his country in his private jet and then, after a few days, later flies off to London with his wife and children, where he and his family are expected to attend several minor functions before the royal wedding.

Claudia has designed their wardrobe, including what they are to wear in the week leading up to the wedding.

The wedding day comes quickly, and all the television networks are filming and broadcasting and describing the event in minute detail. Finally, the guests arrive, and the broadcasters describe their outfits. I described various celebrities wearing St Vincent de Paul garments even though they were designed by recognized designers, very expensive, however, they do not impress the gallery as the artistic features are obscure and the garments are, in reality, not suited for the occasion.

Finally, the president's car pulls up, and he steps out with his wife, daughters, and son stepping out behind him. They are described in favorable terms and make a hit with the fashion-conscious reporters. The simplicity of their design and the flow of the garments attract many favorable comments. The president's wife's dress and his daughters' dresses make an impression, and reporters scramble to find out who had designed them. Claudia's name is mentioned, and Beth and Anna's names associated with hers and her designs are well recognized, and so is her fashion house, MI.

The queen greets them, and they could see that they impress her with their appearance and speaks with them for a few minutes before moving to her official seat.

The bride arrives amidst much fanfare, and the couple are married with the eyes of the world upon them. There are comments made about the contents of the sermon delivered and the time it took, but considering the occasion, no one minded.

Orders come in for copies of the dresses and the designs to be licensed, and Claudia and Marque International receive a lot of accolades for their design. Young couples who are to get married want copies of the wedding dress and the bridesmaids' dresses.

Other major events during the year also exhibit Claudia's designs and that of her team. The company attracts a lot of positive publicity for their unconventional designs and a reputation of looking after their clientele.

While the demand is constant, the fashion house gains a reputation for innovative designs and attracts a lot of attention, especially from Charles Henry's people, who seemed to come off second best in designs, awards, and publicity, making Charles Henry very nervous.

Robert has received several telephone calls warning him what to expect if he continues to win fashion shows at the expense of Charles Henry and has his tires slashed on his car a few times to show that things are getting to where someone would be hurt if Marque International continues its presence on the world stage.

He arranges for all his designers and key personnel to be driven to and from work and security guards to be placed in their homes.

Robert arms himself just in case he finds himself in trouble and employs a further bodyguard as a chauffeur as an extra precaution.

The recognition of the fashion house brings in more orders from the rich and famous who are all scrambling to say they are a client of Marque International and possess one of their exclusive garments.

29

Claudia is nearing completion of her IFS designs, and Anna and Beth have designed the phantom wardrobe, which incorporated a lot of other designers' recognized concepts and features.

The time is nearing when the IFS is to be staged in Paris and when all the world's eyes would concentrate on the designs by the various recognized leaders in the industry.

Claudia works away on her last design when she receives a telephone call from one of her old friends in Paris who advises her that her uncle and benefactor, whom she had known since childhood, is very ill and has been hospitalized. The caller advises her he may not have much time left as his health is deteriorating and was not expected to live beyond the next few days.

Claudia is visibly upset and goes to see Robert.

Claudia says, 'Robert, I have to go to Paris. A member of my family is very ill, and I have been told that they do not expect him to live beyond the next few days. I must see him before he dies and then plan afterwards for his funeral. He lives alone, and there are no relatives in France that can help him. I will most probably will be away for about three weeks, possibly longer.'

Robert replies, 'By all means, take whatever time you need. Do we have to arrange for one of the other designers, Beth or Anna, to take over and finish the designs for the IFS?'

'No, they are all done. The finishing touches I will do before I leave or give Beth and Anna instructions as to what is to be done. My mother will come with me, as I am sure she would also want to see her brother before he dies.'

'Sharon, better go along with you just in case there is trouble. She can get backup from their European division if she needs it. Tell me of your flight details and where you will be staying. Also, after the funeral, I want you to scout out where we can set up a base in Paris for our people and where we can warehouse our garments. This will then make it a business trip, and MI will pay for the lot. You better get on and start making plans. Do you want Emma and Pat to go with you to help in finding us a place? They know Paris well and can assist you by doing some of the legwork and give you support if you need help with your family. There would be less chance of unpleasant interference if you were not alone over there.'

'Great idea. I will ask them if they can spare the time.'

Claudia then moves closer to Robert and gives him a big long kiss and says, 'You know I love you, and that's for your understanding.'

Robert replies, 'Yes, I know, but we can't let it out as it will put your life in danger if Charles Henry knew we were in love.'

Claudia says, 'I understand, but I still want one last kiss.'

They kiss and stare into each other's eyes and kiss again passionately. Claudia then leaves and goes back to MI's office. She asks the primary team to come into the meeting room and advises everyone that, owing to the ill health of her uncle, she must go to Paris to take care of his affairs. She advises the team that Robert thinks it would be an opportunity for Emma and Pat to accompany her to ensure that Charles Henry does not arrange for some mishap, and while there, Emma and Pat can start looking around for accommodation for the team to set up a base and where they can warehouse their garments.

Pat and Emma are delighted to look up on the internet as to what is available in Paris, and Sharon is also happy to accompany Claudia as long as they stay together.

Claudia makes the arrangements, and Sharon advises her European division of their plans and arranges for security to meet them on arrival.

Claudia goes home and advises her mother, who is keen to go to Paris to see her older brother and packs as they are due to fly off in two days' time. All the flights are booked, and everyone wraps up what they are doing so they don't have to come back to a mountain of work. They saved all their designs into the cloud, so they could have access to their database.

The day of departure comes quickly, and Robert asks the team to meet him in his office before they go to the airport.

Robert says, 'I know Claudia and her mother are basically going to see their relative, but I must again caution you as to the danger that you may confront from Charles Henry's men. Stay together or at least in a group of two or three so that they will not approach you or do anything to you, and this specifically means one of our own or security accompanies you to the restroom.' Sharon replies, 'Our European division is meeting us at the airport and will chauffer us around. They will have two of their people in the car at all times and with each group, so we will be well protected.'

Robert says, 'Take care, and may God be with you.'

The group moves out of Robert's office, and Claudia looks back at Robert.

Pat says, 'Well, for heaven's sake, give him a kiss. We all know about you two.'

Claudia and Robert kiss and hug each other momentarily and then let go, and the group makes their way out and into a minibus that is waiting to take them to the airport. They board their plane when it is announced, take off, and finally touch down at Charles De Gaul Airport.

They are met by security, and after they have made introductions, they are taken to their hotel and allowed to unpack and freshen up.

Claudia and her mother decide to go straight to the hospital to see her brother and check on his condition. Sharon accompanies them and phones through for a car to pick them up.

They were taken to the Paris Metropolitan Hospital, and make their way to where her brother was lying. As they approach his bed, he opens his eyes and immediately recognizes them and stretches out his arms to give them a big kiss and bursts into tears. He tries to say something, but his emotion overcomes him, and he ends up sobbing on their shoulders.

It is a tearful reunion, and after everyone has quietened down, he describes he had a stroke, and during the examination, they noted he has a large cancerous tumor on his liver, which is inoperable. The doctors could not tell him how much time he had left other than to say it was days rather than weeks. He does not want to die in hospital but rather at his chateau where he and his wife always stay and where Claudia would come to stay with them when she was a young girl and when she was in Paris doing her fashion shows or attending to design work.

Claudia goes to speak to the doctors, who advise her they can do nothing more for her uncle, and all that could be done under the circumstances is to ensure he is comfortable and control his pain. The doctors have no objections to him going home if there is a nurse on hand to attend to his needs. When he was ready to die or if he dies, they will have to call the hospital, who will send a doctor to his home and, once examined, would issue a death certificate. There would not need to be an autopsy, as the cause of death was known. The hospital would arrange for a doctor to visit twice a day to ensure he is comfortable and his pain is under control.

Claudia speaks to her mother, and both agree to move him back to his chateau so he could die in peace, in familiar surroundings. They would stay with him, as they are familiar with his chateau. It is home away from home for them.

Claudia and her mother go back to the hotel and advise Pat and Emma that they would stay with their brother during his last days. They all arrange to meet in the dining room of the hotel that night for dinner and would decide to move him from the hospital the next morning. Pat and Emma plan to scout out the suburbs of Paris the next day to see if they could see a place that would be suitable as a home base.

They have their meal in the evening, which is a somber affair, and once this is finished, everyone makes a move to their rooms, as the next day is going to require a lot of energy and footwork.

Pat and Emma agree to meet in the hotel's foyer at eight thirty. Their security team was waiting for them off to see if they could find suitable premises to be used as a French base.

Claudia and her mother agree to meet in Claudia's room at nine, and they would head off to the hospital and arrange for ambulance transport to move her uncle to the chateau. They get up and have their shower and breakfast and as planned, meet in Claudia's room. Sharon joins them, and they walk outside to wait for their security team, who are parked outside of the hotel. They drive to the hospital, and Claudia and her mother go upstairs to where her uncle is resting. Claudia greets her uncle with a kiss, and he tells her that the doctors have already arranged for transport to the chateau, which should collect him from the hospital in about half an hour's time. Her uncle gives her the keys to the chateau, and they collect his things and decide to head off and wait at the chateau for him.

They drive to the chateau, which is only some twenty minutes from the center of Paris. It is kept in good condition by servants who look after the cooking, cleaning, and gardening. Claudia's uncle is not a poor man and has made a lot of money in his early days. He bought the chateau for reasons of privacy, plus it has many rooms and is secured by a large brick wall all around and security gates at the front. Security drives up to the gates, and Claudia opens them by a remote controller, which was given to her by her uncle. They drive up to the chateau and are warmly greeted by the butler, who recognized Claudia and her mother.

Claudia asks for all the servants to assemble inside and, once their bags are placed in their rooms, goes downstairs to address those assembled.

Claudia says, 'I must first thank you for looking after my uncle and for calling me to advise me of his hospitalization. Unfortunately, the prognosis is not good, and they say that he will not live beyond a few days. I am telling you this as he already knows, but does not want to be treated any differently just because he is dying. I know this will be hard for everyone, so I will only ask you to do your best for him and look after him as you always have. My mother and I will keep him company in his last days. Are there questions?'

One servant asks, 'What is going to happen after he dies? Are we going to be dismissed, and if we are, then can we start looking for alternative work now as most of us depend on a weekly income?'

Claudia replies, 'I don't know what is going to happen after he dies or what arrangements he has made regarding the chateau. As soon as I know, I will tell you so you can decide what you must do. Until then, I can only ask you to trust me. Most of you have known me for many years, and I will let you know as soon as I find out. Until then, do your best to make him feel at home and cared for.'

Shortly after, the ambulance arrives, and they pull up outside the front door. Claudia shows them where her uncle's room is on the ground floor, and they take him there and put him to bed, sitting him up with the support of some pillows. They place him on oxygen and check his heartbeat and oxygen levels. The staff all come in, and Claudia's uncle looks at them and says, 'First, I must thank you for looking after me when I had my attack, and you called the ambulance and my niece and sister.

You truly are very loyal, supportive. No doubt you have already been told that I have very little time left, and I wanted to pass in my home rather than in unfamiliar surroundings. You never know what unpleasant things you can pick up in the hospital.' Everybody chuckles at this mild witticism. 'You must be wondering what is going to happen to you when I die. Well, you should not worry, as I have already made a will, leaving $10,000 to each of you and the rest of my estate to my niece. My sister refused to have any of my assets, saying that my niece would be able to handle my estate far better than she could, and I know she will always be welcomed here. I know my niece Claudia loves this place and treats it as home and will keep it, so therefore I assume your employment is secure in the future. The only thing I ask is that you stop worrying about me and go about your duties as normal.'

As Claudia's uncle, Mr. Montel, is speaking, there is a knock at the front door, and the servant comes in and says the doctor is here to make sure everything went well with the transportation and that Mr. Montel is not in pain.

Everyone moves out of the room, glad to hear they still have a job, and leaves the doctor with Mr. Montel. Claudia and her mother stay behind to see what the doctor says.

The doctor examines Mr. Montel and notes that he has a higher than normal temperature and that he seems to breathe irregularly. He gives him an antibiotic injection and orders him to take a nap, as he may have used up his energy reserve during the day. The doctor says he would return in the afternoon and leaves.

Claudia asks, 'Uncle, why did you leave the chateau to me and not Mum?'

Mr. Montel replies, 'She didn't want it and felt you would appreciate it more than her. Besides, she will use it whenever she is in Paris, whoever owns it. There is enough room here for both of you.' Claudia's mother says, 'I am sure you will keep it in memory of your uncle. No arguments. I get some money and you get the rest, including all investments, including warehouses and several factories and retail premises.'

Mr. Montel adds, 'Claudia, after my death, you must go to my solicitors, and they will attend to transferring all the property and monies to you. Sell the investments as soon as you can, as there will be a financial crunch in a year's time or two affecting the world's economies. Things are not going well in America with their banks selling junk bonds, which will cause a worldwide crisis. You do not want to hold shares during that period, but rather sell them now and get the best price. Under no circumstances are you to invest in the bonds being promoted by Lehman Brothers as they are worthless. Here is the name of my broker. He has been told what to do, and I have given him your name. He is an honest man and will look after you. Sell while the market is high and then buy in again when it hits rock bottom. It is a pity you are not married or considering marrying someone. I would rest better knowing you have someone to help you through the process and be with you when I pass.'

Claudia replies, 'There is someone, but because of the opposition to our efforts to present a fashion show at the IFS, we have decided not to tell anyone until the IFS is over and the outcome known. We have had splendid success so far, and the Marque International name is recognized worldwide and is gaining more support every day. This has annoyed our main competitor, Charles Henry, who will stop at nothing to win.'

Mr. Montel says, 'I am glad for you and hope you win. I wondered why the security guards were around with guns. You should be careful. That mob plays rough.'

Claudia replies, 'Yes, I will, and now you must rest before lunch.'

Both move out of Mr. Montel's room to allow him to rest.

After two hours, Claudia goes back in to check on her uncle. She enters his room and stands at the door to see if he was awake. She notices he is not breathing and runs to tell her mother. They both go into his room and feel his pulse but could not find one. They ring the doctor, who came over immediately. He checks Mr. Montel's heartbeat but could not detect one. He looks at the two ladies and says, 'I'm sorry, Mr. Montel has passed away.' The doctor writes out a death certificate.

Both Claudia and her mother stay for a few minutes with tears running down their cheeks but glad that he did not have to suffer before death overtook him.

Claudia telephones the funeral home, advising them that her uncle has died and asking them to collect the body and prepare it for burial. Claudia then phones Mr. Montel's minister at his local church and advises him of the passing of her uncle. During her discussions with him, they set a time for the funeral to take place in three days' time. Claudia then gathers all the staff together and says, 'I am sorry to tell you that Mr. Montel has died in his sleep. The funeral will take place in three days' time. Those who want to attend may do so.' Some wept, while others remain dry-eyed. Claudia goes to her room and cries. She could hold her emotion intact until now but finds that finally she could not control them. After about fifteen minutes, her mother comes into her room and sees she is crying and tries to console her telling her that her uncle would not want her to get emotional but think of the good times she had at the chateau before her uncle took ill.

Claudia goes into the bathroom and washes her face and combs her hair and goes downstairs to see what is happening. Most of the staff have gone home, and her uncle's body is still in his room waiting for transportation.

About an hour later, a vehicle arrives from the funeral home, and two men with a body bag enter Mr. Montel's room and collect the body to transport it to the funeral home.

Claudia telephones Mr. Montel's minister to discuss what will be required at the service. The minister was expecting the call, as he knew it would be left up to him to arrange this. He calls in the next day to discuss the funeral arrangements.

Claudia realizes that with all of what has happened, she has not telephoned Pat and Emma and does so to get her mind off the death and funeral arrangements and to give her emotions a chance to settle down.

She telephones Emma, who has just gotten back to the hotel and is with Pat in her room discussing the day's events.

Claudia says, 'Emma, it is good to hear your voice.'

Emma asks, 'How are things with you and your uncle?'

Claudia replies, 'We brought him home and to get him in his bed, but the excitement must have been too much for him. When he went to sleep, he never woke up. The funeral is three days' time.'

Emma says, 'I am sorry to hear that. You must be upset. Do you want Pat and myself to come over and keep you company for a while?'

Claudia replies, 'I would like that, but the staff are also upset, and I gave them the rest of the day off, which means we would have to fend for ourselves.'

Emma asks, 'Why don't we meet at a restaurant somewhere and we can catch up with what we found out?'

Claudia replies, 'No, it is hard to get privacy at a restaurant, and security is concerned about our safety in a place as public as a restaurant. I think the best idea would be for Pat and yourself to come out here so we can talk privately. I will arrange for some take away to be delivered, and we can talk while we have dinner. What would you like to eat—chicken, beef, lamb, pasta, rice, you name it, and I am sure we can arrange for it to be delivered?'

Emma asks, 'Why don't you order a plate of each, and everyone can help themselves with whatever they want? Also, order some salad and bread and maybe a few bottles of wine to take the pain away.'

Claudia replies, 'I can arrange all of that. We will see you within an hour.'

Claudia, who knows Paris well, makes several telephone calls and then goes down to the dining room with her mother. They take a tablecloth from a nearby cupboard and spread it over the large table and take some plates from another cupboard along with some knives and forks and glasses.

Pat goes to her room, and both girls get out of their formal clothes and change into casual clothes and make their way out to security, who has been advised about what is happening. Security drives them to the chateau and was given access once Claudia verified their identity.

Claudia meets them at the front door, and everyone hugs each other as if they had not seen each other for ages. They walk into the dining room followed by security. Claudia's mother is there, as is Sharon, who greeted everyone.

Emma says, 'We're sorry to hear about your uncle. It must have been a big shock that he died on the same day they brought him home from the hospital.'

Claudia replies, 'It was. It is good to see you, and thanks for coming over. I felt you may be tired and not willing to come over.'

Pat says, 'We were going to say we will see you later on, but you sounded very down, and we thought you may want some company.'

The doorbell rings, and security goes to the door and comes back with several boxes containing plates of food and about six bottles of wine. Claudia goes out and pays the people and thanks them for being punctual.

Claudia says, 'We had better get stuck into it before it gets cold. Take a plate, everyone, help yourselves. I ordered a lot, so don't worry about not having enough food.'

They all tuck into the food, and Sharon fills the glasses with the wine, and everyone talks about their experiences in and around Paris. After an hour, everyone has enough, and they took the plates into the kitchen, where one of the girls finds some coffee, and everyone makes themselves a cup of coffee or tea and settles down in the dining room.

Claudia asks, 'How did you get on with your searches?'

Pat replies, 'We began by going to the hall where the fashion parade was to be held and looked around, trying to familiarize ourselves as to how the parade was going to be held and where we were to enter and exit from. We noted the change rooms were away from the catwalk, which made things awkward. We have an estimate of the costs, which we were going to send off to Robert, but maybe it is best that you look at it first, and if you are happy with it, you can email it to him.'

Emma says, 'As for where we can stay, that is another story. We looked at a couple of places that will come up for rent in the next month, but they are asking the earth for a two-month period. It would be cheaper to buy a place of our own in the suburbs and bus ourselves in rather than pay their prices. We will have to continue our search, as most of the places close by are already taken by the other fashion houses, including Charles Henry, who has taken two adjoining places and a small warehouse close to where the fashion show is to the venue.'

Claudia says, 'Girls, what about this place? There are two guest houses on the estate, which are currently unoccupied, which will give us about thirty rooms in which to accommodate our entire team and provide around-the-clock security. We can bus people to and from the venue and make sure everyone is safe.'

Emma replies, 'It seems a good idea, but we will have to still look around to see if there are any alternative sites.'

Claudia asks, 'Look around where? The other fashion houses have snapped most of the decent places up, which means people can charge premium prices for what they have on offer.'

Emma says, 'Look around the Eiffel Tower and other sites of Paris.'

Everyone laughs.

Emma asks, 'How else are we going to see the sights of Paris?'

Sharon replies, 'I think you have a good idea, and if we are based here at the chateau, we won't have multiple sites to secure.'

Pat says, 'Let us have a look at the facilities tomorrow, and then we can compare the quality and price so we can all report back to Robert. I estimate we will need a team of thirty to thirty-five people to put both fashion shows on. We have only two months to go and then we are on centre stage.'

Emma asks, 'When is the funeral?'

Claudia replies, 'Three days' time. His old friend and minister of the local church, Jacques DeVidia will hold it. You will come, won't you?'

Pat says, 'Well, we didn't know your uncle, so I don't think it would be right for us to attend. Besides, neither of us has clothes to wear to a funeral. We will look out of place.'

Claudia says, 'I understand. I just thought you would attend to give me moral support and help me through the service.'

Claudia cries, and the other two could see she was upset.

Pat says, 'All right, you can stop the waterworks. We will attend the funeral. We will have to go shopping for black dresses.'

Claudia replies, 'I know a very good shop near to here. I will take you both there tomorrow so you can buy what you need. We could use the outfit you select for the time we need to be in formal attire during the fashion show. I will pick you up at around ten tomorrow morning. But I have a better idea. Why don't you and Emma check out of your hotel tomorrow and come and stay here with us? There are plenty of rooms, and all the servants will be here tomorrow. I can get them to prepare two rooms, and you can move in tomorrow morning before we go shopping. You will save on the hotel bills.'

Sharon says, 'That is a good idea, and I can monitor you both. From a security point of view, it would be better to have everyone here rather than separated.'

Emma replies, 'It is OK with me.'

Pat says, 'It makes sense. So, we will check out of our hotel tomorrow. We will expect you at ten.'

Both Emma and Pat get up and walk to the front door and give Claudia and her mother a kiss and get into their security car and drive back to their hotel. They advise the reception that they will check out tomorrow at ten and if they could have their account ready. Both go up to their rooms and get themselves ready for bed. The next morning, they check out of the hotel and go down to the foyer to wait for Claudia, who arrives fifteen minutes later with Sharon. They get into Sharon's car and drive off to the chateau. Once there, they are shown to their rooms. They unpack their clothes. Claudia comes into Pat's room and says, 'Well, does it meet your expectations?'

Pat replies, 'Yes, it is roomy and bright. Very nice.'

Claudia says, 'I will leave you to unpack, and we can meet downstairs in twenty minutes and go off shopping.'

Claudia goes out of Pat's room and walks into Emma's room, who was unpacking her clothes, and advises her they would go shopping in twenty minutes and they were going to meet downstairs.

They all meet downstairs and go off to the shops. Each purchases a black or navy dress or slacks and a white or blue blouse with a black or navy coat to match. Those that bought a dress also purchase black stockings to complete their outfit. Once finished, everyone goes back to the chateau for lunch and to relax.

30

obert has completed a hard day at work and is keen to get home so he could unwind. He reads an email from Claudia, who is keeping him up to date with what was happening in Paris and that they are all together at Claudia's chateau. He reads her report about the premises where the fashion parade is being held and the rooms allocated to them on the day of the fashion show.

He emails her the update from Beth and Anna on the finishing touches made to the last garments and that the phantom clothes are ready to be shipped. He closes his computer and switches off his light and walks to the foyer, where he is met by his driver, who is a security guard. He also notices another man standing near his driver and approaches them.

Robert asks, 'Are we ready to go?'

Driver replies, 'Yes, and head office has received a tipoff that there may be trouble as we are getting close to the fashion show. They believe we both should be around you from now on until you fly off to Paris.'

Robert says, 'I think it is an overkill, but I will leave it to you to manage the safety issues. Well, let us get going.'

The three men enter the lift to go down to the car park.

When the doors of the lift open, all step out and walk to the security car when, suddenly, a loud bang is heard, which is followed by two more bangs. Each of the men move behind some cover, and the security guards, who recognize the bangs as shots, draw their guns. As Robert reaches for his own gun, he feels a sudden burning in his shoulder, and he realizes they have hit him. The bullet has gone through him and wedged into the back wall. Robert grabs his handkerchief and places it over the wound area to stop the bleeding. He feels the pain as he presses the handkerchief over the wound into the gaping hole.

Robert could see a man hiding behind a car, so he moves closer to where the man was. As the man moves up to take another shot at the security guards, Robert raises his gun and fires in the shooter's direction. There is silence, so he moves up to where the man is hiding and yells out, 'Call the police! I have shot him. He is dead.'

The police are called and are at the scene within ten minutes of being informed. The police take statements from each of the men and call an ambulance to attend to Robert's wound.

The paramedics arrive and dress the wound and then transport Robert to the hospital to have his wound properly treated. Robert is unsteady on his feet because of the loss of blood.

The dead man was recognized and known to police as a gang member. Robert is an obstacle that Charles Henry is not prepared to tolerate. People acting on behalf of Charles Henry are making sure there is no opposition. As the police put it, the intention is to take out the opposition and eliminate the competition.

Robert is brought to the hospital and is taken immediately to the operating theater, where he undergoes a three-hour operation to repair his shoulder. He is then taken to a private room. They sedated him to ensure the pain does not get the better of him. Security has placed two men in his room and keeps guard around the clock to ensure no one makes a second attempt.

News of the shootout makes headlines around the world declaring a well-known gangster was shot dead in a shootout by Robert Somerset, who was the principal of Marque International.

Claudia, who is with the girls after dinner watching the news, hears of the shooting and is deeply distressed to the degree that she is going to take the next flight back to the States to see how Robert was. The girls convince her she should not put herself in danger and draw attention to herself, as this is not what Robert wants. Claudia telephones the hospital and is able to speak to the doctor, who assures her he is all right and out of danger but couldn't speak to her, as he has been sedated by the pain and is still groggy and slurring his words.

The next morning, police come to interview Robert and, after they have completed the interview, advise Robert that they will not press any charges, as this is a simple case of self-defense.

Claudia rings Robert the next day.

Claudia asks, 'Robert, are you all right? Do you want me to come back to the States?'

Robert replies, 'It is good to hear your voice. No, it is best you do not come back, as it will give the gang another avenue to get us to throw in the towel. If they get at me through you, they know I will not risk your life for a fashion show, so it is best that we are not linked until the show is over. I know it is hard on both of us, but you must stay in Paris and look after the group who will be progressively coming over to assist you in the show. I have Beth and Anna here to attend to the requirements from this end, and they are both protected by security.'

'So were you, but they still got past security and shoot you.'

'No, that was not the case. We never thought that Charles Henry would try to kill me in such a blatant way. Now that he has shown his hand, everyone is on their toes, including the police, who have given me round-the-clock protection, and that includes our people, our business premises, and our homes. Our own security now knows what to expect and has the team to take care of it. The police advise they will not be charging me for killing the gangster, but consider there will be retribution against us for doing so. Under the circumstances, you and your mother had better not come back here but stay over there and start planning on where we are going to house the team of thirty-five, which will come over shortly, as the fashion show is only six weeks away.'

'Yes, I know you're right, but I would like to see you just to hold you in my arms.'

'So would I, but the danger is too great, and we can't let on the fact that we have a relationship. Otherwise, Charles Henry will win, and we will all end up in the hospital or the morgue. Lets' make sure the bastard loses big time and that no one member of our team gets injured.'

'Are you coming over for the show?'

'Yes, but I don't know when. Possibly when our garments are shipped over. What is happening with accommodation for all our people?'

'My uncle has bequeathed his entire estate to me, so all of our team can stay with me at the chateau. There are two guest houses on the estate giving us enough rooms to house all of our staff and allow us to protect them while they are here.'

'That sounds great. Keep Emma there to help with the venue and the fashion shows and send Pat back so she can arrange for the rest of our team to fly over. Pat can come back with the team to give you a hand.'

'Darling, please take care. I must go to my uncle's funeral tomorrow. I don't want to go to my future husband's as well.'

'Are you proposing?' 'Yes.'

'I accept. I love you. Take care.'

Robert is kept in hospital for a week and then is discharged. He goes to his apartment and the next day attends work to catch up with the work he has missed.

Charles Henry rings him and says that he heard that there is some trouble and that he is concerned whether Robert is intending to pull out of the competition.

Robert says, 'It is nice of you to ring, but, no, we are still on track to attending the show and would be shortly sending over our garments that we intend to display at the fashion show.'

Charles Henry replies, 'Well, it's good that you are still thinking positively. I would have thought you would be concerned about the safety of your team and might decide that the risk was too great.'

Robert says, 'No, I have a clear picture as to who is at fault here and don't have to worry about my staff because the first sign of them being threatened or harassed, I will be in your office with a gun stuck down your throat, and believe me, I will not hesitate to pull the trigger. I was in Afghanistan and know what tricks they pull, which I can tell you, or your gangsters could not match these. So don't start threatening me or my people, as I will come after you and you alone, and I won't miss when I pull the trigger.'

Charles Henry pauses for a moment and then just slams the phone down.

Robert intentionally referred to the shipment of their garments to make sure that Charles Henry would take the bait.

Beth and Anna advise Robert that they have completed their task and are ready to ship their garments over to Paris.

31

The last speaker steps down from the pulpit after making his speech about his close friend Henry Montel, whom he had known since early school days.

Mr. Jacques DeVidia, the minister of St Timothy Church, steps into the pulpit and surveys the packed church.

Minister says, 'Funerals are always difficult, especially for the relatives because they are forced finally to accept that their loved one is gone from them. All they have now are memories.

'Funerals are hard to accept for those who have not made peace with the Lord. They tend to feel uneasy as they think, "I could be next, and I have done nothing regarding my relationship with God." And some will question if there is a God.

'For relatives, there is emptiness, as recently, the person was talking to you or playing ball or some game with you, but now nothing, no one to take their place. Many relatives find this emptiness hard to accept and often, momentarily, see their loved ones in their favorite chair or at the dinner table or standing in the hallway. This is a mirage, and they soon realize that at that moment, they are alone with memories and grieve their loss.

'Others, of course, would not care, as they don't believe in a God or life after death and think that they will just disappear once they die. They are betting on the fact that they will not have to see God, as they believe there is not one. Unfortunately, they will have to confront the Almighty God and give an account of what they have done with their life and be told, "Begone with you to hell as I don't know you.'

'Henry Montel was a religious man who believed in Jesus Christ and who had faith in Him. He was tested many times through trials, but always believed God would see him through them and trusted God. He never used the Lord's name in vain and always tried to help the poor and needy, both financially and time wise, providing a mobile kitchen that went from park to park each night feeding the poor and homeless. This work is being supported now by his niece Claudia, who will carry on her uncle's tradition in supporting those who sleep in the parks under a bench who do not have anywhere to go and have no means of support.

'At funerals, invariably the question comes around as to where is the deceased's soul heading? To heaven or hell?

'Many try to avoid this question by saying there is not a heaven or hell. But it does not take much to convince those willing to accept the evidence and truth that this is really an attempt to fool oneself in believing what Satan wants you to believe.

'Where does a person go when they die? The question is relatively easy to answer. If the person believed in God and had faith in Jesus Christ, then the Bible tells us he will have an eternal life after death and will go to heaven. If they do not believe in Jesus Christ, they won't end up in heaven, but hell.

'Some people foolishly believe that their good deeds will be enough to give them eternal life, but this is not the case. There is only one path to heaven, and that is by having faith in the Father. It is a narrow path and only for the faithful.'

'Some people think heaven is a democracy where they will present their case to the Lord, and since they feel they are good talkers and persuasive, they will present a compelling argument to the Lord if He exists, sufficient to get them across the line. The reality is they will not be given the opportunity, as they will be told, "Begone with you. I never knew you."

'Heaven is a dictatorship run by God. It is the same God you get to know here on earth and the same God in whom you have faith in. 'God created mankind, not the other way around, yet most times, man has created a different God in their minds to the one that is described in the Bible.

'You would not think God to be a dictator, would you? But this is the case. Yet He gives you a choice on earth to either follow His ways or Satan's. He does not tell you which way to go and leaves the decision for you. You either follow Him willingly and have eternal life or go with Satan and go to purgatory. Yet with such a clear-cut decision to make, you would think that the majority would say yes to eternal life, but that is not the case. Most, in fact, are hesitating, not knowing which way to go and at the end, die in torment because they did not understand that this decision was for them to make alone. No decision is to deny God and suffer the consequences.'

'We have yet to address the question, what happens when you die? 'Well, there is no definitive answer, as no one has come back to tell us except Jesus, who was resurrected. So, we rely on two sources of evidence—His word and the Bible.

'We are told that when you die, you temporarily end up in purgatory, where the righteous and wicked are separated until the last judgement. It is neither heaven nor hell. Jesus, who has the key to unlock the gates of purgatory, releases the righteous.

'We must not construe Hades as the last place for the condemned. Once all the believers have been resurrected into heaven, they will throw Hades into "the lake of fire comprising burning sulfur", which is called hell. That means that the non-believers will experience a second death.'

'All of this is clearly set out in the Bible, yet many do not care to find out what awaits them if they do nothing. If you ignore what the Bible says or if you come to church every Sunday and are a one-hour Christian, then you will end up in hell. If you fit into this category, I urge you to find faith in Jesus before it is too late. It could be tonight or tomorrow when it is your time, and then you will be on your own, not able to rectify your indecision or where you are going to end up.'

'You have been given a free will, and Jesus levies no pressure as to which path you take. The dictator stands back and allows you to decide. The deceiver rushes in to ensure you stay in sin by offering you what this world has, which stays with this world when you die. Jesus offers you eternal life and riches in heaven, which last forever. Do not be deceived as to what this world offers you, but look beyond it, so you too will stand before God and have your sins pardoned by his death on the cross.'

'We stand and look at Henry lying in this coffin, knowing his body will be returned to the earth and is soul readying itself for the resurrection and final transformation to heaven. I know this is the case, as I knew the man. But unfortunately, I know some of you have not taken up the faith and will not see Henry again unless you change and follow the Lord. Ponder for a moment and think, are you that much different from Henry? Do you also want eternal life, or are you prepared to take the risk and end up in hell?'

'I ask you to seek the Lord and ask for His help to find the right path and see you on it before it is too late.'

'I hope when it is your time that I do not have to stand before your loved ones and, when asked by them, say, "He was a candidate for hell, and that's where he will end up. You will never see him again." The service can be great. The coffin can be expensive and the hopes high, but if you are not a God-fearing person, you will never make it even if the send-off is first class and your comrades speak eloquently of you.'

'Let us pray . . .'

32

Pat has returned from Paris and is glad to be home.

She makes sure everything that they need for the fashion parade regarding the phantom garments was packed and the sequence in which the garments are to be displayed, clearly marked.

Robert telephones the freight forwarding company and arranges for them to collect the garments under security and to ensure they are air freighted to a warehouse that is close to the fashion venue. They made arrangements to have them securely wrapped and strapped to ensure no one could tamper with the garments. The company that is given the task of shipping the garments to Paris is a world- renowned freight forwarder and has a reputation of excellence. The IFS sent one of its auditors to examine the garments and to mark them appropriately as being the garments for exhibition, and they each were catalogued and registered in the IFS database. They collected the garments with security staying with them at all times until they were loaded on the plane for Paris. They secured the upright cases with padlocks and bubble wrapped to ensure no one could open them. They were appropriately labeled and addressed to a warehouse near to where Claudia was staying. They placed the shipment on board an air freighter and it took off for Paris.

The real garments that were to be used for the fashion parade were divided into ten smaller shipments and were placed in special waterproof bags and crated up and sent to a different warehouse, which is owned by the freight forwarding company, and does not look like anything of great value. They could be taken easily for supportive garments and not the prime garments. They, too, are audited and appropriately marked by the IFS audit team to ensure they could be used during the show. These were progressively shipped over to Paris over a four-week period and were delivered to Claudia's chateau, where they were housed in a special room and left to hang to ensure they were right for the show.

About a week after the first lot had been air freighted, Claudia makes enquiries about the whereabouts of the phantom shipment, as they have not received it. The freight company checks its records and notes it has been dispatched and received at the warehouse, but its whereabouts are not known. They made an investigation as to what had happened to the goods, but no one could locate them. After a further frantic day of searching, no one could advise what had happened to the garments that were shipped over.

Claudia goes to the fashion committee and reports the situation, declaring that their designs have gone missing and, unless found, they could not take part in the show. The committee makes it clear that they don't care what the problem is as it is for the participants to ensure they can put on their fashion show, and if they do not, then there would be penalties levied against that fashion house for breach of contract.

The freight company could not explain the disappearance of the shipment and put on extra people to find what had happened to the shipment.

Claudia reports the matter to the other participants and makes a big show of the fact that their designs have been stolen and calls in the police, who start an investigation.

Charles Henry has arranged for the shipment to be intercepted at the warehouse, and several people working for the forwarding agents are paid off to turn a blind eye while they transferred the shipment to Charles Henry's warehouse.

Charles Henry does not have faith in his own designers to win as they had lost several shows and thinks that Claudia would design something far better than his team could ever do. He is determined to hijack the shipment and use this as if his own people had designed them. If anyone objected to his show, he would just say it was sour grapes from the loser. He has the shipment brought into his warehouse and unpacked and the packaging dealt with to ensure no one could point the finger at him for stealing the garments. He swaps the auditor's registration number on each garment as if it were his garments that were sent over. He keeps all the garments under wraps and away from his designers.

Robert arranges for all the design and modeling team to prepare to go to Paris and books a small executive jet to take everyone over to Paris and to ship the rest of the fashion parade garments over with him.

Three weeks before the show, the party leaves for Paris and, after a turbulent flight, arrives at the airport and boards a bus for the chateau. Once there, they all greet Claudia and Emma as lost friends, and all are shown to their rooms and allowed to settle in. That night, they have a get-together party, and at that function, Claudia advises them of the missing garments, the police has been informed along with the fashion show's own security, and that the authorities have great expectations of the garments being found before the commencement of the fashion show.

The next day after breakfast, the group is taken on a tour of Paris and shown the tourist attractions and landmarks of the city. At night, they attend a nightclub, and all enjoy themselves thoroughly with a few having too much to drink and making a nuance of themselves. The day after is a rest day for everyone to get their energy back and to concentrate on the show ahead.

On day two, they are taken to where the fashion parade is to take place and are given time to familiarize themselves with the layout and what facilities are going to be at their disposal.

The models walk the catwalk to get familiar with its size and how long they have to show off their garments. Emma makes sure they are familiar with the position of TV cameras and those filming the show for international broadcasters.

Back at home base, Robert and Pat make their way to the airport and board their flight to Paris. Security meets them at the airport, who whisks them off to the chateau, where they meet up with the previous group, Claudia, and Emma.

Claudia takes Robert into a private study on the pretext she is reporting to him, but she wants to hold him and give him a big kiss and make sure there is no permanent injury following the shooting. After half an hour, they reappear composed as if they had a meeting, and they brought Robert up to speed with what had happened.

The models are taken into a private room where they try on their garments and Pat makes the final touches with her team to ensure proper fit. Everyone is busy making sure that they have delivered all the garments and that they are placed on the rack in sequence order and that none are missing.

At the end of the day, all had been attended to, and everyone settles down to dinner comprising a smorgasbord of various dishes and meats.

After everyone has eaten and the plates put away, they bring in coffee and tea, and again, those who want beverages help themselves to their drink. Some go for a brandy, while others scotch, but most have coffee or tea. When things quieten down, Robert asks everyone to be quiet for a minute as he wants to say a few words.

Robert says, 'Before boring you with my speech, I would like to thank you for having the faith in Marque International and giving your best to ensure we become the winners in this year's IFS design award.'

'We started off with a bankrupted company that no one wanted, and you have resurrected it to a position of excellence and respect. I must give recognition to Vicki Santana, who started off resurrecting the reputation of Marque International and who died in tragic circumstances.'

Some of those present start to cry, while others could be seen to become emotional.

Robert says, 'Tomorrow, we will present her work in the first show followed by Claudia's and your works. Tomorrow, we have the chance of demonstrating our designs and that the thugs of this world cannot intimidate us. We overcame problems with designers and found out that we could not get models. Well, now we have world-class models that will carry our brand down the catwalk and, I hope after tomorrow, stay with us rather than accept the lucrative offers that will be made to them after we win.'

There is applause, and the models are embarrassed to think they would leave Marque International.

Robert adds, 'Claudia would like to say a few words to you before we close.'

Claudia says, 'We have all worked hard to achieve what we have designed and will present tomorrow. One of Vicki's ideas for Marque International was that senior designers were not to take the credit from the junior designers. That tradition will be part of our attitude to training and nurturing new designers and allowing them to show off their designs while still developing their skills under the umbrella of a recognized fashion house. Tomorrow, the designs created by each of you will be shown under your names, so be prepared to stand at the entrance as you are called out. As most of the designs were done by me, then I will lead the second show, the first show comprising Vicki's designs and then my designs, followed by Beth's, Anna's, and then each one of you who contributed by providing outfits for the show. Me or anyone else will not take the credit for your designs, and you will get recognition for your ingenuity. Good luck, everyone, and now it is up to our modeling team to carry our creation to the public down the catwalk. Good luck, everyone.'

Applause rings out, and everyone is excited as they thought Claudia would claim their designs, as was the usual tradition. The junior designers gather around Claudia, thanking her for having faith in them and allowing them to be recognized.

Everyone finishes and slowly goes to their rooms to ensure they get a good night's sleep, as they know tomorrow would be hectic.

33

t about midnight, Claudia was awakened by what seemed to be an engine noise outside the chateau gates. She looks out and sees her three principal models walking up to the big gates with a suitcase in hand and stepping into a car, which drives off. She does not understand what is happening, so she goes to one of the model's rooms and knocks on the door; no answer, so she opens the door and goes in. The bed is not slept in, but there is a note near the bed, which she opens and reads, 'Dear Claudia, sorry to do this to you, but Charles Henry has made it clear that if I don't withdraw from the fashion show, he will put my parents into hospital and possibly ensure they are not around to see me become a model. He has tried to buy me off, but I refused to accept his money. He has arranged for me to fly back home tonight on a commercial flight and guarantees he will not hurt my parents. Sorry, and love to all.'

Claudia grabs the note and runs into Emma's room, waking Emma. After Emma has woken up, she explains to Emma what she saw and gives her the letter to read. Emma is shocked and says, 'Quick, we have to tell Pat.' Both go to Pat's room and wake her up. Emma says, 'Pat, we are in trouble. Henry has got at our top three models, and they are on their way back home, leaving us short for the tomorrow's show. Here, read this.'

Pat reads the note. 'Oh my god, how low can someone get? We have to tell Robert.' All three go to Robert's room and, without knocking, open the door and walk in. They switch the light on and close the door behind them. Robert is startled and surprised to see them in their pajamas and says, 'All three? I must be dreaming, or we have already won.'

Pat says, 'Stop dreaming. We have a big problem on our hands. Three of our top models have left us the night before the show and have returned home. We cannot manage the catwalk on the team we have.'

Robert asks, 'How do you know this?'

Claudia replies, 'I was awakened about twenty minutes ago and looked out the window and saw our top three models walking towards the chateau's main gate where a vehicle was parked with its lights on and engine running. I went to Sue's room, and she left this note, which said that she must withdraw from the show because Henry has threatened her parents.'

Robert reads the note and looks at Emma and says, 'What do you think, Emma?'

Emma says, 'That bastard has got at our girls and has crippled us where we least expected.'

Robert replies, 'First, you will all have to put on robes, as three near-naked women are becoming hard to constrain after midnight. No, two can get a robe on. The third can come and stay with me.'

Claudia says, 'Robert, are you mad, worrying about sex when we have been hit midsection and cannot do tomorrow's show?'

Robert replies, 'All right, this is what we do. Get a robe on and check the other girl's rooms and see if they have left any notes. Then come back here and we will talk about it. And be quiet, as I do not want anyone else to know about this.'

All girls go off to their rooms and put on their robes and go to see if there are any notes left by the other girls. There are none. They then go back to Robert's room and close the door behind them.

Robert asks, 'Were there any other notes left?'

Claudia replies, 'No.'

Robert asks, 'Emma, you have your laptop with you, haven't you?'

Emma replies, 'Yes, I always carry it around with me. Why?'

Robert says, 'check Sue's employment record and see where she lives and who her parents are.'

Emma goes out of Robert's room and in a few minutes, comes back with her laptop. She goes to the section that contains employees' details and sees that Sue is a foster child and does not know her parents.

Emma says, 'She is a lying bastard. She doesn't know who her parents are. She is lying.'

Robert says, 'After I got shot, I was in hospital for a week and then went back to work. I received a telephone call from Charles Henry, who clarified that he will not allow us to win the show and be prepared to pull out. I knew he had something up his sleeve, and it has been proven that he stole our garments as we predicted he would. I then thought where else could he try to cripple us, and, of course, I came back to the modeling of our garments.'

Pat says, 'But if he had stolen our shipment, we would not have had to worry about the fashion show. There would be nothing to show off.'

Robert replies, 'Yes, but Henry makes sure. He doesn't leave anything to chance.'

Claudia says, 'So that still leaves us in a no-win situation.' Robert replies, 'Not really. Two days before I left for Paris, I had a garnishee order drafted by my legal team and asked them to serve it on each of our four top models' banks where we deposit their modeling fees. The order was for information from their bank as to the amount in their accounts and details of any recent deposits and to freeze their accounts and pay any moneys they received to my company for modeling commission and fees. The day before we flew out, all four of our top models' bank accounts received deposits of $350,000 each, and this was transferred to MI under the court order. If the girls want the money, they will have to begin proceedings against MI. Otherwise, I am claiming the money as fees in training them. Henry has paid them to throw a spanner in our works and to prevent the show going ahead.'

Pat says, 'Well, he has done that, hasn't he? We can't leave it to the others to carry the load.'

Robert replies, 'We won't have to. I arranged for six of our other girls to be flown over on a different airline, and they are in Paris in different hotels ready for your call.'

Pat says, 'Six, you said? That's great. Is Kim with them?'

Robert replies, 'Yes, and Anna, who has just become recognized by Vogue.'

Claudia says, 'I will ring them now and get them over here so we can make sure they are up to speed.'

Robert replies, 'No, you won't. Remember, three girls walked out, but one is still here. Charlotte is yet to tip her hand, and I believe she will make her move tomorrow. She was left behind to report back to Henry to confirm we are not going ahead with the show.'

Emma says, 'Well, if she does this, she really will be a Charlotte. What are we going to do?'

Robert replies, 'We are going to get some sleep, as tomorrow is a big day, and we have to play it right. Act as if you do not know what is going on and go downstairs and have breakfast. When the models do not come down, say you will go upstairs and wake them and put on a scene. See what Charlotte says, and we will then take it from there. Now, who is sleeping with me tonight?'

All girls walk out of Robert's room, leaving him alone, and close the door behind them.

The next morning, everyone assembles for a quick breakfast, and after a while, Claudia says, 'Where are the models? They're not here. Looks like they have slept in. I will wake them.'

'She goes up to their rooms when Charlotte yells out, 'Don't worry, I have finished breakfast, I'll go up and wake them.'

'Charlotte goes upstairs and shortly comes down and says, 'The girls are not in their rooms, and their beds don't seem to have been slept in last night.'

Claudia asks, 'Was there a note as to where they had gone? They know the show is on today and we need them. They must have gone ahead of us to the venue to get over their nerves.'

Charlotte says, 'It may be best that I go there now and seek them out to make sure they are there.'

Claudia replies, 'No, that is not a good idea. We should all stay together. Today is going to be hectic enough without everyone getting lost. The bus will be here soon to take us to the show.'

Charlotte says, 'Well, I am ready now, so I still believe I should head off.'

Claudia replies, 'No, we won't be long. Everyone has finished breakfast, so we will all be headed off soon. They must be contactable by mobile.'

Charlotte says, 'Yes, I will ring them and find out where they are.'

Claudia replies, 'Good. You do that. I will just wash my face and be down in a minute.'

Everyone moves to their rooms to get themselves ready, leaving Charlotte to make her call.

After about ten minutes, they all assemble, and Charlotte is in a corner on her own. As soon as Emma comes in, she goes up to her and says, 'I phoned the girls, who advised me they have returned home and will not be taking part in the show.'

Emma says, 'What are you telling me—that they have left us high and dry without models?'

Charlotte replies, 'That's what they told me. I phoned all three of them.'

Pat walks into the room with Claudia and Emma, goes up to them, and tells them what Charlotte said.

Claudia asks, 'Charlotte, what is this about the girls going back home?'

Charlotte replies, 'They returned home last night on a commercial flight.'

Claudia asks, 'Who arranged it?'

Charlotte replies, 'Charles Henry, I don't know.'

Robert comes downstairs, and Claudia goes up to him to tell him what has happened.

Robert asks, 'Charlotte, what are you saying? Charles Henry has done this?'

Charlotte replies, 'It looks like he has flown the girls back home.'

Robert asks, 'But why? He has his own parade to take care of. Why would he do this?'

Charlotte says, 'Well, just think about it. You cannot go ahead with the show without models, can you?'

Claudia replies, 'You're right, we don't have the numbers to carry the show. Unless we double up on some exhibits.'

Charlotte says, 'Not when you have three shows to put on. One, yes, but not three.'

Claudia says, 'No, we will do our best with what we have. Come on, everyone, we still can put the show on.'

Charlotte replies, 'No, I am not prepared to do that on my own. You must accept the fact that it is all over. I don't want to stay here and cop the flack. I am going home.'

Claudia asks, 'How? You haven't got a flight. You came with the group on the company's jet, or are you with the others?'

Charlotte says, 'I have had enough of this. I am getting out of here. I don't need the third degree.'

Charlotte grabs her bag and walks out of the chateau and makes her way up the driveway.

Sharon follows Charlotte up the driveway, staying out of her sight. She notices Charlotte taking out a mobile phone out of her pocket when she got to the top of the gate and dialing a number and beginning a conversation. 'Charles, I have quit on the pretext that I can't do three shows and it is not right of them to ask me to do this, as it is too demanding. I have walked out and waiting for a lift to the airport. Yes, I can see a car approaching now. Right, I believe that they still want to put the show on, but that will be impossible with the team they have. All the top models have walked out on them, and it will be a disaster if they go ahead with the show on that basis. Yes, I am leaving now and will collect my flight ticket at the airport.' Sharon notices the car was being driven by one of Charles Henry's men, and there is another man in the front with a hat on his head. Charlotte gets into the back seat of the car, and it drives off.'

Sharon goes back to the chateau and tells Robert what she observed and what she overheard.

Robert asks Sharon to get Emma and to meet Claudia and Pat in the dining room in ten minutes. They all assemble as asked.

Robert says, 'We now know that Charlotte was part of the girls paid off by Charles Henry. I have checked to see if they also paid off any of the other girls we have brought over, and I am glad to say they have not. We therefore must assume they are clean and will support us. However, we don't know who else in our team has been paid to report what we are doing to Charles Henry.'

Claudia says, 'I don't believe anyone else in our team would turn against us and be a spy for Henry. How many girls did you bring over?'

Robert replies, 'Six of our best models. Here are their mobile numbers. Call them and tell them that Sharon will arrange for them to be collected from their hotels in half an hour. They are to book themselves out of their hotels and will stay at the chateau from here on. Pat and Emma go to the venue and meet the girls and keep them under lock and key until the show begins. We now have two more girls than previously planned, which should make it easier to run your shows, but you will have to fit the model to the garments to ensure they fit and don't look out of context.'

Pat says, 'I know the girls, so we should be all right. Emma and I will go with Sharon to the pavilion after she has made the arrangements, and Claudia can follow us with the team on the bus, and we will meet you there. What do we say to Charles Henry if we see him there?'

Robert replies, 'Act as if the world is on your shoulders and we are facing defeat at Napoleon's hands. Let us play the game until we are ready to put the show on. Emma, make sure the six girls are registered with the IFS so we do not find we have broken the rules. I will go with Claudia and tell the others of what is happening but will not mention the other models. Questions? Well, let us get the show moving.'

Claudia and Robert make their way to where the group has assembled, and Sharon makes some phone calls and arrangements for the girls to be picked up by the security team. Pat and Emma go back to their rooms and get their things and meet Sharon near her car, and all drive off to the pavilion.

Robert stands in front of the group and speaks. 'Can I have your attention, please? Thank you. No doubt you have heard some rumors as to what has transpired over the last few hours. Let me fill you in so everyone knows what is happening and what we intend to do about it. Last night, three of our models left us and went back home. We do not really know the full story as to why, but I believe Charles Henry has paid them off to stop us from putting on our show today. We have been told this morning that Charlotte was also part of the team paid off, and she has left us this morning and will not be attending our show as a model.'

Some within the group start to talk, and you could see they are concerned as to how the show could be continued with four models leaving. One of them says, 'Robert, how are we going to put on three shows without our top models? We are done for. It's not possible.'

Robert replies, 'We have a plan, and we will reveal this to you when we get to the show and after we have firmed things up. All we are asking you to do is trust us and do that little bit extra to ensure we win all the shows today. Trust us, we won't let you down, and we are asking you to do your best today and report anything to us that may happen to you or that may seem unusual or detrimental to our efforts. Questions? All right, everyone, make yourselves ready, and we will reassemble in ten minutes to catch the bus to the show.' Everyone goes to their rooms followed by Robert and Claudia, who end up in Robert's room and close the door. Robert says, 'We have time.'

Claudia says, 'Men. You only have one thing on your mind.' She gives Robert a big kiss and a hug and says, 'Thanks for taking care of the models. I never thought that Henry would pay the girls off to make sure we would lose the show. I thought all of our people were trustworthy, but it appears money talks.'

Robert replies, 'It sure does, especially on world stages.' Robert gives Claudia a kiss and says, 'You better get ready. It is going to be a big day for you.' They kiss again, and Claudia goes off to her room. Robert quickly takes his bag, which contained his notes and mobile, and puts on his coat and puts his wallet in the inside pocket of his jacket and walks out of his room, closing the door behind him. He walks out to where the bus is standing and boards it. Shortly, Claudia comes out of the chateau and boards the bus and sits alongside one girl near the driver. The doors are closed, and they drive off. Once at the show, the models make their way to the make-up rooms and are stopped in their tracks when they see the other six models sitting in the chairs, having their faces done and Pat and Emma nearby. Surprise changes to thrill, and they exchanged hugs and kisses with excitement. Robert appears at the door and says, 'Well, girls, do you think we have a chance now?' Girls say, 'Very much so. We will show them.'

Claudia says, 'Robert, get out of here. The girls have to finish with their make-up and get dressed.'

Robert walks out of the room and down the corridor and is confronted by Charles Henry, who momentarily is surprised to see Robert.

Charles Henry says, 'Well, Robert, when will the announcement of your withdrawal be made? No doubt my team will be required to put their show on in your place, which means we have to be ready.'

Robert replies, 'Why, I don't know what you are talking about, Henry.'

'I understand your top models have walked out on you and you haven't got the staff to carry on.'

'I don't know who told you that, but we are still on schedule and will do our three shows as planned. In fact, I understand the first one will start shortly.'

'That is impossible. You don't have the models.'

'How do you know what I have or haven't got? Have you paid someone to report back to you?'

'No, but I understand your four top models have left you and you don't have the people to carry on.'

'I hope you didn't pay too much money for that information. No doubt you will be in the audience looking at our show, so see for yourself as to whether what you have said is true.' Robert walks off, leaving Charles Henry.

The girls get their hair and make-up on, which takes the longest time. The rest of the team makes their way to where the garments are stored and waits for Robert, as no one can collect the garments other than Claudia and Robert. Both appear momentarily and are recognized by security, who let them in. The garments are inspected and handed to the person who is to ensure they are sequenced on the rack correctly in order of model and time of appearance.

Charles Henry's models, who are all recognized worldwide, have just completed their preparations and moved off to be fitted for their first round down the catwalk.

Charles Henry is to appear after the second show of the day has completed their presentation in the morning and before Claudia's fashion parade is to begin, and as expected, he presents the stolen garments to his models to wear down the catwalk.

They, of course, do not know of the history of the garments, only that they are expected to parade them down the catwalk. One problem that cropped up early in the piece is that some garments did not fit the models, and questions are being asked why. Are they the same that were fitted back at home base when they were hung off the models? No one could answer, with Charles Henry blaming the seamstress for mixing up the garments and telling them to fix it as best as they can, as quick as they can. Every one of his team are on edge, as there is always something going wrong and nothing seems to work out. All are doing their best to accommodate the situation, and all are working under a mountain of stress.

A large gathering of influential people, press, and television channels gathers to see his show, as he has insisted on them being there to witness his winning collection.

In the audience are the committee members and designers from all the other shows that had already presented their designs and those who were yet to present their designs, all expecting a great show from Charles Henry as he is expected to win this time and has a reputation of presenting first-class garments with the best models.

The parade begins with the names of Charles Henry's designers relayed over the loudspeakers and the designers standing at the entrance accepting the crowd's applause before the models are due to step out. Then come the models dressed in their outfits, walking down the catwalk.

As the models pass some of Charles Henry's designers, they immediately notice that these are not their designs. They get up and move to where Charles Henry is standing and advise him that something is wrong, that these are not their designs, and they want to know what is happening. Why the substitution? Charles Henry says, 'Your designs have lost me the last four fashion shows, and I will not lose another one because of your failings. Your designs have been destroyed, so you better accept these in substitute, as they seem to be the winning designs. Look at them. They are far better than what you could produce and are well accepted by the audience.' The designers look at the designs and agree they are better than what they could come up with, but something is familiar about the garments. There is something that they couldn't put their finger on about the designs that cause them concern.

As the models come out, each would get a large applause and would stand momentarily at the entry point before proceeding.

In the audience are several designers from well-established fashion houses. As the girls come down the catwalk, you could hear that a discussion is taking place between them, and their voices are getting louder and louder, so much so that their comments are being picked up by the television broadcasters.

As more models come on stage, more designers come in to see the show and recognize that they have used their designs from previous shows without license or authority. The television broadcasters, noting what is being said by the other designers, make it clear that they gained the ideas from other fashion parades and are not new ideas. As more models pass, they would point out that the design has been used elsewhere and name the designer who first introduced the concept and the show it was first modeled at.

Charles Henry and his designers hear the discussions and consider them sour grapes, in that the designers in the audience are envious of the designs being portrayed. This goes on for an hour until the parade is near its end. The director of the IFS steps up to the microphone and announces that Charles Henry's entry is considered in breach of the rules in that the designs are taken from other designers and are considered not new designs but ideas from other designers' works. They accused Charles Henry of plagiarism and told him that if they find the concepts to have come from other designers' works, then he is in breach of the rules and would be forced out of the show and required to pay a hefty fine.

He could not say he stole the designs and garments, as that would land him in jail. All he could do was blame his designers, as he was not the one who was employed to attend to the designs.

Charles Henry's designers go to the committee, declaring they are not to blame, as the garments they designed for the fashion show are not those shown on the catwalk. They declare they would not have copied other designers' works. They are all professional people and know of the consequences of plagiarism. They do not know who designed those garments, nor where they came from. Charles Henry, of course, is saying the opposite, stating his team has been working on their designs for over a year, and, best to his knowledge, they are the garments designed by his team. They have a free hand and are not dominated by management. The IFS audit team is called in and declares that each of the garments has the distinctive catalogue and audit number and therefore comes from Charles Henry's design team.

The committee meets and hears from the broader community of designers and agreed that the works presented by Charles Henry are not original but taken from other ideas, conceived by other designers. Charles Henry is thrown out of the fashion show accused of plagiarism, is discredited and disgraced, and is forced to pay a hefty penalty to the IFS and is banned from presenting any designs to any International Fashion Show for five years. His designers are named and would not be able to get employment in the fashion industry as their credibility is trounced.

The mob controlling Charles Henry is annoyed with the development of events and the fact that with his reputation as a cheat, they could no longer freely launder money as they did in the past. They now consider Charles Henry to be a liability and a problem for their business.

The committee agrees they are to hold the last two parades that are scheduled for that day as arranged, which is Claudia's team's presentation. They are advised to garment up and present their show. Robert goes to the committee with Claudia and Pat to protest, asking for a delay to ensure they have an equal opportunity that was given to other presenters.

Robert says, 'Committee members, we apologize for our outburst and insistence on making our presentation to you personally, but considering the extraordinary events that have just taken place, we believe that our show will be tainted by what has just transpired, and we ask that the rest of the day be canceled and we be allowed to present our show first thing in the morning. By then, the sentiments of today would have abated, allowing us at least a fair and unbiased review of our work by the judges and the public at large. Otherwise, we will be tarnished by the brush of Mr. Henry's extraordinary parade, which has ended in turmoil.'

Committee chair says, 'I gather you have not had the opportunity of speaking to Ms. Simpson. If you had, she, no doubt, would have told you that the show goes on irrespective of what transpires, as most people here have other commitments tomorrow and they will not be around. This is not the first time we have thrown someone out of the IFS, and we had set precedents, we do not defer the program, but continue until we have completed all the shows. Your protest, while understood, has been rejected by the committee, and you will present your shows within the next fifteen minutes or forfeit the right to do so.'

Claudia steps up to the speaker's table and says, 'Thank you for hearing our concerns, and we understand the rules of the show. We are concerned that one of our designers who is deceased, that her last designs would not be appropriately viewed in considering what has transpired in the last hour, and therefore we lodged our protest. However, we will abide by the committee's decision and will make immediate arrangements to present our two planned designs. Thank you.'

Committee chair replies, 'Ms. Simpson, we understand that you have lost four of your top models and cannot present your shows as planned. Is this the real reason for the request to set the show off until tomorrow?'

Claudia says, 'I will speak bluntly with you. We have found out that four of our models were paid monies to lead us on and to leave our service the day before we were to present our designs to ensure we lost. However, what they did not realize is that we expected the dishonesty of the persons concerned and ensured additional models were here on hand to take their place. All our models are registered with IFS for this show. This information has been kept secret and was not told to anyone. May I ask how you came about the information, as it seems, sir, you have some connection with Mr. Henry and his associates, and I wonder whether our shows would not be treated fairly, subject to your biased opinions or your affiliation with the mob?'

Committee chairman replies, 'I was told by Mr. Henry that they had left but not the circumstances of their departure. I am not associated with Mr. Henry and will not step down unless other members of the committee require me to do so.'

The committee members spoke between themselves and within a minute ask one of their members to speak on their behalf.

Committee representative says, 'they have asked me to advise that the committee believes that under the circumstances and to ensure an unbiased decision is finally reached, that the chair be asked to step aside and that I take the chair.'

Committee chairman replies, 'As you have requested, I will go one step further and immediately resign my position.'

Newly elected chairman says, 'Ms. Simpson, you have fifteen minutes to begin your first show.'

Claudia, Robert, and Pat get up and walk out to advise the staff that their show is going on immediately.

They walk to where everyone is gathered, wondering what is going on, and Robert steps in front of them and begins speaking. 'We tried to have our show postponed until tomorrow morning, but, unfortunately, the committee refused our request. We have been ordered to start our first show in fifteen minutes, so let us get on with it.'

Everyone scats in all directions to get themselves ready. Pat, Emma, and Claudia move to dress the first girls, while the others finish of facials and hair to ensure maximum exposure.'

The production line moves into high gear, with everyone moving to ensure a trouble-free presentation.

Charles Henry, who believes he has stolen Marque International's garments and designs for the parade, is surprised to hear that MI is presenting a fashion parade but knows the penalty is very severe monetary wise if they do not. He thinks they would come up with several old and tried designs used in the past just to get themselves across the line. However, if they do this, they would risk losing their reputation for innovative design and would lose a lot of business.

He sits in the front row to see what is to come along the catwalk, even though he is not welcome there.

The show begins with Robert stating, 'Ladies and gentlemen, my name is Robert Somerset. I am the managing director of Marque International and have great pleasure in presenting our designs over the next three shows. The first show is in memory of Vicki Santana, who was our leading designer before she developed pneumonia and died because of related complications. The last part of this show was completed by our current head designer, Claudia Simpson, in consultation with her team comprising Beth Allen and Anna Bird, who have tried to interpret Vicki's ideas from sketches and notes she had made. Please welcome our models to the catwalk.'

The model's names are read out along with the names of all of those who took part in the show. A fashion parade begins after the crowd applauds. The models walk down the catwalk to the applause of the crowd, who are thrilled with the designs, and as each model comes out, the applause grows louder, and the audience notes the features of the garments.

Charles Henry, who realizes he has been set up, gets up and walks out.

The parade continues for about an hour, and then the chairman advises everyone that the second parade would be held after a half- hour break. The models go back to their dressing rooms and have some light refreshments and rest, for they know they had to be back on the catwalk soon.

Claudia prepares her garments in the order she wants them presented and stands at the front of the stage for the chairman to introduce her. Her name is called out, and they hand the microphone to her to introduce the models, acknowledge the credits, and describe her designs.

Claudia says, 'Ladies and gentlemen, before I introduce the second fashion parade, I wish to advise that we will follow the tradition that had been established by Marque International in that the designs initially to follow will be the senior designer's work— namely, mine. Thereafter, we have allocated a segment where the junior designers will present their works under their own names in the third show. To begin, we have our first model showing a formal dining dress with a low front.'

The model steps out with the applause of the crowed and the television cameras beaming pictures throughout the world. At the end of Claudia's show, they present the third show advising the audience that this segment is to show the works of young designers within MI under their own banners. Beth's designs are shown for about fifteen minutes, followed by Anna's and then several other up-and-coming designers. Each model is applauded, and at the end, Claudia and the other designers come out for a rowdy applause, which lasts for about five minutes. Everyone is impressed with the show and MI's attempt to introduce new concepts in design, even if some ideas were currently deemed futuristic.

After everyone has settled down and after about ten minutes, the chairman takes the stage and advises everyone that the committee, aided by several distinguished designers and schools specializing in design and fashion, has finally decided as to the winner of this year's design awards.

Chairman says, 'We have considered all the entries, and the committee has, on this occasion, been aided by expert designers and teachers from several recognized design schools in Paris who have been gratuitous in giving their opinions and criticisms and have concluded that the prize for the best designs this year must go to two designers Vicki Santana and Claudia Simpson. Each of their works has been breathtaking and has taken design to a new level, and Ms. Simpson's work in the presentation of Ms. Santana's designs was outstanding in allowing us to see these as Ms. Santana wanted them presented rather than have them left on a shelf without being recognized or altered by other works. We therefore present the prize to Claudia Simpson as the designer of the year.'

Claudia comes up on to the stage with the crowd applauding loudly to support the decision and hesitates at the microphone for a few seconds and says, 'I am emotional humbled by the recognition given to me, and I know Vicki would be extremely proud to accept the prize and recognition of her work. On behalf of Vicki and myself, thank you, but in reality, the prize should go to all of those that worked so hard in Marque International against unbelievable odds that nearly crippled the business and the name of this great institution. Thank you to all the models and employees that worked under threat of personal injury and sacrifice.' Claudia then bursts into tears and is immediately joined on stage by Pat, Emma, and all the other team members, who receive a loud round of applause. A cup is handed over to Claudia, and the event is captured on television and beamed around the world.

They held shortly afterwards a party, which is attended by all the participants and committee members. Charles Henry does not attend and goes back to his hotel room and arranges for his crew to return home.

Robert, fearing retribution by Charles Henry, decides to fly back home on the next available flight the next day. He advises Claudia of his plans, who is upset as she thought that the worst was now over and that Charles Henry would give up his onslaught against Marque International and Robert and they would have some time together in Paris.

Claudia says, 'But, Robert, surely he wouldn't be so stupid to do anything now that the IFS is over?'

Robert replies, 'If I am right, he owes a lot of money to the mob, who will demand payment from Charles Henry, as they have supported him over the years. I do not want him to know that I love you and we intend to get married, as he will come after you as he did with Vicki. I do not want another fiancée living under a park bench. Let us see what he does before we declare we intend to get married.'

Claudia asks, 'Are you proposing? Where is the ring?'

Robert replies, 'No, you did that, remember? But if you wish, I will propose after all this is put to bed and we can get on with our lives without worrying about who is coming after us. Keep everyone here in Paris for a week as a bonus for all the hard work they put in to get the prize and the recognition given to us. Make plans to come home in a week or two so we can see what Charles Henry is going to do. Make sure security doesn't drop their bundle and ease off thinking the danger is over.'

Claudia says, 'But you are going to draw all of Charles Henry's wrath onto yourself.'

Robert replies, 'I know, but it is best that I do it rather than have him come after you and the rest of the team. If I am right, the mob will try to get their money out of Charles Henry, who will have to sell down a lot of his assets to pay what he owes, as he cannot pay it out of the prize monies that he expected getting from the fashion show.'

Claudia says, 'Robert, please be careful. I don't won't to organize another funeral, especially yours.'

They hug each other and kiss, and Robert leaves Claudia and goes back to his room to make plans to fly back home.

After a few minutes, Claudia goes out and addresses the girls and says, 'Unfortunately, Robert had been called back home to attend to some urgent business and couldn't stay with us. However, he had asked that I pass his congratulations on to everyone and thank you all for your hard work to achieve the win and is insisting on you all staying at the chateau for at least a week's holiday as a gesture of appreciation. Those who want to stay two weeks can, but they will have to take the time from their accrued holiday pay. We will supply accommodation and food free for the second week.' Everyone is very grateful and thinks it is a kind gesture. However, Pat and Emma could see the real reason behind Robert's decision to leave everyone here and go back by himself. Pat and Emma pull Claudia aside to speak to her.

Pat asks, 'Claudia, what is the true reason for Robert going back home?'

Claudia replies, 'He is worried about Charles Henry taking out retribution against us and believes he will be better off on his own without putting us in danger. He believes the mob may come after Charles Henry, as the word around the traps is that Charles Henry relied on the winnings from the fashion show to settle with the mob. He wants us out of Charles Henry's reach.'

Emma asks, 'What should we do?'

Claudia replies, 'Look after the team and let them have a good time exploring Paris as a gesture of thanks from the boss.'

Pat asks, 'Has he proposed yet?'

Claudia says, 'It is that apparent, isn't it?'

Pat replies, 'Not to most, but it is to us. Be careful. We don't want them to get at him through you.'

Claudia says, 'Sharon and Sue are with me at all times, and they know what is happening and what is going on.'

The girls join the others, and after an hour, everyone makes their way to the bus for the journey to the chateau.

At the chateau, the party resumes well into the night.

34

Charles Henry is still suffering from jet lag when he arrives at his office. He makes some arrangements to hide some cash in an account that no one knows about, just in case things get nasty with the mob and he has to make a quick exit out of the state and go into hiding.

He diverts some money to his private account when the door flies open and three men stand glaring at him. They come in, and the boss, Tony Cirillo, sits at the table.

Charles Henry says, 'Nice to see you, Tony. What brings you around so early? A social visit, I hope?'

Tony replies, 'We heard they threw you out of the show for cheating. You tried to take other designers' work and pass it off as your own.'

'That was not the case. I can explain what happened. They set me up.' 'The organization is not happy with your dealings in this matter and believe you are losing grip on things. We have had one of our bosses killed, and you have consistently underperformed, especially on the international scene. You owe us $2 million, which I have come to collect.'

'I don't have that much money lying around. I used all of my surplus money to acquire investment bonds, which are performing well.'

'Transfer the bonds over to our organization. How much have you got?'

'The last lot I purchased was before we went to the fashion show, as I got them at a 30 percent discount, which would give a good return over time as they are based on thirty-year mortgages. I thought we would win the show and was prepared to extend myself. I purchased a further million dollars' worth, which makes a total of $3 million I hold in mortgage bonds.'

'Good. We will want the lot transferred to our organization.'

'But you said you were after only $2 million?'

'We will take the extra amount as security on advancing our services to you. Have you got the certificates?'

'Yes, they are in my safe.'

'Get them out and sign them over to us so I can go back to the office and confirm the legitimacy of the bonds.'

'Don't you trust me?'

'Get the bonds and sign them over to us so we can get on our way.'

Charles Henry goes to his private office and opens his safe and takes the bonds out. He signs them and brings them to Tony and hands them over to him.

Henry asks, 'Aren't you going to check them?'

Tony replies, 'No. If they are junk, then I will be back with some boys.'

Tony gets up, and the three men leave Charles Henry's office.

Charles Henry is worried as he knows he could not break away from the mob as they helped him build up his business while laundering their money. He knows he would have to use them to scare people into using his organization, especially after being thrown out of the IFS and accused of plagiarism. Clients that want to distance themselves from Charles Henry would get a visit from the mob, encouraging them to stay with Charles Henry. He knows he could build the business up if given time, but he needs some working capital to get him over the next few months. He decides to get a loan from a bank using some of his properties as collateral. He phones the manager who advises the money would be in his account two days after the papers have been signed and approved by the bank.

The manager would arrange for the mortgage papers to be drawn up and delivered to Charles Henry's office before twelve.

At about one in the afternoon, an assistant to the bank manager comes to see Charles Henry, and he explains the documents and has Charles Henry sign the mortgage papers and takes them back to the bank.

The money is deposited in Charles Henry's account two days later, relieving his anxiety as to how he was going to pay for the fixed expenses of the business.

Charles Henry sits back in his chair thinking he has covered all his bases and that he could build the business back up from here, given stability in the economy and support from the mob. Robert also returns from Paris earlier than expected to make sure any attempts by Charles Henry to take retribution would be made against him and not his staff or Claudia.

On the second day, Tony pays Robert a visit, who says he wants to discuss some business.

Robert asks, 'Mr. Cirillo, what can I do for you?'

Tony replies, 'You have it wrong. It is not what you can do for me, but what I can do for you. We are not very happy with Charles Henry and what he did at the IFS and would like to invest in your business as it seems the winner that has the reputation will lead to success.'

'Thank you, but I can fund my business, especially after winning the IFS. The winning prize amounted to more than what we anticipated, which has given us a return on our investment far greater than what we expected.'

'We also offer protection and can ensure success in any dealings you may want to make.'

'Yes, I can well imagine how the protection racket works, as it wasn't so long ago when I had to kill one of your people who came gunning after me.'

'We can guarantee you stay alive if you join us. Otherwise, anything may happen, and your business will amount to nothing without you. Think about it. I will ring you in a day or two and we can discuss it further.'

Tony gets up and walks out of Robert's office, followed by his other two gorillas.

Two days later, Tony phones Robert.

Tony says, 'I hope you have considered our offer. Can we do business?'

Robert replies, 'Yes, I have considered what you have said, but I am not interested in aligning myself with the mob. You had control of my former designer's husband's business and caused him to commit suicide and hounded his wife to her death. No, I don't want to have anything to do with you.'

Tony says, 'I see. Maybe we can change your mind. We will call you shortly.'

That evening, the electricity to the entire block is cut off, preventing Robert from doing any work. He goes home after he has phoned up the power supplier, threatening them with moving to an alternative supplier, but they really didn't care. They said they were looking into the problem and would get back to him. Robert goes to the basement with security to drive home. All the lights are off, so they use torches to get around. When he gets to his car, he notices his tires are slashed and white paint sprayed on his bonnet. As he walks away from the car, he is grabbed from behind in a headlock. The other two men with him move to assist Robert, but they are stopped by two men with guns drawn advising them not to move.

Robert fights with the man who has him in a headlock. He hits him in the head with the end of his torch, and the man loosens his grip, allowing Robert to get free. He draws his gun and, as the man lunges to grab him, fires a shot, and the man falls to the ground. Robert then moves over to where the other thugs are standing with guns drawn. They think it was their boss who has shot Robert and are surprised to have a gun placed to the head of the first man and Robert saying, 'Lay down your weapons or I will shoot you like I shot your boss. You will follow him if you don't put your weapons down.' The men being confronted turn around with their guns aimed at Robert. Robert, anticipating what they were going to do, does not hesitate to fire a shot at one of them and another shot at his mate, who is watching on, killing them both.

Robert goes up to the first man and sees he is dead. He was shot at close range, and it was unlikely that the bullet missed him as he lay in a pool of blood. Robert and the other men go to check on the other two and believe they are dead. All three men walk out of the car park and call the police, reporting the incident.

The police arrive about a half an hour later and want to know what has happened. They contact the electricity company, who advises that they cut the electricity off because of an outage problem, which has now been rectified, and they turned the electricity back on. They go into the car park and interrogate each of the security men, who tell the police what had happened. They ask the men to accompany them to the station so they could give a statement. The police confirm the man that was shot was Tony Cirillo, a kingpin with the mob, and his two friends are his lieutenants.

The police advise Robert that it is unlikely that charges would be pressed against him, as it was a matter of self-defense. However, they warn Robert that the organization doesn't allow those who take action against them to go without retribution, and since Robert had killed three of their key men, the likelihood would be that they would put out a contract on Robert. The police refer the matter to the coroner, listing the incident as self-defense.

After two more days, the team arrives back from Paris and is alarmed to hear what has happened with Robert. They are scared about their own safety but are told at a meeting by police that it would be unlikely that the mob would worry about them as they mainly go after the person in charge, who is Robert.

Claudia does not return with the others, as she is still trying to wind up her uncle's affairs but flies back with Sharon when told about the killings. Robert is concerned, as he would have preferred her out of the way until he gets rid of the mob. They touch down two days after the others have arrived and go straight to the office.

Claudia walks into Robert's office and closes the door. They hug and kiss each other and, after a while, open the door and talk as if it is a business conversation.

Robert says, 'It is good to see you, but you are putting yourself in too much danger. You should go back to the chateau until it is safer. They don't care who they hurt and, once they know about us, will use you to get at me.'

Claudia replies, 'If we are going to get married, we're better off tackling these things together. Otherwise, it won't be much of a marriage. No, my place is beside you, and both of us will do what we can to get rid of these bastards. Mum is at the chateau, and she will handle things there for me. I will have to fly back to complete uncle Henry's affairs, but at present, the solicitors advise me that all is in order and they are processing the application with the court to transfer title of all the properties to me and the $5 million in investments and cash Uncle Henry had.'

'You're a wealthy woman. You do not need this trouble. You can live at the chateau on that money for the rest of your life. Think about it.'

'Yes, the money is there, but I want you and a family, which money can't buy.'

'They will come after you, as you are one of the designers mentioned by the IFS. They will most probably want you to move over to Charles Henry to add credibility to his organization as if he is restructuring his design team, or they may repay you for setting up Charles Henry in designing the clothes that caused him to be recognized as a cheat.'

'I have Sharon and her assistant with me wherever I go, and they are both armed and have had military training, so they won't worry about shooting someone who pulls a weapon. Also, I have a gun in my bag if I need to use one.'

'Do you know how to use it?'

'Yes, you point the gun at the person and pull the trigger.'

'What about the safety switch and making sure it is loaded?'

'They're just minor details.'

'Yes, I can see I will have to get Sharon to take you down to the shooting range and explain and show you how to correctly use the gun you have. You may need to use it someday.'

'I am going home to unpack, and I will see you tomorrow.' They both get up, kiss, and Claudia goes to look for Sharon.

As expected, former clients of Charles Henry are requesting cancellation of their contracts, as they do not want to be associated with a cheat. Charles Henry arranges for one of his associates to call on them to encourage them to rethink their position. Over the months that followed, there are many reports of assaults on public figures, but no arrests are made, and some are hospitalized and refuse to name their attackers or describe them to the police for fear of retribution against them and their family.

Robert also has repeated visits from the organization but refuses to do business with them. They also followed him when he goes anywhere and therefore makes sure he does not meet with people in the open where he could be a target.

Security is tightening up considerably around Marque International's office, and the CCTV is upgraded to ensure the exterior of the building could be monitored around the clock, seven days a week.

There are instances where suspicious fires are started in the back of the building, but these are extinguished quickly with minor damage. There are cybercrimes where emails have been copied along with client records, but these are minor problems that did not disrupt the business.

The mob appoints a new manager to replace Tony Cirillo, and he increases the scare tactics to ensure Robert eventually falls into line. Again, some men are sent to speak to Robert with offers, and on each occasion, they are told, 'Not interested.' Robert receives the usual threatening telephone calls, as do most of his senior design staff, but no one other than Robert has been physically threatened.

35

Charles Henry reads the newspaper, which declares that a major financial institution has gone into liquidation and that the bonds that they have been selling over the last three years are of no value. They are described as junk bonds. Charles Henry switches the television on, and all channels are covering the crisis declaring that the collapse of the bank has major international repercussions as the bank sold the junk bonds to a lot of superannuation and sovereign funds and that people would lose a lot of their wealth owing to the company's corrupt and fraudulent dealings.

Charles Henry folds his newspaper and worries about what may happen to him if what they have reported is correct. He realizes he has made a big mistake in putting most of his spare cash into these bonds and in fact, used the bonds as collateral to get loans and pay off debts. The bank that sold them was a reputable bank with an international reputation and no one would ever have thought they would be involved with a scheme to sell junk bonds, but this was the case. The US government had ordered an investigation, and the stock market worldwide went into meltdown, causing equities to crash, and many lost most of their share portfolios, as a consequence. Charles Henry not only had invested in these junk bonds but also had borrowed monies from various banks on what is called 'margin call' where further monies must be paid back to the bank should there investments fall more than 10 percent. This was all right if you had the money, but if you had most of your investments in equities, then you had to sell your shares at a loss to repay the bank.

Charles Henry had arrived at the office early to attend to some minor matters before his staff begin their day. He is concerned as to what is going to happen to him, as, no doubt, the news would have spread. As he gets up from his chair, he receives a telephone call from Vick Soprano, Tony's replacement, who advises him he is on his way to discuss the financial crisis reported in the morning news.

Ten minutes later, Vick is in Charles Henry's office wanting to know how Charles Henry is going to pay back all the monies that were paid by junk bonds by Charles Henry. Also, the organization has bought a lot of bonds from people Henry has introduced to them, which are now worthless, and they hold him accountable for their losses, as it was on his recommendations that they bought them.

Charles Henry says, 'You can't blame me for those investments. I had nothing to do with them other than make the contact.'

Vick replies, 'It was on your recommendation that we bought them, and we expect you to make good our loss. We will give you two days to come with an answer as to how you intend to make good our losses or we will make sure your estate does. We will be back.'

The men get up and walk out of Charles Henry's office.

Charles Henry knows he is in terrible trouble. His real estate is losing value and would not realize enough money to pay for his debts. He knows the bank would call him wanting to know how he intends to make good the losses on his investments as the value of his share portfolio has fallen 60 percent.

Charles Henry knows his life is in danger from the mob. With the bank, he could declare himself bankrupt, but not with the mob. You either pay up or else you get fitted with a body bag. He thinks briefly about his family. He does not worry about them too much and what they would go through, as he is only thinking about himself. They have had a good life up till now. A bit of discomfort will make them appreciate the good life if ever they come back to their current status in the future.

Charles Henry goes to his online bank account and tries to transfer some money over to his credit card so he could take out some money from an ATM but finds out that his accounts are frozen. The bank is onto him. He checks his property portfolio and finds out that each of his titles is held by the bank or the organization, who has lodged caveats on them, stopping him from selling them. He has no way to get some money other than what he has in his pocket, which amounts to a few dollars. Emails come in from the bank insisting on him making good on the losses made on his margin call accounts.

The Futures Market, which is down four hundred points, shows that the share market is going to open considerably down with massive losses from the start of trading. He could ride it out for the next few days and hope there will be a bounce, giving him a clearer picture as to what will happen and what his options are. He knows he does not have the grace of time on his side, and it may not recover but drop continually for the next week, making things even worse. The bonds compounded the problem in that a lot of investors worldwide took Lehman Brothers at their word and considered they were buying quality investments, not junk bonds.

Charles Henry does not know what to do.

If he stays, he would be killed, so he knows he would have to get out and hide somewhere so they couldn't find him. But where? He could not fly off somewhere as he doesn't have the money and facial recognition would pick him up at the airport. He could drive interstate, but they would locate him by the number plate of his vehicle. He looks out of his office window and sees a street beggar on the opposite corner across the street from his office with a bowl on the ground and sign asking for donations. He decides to become one of them as they all look alike, and no one ever confronts or even wants to approach one of them. He has to decide quickly, as his staff will arrive shortly. He quickly changes into some street clothes he has at the office, a dark top and track pants and a black polo shirt and makes a dash for the park, which is some two miles away, where no one would expect him to go. He does not consider whether he could make it on the street, only that he would be alive and have the opportunity of trying to make a comeback.

Charles Henry grabs his bag, wallet, his gun, mobile, laptop, and iPad and some money he has in his office drawer and makes his way out of his office down the rear stairwell and begins walking south, down the street towards Central Park. He is determined not to be one of those bums that he frequently sees on the street. He picks up his speed as his Rolex shows it is eight fifteen and it would be time for most people to make their way to work. He does not want anyone to see him or stop him for a chat. He sticks to side streets to ensure he is not recognized.

About half an hour into his walk, he is passing an old industrial site when two men move to block him from going any further. The taller of the men says, 'What have you got in the bag?'

Charles Henry replies, 'None of your business, so let me pass.'

Taller man says, 'Since you won't tell us, we will have a look ourselves.' They move to grab the bag, but Charles Henry hits the first man across the face with the bag and slams his fist into the midsection of the second man, who falls to his knees. Charles Henry reaches into his bag and withdraws his gun. He aims it at the first man and pulls the trigger, shooting him through the heart, and then shoots the second man in the head while he is down. He looks around to see if there are any witnesses and then moves off, leaving the men. He does not care about them as he presumes both are dead or would die from the loss of blood by the time help arrives. No one could trace it back to him. He checks their pockets and sees they have some money, so he takes it so it would seem a robbery and walks on.

He reaches Central Park and walks to the leased frequented area at the south end and sits on one of the park benches, contemplating what to do next. He does not look like one of the inhabitants and decides he needs to get a supermarket trolley and some rags, so he fits in with the undesirables that call this home.

He goes to the supermarket and takes a trolley and buys some tin soups, plastic bags, and a towel, and after paying for these, takes some cardboard boxes on his way out. He wheels the trolley back into the park and back to his bench that he has previously selected and makes himself comfortable. He throws his boxes and plastic bags under his bench and sits on the bench, thinking about what to do next.

Charles Henry's employees turn up for work unaware of what is happening and that they would not get paid for the week or their entitlements. No one knows where Charles Henry went or what has become of him. The mob checks the airline bookings and could not find any flights that he had booked himself on. The bank continually tries to locate where he is and, after a few days, files for an administrator to be appointed to his business. Within a week, they are forced to appoint a liquidator as things were worst then first expected. A trustee is also appointed to his personal estate, and they declared Charles Henry bankrupt.

All of Charles Henry's assets are auctioned off or sold at the best price, and the funds raised paid approximately 20 percent of the amount owed to his creditors, including the mob. As most of the loans were guaranteed by Charles Henry, his personal assets including his family home, were confiscated and sold to pay his debts. His family was deprived of any means of support and were forced to seek help from charities and tried to live off the pension. His children were forced out of private school and had to go to state school and found this very hard to cope with.

They bullied his son at school to the degree that he could not take it anymore and one day takes an overdose of drugs. The coroner's court declares it is a tragedy that schoolchildren could force another to commit suicide, but this is clear from the facts of the case.

His daughter also finds it hard to cope with the reality of life, especially after her mother died from unknown causes after attending a party hosted by Vick Soprano, where she was expected to act as an escort for one of Vick's mates. They placed the daughter in foster care but she ended up on drugs and a lifetime of mental problems.

The mob has lost a lot of money as they have invested heavily in the junk bonds, which become worthless, and must move out of their traditional areas of activity as the economy shrinks and people wouldn't or could not pay the extortion fees demanded by them.

Robert, who hasn't invested in junk bonds, was not affected by the global financial crisis and manages to pick up some prime property at very low prices, as many of the rich and famous are in a similar position to Charles Henry and are also declared bankrupt, losing all their wealth. They sold their assets off at auctions at prices substantially lower than their purchase price.

The mob withdraws from their activity, and things get back to normal, and the idea of retribution being inflicted by the mob on Robert and his team becomes less likely.

The mob phases out of existence, keeps a low profile, and regroups, waiting for things to get better. The only thing they have to control are the young entrants who are trying to muscle in on their territory.

Charles Henry sits on the bench and watches the world go by. If anyone gets near to him, he will move under the bench to make sure no one recognizes him. He still has a trendy haircut, and his skin has not aged. He does not look like a park dweller or like a person who is in difficulty, but quite the opposite. If anything, he looks like an upmarket tourist spending a day in the park. While he is like this, someone who has seen his photo in the news could recognize him. He must make sure he keeps a low profile until his hair and beard grow. He lies under the bench and covers himself up with plastic and falls asleep and dreams of the days when he had money and a dignified position and sees himself walking to his office in an expensive suit past the Town Hall steps. He remembers the girl that was always there with her box, which he would kick out of the way into the gutter, scattering her money. He considered her a lowlife, a burden on society, someone who should be looked down upon and not allowed to show herself. Now he has become one of them and has a different opinion, especially when the shoe is on the other foot.

He wakes up, realizing that he has not seen her for a long time, and wonders what had happened to her. Never mind, she is not worth worrying about. He has other problems to concentrate on. The evening comes and the sun sets in the west, and he soon looks up at the stars, wondering what to do next. At about eight in the night, a man approaches him from the shelter, asking whether he wants to have a shower. He declines and says he wants to stretch his feet and get a coffee. The man directs him to the public facilities in the park and advises him that the soup kitchen would be in the center of the park in an hour's time. The man then leaves. Henry opens one of his tins of soup he bought from the supermarket and makes a small fire with sticks fallen from the trees nearby and warms the soup up and eats it out of the can. Afterwards, he stays up for an hour, hides his bag in a bush nearby and walks to the center of the park to get a coffee. He approaches the soup kitchen, and they offer him some soup, which he takes, and coffee and walks away. He sips the soup but finds it tasteless and tips it out under a bush. The coffee is awful, but he drinks it as there is nothing else for him to drink. He goes into the toilets nearby, but as he enters, he is grabbed by two men and thrown to the ground with one man pressing his chest down on the ground. He turns. As he turns, he hits the first man on the side of his face, sending him backwards into the wall. He grabs the second man, holding his chest down, and kicks him midsection and then kicks him in the groin and then again and again, yelling out to him, 'This will stop you from f——king around.' The other man gets to his feet and runs out. Charles repeats the kicks several more times and then lets the man fall to the ground. He walks out of the toilet block, noting no one else is lined up to go in. He goes back to his bench and notes that someone had ransacked his rags. He goes to the nearby bush and feels around for his bag and finds it. It has not been touched, and all of his money, gun, and other items are all in there.

He cleans himself up as best as he can and then boxes himself in and go to bed.

At about midnight, he hears some noise as if several people are moving around close to his bench. He gets up and grabs his bag and runs off near a tree near to his bench and hides. Sure enough, they come across his bench and shine a torch on the rags and plastic left under the bench. They go through what is there and shine their torch on the tree to see if anyone is there. They take the plastic and fold it up and take it and move on. They walk about three hundred meters until they come to the next bench and notice that someone is sleeping there. Charles Henry follows them to see what they are up to. They grab the occupant under the bench and start to hit and kick him. The person does not have time to wake up and defend himself before they lay into him. Charles Henry quickly reaches into his bag and withdraws his gun, and fires at the men. One falls to his knees, while the other stands momentarily looking at his mate and then realizes he has been shot and runs, leaving his mate on his knees, bleeding from a wound to the gut. The bench occupant quickly gains his composure and gathers his things and moves off to another part of the park, leaving the wounded man. Charles Henry walks up to where the man is lying and picks up his plastic sheets that were taken from his bench and walks back to his bench, thinking to himself, *It is a pity I didn't shoot the other one as well.* He gathers his things and moves himself to another part of the park, away from where he shot the man.

In the morning, Charles Henry gets up and walks to where the charity kitchen is located and gets a cup of coffee and, on his way back, notices the news headlines: 'Man Found Dead in Central Park'. The article advises the person was male, aged twenty- three years of age, who had come from a wealthy family, and they are trying to put the pieces together as to what he was doing in the park. Charles Henry thinks to himself, *good riddance to the bastard,* and walks on to where his bench is located. He could not move around freely as his beard was not grown and his hair was still short. He has a cap on over his ears and a scarf on, which he pulls up when he approaches anyone. He checks his bag and notes he still has $300 in cash and four more bullets left in his gun. He goes to the supermarket and buys himself some tins of various soups and casserole dinners and goes back to his bench. The weather is warm, but by midday, clouds come in and it rains. Charles Henry gathers his things and moves to a bus shelter while the rain pours down. He sits there noticing everyone has moved away from him, leaving him alone. The rain lasts all night and into the next day. He goes back to his bench but could not sleep under it as the ground is wet, so he wraps the plastic around him and settles on top of the bench. He stays secluded for a couple of months until he becomes unrecognizable and looks like a derelict. His beard grows longer, and his hair becomes thicker and scruffy, and he fits in with the other street dwellers at the park. His cash reserves are dwindling. So, he does the rounds of the soup kitchens and finds out where they are each night. He knows the restaurants in the area and would go around and see what they throw out as leftovers and, if it is edible, would take it and eat it rather than buy his own.

Life in the park is not a picnic, and you must be on your toes every minute to ensure you did not end up robbed or dead or both. It is Saturday night about one in the morning when he is startled by a man standing over him talking to himself. He could see the person was out of his mind and on drugs, referring to things he imagined he could see. What he describes are monsters who are teasing him, and he wants to get hold of one of them and kill it to teach them a lesson. The person sits on the bench and is discussing things with his imaginary world and then runs off, presumably chasing one of his creatures. Charles Henry gets up after the person has left and walks to a nearby bush to relieve himself when he sees some men walking his way. He dives behind the bush as they pass him, headed for his bench. They stop there and search his pile of rags and plastic bags and see his bag. They open it and note there is $250 in the bag and a gun. One man takes the cash and the other the gun out of the bag. The one with the gun waves it around, pointing it towards the nearby bushes when the gun goes off. They stand momentarily and then spontaneously run off towards the park exit.

As the men exit the park, they run onto the main street, which on Saturday is always patrolled by police. On this occasion, there are two police cars heading back to the station when the men run out of the park and straight in the police's path, who have to abruptly stop to avoid hitting them. The police get out of the car and orders the men to put their hands on the bonnet of the police car, which they do. All are searched and their names taken. The police notice one of the men has a bag with a large sum of money and the other man a gun. They check the gun and notice it has been recently been fired. They ask the man if he has a license for the gun, and he does not. They radio the station and check the gun and the bullets and find the bullets match the ones that have been involved in several murders throughout the neighborhood. All the men are arrested and taken back to the police station. After further investigation, they are advised that they would be refused bail. The one with the bag tells the police that they went out for a night on the town and decided to walk through the park and came across this bench with the bag hidden under some old rags. They decided to take the cash and the gun, and in playing around, the gun discharged into a bush in the park. The police decide to take the men back to the place in the park where they said they found the cash.

The police drive the men back to the park, but they could not remember which bench they found the bag under. In looking around, the police notice a person lying on the ground motionless behind a bush. They walk up to the person and shine their torch on him. They notice he has been shot in the head and is bleeding profusely. They immediately radio for an ambulance. The ambulance arrives and notices the man had lost a lot of blood and is near death. They decide to take him to emergency and radio for help on arrival. The police take both suspects back to the station and advise them they believe they robbed the homeless man and shot him. The police records showed that they had shot several people with this gun, and as the man had killed other people, one more didn't matter. They advise him they would possibly charge him with manslaughter, but if the man dies, it will be murder with robbery and that they would implicate both in the murder.

They rushed Charles Henry into the operating theater upon arrival in emergency at the hospital with the prognosis that he would not live. The operation takes six hours, and he is in hospital for two weeks on life support. Police come to see him, but he recalls nothing and in fact has lost his memory from the surgery. He does not know who he is or his name or anything about his history. After a further two weeks, the hospital decides they couldn't do any more for Charles Henry and arranges for him to be put into a nursing home. He has no money and, because of an administrative bungle at the nursing home, he finds himself out on the street and is told not to return to the nursing home.

Charles Henry walks the streets not knowing who he is, where to go, or what to do. He passes an elderly beggar on the corner of the street and kicks his box of coins down the curb only because he thinks this is the right thing to do. Something tells him this is what he should do. The old man gets up and grabs him and is ready to a punch him when he sees Charles staring at him, not understanding what he has done or who he is. He lets go of Charles and collects his coins. Charles goes down on his knees to help the man and bursts into tears. They collect the money, and the old man says to Charles, 'Why did you do this?' Charles just looks at him in emptiness, not understanding or responding to the question. The old man could see Charles was not normal and told him to sit near him, which Charles does. He goes through Charles's pockets and finds a nursing home letter addressed to Charles and gathers that is his name. At five o'clock, the old man gets Charles to his feet, and both make their way to the park and make their way to where the charities have their soup kitchen. The old man introduces Charles to everyone, and all could see that Charles needs a lot of help, even to feed himself. He cannot speak properly, and everyone thinks he is retarded and lacks intelligence, but where possible, most try to help Charles, realizing he is not acting but in genuine need of help.

Charles stays with the old man for a year until one day, the old man does not wake up in the morning. Charles does not know what has happened but knows the routine well enough to know he has to get up in the morning and go out on the street to beg for money. Charles takes the cardboard box and the sign they carry with them and goes to the Town Hall steps, where they usually sit begging all day.

He sits and waits, unable to comprehend what he is doing or understanding the purpose. Physically, he is there, but mentally he is gone.

36

Claudia and Robert finally can get back to normal life and set a date for their wedding. It is to be officiated by Allen, and Claudia has designed her own wedding dress.

The week before the wedding, they attend church, along with their respective mothers and the groomsmen and bridesmaids.

The service takes its usual structure, with songs being sung and reading from the Bible. Then Allen takes to the pulpit.

Allen says, 'Today, I would like to speak about settling the score or, in a nutshell, retribution.'

'It is a topic that means different things to different people, but one clear understanding that most people have is that the person aggrieved seeks revenge against the perpetrator. If you are a true Christian of the faith, then your emphasis would be on Christ attending to the retribution. However, if you are a non-believer, you basically look towards yourself to attend to it the retribution, as you act as your own god.'

'One clear aspect of retribution is that most people seek retribution within a short period after the infliction of an event, and this is when most people regret their actions as they recognize that they have overreached the mark in taking matters into their own hands. If they would have held off, they most probably would not have sought retribution or would have had dealt with the matter differently.

'The Bible tells us that the history of Israel was a continuous cycle of taking retribution. Cain was punished by being forced to leave his home. The earth is punished by a devastating flood for widespread sin by the "Sons of Gods". Abraham and Sarah are rewarded with a son, Isaac. Moses led the Israelites from bondage out of Egypt, but the people rebelled against God and were punished by being denied entry into the Promised Land.'

'Retribution, whether it is between God and humans or between human beings, is considered by most as the act of getting what one deserves, either by human standards or by divine decree. Both the Covenant Code (Exod. 20–23) and the Holiness Code (Lev. 17–26) are the classic texts for seeing the clarity with which they wrote the laws regarding retribution. In the OT, breaking any laws was detrimental to your personal relationship with God.'

'The most famous expression of the law of retribution is stated in Deuteronomy (19:21), "A life for a life, an eye for an eye, a tooth for a tooth, a hand for a hand, a foot for a foot." The principle is to show pity, but its application in Israel's law shows that the primary function was to limit retaliation and guarantee punishment would not exceed the crime rather than prevent retaliation.'

'Retribution has been a topic going back to pre-Christian days when God made it clear it was His and only His responsibility to make judgement and to settle the score. On the mount, Christ again emphasized it was God's prerogative to render retribution and not that of mankind. In Jeremiah (46:10), it is stated, "The day of the Lord will be the day of retribution against God's enemies." From this develops the concept that humans should trust in God to bring about settling the score or retribution against those who have wronged them, rather than seeking to effect this themselves.'

'Why? Well, the main reason centers on the fact that we are created by God, and He is responsible for the action of his creation even though we have a free will. So if one sins against you, then you should look towards God to punish the person and not handle the matter yourself. It is also believed that God's judgement would be more just and will fit the sin (the crime) than as devised by mankind and be more relevant and proportionate.'

'The problem with God entering the picture is that most people expect retribution to be immediate and not in the future. If we are sinned against, we expect the other person to receive a bolt of lightning to teach them a lesson or as payback. Unfortunately, this never happens, and most people lose faith in God as they see no such judgement being made and it seems as if the person has got off scot-free, whereas you have been injured or sinned against and expected to suffer.'

'The question raised is, why does God wait to inflict judgement? Well, it is because we are all free willed and we may, over time, decide what we did was wrong and remedy the wrong. We may ask for forgiveness, and therefore, no judgement is required by God if we are genuine. However, if this is not the case, God does not institute retribution immediately, but over a period. He may in fact not do this in our lifetime, but judge the person after death. He gives you an assurance that the sin will not go unpunished and will be judged and retribution inflicted in His time. You must have faith in God that He will honor His promise to you even though you may not bear witness to His actions and must have faith in Him, that He will not let the matter go unjudged.'

'To those who believe in Satan and follow him, then retribution is in their hands and follows immediately after the occurrence of the event. They do not look to God but themselves to carry out retribution, which in most cases is disproportionate to the sin dealt with. To them, this is immaterial, as long as they inflict retribution in some form or another. They are their own God and will attend to the matter themselves.'

'Behind the call of the retribution is Satan. He will not only be at the cause of the sin but also be at the call for retribution to ensure that mankind deals a blow to the Christian, and if by chance it is disproportionate and the person is fatally injured or killed, then that is even better. It means one less Christian to worry about or one less person to prevent going over to the other side.

'The "retribution principle" is based on OT convictions that the righteous will prosper, and the wicked will suffer, both in proportion to their respective righteousness and wickedness. In Israelite theology, the principle is integral to the belief in God's justice. Since God is just, the Israelites held it was incumbent on Him to uphold the retribution principle, and over time, they developed the inevitable converse corollary: those who prosper must be righteous (i.e., favored by God), and those who suffer must be wicked (i.e., experiencing the judgement of God). Thus, the retribution principle was an attempt to understand, articulate, justify, and systematize the logic of God's interaction in the world. The fact that human experience often seemed to deny the belief of the retribution principle required that it be qualified for it to be understood realistically. How can God be just if He does not punish the wicked?'

'Whenever retribution is considered, the discussion is centered on the book of Job. As some readers will be aware, the story of Job is two stories preserved in one book. Job is a man who stands righteous—"blameless and upright"—before God, who fears God and rejects evil. Job is also very wealthy—"the greatest of all the men of the east" (Job 1:1–3). One day, he is accused before God in the court of heaven: he fears God, the Accuser ("Satan") charges, only because God rewards him with wealth—let him suffer and Job will curse God. To test the accusation, God agrees to hand Job over to suffering (vv. 6–12). During his suffering, Job's friends come to comfort him and sit with him in silence (2:11–13). Despite losing all his property, family, and health at the Accuser's hand, he passes the test of suffering, refusing to curse God. God thus rewards Job's steadfastness, giving back all he had lost times two. Job then lives a long life and dies a happy man (42:10–17). In this story, Job's suffering has a known cause and a divine purpose: God allows Job to suffer as a test of faith. What is more, and of importance here, Job does not question God's justice on account of his suffering: "In all this Job did not sin or charge God with wrongdoing" (1:22).

'It is the "other" story of Job rather than this one that concerns us, for here both the justice of God and the piety of Job are called into question. This less familiar story is a lengthy poetic dialogue between Job and his friends. Job does not accept suffering with calmness and composure—in the opening speech of the dialogue, he curses the day he was born. And Job's friends do not sit with him in silence. They offer him no comfort in his suffering but counsel him, "If I were you . . ." Here, the cause of Job's suffering is unknown, and its purpose is impossible to understand from the initial information provided in the Bible. Such ambiguity opens Job's suffering to interpretation: Who is at fault, Job or God? Job and his friends thus hold court in search of a proper judgement of the matter. 'Job and his friends present conflicting cases. The friends question not God's justice but Job's innocence. They accuse him along traditional grounds of having sinned and thus judge him as deserving of his suffering—it is not God who is to blame but Job himself. They assume he is receiving only his "just deserts" for his sin and thus declare that he must confess his guilt to God and repent of his ways to put things right and so find favor with God.'

'Job persists throughout the dialogue in protesting his innocence before both his friends and God and thus maintains his complaint against what he sees as God's injustice. The earth is given into the hands of the wicked. He covers the eyes of its judges—"if it is not God, who then is it?" God is unjust, Job complains, because the order of things treats the innocent and the wicked, not according to their deeds, but in the same way. The cosmic order appears indifferent to innocence and guilt, and God alone is responsible for the order of things: "if not he, then who?"

Further on in the dialogue, Job strengthens his case by appealing to the strength of the wicked as evidence of the injustice of God: "Why do the wicked live on, reach old age, and grow mighty and powerful? . . . Their houses are safe from fear, and no rod of God is upon them . . . They spend their days in prosperity, and in peace they go down to Sheol." If God's ordering of things permits the wicked to prosper in life and then die in peace, without fear of punishment from God, then what is the purpose of serving God? Job asks. Again, he points to the crux of the issue, the natural order that God has created and supervises compounds injustice with injustice, not only allowing the wicked to prosper but also treating the wicked and righteous alike in the end: "One dies in full prosperity, being wholly at ease and secure . . . while the other dies in bitterness of soul, never having tasted of good but only from misfortune. They lie down alike in the dust, and the worms cover them."

'What Job and his friends share, which none of them questions, is the retributive paradigm, evident in both Job's complaint and his friends' arguments. They presume the existence of a divinely created cosmic moral order that rewards good and punishes evil. Job and his friends differ only on the question of *which party* has contravened the retributive order of things, God (Job's claim) or Job (his friends' claim). Surprisingly, although God rebukes Job for presuming the right to challenge the justice of the Creator, and although Job falls prostrate before God in humble repentance in response to this rebuke, in the end, God vindicates Job and rebukes his friends.'

'Notice how remarkable is this outcome: it is Job that has spoken rightly, not his friends. God thus rebukes Job's friends for their speeches in *defense* of God! Their defense of God and judgement of Job were based upon the assumption that the cosmic moral order God has created and governs is a retributive system. According to this paradigm, Job's suffering entails one of two possibilities: *either* Job has sinned, in which case Job deserves his suffering and God's justice is vindicated, *or* Job is innocent, in which case Job does not deserve his suffering and God is proven in this instance to be unjust. We thus expect God to affirm one or the other of these alternatives. God's ultimate response, however, affirms *neither* alternative. Job is innocent, as he has insisted, such that he does not deserve his suffering, and yet God's justice is vindicated. Job's friends have *both* judged wrongly of Job *and* spoken wrongly of God. The inference to be drawn here is that the fault lies neither with Job nor with God, but with the default paradigm within which we understand the ways of God and so frame the problem of evil. The conclusion here thus upsets the retributive paradigm of human thinking about God, the cosmos, and justice: the cosmic order ordained by God is not necessarily a retributive system.'

'This conclusion carries a profound implication. God's just governance of the cosmos allows innocent human suffering—the story of Job, *affirms* the reality of undeserved (innocent) suffering in the God-created cosmic moral order. Such a conclusion, of course, leaves us with no explanation for Job's suffering. The meaning of innocent suffering remains as mysterious as the God who speaks from the whirlwind. Nonetheless, this conclusion reveals that God's ordering of the cosmos and dealing with humanity goes beyond human standards of what is reasonable and right and, hence, that God's justice does not necessarily accord with the law of settling the score or retribution.'

'In the Sermon on the Mount, Jesus teaches that the cosmic order confirms what the cross reveals—that God does *not* rule by the law of retribution. Jesus does not conclude that we cannot know anything about the ways of God. Instead, Jesus teaches us to see the workings of the cosmos as confirming the grace-rooted, enemy- loving, redemption-seeking justice of God that is revealed through the cross. The "hand of God", Jesus teaches, is both loving and just to all—but seeing that it is so requires us to see God's justice as going beyond retribution and to the cross.'

'Two of the original gifts of God to his creatures are the sun and the rain, and God has bestowed these natural gifts, which were necessary for life, on all creatures equally. As anyone can readily observe, patterns of sunshine and rainfall do not vary with the righteousness or wickedness of the recipients. True, sunshine and rainfall are not distributed equally across the globe; but in any one location, the sun shines and the rain falls on everyone the same. Sunshine and rainfall in farm-based economies symbolize all the God-provided necessities of life that the natural order distributes on an equal-opportunity basis regardless of moral qualification. Thus, through the created order of nature, observation tells us God providentially bestows the goods necessary for human flourishing on everyone the same, making no distinction between who is righteous and who is wicked. We can then draw the inference, if God ruled the cosmos strictly by the law of retribution, then we would reasonably expect the righteous to enjoy an abundance of sunshine and rainfall and the wicked to suffer deprivation of sunshine and rainfall. But that is not what is observed. Therefore, God does not rule strictly by the law of retribution. The evidence of the cosmos therefore leads us to conclude that God's providential governance goes beyond retribution— for a strictly retributive cosmic order would lead us to expect to see all (and only) the righteous being rewarded with sun- and rain-generated prosperity and all (and only) the wicked being punished with sun- and rain-deprived suffering, which is not what is observed to happen. Retribution, observation, and reason therefore tell us it is not the law of nature.

'We hasten to note here, as Qoheleth, Job's friend, observed, that the natural order does not discriminate between the righteous and the wicked. Nature distributes from its storehouse good and bad to alike.

Floods, earthquakes, hurricanes, tornados, and tsunamis sweep away the righteous along with the unrighteous, despite the pleas of the righteous for rescue from God (Ps. 26). We must add here that human choices often aid and abet the disastrous effects of natural disasters. It is not by the sheer whim of nature alone that the primary victims of Hurricane Katrina in New Orleans in 2005 were black and poor. Yet the human suffering caused by natural disasters cannot be completely accounted for by human sin. Concerning both good and evil, then biblical wisdom discerns that the natural order is not a strictly retributive system, and the order of things that God has ordained in creation does not reward us according to our deeds.'

'What, then, are we to conclude? Logically, we have three options: either deny that anyone who suffers is truly righteous or deny that the natural order has any moral ordering or affirm that God has ordained a natural order that does not conform to the law of retribution.'

'The first option is that of Job's friends, who believed human suffering is divine punishment inflicted by God on the deserved for their sins. This goes back to the theory that the rich are in favor with the Lord and the poor basically get what they deserve because they lack available protections from the forces of nature because of patterns of injustice and practices of oppression. Unless we are to regress to the view that the poor deserve their poverty and the ills that go with it, then this argument is impossible to maintain. The identification of divine judgement in natural events is thus fraught with the danger of self-righteousness, the presumption that "they" deserve their suffering while "we" deserve our comfort.'

'The second option is that of the natural order, which considers punishment follows the crime and is administered by God. The last option leads us to a conclusion that we inhabit a morally indifferent cosmos, and it is no more reasonable to believe that the sun and the rain are signs of God's love than to believe that pain and suffering are signs of His punishment.

'The third option is that of Jesus, who rejects all these views and declares God's justice distributes good and evil in nature, neither according to the law of retribution, nor according to laws of chance, but according to the "law of love" (Matt. 5:43–48). Thus, yes, sun and rain are gifts of God's love, dispensed equally upon the righteous and the wicked, but pain and suffering are not necessarily the punishment of God dispensed upon the wicked. These can be self-inflicted.

'The latter point deserves some discussion. In Jesus's view, human suffering does not necessarily bear divine judgement and, hence, does not witness to the sin of the sufferer. To the contrary, suffering may become the blessed way of having divine approval— when it results from the faithfulness of the sufferer to God's will in the face of the injustice of the world. In revealing the way of divine wisdom, Jesus teaches that those who endure persecution on earth for the sake of righteousness or on account of loyalty to himself are blessed in the kingdom of heaven (Matt. 5:10–11). Peter teaches likewise, far from being the sign of God's judgement, to endure suffering "for doing what is right" or for loyalty to "the name of Christ" receives divine approval (1 Pet. 2:20; 3:14; 4:14). Indeed, Jesus says, those who suffer on his account are to "rejoice and be glad, for [their] reward is great in heaven" (Matt. 5:12; cf. Jas. 1:12; 5:10–11). And, Peter adds, such suffering in the way of righteousness and faithfulness is both an imitation of and a participation in the sufferings of Christ (1 Pet. 2:21: 4:13).

'The correct conclusion is not that the cosmos is morally indifferent, nor that suffering is divine punishment, but rather that the moral order of the creation is not strictly retributive—and that by the design of its creator. The moral order of the creation, according to the personal character of its creator, goes beyond the law of retribution, in that God loves both the righteous and the wicked, and because Jesus was crucified on the cross for our sins, the retributive paradigm makes no sense to human reason apart from faith in the God, who is both Creator and Redeemer, who shows through the cross the justice that redeems the cosmos. Contrary to human expectation and moral calculation according to the law of retribution, the cross of Christ reveals the justice of God by dispensing divine good (righteousness, justification) in exchange for human evil (sin, transgression) (Rom. 3:21–26). Indeed, the cross reveals God's justice precisely through Christ's costly demonstration of divine love for "the ungodly" and "sinners" and "enemies". Jesus is saying that his death at the cross pays for any need for retribution towards sinners who believe and have faith in him, and therefore the retribution paradigm is not a strict rule but is dealt by Him as to your belief in Christ. Having our perception and thinking reoriented by the cross, then we can make sense of what Jesus teaches us to see—that the cosmos confirms God's retribution is beyond justice, demonstrated through indiscriminate love for all mankind.'

'We now take up our second question concerning retribution and the "natural law" of justice—whether *human*-executed retribution accords with the God-created nature of things. Once we have recognized that the cosmic order is not governed strictly by the law of retribution, such that retribution is not executed in human affairs as a matter of course, we might maintain that justice requires retribution and so regard it as the obligation of human authority to execute retribution, where nature has not done so. Most people believe we do what is both right and good when we "pay back" evildoing to evildoers, and giving "payback" is right and good, we think, because that accords with "the nature of things". Is that so? Two ancient philosophers, one Greek and pagan (Socrates), the other Roman and Christian (Lactantius), thought it far less than obviously the case precisely for reasons of natural law.

'The Bible tells us the earth was created by God and it was made "very good" so was man who was made in "God's image". God is saying that we should not seek retribution in our own right but pass the matter to Him and allow Him to handle it for us. We love the Lord and therefore should love those created in His image, for He created them as He has created us. To take action against the person is to take action against God, for He created the person, and while that person has a free will, God is still the creator of that person and is responsible for that person's actions. God is the one that has given that person the free will, not you, and God is the one that gives you the assurance that if you leave it to Him, He will attend to the matter. "We are then advised that Jesus died on the cross for our sins, which has made the universal strict theory of retribution not possible. Anyone who believes in Jesus and has faith in Him will have eternal life, and that includes the person who has wronged you and later seeks the Lord and has faith in Him. For example, the criminal that was crucified along with Jesus. God is saying that, generally, retribution is not administered immediately as the person can change their ways after taking time to contemplate what they have done and seek forgiveness for their sin, and therefore God wants to give them the opportunity and time to do so. God advises He loves both the perpetrator and the innocent person, as He created both of you in His image.'

'Where it is obvious that the person has no intention to seek God out but remain in the company of Satan, God will take whatever action is necessary to inflict retribution on that person while persuading them to change their ways and to bring them back to their senses. His retribution may be disproportionate to what has been done to you, as it may be over a long period and with varying degree of grievances from personal to his family and could affect their lifestyle and wealth. You cannot do this, as you do not control the universe or what is happening in this world, but

God does. Therefore, God is saying, hand the problem over to Him and allow Him to handle it in His way and on His terms and in His time.'

'The other aspect discussed and confirmed by Jesus is that the retribution doctrine is not a strict universal doctrine that applies to all events in a strict order. The wealthy cannot be said to have the grace of the Lord, nor can the poor and misfortunate be said to be under the wrath of the Lord. People are dealt with individually by God under how He believes they should, to ensure they gain solid rock faith in Him and can judge this for themselves through trials. So there is no universal theory that applies other than the theory of having faith in the Lord, and this is the only way you can ensure He will attend to the grievance and you maintain your faith and love of the Lord.'

'God will settle the score His way and by His discretion. It may end at the death of the person in that they may have to appear before God and explain their actions and be punished in hell. This is for God to decide and not for you to offer solutions or seek progress reports from God as to what has happened. Yes, you may see the person prosper and gain further wealth while you may struggle on this earth, but this is God's will and not theirs, and you must have faith in God's judgement. He created both of you and will answer for both.'

'It is clear in today's age where we are in serious moral trouble because every type of lifestyle is now regarded as legitimate, and that most of the population have moved from having a relationship and faith in God to a position of "do what suits self". Since there is no Creator or higher order in their life, they look towards the State to attend to the matter of retribution. Our government has been playing the role of God and is openly declaring people are free to act as they please and attend to legislating laws to attend to retribution on a default basis. In these instances, it is not discretionary or delayed, but basically, punishment follows the crime and is not referred to as a higher order to God, but is dealt with by the courts. Most people seek retribution through these avenues rather than seeking God's help and leaving the matter to Him to handle. Even Christians have resorted to the legal system to attain retribution rather than referring the matter to God for His eventual judgement. Why? In most cases, they lack the faith in God, and second, they are not prepared to leave it to God to attend as the person may not receive the punishment but ask forgiveness from God. The need to see punishment inflicted is great even amongst Christians. The third reason is that the person's relationship with God has not developed to the extent that they are prepared to accept that God is the Creator and therefore responsible for the other person's actions. They want the state to take this responsibility as they can see what is transpiring, whereas with God, it takes faith and time and may not occur in their presence or time.

'The result in this is that more and more people are taking retribution into their own hands—Christians through the court and non-believers attending to this personally or again through the judicial system. With these events happening, there is no wonder that the Christian faith is not well understood or supported and there is a general lack of faith in Christ.'

'Jesus leaves the decision to you as a Christian. He has given you a free will for a reason, and you must act according to how you believe it should be handled. In a similar instance, Jesus was approached by the Pharisee and given a loaded question regarding payment of taxes. He called for a coin that was commonly used in commercial transactions in those days. He asked whose image appeared on the coin and was told by the Pharisee that of Caesar. Then He said, "Give unto Caesar what is due unto him and give what is due to God that what your heart believes is Gods.'

'God's justice may take a lifetime, whereas the courts are reasonably quick and sentence predictable depending on the act done. In a court, you can witness the evidence presented and the sentence or judgement proclaimed. The actual punishment may not take place except in criminal matters. If it is a commercial matter, then the person may not have the means to pay and could declare themselves bankrupt and avoid any liability. With God, you leave the matter in His hands and walk away from it, knowing God will never let you down and will, in His own time, attend to the matter of retribution. The person cannot avoid the Creator, nor shall they be able to avoid punishment on technical grounds. God will deliver judgement. Believe in Him and have faith in Him.

'Let us pray . . .'

37

The day finally arrives for Claudia and Robert's wedding, with all at MI attending and gathering around the church in preparation. The groom in his best off-the-shelf suit, while the bride in the wedding dress of her own design.

The media do not miss the occasion, and world reporters are on the scene recording the event. Claudia has become news since winning the prestigious IFS award.

Claudia makes her way up to the entrance of the church with flashes from the cameras and finally stands at the entrance waiting for the music. Tim, Pat's husband, was waiting there to escort her down the aisle. Unfortunately, there was no great orchestral presentation but rather Mrs. Jones on the church piano, which really needed a tune-up and Mrs. Jones some music lessons.

Claudia moves slowly down the aisle with Tim until she reaches the altar, where Robert is standing. Robert looks at her and thinks she is an angel looking so young and beautiful in her wedding dress. They hold hands, and Allen conducts the ceremony, which culminates in the exchange of vows.

The couple walks out of the church as man and wife and are whisked away for photographs. Shortly after, they attend a reception, and everybody enjoys themselves.

After the birth of their first child, Robert sells Marque International, as it is getting very demanding and requires a lot of his and Claudia's time. Claudia wants to have a second child and to look after her children rather than place them under the care of a nanny.

They live in the chateau for approximately six months of the year and are back in their usual residence when not there. Robert continues with the nursing homes and sees this as a growing long-term business. He hires a young CEO to run the day-to-day operations and concentrates on the amalgamations and takeovers, as he was very good at negotiating.

Robert still has an office in town and arrives at work early one day to meet with some advisers. After reading reports for an hour, he goes out and gets a cup of coffee and stretches his legs for a while.

As he walks up to the steps of the Town Hall, he notices someone was sitting at the same spot Vicki Santana used to sit when she was on the streets, and he has a similar box just like hers. He has a sign stating, 'Homeless and would appreciate some help'. Robert walks up to where the person is sitting and is ready to throw in some coins in the box when the person raises his head and says, 'Thank you.' Robert stands there momentarily, wondering where he has seen that person before. He throws his coins into the box and walks on for about twenty yards and then realizes it is Charles Henry. His blood pressure rises, and he could feel himself getting anxious and angry. He wants to go back and kick the box down the steps as Charles Henry had done to Vicki. He stands for a moment and feels Vicki's spirit with him.

Vicki tells him not to let bitterness and thoughts of revenge take hold of him. She wants him to leave Charles Henry to the Lord.

Vicki says to him, 'You see how far Charles Henry has fallen and the misfortunes that have befallen his family. God has punished him for his sins. At best, you could have only taken his life and sent him to hell. He will now experience the worst of life until his dying days on earth, and he has brought this on himself. Leave it to the Lord as you previously agreed. "Retribution is mine", said the Lord. I will settle the score "and not yours, Robert.'

Robert stands for a moment with sweat coming from his forehead pondering the situation and then says, 'I would get more satisfaction right now in punching his lights out.'

A voice is then heard, 'What did you say, mate? You want to punch my lights out?'

Robert looks up, and where he saw Vicki there stands a man looking at Robert, who says, 'Are you all right, mate? You seem to talk to yourself. Maybe you need some help. I can call for an ambulance, and they can take you to a hospital to get you checked out.'

Robert replies, 'No, mate, I am all right. I just saw a ghost.'

The man says, 'That is nothing. I see them all the time, especially when I have a few drinks. You haven't been drinking, have you?'

Robert replies, 'No, mate, thanks, just in spirits. I will be all right.'

Robert walks on agreeing with what Vicki had said to him and remembers he agreed with Allen that he would leave the retribution to the Lord.

He thinks about what Vicki has said and agrees that no one could have arranged Charles Henry's affairs in this way to force him to change places with Vicki except God. Charles Henry had lost everything he ever owned, including his family, investments, assets, mansions, and reputation. Even if he attached himself to Satan and got out of his situation, no one would want to have anything to do with him or would ever deal with him. All that he could expect is a quick death from the mob if they ever catch up with him.

Robert says a prayer promising to leave it to the Lord to handle and walks on and vows never to pass this way again and understands why he is told to have faith in the Lord and leave the retribution to Him.

Robert goes back to his office and considers his situation as to what has happened with Charles Henry and gives thanks to the Lord in a short prayer for what he has gone through and what he now has in the way of a family and fortune and understands in some ways the trials Job went through.